MYSTERIOUS TALES OF OLD MINNEAPOLIS

ALSO BY LARRY MILLETT
PUBLISHED BY THE UNIVERSITY OF MINNESOTA PRESS

Mysterious Tales of Old St. Paul
Rafferty's Last Case: A Minnesota Mystery
Strongwood: A Crime Dossier
The Magic Bullet: A Locked Room Mystery
Sherlock Holmes and the Eisendorf Enigma
The Disappearance of Sherlock Holmes
Sherlock Holmes and the Secret Alliance
Sherlock Holmes and the Rune Stone Mystery
Sherlock Holmes and the Ice Palace Murders
Sherlock Holmes and the Red Demon

MYSTERIOUS TALES OF OLD MINNEAPOLIS

LARRY MILLETT

University of Minnesota Press
Minneapolis
London

Published by the University of Minnesota Press
111 Third Avenue South, Suite 290
Minneapolis, MN 55401-2520
http://www.upress.umn.edu

ISBN 978-1-5179-2047-0 (hc)
ISBN 978-1-5179-2048-7 (pb)

A Cataloging-in-Publication record for this book is available from the Library of Congress.

Printed in the United States of America on acid-free paper

34 33 32 31 30 29 28 27 26 25 10 9 8 7 6 5 4 3 2 1

Once again, to Jodie

CONTENTS

MURDER AT THE FALLS

"But let justice roll down like waters, and righteousness like an ever-flowing stream."

—BOOK OF AMOS

PROLOGUE
"A MIGHTY SPECTACLE"

OWÁMNIYOMNI, a place of turbulent waters, was one of many names by which the Mdewakanton Dakota called the cataract that would later come to be known as St. Anthony Falls. The Dakota and their frequent enemies the Ojibwe viewed the falls as a sacred site where dreams and legends swirled in the mist. Belgian-born Father Louis Hennepin, a great traveler and perhaps an even greater fabulist, was possibly the first European to see the falls, in 1680, and he promptly named it after his patron saint. The native names, flowing with music and magic, were thereafter rejected, and the waterfall's new name soon appeared on maps of the northern wilderness that would become Minnesota. In time other travelers came to see the cataract, one of them describing it as "a mighty spectacle outdone only by the great Niagara."

Receding steadily upstream, the falls was 1,500 feet north of where Hennepin had seen it by the 1840s, when ambitious men from New England arrived to turn its frothing power into money. A hardheaded lot, they had no use for the ancient myths of people they regarded as mere savages. Instead, their preferred myth was that of divine providence, and they saw the Almighty's hand at work in the waterfall so perfectly placed on the Mississippi River at the heart of the continent. Vast pineries awaiting the ax lay to its north and east, endless prairies awaiting the plow to its south and west. The logs would have to be sawed into lumber, the wheat ground into flour, and it would all happen at the falls, where the Mississippi, placid for most of its course, dropped seventy feet in the span of a mile, providing a source of power greater than any available in the fabled mill towns of New England.

It did not take long for the falls to be harnessed, "like a wild stallion put to work with a plow," as one perhaps too colorful writer put it. Dams, walls, raceways, flumes, canals, tunnels, and deep pits carved from solid rock soon enveloped the ancient cataract in a web of industry, turning what had been one of the beauty spots of the continent into a vast, roiling factory on water. Meanwhile, the city of Minneapolis grew with stunning speed around the newly empowered falls and became, in little more than two decades, the world's colossus of flour.

There was no place for the Dakota amid the city's bustling mills, and they were soon evicted from their ancestral lands and sent far away to live in impoverished resentment. Their legends, however, remained. One spoke of Oanktehi, a spirit of water and evil who dwelt beneath the falls, and some would come to wonder whether its dark presence still haunted the cataract when, in June 1872, a prominent miller came to a violent end under circumstances not easily explained.

1.
DEATH AT THE PERFECTION

IN A CITY WHERE FLOUR WAS AS GOLD, the Perfection Mill had no equal. Built of massive limestone walls rising to a height of six stories, the Perfection was the pride of Minneapolis, towering over the Falls of St. Anthony like a medieval fortress. Within its confines thirteen of the finest French buhrstones ground wheat into 100,000 pounds of flour every day amid a bewildering maze of gears, belts, pulleys, and shafts tended by men in white dustcoats who moved cautiously about their business lest an arm or leg or life itself be sacrificed to the roaring machinery. "It is a wonderland of human ingenuity," wrote an awed correspondent from *Harper's*

Weekly who toured the mill shortly after it opened in 1867. "There can be no doubt that the Perfection lives up to its name or that Minneapolis, which sprang up like an exhalation from the prairies a mere decade ago and which is already an extraordinary beehive of industry, is sure to become the greatest metropolis of the Northwest."

Two transplanted Easterners of very different character, Stoddard Chase and Ransom Everleigh, had built the mill and remained its owners, although they had long been at odds and usually communicated only through subalterns. The son of a Massachusetts industrialist, Chase was broad of body and fierce of demeanor, with heavily hooded eyes and a long black beard that gave his face a dark and brooding cast. He was also a mechanical wizard who'd overseen construction of the Perfection down to its last detail. A terrifying glare was his chief instrument of domination, and he brooked no dissent from his subordinates. When he spoke—in a deep, menacing voice—it was wise to listen, for he was one of those men who sit hard upon the world and believe they can subdue it with an iron will.

Everleigh stood in utter contrast to Chase. As thin and quick as an elf, he hailed from New York, where his father had been a silver-tongued Wall Street broker until an indictment for fraud caused him to flee to the tropics, never to be heard from again. Navigating the treacherous world of high finance and luring in investors were Everleigh's chief talents. Unlike his humorless partner, Everleigh loved to jape and josh, and no social event among the better classes in Minneapolis was complete without his scintillating presence. Exceptionally handsome, with a lush head of hair that seemed to grow only lusher with age, Everleigh was also known for his many entanglements with women, none of whom had managed to snare him as a husband.

The Perfection was one of more than a dozen mills—"pigs at a trough," one wag dubbed them—that drew water from a canal paralleling the Mississippi River just below the falls. The Perfection's pumping hearts were two bladed, 350-horsepower Boyden turbines made in Massachusetts. Mounted horizontally at the bottom of a pair of forty-foot deep, iron-lined pits carved out of the same limestone from which the mill had been built, the turbines turned falling water into power, producing so much torque that it seemed at times as though they might twist the mill off its very foundations and send it into a wild, whirling dance. Perpendicular shafts connected to the turbines distributed power through the mill, and once the plunging water had done its work tailraces returned it to the river.

On the morning of June 6, 1872, workers at the Perfection began their shift, as they always did, by opening metal gates in the mill's basement. As a horn sounded to alert the men that the mill was about to spring to life, water from the canal rushed through the open gates into short headraces before thundering down into the pits where the four-foot-diameter turbines awaited their daily duties. Within seconds the turbines began to spin, setting the mill's machinery in motion. One of the turbines, known as the A, controlled the mill's grinding stones, while the other, the B, powered auxiliary machinery.

The Perfection's foreman, Peter Nichols, knew the throaty hum of the turbines as well as anyone, and his ears told him almost at once that something was wrong. An ominous shudder pulsed through the mill, and instead of starting to grind at speed the paired millstones arrayed in ranks on the Perfection's upper floors struggled to gain momentum, as though slowed by an invisible brake. Seconds later, the millstones stopped altogether.

Letting out a string of curses, Nichols headed for the basement to see what the problem was. "What the hell is going on?" he asked the first millwright he encountered. "Has some damn fool dropped a tool down into the A turbine?" It had a happened before, and if the turbine was damaged there was no option other than to replace it, a costly and time-consuming job that would force the mill to shut down for days.

"I don't know, sir," the millwright said. "But it ain't turning, that's for sure."

Shaking his head and dreading what would happen if he had to deliver bad news to his bosses, Nichols instructed the millwright to shut the headrace gates to both turbines and stop the flow of water. "Be quick about it," he added. "I have to see what's going on."

The millwright scurried away while Nichols made his way through the poorly lit basement to turbine A's wheel pit, where only a thin iron railing protected workers from falling to an all but certain death. A hurtling flood of foaming, brownish water poured from the headrace into the pit, which was ten feet in diameter, and so powerful was the force of it that Nichols felt the railing throb against his hand. Then, as though the Mississippi had abruptly run dry, the flow of water stopped, the last of it trickling away down into the inky depths of the pit.

The worker who had closed the headrace gates returned as Nichols peered down into the pit and said, "Can you see anything down there, Nick?"

"Too dark," Nichols said. "Get me the lantern and rope, and we'll have a look."

Although an iron ladder was mounted inside the pit to provide access to workers, Nichols knew the rungs would be wet and treacherous. Before risking a harrowing descent, he thought it wise to drop the lantern down to see what the light might reveal. Nichols lit the lantern and with both hands on its attached rope slowly lowered it into the pit as he and the millwright peered over the railing.

What they saw as the light neared the bottom of the pit was something so grotesque that Nichols lost his grip on the rope, sending the lantern clattering to the bottom. Both he and the millwright jumped back as though they'd seen Lucifer himself coming up from Hades for a visit. Nichols fought the urge to vomit as he went down on his haunches. "Oh Jesus," he said, crossing himself. "Oh holy Jesus." The millwright, meanwhile, just kept backing way, wanting no part of the scene in the pit.

Screwing up his courage, Nichols took a deep breath and went back to the railing. Although the lantern had fallen to the bottom of the pit, it remained intact, its light still shining on a scene the likes of which Nichols hoped he would never see again. A crumpled body lay face up at the bottom of the pit where it narrowed to funnel water into the turbine. The body was that of a man, his dark suit and white shirt soaked in water, his right arm torn off at the shoulder and his long gray hair yanked from his head so violently that most of his scalp was gone. The vanished arm had presumably been sucked into the turbine, along with the hair and scalp, causing it to jam and stop.

What made the sight even worse was that Nichols knew the dead man, for it was none other than Ransom Everleigh, his face distorted but recognizable. How in God's name had he ended up at the bottom of the wheel pit? Nichols didn't know, since Everleigh rarely visited the mill. Even so, he certainly knew the dangers posed by the powerful turbines. But why would he have been in the mill overnight, when only a watchman was on duty? It made no sense.

On the other hand, if Everleigh had met with foul play, as seemed likely to Nichols, there could be only one prime suspect. It was no secret in the milling community that the relationship between Everleigh and Chase had completely ruptured in recent months because of a simmering dispute over how the substantial profits from their enterprise were being divvied up. It was also no secret that under the terms of the partnership agreement, Chase would assume sole ownership of the Perfection upon Everleigh's death. Even so, could Chase have so cruelly murdered his partner? Nichols wasn't sure. What he did know was that Chase had money beyond measure and lawyers as fierce as circling wolves. If he had murdered Everleigh, who in all of Minneapolis could hope to stand up against such a man and make him pay for his crime?

2.
THEORIES AND TESTIMONY

The news that Ransom Everleigh had died under most mysterious circumstances in his own flour mill was naturally grist of the tastiest sort to the people of Minneapolis, then a community of fewer than twenty thousand souls. The youthful city's newspapers, led by the *Daily Tribune,* seized upon the story of Everleigh's spectacular demise with such unseemly enthusiasm that preachers in their Sunday robes felt compelled to chastise the Fourth Estate for its dearth of simple decency. But as decency did not sell newspapers, the *Tribune* and its smaller rivals saw no need to stint on their coverage or to be overly impeccable when it came to separating fact from fiction.

The first round of stories, naturally enough, focused on how Everleigh had come to end up at the bottom of the wheel pit. A reporter tracked down the mill's elderly night watchman, but he reported seeing nothing unusual, and in any event, he'd made only two brief visits to the basement during the course of his rounds, or so he said. In truth, the watchman had slept through much of the night, a luxury he was able to enjoy because the mill's telltale clocks, designed to record his activities, weren't functioning. No other potential witnesses surfaced, and with little real evidence to work from, the press was left to speculate as best it could.

So it was that all manner of theories sprang up like apparitions rising out of the trapdoor in a bad stage play. One idea was that Everleigh, a well-known figure at the city's gambling halls, may have taken his own life, or even been murdered, because of huge debts he'd supposedly amassed at high-stakes poker games. "I have been led to believe he played frequently and liked to place very large bets," Chase told the *Tribune.* "I would not be surprised if he owed many thousands of dollars to some very rough characters. Perhaps he saw no way out of his situation and so chose the path of self-destruction. It is all extremely tragic."

Others suggested that Everleigh's thirst for sexual adventure had finally caught up with him. Had a wrathful husband or boyfriend exacted revenge after discovering Everleigh in a bed where he had no business being? It seemed possible. Yet a flour mill was hardly the place anyone would expect a crime of passion to play out, and the cuckold scenario had only a few proponents.

Yet another theory, perhaps the most far-fetched of all, was that Everleigh had gone to the mill with the idea of sabotaging the turbines to strike back at his partner. While going about his secret business, or so gossipmongers hinted, Everleigh had somehow fallen into the wheel pit. There, he'd supposedly died at once or suffered such grievous injuries that he could not escape before the water gate opened and the turbine tore him to pieces.

Scoffers—Peter Nichols prominently among them—dismissed all such talk as arrant nonsense. If Everleigh killed himself, why would he have done so in such a brutal fashion? A simple shot to the temple would have been a much easier way to go. As for the gamblers he was said to be in hock to, why would they have killed him when they needed him alive to get their money back? Roughing him up would have made much more sense. Nichols also doubted Everleigh's bedroom antics had led to his demise. It seemed far more likely that a seething, cuckolded husband would have killed Everleigh on the spot rather than staging an elaborate execution at the mill. Nor did Nichols think it even remotely possible that Everleigh would have tried to sabotage the Perfection, from which he derived most of his income.

*

As the press wallowed in theories and rumors, the city's small police department, which was not generally regarded as the Scotland Yard of the northern prairies, launched what it promised would be a thorough probe. Chief Michael Riley, a thumper of the old school with no real investigative experience, announced he would "leave no stone unturned" to find out what happened. The turning of the stones, however, produced little in the way of real pay dirt.

The police did manage to establish Everleigh's whereabouts on the night before his death. A wooden chip found in one of his coat pockets proved to be especially helpful. Painted red and stamped with "$5" on one side, the chip was traced to an illicit but well-patronized gambling hall in the back room of a saloon operated by a rough character named Ned Camp.

Camp, who wore a patch over one eye and resembled a landlocked pirate, confirmed that Everleigh had indeed been at the saloon. Numerous patrons had also seen Everleigh, who'd arrived that evening around eight. A skilled poker player who was a regular at the saloon, he sought out high-stakes games, and unlike his wealthy business peers, he had no reservations about mixing with the rugged crowd who frequented the establishment. But the witnesses, few of whom could be counted among the city's most respectable citizens, claimed not to know where Everleigh had gone after leaving around eleven o'clock. Nor had any of the witnesses noticed anything unusual about his appearance or demeanor. "He was his usual jovial self," said one man, "and he didn't appear to have a care in the world."

Further inquiries revealed Everleigh had won a sizable pot of money, a hundred dollars or more, that evening. This led the police to wonder whether Everleigh had been waylaid and robbed after leaving the saloon, since neither his wallet nor the valuable gold watch he always carried had been found on his body. But it was hard to believe that strong-armed robbers, who were usually quick about their work, would have dragged Everleigh into the mill and killed him there. As for the missing wallet and watch, the police were of the opinion that both items had been sucked away by the turbine and were now at the bottom of the Mississippi.

*

With the police making only modest headway, the immediate task of trying to figure out the circumstances of Everleigh's death fell to the county coroner, Charles Chilstrom, whose chief qualification for the job was that he had won just enough votes to be elected to the lucrative office. Autopsies were rarely performed in those days, but Chilstrom, a homeopath by trade, was as curious as everyone else about Everleigh's death. On the Monday following the discovery of Everleigh's body, Chilstrom convened a coroner's inquest, knowing it would garner the undivided attention of the press.

Three days of testimony from more than a dozen witnesses followed. A physician who had been called in to help Chilstrom was the first to testify, but his findings only added to the mystery. Everleigh's injuries included a head wound thought sufficiently severe to have caused his death, but the physician could not say whether the wound was the result of Everleigh's fall into the pit or whether he had been struck first and then hurled down into the turbine. "Either is a possibility," said the physician, whose statement was immediately ridiculed in the press as "being of no more value than the proverbial glass of warm spit."

Peter Nichols came next, recounting in detail how he'd discovered Everleigh and then gone down the slippery ladder into the pit to see if he could be of any help. "But there was nothing to be done," Nichols said. "Mr. Everleigh's body had taken a fearful battering. It was an awful sight. That's all I can say."

Police detectives also testified, recounting their efforts to trace Everleigh's movements in the days and hours before his death. A butler and maid at the fancy rowhouse where he lived reported last seeing him around noon on June 5, when he'd left "to do some business," as he told them rather vaguely. He never showed up at the small downtown office he maintained, however, and detectives couldn't find anyone who'd encountered him that day before his appearance at Camp's Saloon. But as testimony would soon reveal, the police made an interesting discovery about Everleigh's activities on June 3, when he'd gone to the city's brothel district on a curious mission.

Since the basic circumstances of Everleigh's death constituted old news, the press was greatly pleased on the second day of the inquest when "two members of our local demimonde," as the *Tribune* described them, took the stand. The first was Mary Polander, a part-time prostitute and regular at Camp's Saloon, who testified she'd seen Everleigh leave the establishment at about eleven on the night of his death. She'd told police the same thing earlier, but now she added a new twist, claiming that as Everleigh stepped out the door, he was joined by "a tall man in a stovepipe hat" and that the two of them walked off together. When pressed, Polander couldn't identify the man, saying she hadn't seen his face. "He was taller than Mr. Everleigh," she added, "but beyond that I cannot describe him."

Polander's testimony didn't galvanize the newspapers, but Nettie Conley's did. As the city's most notorious madam, she preferred flamboyance to the tedium of quiet good taste, and she did not disappoint when she took the stand in a flowing red gown with a lacy, low-cut bodice. "A magnificent diamond pendant dangling from her neck provided glittering evidence that her profession, so odious to the decent people of this city, has made of her a wealthy woman," the *Tribune* wrote, trying to gin up some moral outrage. What Conley had to say caused a much greater stir than her bejeweled presence, for she testified that Everleigh had come to her establishment on June 3 in search of a prostitute named Sally Sharpe.

"Did he say why he was looking for her?" the coroner asked.

"No. But he told me it concerned an urgent matter and that he would 'pay handsomely'—those were his exact words—for any information as to her whereabouts."

"Had he availed himself of her services while she worked for you?"

"No. I had never met Mr. Everleigh before that night. He was not a customer, and I have no idea why he was interested in Sally." Conley went on to state that she never saw Everleigh again after their brief encounter. "As for Miss Sharpe, who is a dear young woman, I cannot say where she has gone, as she left my employ some time ago."

Other madams told similar stories. Everleigh had come looking for Sharpe, but in each case the madams, none of whom reported ever seeing Everleigh before, replied that they could be of no help to him. It was all very curious, but no one could say whether Sharpe knew anything about Everleigh's death.

Sniffing the sweet scent of postmortem scandal, the newspapers speculated the missing prostitute might be a pivotal figure in the case. "Could it be that a soiled dove who's flown away holds the key to the Everleigh mystery?" asked the *Tribune,* which didn't spoil the mood by trying to answer its own question. The newspaper went on to note that Everleigh had never been married but was said to "possess a sporting nature," a phrase well understood to mean he was promiscuous. The *Tribune* didn't explain why these supposed revelations were of any consequence in Everleigh's death, but as the merest whiff of sexual profligacy stimulated readership, it saw no need to do so.

Stoddard Chase was among the last witnesses to testify, and he reinforced his contention that Everleigh's death could have been a suicide. "I have read all the idle speculation in the press, but I believe Mr. Everleigh very probably took his own life in a moment of derangement. I cannot be sure of this, of course, for who among us knows what goes on in another man's mind? But I had detected some darkening of his mood of late, and I fear he succumbed to the kind of hopeless gloom that can affect any man in troubled circumstances."

Asked whether he believed gambling debts could have led to Everleigh's being murdered, Chase said he doubted that was the case. "Still, one never knows. Perhaps he was indeed under great pressure from the unsavory men who run gambling parlors. I only wish now he had asked for my help, which I would have freely given despite our differences."

Peter Nichols, who had taken the day off to listen to Chase's testimony, could hardly help from breaking out into derisive laughter when he heard those words. Ransom Everleigh, he believed, would have been the last person to receive a helping hand from Chase. It was far more likely that Chase had helped his disaffected partner to the grave.

Once the testimony was complete, it took but a few hours for the coroner's jury to render a verdict that satisfied no one. "We find," stated the foreman, "that Mr. Ransom Everleigh died of injuries received at the Perfection Mill in the city of Minneapolis in the early morning hours of Thursday, June sixth, 1872. However, we are unable to say whether his death was the result of suicide, homicide, or misadventure."

*

C. Thomas Dowd, whose first initial was a mystery, was known around Minneapolis as the "Undertaker" because he always wore a black suit and spoke in the soft, soothing manner of someone paid to mourn the death of strangers. No one seemed to know exactly what he did or even who employed him, but where there was rough work to be done, he could be counted on to do it, for a suitable price. He had built his business, if it could be called that, on the basis of absolute discretion. "If you hire me, it will be as though you have hired an invisible angel," he would tell prospective employers. "I speak to no one about what I do or for whom I do it."

Over the years he'd done "odd jobs," as he called them, for everyone from Stoddard Chase to Ned Camp to the occasional husband looking for evidence of a cheating wife. Tall, powerfully built, and well versed in the fine art of street fighting, Dowd did not shy away from extralegal means to accomplish his work. He always kept brass knuckles and a pistol close at hand in the event someone needed persuasion. "Fear is what moves men," he liked to say, "and it will keep them in line when all else fails."

A product of Manhattan's notorious Five Points neighborhood, he'd run with the gangs there before moving on to Chicago, whose rough-hewn businessmen found use for a man of his talents. But after an unfortunate incident involving a twelve-year-old girl, he'd found it necessary to leave Chicago. Once he reached Minneapolis, Dowd talked his way into a job at the Perfection Mill as a company spy. He performed so admirably that Chase gave him more assignments, as did other millers anxious to quell any unrest among their workers.

Dowd had been working on an especially sensitive assignment at the time of Everleigh's death. Chase had come to believe his young wife, Bridget, was having an affair and he wanted proof of it. So he'd ordered Dowd to tail Bridget whenever she left the mansion to see if she was meeting anyone. But after two weeks on the job, Dowd reported that he'd found no indications Bridget was involved with a man.

A few days after the inquest, Dowd went to Chase's office next door to the mill to deliver his latest update on Bridget. "I have found nothing improper as yet about your wife's behavior," he said, "but I do have some news I believe you will find of great interest. It concerns Sally Sharpe who, as I understand it, was once in your employ. It seems she has been saying some unpleasant things about you."

Although the public at large didn't know it, Sharpe had worked briefly as a maid for Chase's late wife, Elizabeth, who'd died two years earlier in a most unfortunate mishap at the family mansion.

Chase felt a small knot forming in his ample belly. He said, "All right, Mr. Dowd, tell me what that rotten little whore has been saying."

"Well, sir, I have been told that on more than one occasion she accused you of most foully murdering your first wife. I learned of this from a man I know who frequents Nettie Conley's establishment. He said that while he and the Sharpe girl were engaged in their business one evening, she suddenly shouted your name at the top of her lungs and called you a 'wife killer.' She became so agitated she had to be removed from her room and sedated. Apparently, something similar happened when she was with several other customers."

Chase's dark eyes narrowed, and he slammed a fist on his desk with such force that papers rustled to the floor. "She actually accused me? Why, that lying trollop, I could wring her neck. I know why she is doing it. The wench stole some jewelry after Elizabeth's death, and I dismissed her at once. She's lucky I didn't have her thrown in jail. Now, she's trying to get back at me and I will not stand for it."

Dowd nodded and said, "I certainly understand your anger, sir. However, the situation may not be as bad as it seems. You see, Miss Sharpe is known to be a regular user of laudanum, and it is doubtful many people will believe the hallucinations of an opium addict. Still, there is cause for concern. If Miss Sharpe continues to make allegations, rumors about your first wife's death will inevitably spread, and that would not be a good thing. As it is, you are already the subject of much whispering over Mr. Everleigh's demise. Ugly rumors of yet another murder would hardly enhance your public stature."

Chase drummed his fingers on the desk, all the while shaking his head. "Damn it, this not fair! Do you know what it's taken to build this business? Work, work, and more work, that's what it's taken. And now a stupid whore is threatening everything. Where is she now?"

"I fear I do not know, sir. She seems to have disappeared after she left the brothel."

"Well, she can't have gone far. I will get in touch with Chief Riley and let him know his men need to find her. The chief has always been very helpful to me."

"I am sure he has," Dowd said. "But I wonder if it would be wise to involve the police. If she talks to the police, she might arouse more suspicion against you. I think it best if you let me locate her."

"Yes, I see what you're saying. All right, go find her and impress upon her how unwise it is to make slanderous allegations against me."

"Very good, sir. I will see to it that she causes you no further trouble. And what of the present Mrs. Chase? Am I to continue watching her?'

"You are. She is up to something, I know it. It is just a matter of time before you catch her at it."

3.
MOTHER AND SON

NO ONE FOLLOWED THE NEWS of Ransom Everleigh's death more closely than Peter Nichols and his mother, Sophia Westerly. The two were very close and talked every day. Of late their conversation had focused on Peter's love life. Still a bachelor at thirty, he'd finally fallen for a strong and beautiful woman named Annie Doherty, who he had to admit reminded him more than a little of his mother. But would Sophia approve of her? To Peter's relief, Sophia had not only approved of Annie but pronounced her to be "quite marvelous and very intelligent"—a judgment that would be borne out years later when Annie became embroiled in a murder mystery of her own in the strange case of "The Death Committee."

"Marry her and be quick about it," Sophia had told Peter. "You will not regret it."

A September wedding was planned, and Sophia and Peter had been busy preparing for that joyful event when Ransom Everleigh met his violent end at the Perfection Mill. His death had shocked both of them. They believed Chase had in all likelihood murdered Everleigh so as to have the Perfection Mill all to himself. But with the police demonstrating little investigative prowess, it was difficult to see how justice might be done.

Everleigh's bloody death had hit Peter hard. Unlike Chase, who cared little for the Perfection's workers and complained constantly of their laziness, Everleigh had always been kind and pleasant on those rare occasions when he stopped by the mill. Once, he'd even helped Peter rescue a worker whose shirt sleeve had become entangled in the machinery, ordering the turbines to be shut down—much to Chase's subsequent ire—before the man risked a fatal injury.

Sophia was equally disturbed by what had happened to Everleigh, for reasons of her own. She'd first met him in the 1860s, when he and Chase were building the Perfection Mill. Everleigh had been wild and dashing then, the most perfectly stunning man she'd ever seen, and a great contrast to his dour, demanding partner. "Air and stone," Sophia had called them, for Everleigh was a charming man of hopes and dreams, a spring breeze, whereas Chase was a rolling block of New England granite, ready to crush anyone or anything in his way.

Both mother and son thought the coroner's inquest had raised troubling questions while providing few good answers. A *Tribune* reporter named Robert McGuire was of the same view, and he interviewed Sophia and Peter, hoping to learn more about Everleigh's troubled relationship with Chase. But McGuire, who in the years to come would figure prominently in a sensational Minneapolis murder case involving Oscar Wilde, didn't make much headway with his inquiries.

The press's interest in Everleigh's death soon waned when a new scandal erupted involving a Lutheran minister and a pretty young member of his church choir. Like bored partygoers who'd learned of better entertainment elsewhere, the newspapers rushed off to write about the wayward minister and the delightfully juicy accusations against him. Everleigh, at least for a while, became old news.

"It's as though everyone has forgotten about Mr. Everleigh," Peter said one night as he and his mother shared coffee and cake at her mansion.

"Well, I haven't," Sophia said. "That monster Chase had Mr. Everleigh killed, I am certain of it. The trouble is, Chase all but owns this city, and he will see to it that the police do nothing."

"I agree. But do you really think Chase is capable of cold-blooded murder?"

"Why wouldn't he be? You know how he operates. He will do anything to advance his fortunes, and I do not believe murder is beyond him. William warned me about him after the falls went out, as I'm sure you remember."

In 1869 Sophia's late husband William Westerly had invested in a project led by Chase to dig a tunnel under St. Anthony Falls to extend the reach of its waterpower. But the tunnel had collapsed before it could be completed, nearly destroying the falls in the process. Chase had responded by casting blame on Westerly and the other investors, claiming they'd forced an alteration in the plans that led to the disaster. William, who died the next year, told Sophia he suspected Chase had created forged documents to bolster his false claims in court.

"The man is a wild boar who wants to devour everything and everybody in the world," Westerly had said. "He is utterly ruthless. Do not ever make the mistake of trusting him." Sophia had never forgotten those words.

"Well, we have to do something," Peter said. "If Chase is behind this awful business, he must be held to account."

"Yes, he must," Sophia agreed, "and it will fall on us to be avenging angels, as I doubt anyone else will dare take on Chase. I have some ideas as to how we might bring the monster to justice. We must begin by discomfiting him. I want him to hear footsteps in the dark, to know we are pursuing him."

"That sounds dangerous, Mother. If he feels cornered, he will strike out at us."

"I know, and that is when we will catch him in a trap."

Peter stared at his mother, taken in as he always was by the force of her piercing eyes, and said, "Well, I hope you know what you're doing. Chase is not a man to be toyed with."

"Nor am I a woman to be disregarded when I have set my mind on something."

"Oh, I know that all too well. But I must say, I'm curious why Mr. Everleigh's death has affected you so much. I thought you hardly knew him."

"There are stories you don't know," Sophia said, patting Peter's knee, "and that is just as well for the time being. Perhaps one day I will tell you more."

*

The stories Peter did know about his mother were so extraordinary that no adventure yarn he'd ever read could match them. By the time they arrived in Minneapolis in 1856—when she was forty-five and he, the youngest of her three sons, newly turned fourteen—she had already led a life packed with extraordinary adventures and more tribulations than she cared to remember. “I sometimes think I am a fantastic accident,” she told him once, “and I do not know that I will ever quite understand all that has happened to me.”

Born in the Swiss canton of Bern to French-speaking parents, she’d crossed the Atlantic in 1821 as a ten-year-old with her widowed mother and two sisters to join the ill-begotten Selkirk Colony on the Canadian prairies. Founded by a Scottish lord, the colony had been advertised to Sophia’s mother and her fellow immigrants as an agricultural paradise, the one problem being that it was an Eden in the middle of a vast, empty prairie where the temperature regularly plunged to forty below and starvation was always in the wind.

Sophia and her family had gotten their first taste of what was to come when ice in the Hudson Strait nearly sank their leaky old ship. By the time they finally reached the colony after a perilous trip up rapids-choked rivers and across Lake Winnipeg, they found food and shelter in short supply and winter approaching fast. A group of former mercenary soldiers known as the Meurons took them in and helped them ward off starvation, but at a cost. The men wanted white wives, the sooner the better, and Sophia was all but forced into marriage at age thirteen to a Meuron named François Nichols, who was twenty years her senior.

“I did not have the opportunity to grow up slowly,” she once told Peter. “I had no choice but to become a woman at a very young age.” Gifted with a strong constitution and a spirit not easily broken, Sophia took to the wild life in the cold north. She and François rode across the boundless prairies with Cree and Métis hunting parties in search of buffalo, and in time she became an excellent shot with musket and pistol. She learned how to make pemmican from dried meat, how to sow and harvest wheat, how to cut wood along the winding Red River of the North. The colony’s small gristmill, with its creaking wooden shafts and slowly grinding buhrstones, fascinated her, and she asked so many questions of the miller that he finally told her to go mind her own business.

Sophia might have lived out her life in the colony had not nature intervened. Lord Selkirk, as it turned out, had founded his colony with big dreams but very limited geographical knowledge. The colony was among the flattest places on earth, and the Red River was extremely prone to overflowing its banks. When an epic flood arrived in the spring of 1826, the colony became a vast inland sea, no trace of land visible for miles.

With their farmland inundated, Sophia and François saw no future in the colony and decided to move on. They journeyed hundreds of miles by oxcart and river raft to Galena, Illinois, where some former Selkirkians had already settled and where America's first great mineral rush—for lead rather than gold—was already underway. Lead mines were also springing up nearby in what would become Wisconsin, and the Nicholses soon made their home in a little town called Potosi within eyeshot of the Mississippi River. There, Sophia gave birth to three strapping sons after her first child, a precious girl, died in infancy. François, meanwhile, found steady work in a smelter, and they were able to buy a small house.

A cholera epidemic claimed François in 1848, not long after the family's two older sons had gone off to California to hunt for gold. Sophia and Peter then relocated to Galena, which was not only much larger than Potosi but also much richer, home to twenty millionaires, or so it was said. Within a year of her arrival in Galena, Sophia—still only in her thirties—married one of the town's wealthiest men, a mine and smelter owner named Darius Hoskinson. But he died just three years later, under peculiar circumstances, and Sophia once again moved on.

When Sophia and Peter reached Minneapolis in 1856, she instantly attracted men of a certain age. Tall and slender, with long brown hair going gray and hazel eyes that radiated keen intelligence, Sophia soon married for a third time, to a flour miller named William Westerly, who had lost his first wife a year earlier. Westerly proved to be the kindest of Sophia's husbands, and when he died in 1870 she was truly distraught.

After his death, Sophia found herself in a stifling world of well-to-do widowhood, which entailed card parties, afternoon teas, and fancy soirées populated by chattering women and elderly men looking for a nurse to take care of them. It was a life her women friends, few of whom she felt especially close to, seemed to find perfectly acceptable. But it left Sophia feeling bored and useless, and she began to wonder if her life had become devoid of purpose.

By the time she celebrated her sixty-first birthday with Peter in March 1872, she was three times a widow, wealthy beyond her dreams, and living in one of the grandest mansions in Minneapolis. Yet happiness eluded her amid deep longings that she feared would never be satisfied. Then, quite by chance, she had an encounter that would bring her elation and a new sense of hope, only to be followed by a shattering loss.

4.
TROUBLE ON CATARACT AVENUE

In 1872 a mansion of any consequence in Minneapolis was built of the local gray limestone in a style that would come to be called French Second Empire, after the monumental buildings bestriding the grand new boulevards that Napoleon III and his prefect, Baron Haussmann, had carved through Paris like the cleaves of a mighty knife. But the Minneapolis versions of this Parisian dream were as coarse peasant bread compared to the baron's rich architectural pastries. The mansion belonging to Stoddard Chase was no exception. Tall, squarish, and heavy, it presented a massive appearance but lacked the leavening of genuine French elegance.

The mansion occupied an entire block along Cataract Avenue, which in line with Minneapolitans' love of numerical order, would soon be renamed Sixth Avenue South. The mansion's most notable feature was a central tower, fifty-five feet high, that culminated in a small library tucked beneath a mansard roof sporting four elaborate dormers. A broad iron balcony extending out from the library offered an excellent view of the Perfection Mill just a few blocks down Cataract Avenue at the falls.

Although a winding staircase rose through the tower, Chase—whose girth had increased as steadily as his fortune—rarely used it. Instead, he'd installed a manlift, run by a small steam engine in the basement, as an easier way to ascend to the top of the tower, since passenger elevators had yet to arrive in Minneapolis. Without the protection afforded by an elevator cab, the manlift—which consisted of steps attached to a continuous, moving belt set within a vertical shaft—could be very dangerous. Handholds were supposed to prevent anyone using the lift from falling down the shaft, but they had not saved Elizabeth Chase's life. She'd plunged down the shaft to her death, a tragic accident—or so it had been determined—of which Chase never spoke.

Chase had remarried, scandalously only three months after his first wife's death. Bridget O'Malley, who was stunningly beautiful, had been a maid in the household and was twenty-five years his junior. It was assumed that, after having his way with her, Chase had been forced into the marriage, and the city's high-toned ladies waited eagerly for Bridget's baby to confirm their awful suspicions. But there'd been no child—not yet. Even so, Bridget was regarded as the kind of low-class sexpot, oozing with moist allure, who inevitably leads men to grief, and she'd never been welcomed into polite society.

Nor had she found a place in Chase's affections. Jealous by nature, he became convinced she was enjoying assignations behind his back, no matter that Dowd could find no evidence of her supposed infidelity. In the days after Everleigh's death, Bridget had become particularly difficult, and one evening as they sat in the mansion's baronial front parlor, the butler hovering nearby, she'd posed a startling question.

"Did you have Mr. Everleigh murdered?" she asked. "People are saying you did."

"How dare you suggest such a thing!" Chase shot back. "And just who are these people you speak of? Give me their names, and my lawyers will teach them the folly of slandering my good name."

"I would rather not say. But you must know I cannot live with a murderer. I cannot!" she said, rushing from the room. When Chase tried to speak with her later in her bedroom, she refused to open the door.

"That damn woman is crazy," Chase muttered within earshot of the butler when he came back downstairs. "I should never have married her!"

*

Late the next afternoon, when Chase returned home after a day of more meetings with potential investors, he was greeted at the front door by his butler.

"If you do night mind me asking, sir, I am wondering if you have seen Mrs. Chase today," the butler said with his usual silky diffidence.

"No, why should I? Isn't she here?"

"I'm afraid not, sir. She did not come down for breakfast this morning as she normally does, and no one has seen her all day."

"Is that so? Well, she's probably off somewhere shopping." Or, he thought, in some other man's bed.

"Yes, perhaps that's the case. However, I must inform you, sir, that the maid noticed this afternoon that some of her clothes appear to be gone from her wardrobe. A suitcase also seems to be missing."

Chase, who could go from calm to cold fury in an instant, glared at the butler and said, "Why didn't you tell me of this at once? Do I pay you and the maid to be fools?"

"No, of course not, sir. I sent a boy with a message to your office as soon as I learned of the situation but received no reply. I—"

Chase gave a snort of disgust, wheeled away from the butler, and went up the mansion's broad central staircase, taking two steps at a time, then strode down a long hallway to his wife's pink bedroom. There, he found empty hangers in her wardrobe, two half-open bureau drawers from which undergarments appeared to be missing, and a jar of cold cream with its lid lying beside it, as though Bridget had rushed off without bothering to screw it back on. But it was another discovery that gave him pause, for next to the cold cream was Bridget's diamond wedding ring.

Chase went downstairs and instructed the butler to fetch the maid, in whom Bridget had presumably confided. When the maid appeared, Chase grilled her so forcefully that she broke down in tears, all the while insisting that she'd known nothing of her mistress's plans. The butler also pleaded ignorance.

Disgusted, Chase said, "The two of you had better be telling the truth. Now, you are to say nothing of this to anyone. If you do, you will not like the consequences. Is that clear?"

"Yes, sir," came the reply in unison.

*

The next day, in his office near the mill, Chase called in Thomas Dowd for a talk.

"My wife has apparently left me, and I don't know where she is," Chase stated as soon as Dowd took a seat. "She's been trouble since the day we were married."

"I am very sorry to hear that, sir."

"Not as sorry as I am. She's a clever one and she may be in the mood to cause trouble. I would not like it if she took it upon herself to begin making wild claims against me."

"Of course not, sir. Am I to assume you would like me to find her?"

"Yes, and hire as many men as you need to do the job. I do not want her on the loose for long."

"And when we find her?"

"Bring her back to my mansion. I'll decide then what to do."

"Very good, sir."

"Now, what about Sally Sharpe? Do you have some good news for me?"

"I regret to say I do not. However, I assure you I will track her down before long."

"I care not for your assurances, Mr. Dowd. You need to find her, the sooner the better. For all I know, she intends to go to the newspapers with her wild accusations, and I cannot allow that to happen."

"I understand, sir. When I have my hands on her, what would you like me to do?"

"Interrogate her, Mr. Dowd, and do not be polite about it. Find out what exactly what she claims to know about my first wife's death. Then deliver the sternest possible warning that if she persists in her slanders, she will have cause for the utmost regret."

"Very good. I will press her hard. She will cause you no further trouble."

*

Two days after Dowd's meeting with Chase, the *Tribune* reported on a grim discovery in a shanty along the river a mile or so north of Nettie Conley's brothel. BODY OF SALLY SHARPE FOUND, HAD TIES TO EVERLEIGH CASE, POLICE INVESTIGATING, read the headline. The story below stated that an unidentified "drifter" had stumbled across the body, and that it appeared Sharpe had been dead for "a day or more" by the time she was found.

Yet even though the story revisited Sharpe's connection to the Everleigh case at some length, it concluded that "there is nothing to indicate at this time that her death was in any way related to that matter. Miss Sharpe, 24, apparently took up residence in the shanty after having been for some years an inmate of Nettie Conley's well-known sporting house. The police state that they found no evidence of foul play at the scene. However, several empty bottles of a nerve tonic containing laudanum and alcohol were found near her body, and it is to be supposed that the poor young woman, destitute and alone, deliberately ended her life or simply drank too much of the tonic."

Stoddard Chase read the story with a mixture of satisfaction and concern. The whore would trouble him no longer. But had Dowd been involved in her demise? Chase put the question to his fixer when they met later that day.

Dowd stoutly denied any role in Sharpe's death. "She was hiding out in that shanty all by herself," he told Chase, "and as she apparently told no one of her plans, I was unable to find her. But nature took its course, and now she is no longer a worry to us."

"Yes, and that is a good thing," said Chase, who felt the heavens had delivered him a favor. "Now then, Mr. Dowd, let us talk about my wandering wife. Are you close to retrieving her?"

"We are," Dowd promised, even though he had no idea where Bridget might be. "My men are making inquiries day and night and scouring her known haunts. I also have men watching the train stations in case she tries to leave the city. We will find her. It is only a matter of time."

"Well, it had better happen quickly," Chase said. "I am paying you good money, Mr. Dowd, and I expect results. So far, you haven't delivered them."

Dowd stood up, gave a small bow, and said, "Do not worry, sir. You will see results very soon."

*

When Sophia Westerly read the sad news about Sally Sharpe, she thought it could hardly be a coincidence that the girl had turned up dead so soon after the coroner's inquest. But if Sharpe had been murdered at Chase's behest, as Sophia suspected, why had she been such a danger to him?

What did seem certain was that poor Sally had died a miserable death, with no one to hold her hand or speak lovingly to her as she traveled to eternity. Sophia decided that at the least Sally deserved a decent burial as opposed to unmarked grave in the rough dirt of a potter's field. Sophia bought a casket and a burial plot at Layman's Cemetery, then hired a minister to say prayers over Sally's body when she went into the ground. And as she left the cemetery, where Nettie Conley and some of her "girls" had joined her for the brief services, Sophia felt more strongly than ever that Stoddard Chase had to be called to account for his evil doings.

That night, back at her mansion, Sophia composed a brief note and put it out for the next day's mail. Chase, she was sure, believed he would get off scot free, that no one ever would be able to bring his evil deeds to light. She planned to disabuse him of that notion. *Let us see what happens,* she thought, *when he begins to feel the hot breath of vengeance at his back.*

*

The following evening, Chase opened his mail as he enjoyed a drink in his study. A small envelope of the size used for an invitation or a thank-you note caught his attention. Suspecting the envelope contained an anonymous diatribe from some disgruntled mill worker—he'd received several such missives over the years—Chase slit it open and received an unpleasant surprise. Hand-printed on a plain white card was this message: "I know you murdered Ransom Everleigh. Do not think you will escape judgment, for as the

Bible says, 'There is nothing covered, that shall not be revealed; neither hid, that shall not be known.' " The note was signed, "Your Nemesis."

5.
A PIONEER AT THE FALLS

LONG BEFORE Stoddard Chase first saw St. Anthony Falls, it glowed like a wondrous mirage in his mind's eye. He'd seen what water could do at the Pawtucket Falls in Lowell, Massachusetts, where his father owned two cotton mills. It was there that Chase, a self-taught engineer, learned how a mill's complex equipment could be tied together to form a huge machine turning cotton into cloth and cloth into money.

Chase, his father assumed, would one day take over the mills. But as he came of age, Chase chafed under his father's oppressive thumb and longed to strike out on his own somewhere far away from the cramped, tradition-bound world of New England. He began to read every book and article he could about new lands opening to the west, and when he came upon descriptions of the great falls on the Mississippi, he had a vision. It could be the centerpiece of a new Lowell, he believed, a place where he might make a far greater fortune than his father had ever managed to amass.

So it was that at age twenty-five Chase made the long journey to see the falls for himself. He finally reached the little village of St. Anthony along the east side of the falls on a cloudy May afternoon in 1852. It was a raw place, only recently carved out of the wilderness. Wandering pigs rooted in muddy streets laced with horse manure, cows wandered in backyard fields amid the stumps of a newly vanished forest, and everywhere men rushed about as though a fortune lay waiting for them just around the next corner. The village itself consisted of rough clapboard cottages built of green wood that still oozed with moisture, along with a handful of small brick shops and stores, all of it as cheaply and hastily built as a stage set. Yet the town itself hardly mattered. Instead, what Chase heard as he walked down Main Street, nodding to occasional passersby, was everything.

Chase had first heard the sound—like "thunder rolling in the air," as one early traveler put it—not long after arriving in St. Paul, the most northerly port for steamboats on the Upper Mississippi. He'd then boarded a stagecoach for the ten-mile trip across the prairies to St. Anthony. As the coach breasted the bluffs above St. Paul, with the wind blowing hard from the west, Chase began to hear the falls. It was a distant hum at first, a whisper of possibility beckoning him. Mile by mile, the sound grew louder, until it became the unmistakable roar of falling water.

When Chase made a careful inspection of the falls, he understood at once that his long trip had been worth the effort. The falls was wider and higher than any he knew of in New England, and the flow of water was very strong, providing an abundance of power. But to Chase's dismay, he saw that the falls was already the site of frenzied development. A small gristmill had recently been built, while a ramshackle colony of sawmills powered by waterwheels extended across the falls on wooden platforms wedged between massive chunks of limestone. Even more mills appeared to be under construction nearby, and Chase began to worry he'd arrived too late to make his own mark at the falls.

After checking into a hotel that was little more than a giant wooden shed, Chase began making inquiries. He soon learned that all the property along the east side of the falls was controlled by a mix of prominent locals and eastern capitalists. Even worse from Chase's point of view, the owners were deeply enmeshed in litigation over a bewildering array of issues, with no end in sight.

Chase didn't see how he could ever gain a foothold in a place drenched with so much bad blood and so many lawyers, and so he cast his eyes across the river to the west side of the falls, where land was rapidly opening to settlement after treaties relegated the Dakota to distant reservations. Would not the west bank be a place where a man of vision and drive might find great success? Chase hoped so, and two days after arriving in St. Anthony, he took a ferry across the river to see the west bank for himself.

*

When Chase arrived on the scene, the west bank, where Minneapolis would soon bloom into a city, was still part of a military reservation established around Fort Snelling at the confluence of the Mississippi and Minnesota Rivers. But by the early 1850s ambitious squatters, known as preemptors, already had settled on much of the land around the falls in anticipation of buying it once it went up for public sale. The preemptors, who were an unruly bunch, occupied their days and nights with arguments, fistfights, claim jumping, and occasional gunplay, for the stakes were very high. Owning the right plot of land, like marrying an heiress, would guarantee a fortune, and no man wanted to miss out on the opportunity of a lifetime.

The choicest property near the falls was controlled by a man named John Hickey, who also operated a small gristmill originally built by the government to serve the soldiers at Fort Snelling. He was a tough old bird, all squawk and strut, and he carried a pearl-handled Colt revolver on his hip to, as he put it, "discourage anyone with land-grabbing ideas." He was, however, much handier with weaponry than the intricacies of finance, and like many of his fellow pioneers he was notoriously cash poor.

Chase, who could be charming when it suited him, quickly ingratiated himself with Hickey. He lent the old man money on excellent terms, helped rebuild a portion of his mill, and even wrote letters for him. After more than a year of careful effort, Chase convinced Hickey to take him on as business partner. Once the city of Minneapolis sprang to life in 1855, he and Hickey purchased the land they'd preempted. Soon thereafter, the partners formed a company with several other transplanted New Englanders to build the canal that would within ten years feed a dozen power-hungry mills. Hickey, however, didn't live to see that day.

"It is with great sadness that we must report the death of John Hickey, one of our pioneers," the *St. Anthony Express* reported late in 1857 as a financial panic roiled the region. "It appears he used a pistol to take his own life at his home in Minneapolis. His business partner, Stoddard Chase, states that Mr. Hickey had become despondent over recent financial reverses and seeing no way out of his difficulties, took the path of self-destruction. He will be missed by his many friends and associates."

Not everyone believed the story, for Chase and Hickey had become uneasy partners. Hickey disliked Chase's supercilious air, while Chase was not pleased that his partner was drunk more often than not. There were also rumors, swirling like the waters below the falls, that Chase was doing some creative embroidery with the partnership's books.

Chase was duly questioned by the authorities, who had their suspicions. It was quickly discovered that he had no alibi for the night of his partner's supposed suicide. Instead, he simply stated he had been home alone, asleep in his bed. But the absence of an alibi is proof of nothing, and with no one able to contradict Chase's story or offer clear evidence against him, he was never charged with a crime.

*

With Hickey gone, Chase was free to pursue his dream of creating an empire of flour at the falls. It took him three years to raise enough money to erect his first mill in 1859. It was a smallish affair modeled on a highly automated milling system devised more than half a century earlier by a Philadelphia-based mechanical genius named Oliver Evans. Chase's new mill, which he called the Cataract, functioned well enough initially, but a series of vexing problems soon began to plague its operation. These issues were rendered moot when the mill burned down on an icy January day in 1863 following an explosion.

What sparked the blast was never determined, and there were some in the business community who suspected Chase had sabotaged his own mill because it was failing. The mill's insurer even advanced that theory in court, but Chase's lawyers brought in experts to describe how easily even the tiniest accidental spark could cause volatile flour dust to explode. Chase won his case, and with a six-figure insurance settlement finally in hand, he began to lay plans for a new, much larger, and more efficient mill.

As he was considering how to raise additional monies for the project, he encountered Ransom Everleigh. Like Chase, Everleigh was a visionary, and in the early 1860s he'd relocated to Minneapolis, which he believed offered unparalleled opportunities for a man of his talents. New mills were rising all around the falls and their owners needed access to eastern capital to build and equip the huge structures. Once he learned Chase wished to build a mill of unprecedented size, Everleigh offered his services over dinner at a tavern. As Chase looked on in astonishment, Everleigh wrote down the names of half a dozen prominent New York and Boston financiers and said, "I can get fifty thousand dollars or more from any of these men, on good terms, to build your mill."

A partnership resulted. It was not what Chase wanted, but Everleigh was adamant that such be their arrangement. Everleigh proved as good as his word when it came to obtaining capital, and by 1867 the new mill, largely designed by Chase, was up and running. Chase named the mill the Perfection as a tribute to his own mechanical ingenuity, and he delighted in explaining to one and all why it was the finest flour mill not only in Minneapolis but the entire nation.

Yet the partnership between Chase and Everleigh was fraught from the very beginning. An engaging personality with a fine eye for the female form, Everleigh spent money as fast as he made it, while Chase preferred to hoard and scheme. He also despised Everleigh's personal conduct. Chase thought of himself as a proper man, in need of a proper wife, but work consumed him until, at age forty-one, he married Elizabeth Neill, the shy daughter of a Presbyterian minister. Although Chase hardly qualified as a model husband, he did not stray from the marital bed, and he found Everleigh's many dalliances to be immoral and quite disgusting.

Far worse, from Chase's point of view, was that Everleigh could not be trusted with money. He thrived on financial trickery, the more complicated the better, and as the years went by Chase began to suspect he was being cheated. In early 1872 Chase hired, in secret, an outside accountant to review the partnership's books. The accountant concluded that Everleigh was helping himself to an excess share of the profits, although the details of how he had managed this alleged feat of embezzlement were murky. Chase, however, had no doubts his partner was a crook, and a huge row ensued.

Seething with anger, Chase threatened to sue Everleigh or even seek a criminal indictment. But Everleigh denied any wrongdoing and even proclaimed that he would countersue Chase should their dispute end up in the courts. It was all very unsettling, and by June 1872 Chase was ready to be done with his partner, telling an associate, "I will be rid of Everleigh if it is the last thing I ever do."

*

"I received this in yesterday's mail," Stoddard Chase said, sliding the threatening note from "Your Nemesis" across his desk so that Dowd could read it. "Who do you suppose sent it?"

Dowd had never suffered from a shortage of work, for a discreet man willing to undertake unpleasant jobs for the wealthy was always in demand. But Stoddard Chase was turning into a very troublesome client, beset by one problem after another and expecting immediate solutions as though Dowd's résumé included the performance of miracles. Dowd felt put upon, but such was the way of rich men, who'd always viewed him as a mere tool whose only value lay in its use.

Dowd kept such thoughts to himself as he pored over the note as slowly as if he were deciphering ancient hieroglyphs. When he'd finished, he said in his usual syrupy manner, "It is hard to say, sir, who might have written this. You will pardon me for saying so, sir, but have you considered the possibility that the present Mrs. Chase wrote it?"

Chase had in fact suspected as much, but he didn't want to share that idea with Dowd. Instead, he was hoping, in a strange sort of way, that Dowd could come up with a better explanation. "No, I do not think Bridget would be foolish enough to make such a ridiculous allegation. It must be from someone else. I have many enemies in this city, Mr. Dowd, many enemies, and I imagine more than a few of them would take great pleasure in tormenting me. Do you have any other thoughts as to who it could be?"

Dowd said, "Whoever wrote it must, of course, be a friend of

Mr. Everleigh. It could be someone who works at the mill, since Mr. Everleigh was very popular with the men there. Still, I would not make too much of the note, sir. As we both know, you did not murder Mr. Everleigh, and as you've said, the note is obviously intended to discomfit you. My only concern is what the person responsible for it might do next."

"Exactly," Chase said, "and I do not like it one bit. Why is it people wish to think ill of me? What have I done to deserve such horrid treatment?"

"Why, you have done nothing, sir, but there are always people who envy the success of others and act out of spite against them. I am sure that is the case here. I will make a few inquiries around the mill to see what I can learn."

"You do that. And what of my wife?"

"We are closing in on her, sir."

"Well, close faster. I need to talk some sense into her. There is much mischief in the air, Mr. Dowd, and I must put a stop to it, by one means or another."

6.
THE PROPHET OF THE MIST

PETER NICHOLS WAS JUST ARRIVING at the Perfection Mill for his regular shift at seven in the morning when John the Baptist, dressed in his usual robe, rushed up to greet him. The Baptist, as people liked to call him, was also known as the Prophet of the Mist and lived on a small island near the mill. His real name, which Peter struggled to remember, was Jonathan Hobson, and he was regarded as one of the great characters of the city.

"Good day," said Hobson, who was gaunt and well bearded. "Can you spare anything for a poor old man?"

"Oh, I'll find something," Peter said. He opened his lunchbox and handed the Baptist a shiny red apple. "I can do without."

"Very kind of you. Very kind indeed. Do you know what I saw?"

"I don't," Peter said, hoping to avoid an extended conversation with Hobson, who was prone to ranting about whatever subject happened to occupy his fevered brain at the moment. Hobson was well known to Peter and the other millhands. They viewed the strange old man as a harmless crank and would often give him food, since he always appeared to be in need of a good meal.

"I saw the tall one with him," Hobson announced as he stuffed the apple in an inside pocket of the long, ragged robe he wore no matter how warm the weather. "I see things no one else does."

"Well, I'm sure you do," Peter said, starting to edge away. God only knew what the old man was babbling about, and Peter didn't have the time to listen to him. "Now, if—"

"He is one of the devil's agents, the tall one is," Hobson continued, his intense blue eyes boring in on Nichols like the lamps of an onrushing locomotive. "It's too bad he killed Mr. Everleigh, as I suppose he did, but murder is always the devil's work, is it not?"

Peter wasn't sure he could believe what he was hearing. Had the crazy old hermit actually seen something on the night of Everleigh's death? "Tell me all you know," Peter said, no longer worried he might be late for his shift, "and I promise I will make it worth your while."

*

Said to hail from an obscure hamlet in Maine, Jonathan Hobson had wandered into St. Anthony in 1847 as an itinerant preacher, looking for new territory to save souls. He had little luck in that regard, but before long the falls itself became his spiritual mission. Unlike his fellow New Englanders who saw only money flowing over the falls, Hobson had been enchanted by its beauty from the moment he saw it and detested the "improvements" that he believed were ruining it. In whatever church would have him—and before long, none would—he proclaimed that the falls lay at the heart of a "new Garden of Eden" and that the men busily turning it into a giant factory on water were "desecrating God's glorious creation."

In a place full of men pursuing the main chance thanks to the power of the falls, Hobson's message did not prove popular. Soon labeled "John the Baptist," he wandered about in a robe with a shepherd's crook, enduring derisive laughter and the taunts of children wherever he went. He roamed the city for several years before abruptly disappearing one summer. It was assumed at first that he had packed up his meager possessions and gone elsewhere to harass the populace. But he hadn't. Instead, he'd simply moved a bit downriver to build a rude cabin on Spirit Island just below the falls.

Rising forty feet above the river in sheer cliffs, the island was a mammoth tilted block of limestone that had been shaped by the force of the river. The Dakota, who called it Wíta Wanáǧi, knew the island well and their women sometimes went there to give birth under its magic spell. A small stand of spruce watered by the mist from the falls had once stood atop the island like a thick clump of hair, but the tiny forest was cut down once settlers arrived. Later, fitful attempts to quarry the limestone met with limited success, and by the time Hobson built his cabin, which he occupied only during the warmer months, the island was deserted save for nesting eagles who hunted fish in the river. Hobson used a small skiff to reach the island and would usually tie it up by the Perfection Mill when he went into the city.

Once Hobson moved to his island hermitage, a newspaper columnist promptly dubbed him "the Prophet of the Mist, bathed in the waters of his own righteousness." The mocking appellation stuck, and in time hardly anyone remembered Hobson's real name. All the public knew was that he appeared to be a beggar of unsound mind, dirty and unpleasant, and no respectable person would have anything to do with him.

*

Hobson was a close observer of the moon, which he believed to be a reflection of God's visage, and he liked to gaze upon its splendor whenever he could. On the night of Everleigh's death, the moon was "being enigmatic," as Hobson liked to say, slipping in and out of view amid scudding clouds that raced beneath the stars. Equipped with a small telescope, Hobson went out to the cliff that formed the island's western face to make observations. It was nearly two o'clock in the morning, but as Hobson owned no watches or clocks, he knew only, as he later told Peter, that it was "a time when the moon was smiling full between two long clouds that looked like serpent devils."

As Hobson swung his telescope around beneath the light of the moon, he caught sight of a curious scene on the river side of the Perfection Mill, where a planked roadway covered the canal that brought water to the turbines. Normally, there would have been no one about at such a late hour, but Hobson saw to his surprise that a horse cart had pulled up next to the mill's rear door. The driver, a very large man dressed all in black and wearing a stovepipe hat, stepped down and went around to the back of the cart. The man walked with a distinctive, shambling gait, and Hobson knew at once who it was. Thomas Dowd, who on several occasions had shooed Hobson away from the mill with threats of violence, walked in just such a way. What Hobson didn't know yet was that Ransom Everleigh lay unconscious in the cart.

Everleigh had left Camp's Saloon half an hour earlier, following a successful night of poker, when he encountered Dowd, who stepped out of the shadows and offered a friendly greeting. Dowd had long known that murder was easy enough if you were careful about it. Stealth and surprise were the keys. So it was that after a brief and uneventful conversation, Dowd doffed his stovepipe hat, said his good nights, and then, as Everleigh turned away, struck him on the back of the head with a sap.

Dowd had already obtained, through trusted intermediaries, a horse cart of the kind normally used to transport human excrement, or "night soil" as it was euphemistically called. As Minneapolis did not yet have a sewer system, human waste collected from privy vaults had to be carted to the river for dumping, preferably in the wee hours of the morning when no one was about to smell the fragrant cargo. Dowd dragged Everleigh to the cart, which he'd parked in an alley, wrapped his limp body in a canvas tarp, and then drove down First Street to the Perfection Mill, ignored by the drunks staggering along nearby.

As Hobson looked on from Spirit Island, Dowd pulled Everleigh's limp body from the cart, hoisted him over his shoulder, unlocked a door, and carried him inside the mill. Once in the mill, hidden from Hobson's view, Dowd delivered another blow to

Everleigh's skull and then threw him into the wheel pit in accord with his instructions. Everleigh lay unconscious at the bottom of the pit until the canal gates were opened a few hours later and the turbine, fed by the inrushing water, tore his body to pieces.

Hobson was still watching when Dowd reappeared outside the mill after accomplishing his lethal mission. As the moon passed beneath one of the serpent clouds, Dowd—now just a moving shadow—relocked the door, climbed back up on the cart, and drove away.

*

"That is quite a story," Peter said after Hobson recounted all he had seen. "You're not making it up, are you?"

"I am no liar!" Hobson said, so loudly that he could have been heard a block away.

"Now, now, I would never accuse you of such a thing," Peter said, emptying his pocket of two silver dollars and pressing them into Hobson's hand. "I just need to be sure, that's all."

"You may be sure," Hobson insisted. "I speak only the truth."

Workers were now arriving at the mill. Peter guided Hobson to a small recess by an auxiliary powerhouse where they could have more privacy and asked, "Could you tell that Mr. Everleigh was the person Dowd carried into the mill?"

"No, God did not grant me that vision. But I read the newspapers, more than you would think, and I hear the buzzings of the world. I know what happened. It was Everleigh who met his end—it could have been no one else—and may God have mercy on his soul."

"Why didn't you tell anyone before now about what you saw?" Peter inquired.

"Why, who would believe my story, except perhaps a kind Christian man such as yourself? This cursed city, you see, has no use for me because I have no part in its business, which is getting and spending and destroying all things beautiful. Besides, God knows what was done that night, for is not the moon His glorious reflection? There will be justice in due time, and that is all that matters. Now, I thank you for what you have given me, but there is nothing more I can give you."

"But you can!" Peter said. "There is justice to be done in this world as well as the next. You must speak of what you saw to the police, or Dowd and his boss will get away with murder. I will even go with you if you want."

Hobson shook his head and began to edge away. "No, it cannot be, and that is my last word upon the subject. Goodbye and Godspeed."

*

That same morning Dowd, following his latest talk with Chase, was nosing about the Perfection Mill. Dowd knew from spies that Peter had more than once said he blamed Chase for Everleigh's murder. But what did the young millwright really know, if anything? Dowd doubted Peter would be interested in answering that question. On the other hand, he just might respond to a suggestion, delivered in Dowd's usual menacing way, that he keep his nose out of matters that didn't concern him, or face unpleasant consequences.

So it was that Dowd stationed himself outside the mill with the intention of taking Peter aside and delivering the kind of warning that would chill his blood, especially if he'd been the author of the note accusing Chase of murder. Dowd also wanted to find out what Peter actually knew, if anything, about the circumstances leading to Everleigh's demise. Or was he simply spouting off about suspicions, with no evidence to back them up?

Dowd had just lit a cigar and was rehearsing exactly what to say when he spotted Peter, at the far corner of the mill, speaking with Hobson. It appeared to be a very animated conversation, and it piqued Dowd's curiosity. He saw a group of millhands coming up Second Street toward the mill, and when they passed, he fell in behind them. As the workers approached Peter and Hobson, they called out greetings. Peter waved at the men but quickly turned his attention back to Hobson, and he didn't notice Dowd going by. Dowd was just in time to hear Peter say, "You must speak of what you saw to the police, or Dowd and his boss will get away with murder."

Dowd wanted to linger but couldn't risk being seen, so he kept walking. By the time Hobson headed back toward the island and

Peter went off to work, Dowd was already thinking about what he might have to do next. He'd assumed no one had seen him with Everleigh's body, but now it seemed that was not the case, despite the great care he'd taken in committing the crime. Dowd weighed his options and decided he'd have to send John the Baptist into the wilderness, permanently.

*

"Well, we have evidence at last, Mother, but I do not see it will be of much use to us," Peter said that evening as he and Sophia enjoyed lemonade and a cooling breeze on the front porch of her mansion. "Poor Old Hobson is probably right in thinking no one will believe him."

"Perhaps," Sophia said. "But we believe him, and that is the important thing."

"I guess so, but what can we do?"

Sophia loved Peter dearly, but she knew she surpassed him in the fine arts of calculation and plotting. He reveled in the tangible work of fixing things, and even the most stubborn pieces of equipment at the mill yielded to his skillful hands. But he wasn't always adept at reading people and their devious doings, and so Sophia took the lead in their discussion.

"There is at least one thing we can do, which is to continue pressing Chase. He doesn't know what we know, that there was a witness to Mr. Everleigh's murder. The question is how we can best use this knowledge to our advantage. We can't go directly to the police and tell them what Hobson saw. They would question his account, as you've said, but I also fear Chase would find out about it because he and Chief Riley are on close terms."

"Like bugs in a rug," Peter agreed. "So what exactly do we do next?"

"We have to keep turning the screws. That note I sent him was merely the first turn. I want him to feel the pressure building, to know he has not fooled everyone. Going forward, our strategy should be to make the public at large ever more suspicious of him, and of Dowd. If the public, and even more so the newspapers, are sufficiently aroused, they will demand a new investigation. And then perhaps Mr. Hobson's story will be heard."

"You already have a plan in mind, don't you?" Peter said.

"You know me too well," Sophia said with a smile and then told Peter what she intended to do.

"That is very clever, Mother. How did you think it up?"

"Let us just say I have a talent for intrigue. Most woman do, even if they won't admit it. Now then, there are other matters we need to discuss, beginning with the death of Sally Sharpe. Do you know she once worked as a maid at Chase's mansion?"

"I didn't. How did you find out?"

"I know many ladies who like to gossip, and one of them mentioned it. I trust you see what this means. I think Mr. Everleigh was looking for the Sharpe girl because he believed she knew something, perhaps something very incriminating, about Chase. And now, suddenly, Sally Sharpe is dead, and it cannot be a coincidence. I have no proof of it, but it's likely Chase sent Dowd to murder her."

"What do you think she knew?" Peter asked.

"I have an idea about that. She apparently left Chase's employ some years before Mr. Everleigh's murder, so whatever she knew must have involved something other than his death. Perhaps she possessed some incriminating information about another death, that of Elizabeth Chase."

"Oh, I remember that," Peter said. "It was in all the papers. She fell down a shaft at the mansion."

"Yes, but what if she didn't fall?"

"My God, do you think Chase murdered her too?"

"I have my suspicions. Remember, Chase married Bridget only a few months later. A man lusting after a beautiful woman—and Bridget is certainly that—is like a charging bull. He will do all he can to mate, and he's capable of anything."

Peter had once been embarrassed by Sophia's blunt talk when it came to sex, but he'd become used to it. "But do you have any evidence Elizabeth was murdered?"

"No, not yet. Bridget Chase may hold the key. A woman who leaves her husband as she did is almost surely a woman in fear. She knows something, and she believes Chase will do whatever it takes to silence her. I don't suppose your sources at the mill have any idea where she might be."

"They don't. Maybe she's left town."

Railroads had only recently connected Minneapolis to Chicago and points east, and Sophia agreed it was possible Bridget had fled the city. "But I really don't think she left. She'd be too easy to trace if she bought a train ticket, and Bridget is no fool. Do you know her at all?"

"I've seen her a couple of times."

"And what do you think of her?"

"Well, she's certainly very attractive."

"That may not be a strong enough word. I saw her at a party once, and men could hardly take their eyes off her. They were like buzzing bees at the honeypot. Bridget is also a very interesting character. As you may recall, she was, like Sally Sharpe, one of Chase's maids until he married her. How that happened I cannot say. But Bridget somehow landed him, and that tells me she is nobody's fool. In any event, we must try to find her before Chase does. I fear she is in mortal danger."

"I wouldn't know where to look for her," Peter said.

"I will make inquiries among my woman friends. Someone in this city must know where she is."

*

The next morning, by one of those circumstances that suggest a tidy universe, a boy appeared at Sophia's mansion with a note in hand. It was from Bridget Chase. "I would like to talk to you," the note said. "I would be most grateful if you could see me at two o'clock this afternoon at the home of the Sisterhood of Salvation."

7.
BRIDGET'S STORY

Sophia Westerly had first met Bridget Chase when they both served briefly as volunteers with the Sisterhood of Salvation, an organization devoted to helping prostitutes, unwed mothers, and other "fallen" women. Sophia thought it clever of Bridget to have taken refuge with the Sisterhood, whose leadership consisted of wealthy women with influential husbands. Not even Chase, she knew, would have the wherewithal to remove his wife, even by force, from such a protected setting.

The Sisterhood operated out of a gloomy old house on Fifth Street South. Sophia rang the doorbell a few minutes before two. "I would like to speak to Mrs. Morrison," she told the girl at the door. "It is a most urgent matter."

When Mathilda Morrison appeared, in a long gray dress cut so tightly around her neck that it was a wonder she could breathe, Sophia was reminded why she'd left the Sisterhood after only a few months of service. A grand dame who took obsessive delight in proclaiming how devoutly she served the Lord, Morrison ran the Sisterhood like a church, with moral instruction—the more hectoring the better—at the core of its mission. This persistent moralizing, thick as a choking fog, hadn't sat well with Sophia, whose faith in God was not especially strong, and after a few numbing months she had opted out of the Sisterhood.

"Why, Sophia, my dear, how nice to see you!" Morrison exclaimed. "I trust God's grace is shining down on you."

"Perhaps it is," Sophia said. "I hope it also shining on Bridget Chase. She has sent me a note and I need to speak with her at once."

"Is that so?" Morrison said, apparently caught by surprise. "Well then, I will show you to her room. I trust you have not mentioned Mrs. Chase's whereabouts to anyone?"

"I have not, since I believe she is in danger."

"Yes, that is what she appears to believe as well, although I am not so sure of that. In my opinion Mr. Chase is hardly a dangerous man."

"Then you do not know him well enough," Sophia said. "Now, please take me to Bridget."

*

Bridget Chase was staying in a small bedroom on the house's upper floor, and when she opened the door and saw Sophia with Morrison her face brightened. Wearing a modest black dress that could not disguise her voluptuous figure, Bridget was just as Sophia remembered her. She was almost ridiculously beautiful—a perfectly formed face, full lips of the kind invariably described as "pouty," electric blue eyes, and light auburn hair that curled down to her shoulders. She was a goddess of midnight, promising bedroom splendors, and it was easy to see why Chase had sought to possess her. Still, it was one thing for a man to seduce his maid and quite another to marry her, and Sophia had always wondered how that had happened.

"I understand you wish to speak with Mrs. Westerly," Morrison said as they stepped into the room. "May I suggest that if in the future you wish to have visitors, you should let me know in advance."

Sophia said, "Thank you for your help, Mrs. Morrison. You may leave us now as our talk must be conducted in private."

"Well, I must say—" Morrison began, ready to lodge a protest, but Sophia all but pushed her out the door, which she then closed and locked.

Sophia took a seat on the bed across from the rocker where Bridget had apparently been reading a devotional tract, which lay half open on a small table beside her. Images of the tortured Christ and of a heavily bearded God the Father adorned the room, which featured patterned wallpaper so darkly oppressive it seemed to sop up every ray of light that came through the only window. A prison cell, Sophia thought, might have been more cheerful.

"It is so good to see you," Bridget said. "The ladies here are nice, but they are oh so starchy, if you know what I mean. It feels like I'm stuck in church. All I hear is God this and God that, and it becomes terribly boring. Thank goodness I brought along some interesting books, but I had to sneak them in. Have you read *The Moonstone* or *Lady Audley's Secret*? I do like a good mystery."

"And now it appears you're in one," Sophia said.

"Yes, you could say that. And that is why I asked you here. I believe you can be of help to me, and help is what I certainly need right now."

"I can understand that. But why did you contact me? It is not as though we are dear friends."

"Oh, I do hope one day we will be so. But there is a very good reason why I reached out to you. I have been told you are looking into Mr. Everleigh's death and that you believe my husband may be behind it. Is that true?"

Sophia was caught off guard. "May I ask who told you this?"

"I would rather not say, as I do not wish to get anyone in trouble. But I will tell you that the information came from a person acquainted with your son, Peter. I was told he was quite devastated by finding Mr. Everleigh's body. How horrible that must have been!"

"It was," Sophia agreed. "And you are right. My son and I are indeed investigating Mr. Everleigh's death, and we are all but certain we know what happened. Are you acquainted with a man named Thomas Dowd?"

A flash of alarm registered on Bridget's face. "Mr. Dowd? Yes, I know of him. He works for my husband, but I am not sure what he does. What about him?"

"I have evidence that he murdered Mr. Everleigh on your husband's instructions," Sophia said and then recounted what Jonathan Hobson had seen on the night of Everleigh's death. "My son believes Mr. Hobson and so do I. He would have no reason to lie. We assume your husband hired Dowd to commit the murder. I am sorry to have to tell you this, but you have a right to know just how truly evil your husband is."

Bridget lowered her head briefly, then looked up and said with what sounded like a sense of relief. "Thank you for telling me this. I suspected from the start my husband was involved in Mr. Everleigh's death. I even asked him once if it was so, but he denied it, and as it was, I had no proof. I knew only that he really hated Mr. Everleigh. I heard him say more than once that he would like to kill him if he could."

Sophia said, "Did you leave your husband because of those suspicions?"

To Sophia's surprise, Bridget shook her head and said, "No, that was not the reason. May I confide in you?"

"Certainly."

"Very well. To begin with, you need to know that my husband desperately wants a son—a daughter would mean nothing to him—but so far that has not happened, and he has grown very angry with me. I have no reason to think I can't have children, and I sometimes wonder—"

"If the problem is with him?" Sophia interjected.

"I do not like to speak of such things but, yes, that is what I wonder. Of course, he would never admit to having such a problem, so I must bear the brunt of his unhappiness. You may not know it, but I was told Elizabeth, his first wife, was unable to have children and that Mr. Chase came to detest her because of that. Well, a few days ago he took me aside and said I'd better be with child soon or he would have no more use for me. The way he said it was so cold and so harsh that I felt a chill run down my spine. But what he said next terrified me. 'You would do well to remember what happened to Elizabeth,' he said, 'lest it happen again.' Those were his exact words."

Elizabeth Chase's death, as Sophia recalled, had been the subject of extensive coverage in the press. The story was that she'd been found dead at the bottom of the manlift in the Chase mansion. There were no witnesses to the accident, or so the newspapers said, but it was presumed that Elizabeth had somehow lost her footing while riding the manlift and plunged more than forty feet to her death. Although Chase was said to have been disconsolate over what he called "an awful tragedy," he'd nonetheless recovered quickly enough to install Bridget in his bed a few months later.

It suddenly occurred to Sophia that Elizabeth's death—a quick, fatal drop down a deep shaft—was eerily similar to Everleigh's demise. She said, "Are you saying your husband murdered her?"

Bridget nodded. "Oh, I know now it wasn't an accident. He pushed her. That is what he did, and it was cold-blooded murder."

"How do you know this?"

Bridget took a deep breath as tears began to roll down her cheeks. "It was poor little Sally Sharpe who told me, only days before she died. Oh, it is all so awful! I now fear she, too, may have been murdered."

Sophia was both stunned and intrigued. "Tell me everything you know," she said. "Everything."

Bridget obliged. She said she and Sharpe were both working as maids at the Chase mansion when Elizabeth died. On the night it happened, at well past eleven o'clock, the servants were all in their quarters, except for Sharpe. Unable to sleep, she went to the tower room, where there was a well-stocked library, to look for something to read. Since she found the manlift too frightening to use, Sharpe walked up the steps. Just as she entered the room, she saw Chase standing at the entrance to the manlift with Elizabeth, apparently insensate, flung over his shoulder. He gave her a kiss and said, "Goodbye, my dear" before throwing her down the open shaft where the manlift operated.

"Poor Sally was scared out of her wits," Bridget said. "She ran back down the stairs before my husband saw her. The funny thing was, Elizabeth did not appear to put up a fight of any kind, or so Sally told me. I suspect now that Mr. Chase drugged her into a stupor before murdering her."

"What happened next?"

"Sally gave her notice the next day, but something she said or maybe just the way she looked must have made my husband suspicious. I cannot be sure, but I think he gave her some money and told her to keep quiet unless she wanted to end up like Elizabeth. Later, he claimed she'd been fired for stealing some jewels, but that was a lie."

"Did Sally tell you what she'd seen?" Sophia asked.

"No, not until much later. I guess she was too afraid to say anything for a long time. But it must have been eating at her, especially after Mr. Everleigh's death. That's when she sent me a note out of the blue and I went to visit her. I must say it was very sad to see what had become of her. I gave her ten dollars and told her to come here if she wanted to make a decent life for herself. She said she'd think about it, and that's when she sprang a big surprise and told me about Elizabeth's murder. Naturally, I was shocked, but I wasn't sure if I should believe her, given her condition. But the next thing I knew, she was dead, and as you can imagine, I became very frightened. I decided the best thing would be to leave Mr. Chase, as I feared for my own life."

"You made the right choice," Sophia said. "By the way, were you aware Mr. Everleigh was looking for Sally just before his death?"

"No, but he must have had some suspicions of his own. I didn't know him very well—he was never invited to the mansion—but he always seemed like a charming man."

"He was," Sophia agreed. "Perhaps too charming for his own good."

"Now, there is one more thing you must know," Bridget said. "Elizabeth and Sally were very close. I don't think poor Elizabeth had many friends—she was quite sickly for a long time—but she confided in Sally that she feared Mr. Chase would kill her so that he could remarry. How I wish I would have known of that before I became his new wife! But I didn't. As it was, Sally told me Elizabeth wrote out a last testament describing all of Mr. Chase's threats against her. It concluded by saying that if she died a violent death, it was because her husband and no one else had murdered her."

"Do you have this testament?" Sophia asked. "It could be of tremendous use to us."

"No. Sally told me about it the last time I met with her. She said Elizabeth had hidden it in the tower library in a novel she was reading because she knew Mr. Chase never cared for fiction. Unfortunately, Sally didn't know which novel the testament was in. I looked for it—I took down every book in the library—but I couldn't find it."

"Elizabeth could have put it somewhere else or even have left it with someone for safekeeping."

"Or Mr. Chase could somehow have found it, in which case it will have been destroyed. Why is it that evil men such as my husband seem to have all the luck?"

"That is a question best left to God," Sophia said. "For you, the question is what comes next. I think you should tell the police what you have told me about Elizabeth's murder."

"And then what?" Bridget asked, a glum look settling over her face. "Mr. Chase is on very good terms with that man—I forget his name—who's chief of police. They're bosom friends, those two. Do you think the police would believe me, especially since Sally is dead? I have thought about going to the newspapers, but they fear Mr. Chase and his attorneys. They know he would sue them over a story accusing him of murder. So I am stuck, Sophia. I'm not sure what to do."

Bridget began to cry again but quickly regained her composure. She said, "My life seemed so wonderful when I married Mr. Chase, and now it is a nightmare!"

"I have often thought about your marriage," Sophia said. "I do not wish to pry, yet I think it is quite extraordinary that he took you as his wife, given how different your backgrounds are."

"Yes, it is strange, isn't it? But I believe he greatly desired me, in the way men do, and as he knew I would never compromise my virtue, he saw no choice but to wed."

"And then your life suddenly changed."

"It did! And at first I felt like Cinderella. I had nothing as a child, except the smell of slaughtered animals in my nostrils day and night, and to become the wife of a great man, and live in a great house, well, it was a dream."

Sophia understood. When she'd married into wealth in Galena, it had been like moving into heaven—all the rough poverty of her previous life magically transformed into a world of fancy dresses, fine linens, and crystal goblets. It had all been very intoxicating, if only for a little while, before Darius Hoskinson showed what kind of man he truly was.

"But fairy tales do not always end well, do they?" Sophia said.

"No, but maybe we can create our own, with a happy ending."

"Yes," Sophia said. "Perhaps we can, so long as you do not give up hope. What we must do now is to make sure you are safe. There are many ears and eyes in this house, and I fear someone will make your presence known to Mr. Chase before long. You could leave town, but I imagine he has men watching the railroad depots. They may also be keeping an eye on the hotels and rooming houses. No, you must stay somewhere Mr. Chase and that ruffian of his, Mr. Dowd, will not think to look, and I know just the place."

"That would be wonderful if you could help. You are a true friend, Mrs. Westerly."

"Call me Sophia, my dear. I am indeed a friend you can rely upon. And you may also be sure that I remain Mr. Chase's mortal enemy. I have been doing all I can to expose his crimes. Read the *Tribune* and you will see soon what I mean. I will not allow that monster of a man to get away with murder."

"You are very brave," Bridget said. "That cannot be said of many women."

"To the contrary, it can be said of more women than you imagine," Sophia said. "Now, here is what we must do."

*

The next morning, Sophia shepherded Bridget to the house of woman she knew across the river in the old town of St. Anthony, now part of Minneapolis. She gave Bridget firm instructions not to leave the house until further notice. "You must think of yourself as a prisoner for the time being," Sophia said. "It is the only way you can be sure to avoid detection."

*

Two days later, as Bridget settled in with Sophia's friend, a large paid notice appeared in the *Tribune* that occasioned much excited talk among the newspaper's regular readers. Positioned prominently at the top of the front page, the notice offered an intriguing message in bold copperplate letters: WE KNOW WHERE C. T. D. WAS ON THE NIGHT OF JUNE 6, 1872, AND WE KNOW WHO HIRED HIM. JUSTICE WILL BE SERVED!

The *Tribune*'s editors, well aware that Ransom Everleigh had died on June 6, would have been reluctant to run the notice had it not arrived in the mail with a cashier's check for one hundred dollars, which was enough to pay for an entire edition's worth of advertisements. And as the notice named no names, it could not be viewed as libelous. Among readers, a great guessing game began as to the identify of "C. T. D." An optometrist named Charles T. Daly soon found himself receiving unwanted attention, as did Curtis T. Daniels, one of the city's occasionally honest aldermen. But among those privy to the details of Everleigh's murder, there could be no doubt that C. Thomas Dowd and his unnamed employer now stood accused of the crime.

*

The notice naturally caught the attention of Stoddard Chase, who called in Dowd for a meeting. "What do you make of it?" he asked bluntly, sliding a copy of the *Tribune* across his desk so that the bold notice pointed at Dowd like an accusatory finger. "It looks like someone has it out for us."

"Indeed it does," Dowd replied, "and I know who it is. I believe it's the same person—'your nemesis,' as he signed himself—who sent you that threatening message."

"Yes, that seems likely. So who is it?"

"It must be Peter Nichols, sir. Ever since he discovered Mr. Everleigh's body, he's been stirring up trouble. Now he has gone so far as to accuse me—and you—of murder, or so it seems. I also have reason to be believe his mother is egging him on. Do you know Mrs. Westerly?"

"Of course I do," Chase said, stroking at his beard as though hoping to find a brilliant thought hidden among the whiskers. "William's widow. I've met her a few times. Quite a striking woman, I must say. Her husband was no friend of mine, and neither is she. Indeed, she never liked me. I don't know why."

Who in all of Minneapolis does like you? Dowd wanted to ask but held his tongue.

Chase played with his beard a bit longer before issuing instructions. "Do some digging, Mr. Dowd, and be quick about it. If Nichols and that meddling mother of his are behind these attacks, they must be stopped. I will not be defamed under any circumstances."

"And what might stopping them entail, if I may ask, sir?"

"Whatever it takes. Make it very clear to them that they will be ruined, or worse, if they persist in their attacks upon me. And while you're at it, perhaps teach young Mr. Nichols the kind of lesson he won't soon forget."

8.
LOVE AT LAST

SOPHIA'S CAMPAIGN against Stoddard Chase had an eerie parallel in her own life. She, too, had once been accused of a terrible crime, in Galena, and it remained an uncomfortable memory. But whereas Sophia was sure Chase had committed murder, her own case was entirely different, or so she would always claim.

Her troubles arrived a few years after she married Darius Hoskinson following the death of her first husband. The wedding elevated Sophia into a world of wealth she had never known before. Hoskinson was a widower with two adult children and occupied a splendid mansion on Park Street in the heart of Galena. With servants to tend to her every need, Sophia set about the task of becoming a cultured woman. She read widely in French and English, learned the intricacies of managing a large household, bought elegant silk dresses for the first time in her life, and even took piano lessons.

Peter lived with her, and he was the one true joy of her life, because Hoskinson did not turn out to be the kind of lover Sophia had always wanted. Instead, he was cold and critical, and prone to terrible fits of temper. He also made a frequent point of reminding her that "the only good women are the ones who always obey their husbands." But money has a way of salving unhappiness, and Sophia kept to her wifely duties, even as Hoskinson grew ever more rude and demanding.

Then, in the summer of 1853, Hoskinson suddenly fell ill with an acute intestinal disturbance. Dysentery, the doctors thought, and within a week he was gone. Sophia put on a black mourning dress, made suitable expressions of grief, and prepared for a new life as one of Galena's wealthiest widows.

Sophia's mourning was soon interrupted by a noisy dispute over her husband's estate. Hoskinson's two children, who had never warmed to their stepmother, contended that their father had left his entire estate to Sophia in a will they knew nothing about. Sophia, they claimed, must have forged the document, an allegation she stoutly denied. They also began to circulate rumors that she had poisoned Hoskinson, perhaps with arsenic, and wherever Sophia went in Galena she was met with cold stares and whispered animadversions. With a long and expensive legal fight looming in probate court, Sophia finally agreed to split the estate with Hoskinson's children, whom she regarded as both greedy and lacking any real affection for their father.

"I have done nothing wrong," she insisted in court, "but I see no value in enriching a pack of voracious lawyers at my expense."

Yet even after the settlement, the whisperings persisted. No longer able to tolerate Galena and its nattering gossips, Sophia moved across the river to Dubuque, Iowa, but the ugly rumors followed her. With the money from her late husband's estate all but exhausted, Sophia finally came north with Peter to Minneapolis, thinking new opportunities might await her there.

*

Peter had been only twelve when Hoskinson died, and all the gossip directed at Sophia caused him great pain. Strong for his age, Peter had had no trouble dealing with the boys who tried to bully him, and he always stood up for his mother. Still, a wisp of suspicion haunted Peter, although he never worked up the courage to ask Sophia outright about Hoskinson's death. To his surprise, the subject came up after Sophia had placed the notice in the *Tribune.*

"Well, I imagine everyone is talking about it," Peter said. "Chase and Dowd must be beside themselves. Do you think other people understand who the initials refer to?"

"If not, they will figure it out before long, and they will talk and talk. The gossip will find its way to both of our targets, and they won't like it, especially Chase. I know what kind of effect an accusation of murder can have. I am sure you remember what happened to me after Mr. Hoskinson's death."

"I will never forget it. I knew you were innocent, no matter what anyone else said."

"It was an ugly time," Sophia agreed, "but I knew you would stick by me. You have always been my favorite, my sweet boy."

Peter would never have said so, but he sometimes wondered whether he knew the full story behind Hoskinson's sudden and rather mysterious death. His mother, he believed, was capable of anything if it was powered by love. He still vividly recalled how he'd once been punched in the face by Hoskinson during one of his violent rages. Sophia had reacted to the assault with astonishing fury. She grabbed a butcher knife, pressed it to Hoskinson's neck hard enough to draw blood, and backed him up against a wall. "Never," she said, "never again will you strike my boy." Less than a month later, Hoskinson was dead. Peter believed it was a coincidence, and yet—

Now she was pursuing Ransom Everleigh's murderer with that same daunting intensity, and Peter thought it could only be because of love. With that in mind, he said, "You were in love with Mr. Everleigh, weren't you."

Sophia took him in with her lustrous eyes and said softly, "Yes, Ransom meant more to me than you know. I will tell you the story, and I hope you will not think ill of me. It was not a thing I expected to happen. It just did."

*

It had all begun at William Westerly's wake, where many of the city's prominent millers paid their respects. Chase, cold and imperious, had already made a brief appearance by the time Everleigh arrived. Looking splendid as always in a finely tailored black suit, his beautiful head of hair flowing in waves, he approached Sophia, kissed her hand, and spoke in a heartfelt way about her late husband.

"I am so sorry about William," he said in a soft voice. "He was a good, honest man, and I cannot say that of many others in this city. Most of us, you know, are just pirates after booty, but William was always fair and square. Do you remember when a small fire damaged our mill shortly after it was built? Well, your husband was the first miller to come to our aid and offer any and all help he could."

"Yes, he was a good man," Sophia said, her hand somehow tingling from the kiss. "I will certainly miss him."

Everleigh nodded and said, "Of course. But I do not doubt a woman as beautiful as yourself will find new companionship in time. We mourn our losses, but we must move on. It is all we can do."

Mourning was supposed to be a nearly unending ordeal in those days, especially for a widow, who would certainly have to wait a year or even two before being seen in the company of a new man. But Sophia's grief was neither long nor deep. William had been like a kindly uncle, so much so that at times she felt more like his ward than his wife, and once he developed diabetes, he'd been too ill to perform in the bedroom.

A week after the wake, Sophia encountered Everleigh by chance as she left a seamstress's shop on Nicollet Avenue. He was strolling along with his customary insouciance and hailed her on the sidewalk. They talked for half an hour, and two nights later, Sophia—both shocked and intrigued by her sudden descent into promiscuity—found herself in Everleigh's lair, enjoying sex in a way she never had before.

Sophia had known, since the first time she pleasured herself as a girl, that sex was a kind of strange magic, but that quality had been notably absent from her marriages. François was a buck for whom sex was a brief, snorting release and little else. Darius Hoskinson hadn't been much better, rough of manner and not the least bit interested in pleasing her. And William, kind as he was, had simply been too sickly to make anything like passionate love.

But Everleigh! How different he was from any man she'd ever known! He kissed and caressed and fondled her, ran his long fingers down her spine as they lay naked, and he was never in a hurry. And when he entered her, it was as though her heart had been torn open to reveal a powerful force long hidden deep inside her. The shuddering orgasm that followed was so intense Sophia cried out with joy. Afterward, Everleigh did not rush to leave the bed or fall asleep, as her husbands had, but instead stayed to talk and touch.

"I have never been with a man like you," Sophia said as she

rubbed his chest. "How is it you know so much about pleasing a woman?"

Everleigh smiled and said, "I think I can answer that easily enough. You see, most men don't like women. In fact, I believe they secretly despise them and only tolerate them for the obvious reason. But I have never felt that way. I really do like women and always have."

"And you seem to particularly like seducing them, as I have just learned," Sophia said.

"No, I do not quite see it that way. You are far too strong and wise a woman, my dear Sophia, to fall for honeyed words and false promises. I think we seduced each other."

"Yes, perhaps we did. And now, I suppose, you will be moving on."

To Sophia's surprise and delight, Everleigh said, "You know, I have been moving on, as you put it, my whole life, and yet now I find myself wishing to stay still for a while. To be a dweller, you could say. I confess you have enchanted me."

Sophia, too, was smitten. She'd thought she and Everleigh would be fireflies in the darkness, together for a moment and then gone. But as they met again, and more times after that, she felt herself falling into a kind of a whirling dance with Everleigh, as though they were planets being pulled ever closer by gravity.

"I think I should like to live with you," Everleigh announced one night as they lay entwined together.

"But would you also make an honest woman of me?" Sophia asked playfully.

"By marrying you, you mean? Why, I just might. You've taken me, Sophia, and I can't escape you. Strange as it sounds, especially to me, I really do think I'm in love."

"As am I," Sophia said, and when she left his townhouse that night, her heart singing, she was sure she had finally found the one thing that had always eluded her. A week later, Everleigh was gone, murdered in cold blood. Sophia had grieved in private, Everleigh's memory like a precious jewel hidden between her breasts, before her loss turned into an anger so intense that it burned inside her.

She knew then that she had to avenge Ransom's death, even at the cost of her own life, if need be.

*

Sophia had spared her son the intimate details of her relationship with Everleigh, but she could tell by his expression that the story of their affair embarrassed him.

"Now, now, don't look that way," she said gently. "We all wish for love, Peter, and we all wish to make that love felt. It is a glorious thing when it happens, and I do not believe there can be any sin in it."

"All right," Peter said, "but I do not need to hear more."

Sophia took Peter's hand and said, "No, I suppose you don't. Just know that I love you dearly. But know also that I owe it to Ransom, to his memory, to destroy the man who destroyed him. Nothing less will satisfy me."

"I see that. So what happens next?"

"I have another surprise in store for Chase, and it may be enough to finally drive him over the edge."

9.
A SCENE AT THE THEATER

ON THE EVENING OF JUNE 28, Stoddard Chase took his usual seat in a private box at the Academy of Music, a newly opened venue that could fairly claim to be the largest and least crudely appointed theater in the city. Over the years, all manner of visiting performers had found their way to the Academy, none perhaps more famous than Oscar Wilde, who in 1882 spoke at the Academy and then went on to solve a murder at the nearby Nicollet House Hotel. But in 1872 plays were the most common form of entertainment offered at the theater. What Chase didn't know as he settled into his seat was that he was about to play a prominent role in the night's drama.

Chase had no particular interest in the stage, but he had long made it a point to attend the opening night of shows as befitting his status as one of the city's certified grandees. The evening's entertainment was a play called *Caste,* which as far as Chase knew had something to do with marriage and class, and he hoped it would not prove as tedious as most of the dramas he'd seen of late.

The play's protagonist was a beautiful albeit poor ballet dancer who'd had to secretly marry the nobleman she loved because his snooty family would have opposed such an unseemly union. As act one neared its conclusion, a friend of the dancer who'd opposed the marriage noted that "people ought to stick to their own class. Life is a railway journey, and Mankind is a passenger—first class, second class, third class."

This observation met with Chase's approval. He thought of Bridget, who hardly hailed from the better classes, and knew it had been a mistake to marry her, despite her astonishing beauty. Perhaps it was just as well she was barren, or seemed to be, for could she really produce the son of his dreams? He even began to think she'd done him a favor by leaving, as he could claim abandonment in any divorce proceedings. Still, he worried that she'd emerge from hiding to make nasty public allegations against him, unless Dowd managed to locate her first. And so far, Dowd had failed miserably at that task.

Chase was sufficiently absorbed in his thoughts to miss the exact moment when a youngish man in street clothes wearing heavy makeup and a long black wig burst from the wings and out onto the stage. As the audience gasped and the cast looked on in confusion, the man turned toward Chase's box and shouted his well-rehearsed lines: "Elizabeth Chase was also a poor woman and look what her rich husband did. That beast Stoddard Chase murdered her in cold blood, but justice will not be denied!"

The man then fled the stage as a loud buzz went up in the audience. Almost immediately, all eyes turned toward Chase, who stood up in his box and shouted, "Why, that is a damnable lie! Someone catch that man!"

Under a headline reading "A Strange Event at the Academy," the *Tribune* described the scene with the utmost circumspection, stating only that "the man, who had disguised his appearance, cast aspersions in the direction of Mr. Stoddard Chase before running from the stage as quickly as he had appeared. Stagehands attempted to detain the man, but were prevented from doing so by a large, bearded bruiser who apparently had come with him. The two of them escaped to a waiting carriage, which raced away down Washington Ave. at such a high rate of speed that no one could follow.

"Mr. Chase said he suspects the stunt was engineered by an enemy in hopes of discrediting him. 'It will not work, of course,' he averred with his usual firmness, 'and it is especially appalling that the name of my late, beloved wife was brought up in such a cruel way.' Asked if he knew who might have arranged for so startling a stunt, Chase said, 'I will only say that I intend to get to the bottom of this obnoxious business, and when I do, you may be assured that the culprit will pay a steep price for his outrageous behavior.' "

Despite a theater full of eyewitnesses—Sophia among them, for she, too, was a regular theatergoer and had a box across from Chase's—the "culprit" made a clean getaway and was never identified. The police suspected he was an out-of-towner hired for the job. But as to who might have hired him, they couldn't say.

*

It had cost Sophia only fifty dollars to engage the young man, an aspiring actor from St. Paul unknown in Minneapolis, whose citizens considered their neighboring city a place rarely worth the trouble of visiting. Sophia had given the actor his lines and made sure he was well rehearsed for his performance. She'd also paid for his burly escort.

Sophia was playing a subtle game, but she believed it was about to give way to something much rougher. Stung by the embarrassment of being accused of murder before a crowd of hundreds, Chase would react furiously, and she would become the object of his wrath, for it could only be a matter of time before he and his minion Dowd figured out who was behind the incident. She wasn't sure exactly what they would do—an attempt on her life was hardly out of the question—and she had to be ready for anything.

Her ultimate aim was to induce Chase to accuse her of defamation. Then her attorneys, every bit as good as his, would attack him relentlessly in court with the evidence of his wrongdoing. And with public sentiment building against him, prosecutors would finally have little choice but to seek a criminal indictment. Such was the plan, and Sophia was confident that, with a little luck, it would work perfectly.

*

"You have read the papers, no doubt," Chase said the next day when Dowd took his usual seat in the mill's office.

"I have, sir. I must say, it was a very peculiar business."

" 'Disgusting' would be a better word. The police supposedly are looking for the man, but as they would have trouble finding tobacco juice in a spittoon, I am not optimistic. But I am beginning to think you are absolutely right about who is trying to besmirch my good name. I saw Mrs. Westerly as I was leaving the theater and she smiled at me in a very smug way. Have you found any proof yet that she and her son are the ones plotting against me?"

"I believe I have, sir, but it is evidence of an indirect nature, you might say, as it also concerns your wife," Dowd said with the satisfying smile of a man who'd found a seam of pure gold after hours of hard digging. "I am pleased to tell you that I know where Mrs. Chase went after leaving your residence. It took all my resources, but I discovered that she stayed at the house maintained by the Sisterhood of Salvation. Do you know of it?"

"Yes. It's where rich old women with nothing better to do try to save the souls of whores, or some such nonsense. Come to think of it, Bridget did some work there until I told her she was wasting her time. You said she 'stayed' at the house. Am I to assume she is no longer there?"

"Yes, she left some days ago, and I am not sure yet where she went. But I did make an intriguing discovery as to the circumstances of her departure. You will be interested to know it was Sophia Westerly who came to the Sisterhood's house and arranged for your wife to leave. Took her away in a carriage, she did. I learned of this, for no more than a few silver dollars, from a woman who's staying at the house. So you see, sir, it is clear your wife has found an ally in Mrs. Westerly. I can only assume the two of them are spreading the story that you murdered the first Mrs. Chase, although they have no proof other than the hearsay testimony of a dead whore. I have no doubt now that Mrs. Westerly, working with her son and Bridget, placed that notice in the *Tribune* and also sent you that accusatory note regarding Mr. Everleigh's death."

"This is outrageous," Chase said. "Why would the Westerly woman do such things?"

"I cannot be sure of her motives. However, I suspect her son convinced her to undertake the campaign against you even before she became involved with Bridget."

Chase rose from his chair, anger boiling up inside him, and said, "I will not stand for any of this! I will see to it that Nichols is dismissed at once. Then I will take him and his mother to court and show them the hard end of the law. They will be finished, the both of them. Finished! As for that lying wife of mine, she will come to regret her perfidy. I will throw her out on the street like the trash she is."

"That may not be the wisest course of action, if I may say so, sir, at least not for the moment," Dowd said with his usual deference. "It has long been said a man should always keep his enemies close so that he knows what they are up to. Perhaps you should do the same. I have a night spy at the mill who is said to be quite friendly with Nichols. We could arrange to put the two of them together to see what we can find out. Knowledge is power, as they say, and the more you know about what Nichols, his mother, and your wife are planning, the better you'll be able to engineer their much-deserved downfall when the time comes."

Chase thought a minute, his fury giving way to calculation, and said, "I see your point. Very well. Learn all you can about the three conspirators. Watch them like a hawk, but do not be too long about your task. The three of them need to be taught a brutal lesson, and I intend to do just that very soon. The lash would be too good them."

"Agreed," Dowd said. "Have no worries, sir. They will pay a steep price for their sins."

10.
DANGER IN THE NIGHT

WHEN PETER NICHOLS ARRIVED at the Perfection Mill a few days after the uproar at the Academy of Music, the general manager took him aside and told him he was being temporarily reassigned to supervise the night shift. "It'll just be for a few nights," he said. "We're staring at some big repair jobs, as you know, and I have to be sure everything is done right." It was an unusual assignment—the mill had a regular night crew perfectly capable of performing repairs on their own—but as it would earn him a substantial amount of extra pay, Peter saw no reason to object.

"I guess I won't be getting much sleep," he said to his mother that evening at dinner, "but I can use the money."

"It sounds that way," Sophia said. "Have you ever been asked before to supervise the overnight crew?"

"No, but the manager told me I'm his best millwright and that's why he wants me to be in charge of the job."

Sophia said, "Well, it's rather curious, if you ask me. But if you need the money, so be it. However, you know what I think. You wouldn't need the extra work if you lived with me. It would be much cheaper for you here."

"I know, but I just prefer to have my own place." He'd been renting a small house not far from the mill for the past several years, and he liked the privacy, especially when Annie Doherty came by for visits.

"You just want to be alone with Annie," Sophia said in a teasing voice. "I know about such things. Love is the most powerful thing in the world and always has been."

"So you've told me," Peter said, thinking back to what his mother had told him about her passionate involvement with Ransom Everleigh. "But you're right. Annie and I are very much in love. I think of her all the time."

"Yes, that's the nature of love, isn't it. To have the other person in your head, day and night, no matter what."

After dinner, as Peter prepared to leave, Sophia kissed him gently on the cheek and said, "Be careful. I could not stand it if anything happened to you."

"Nothing's going to happen to me," Peter said. "It's you I worry about."

"Then let us worry about each other," Sophia said, and kissed him again.

*

When Peter showed up for his first night shift, the team of millwrights he was supposed to supervise were surprised to see him. But they welcomed his help—it meant less work for them—and by midnight they'd managed to fix two bolters, a misaligned buhrstone, and a badly frayed belt that looked ready to snap at any moment. It was the kind of work Peter loved—setting things right—and he always drew satisfaction from a job well done.

Most of the crew went out for drinks afterward, but Peter was tired and headed directly home. The night was cool and pleasant, but also very dark, for there was no moon. Gas streetlamps had recently been introduced in parts of the downtown area, but most of the city offered little illumination beyond whatever light leaked out of buildings and houses.

Peter's route took him along Cataract Avenue toward Washington Avenue, where a raucous saloon called the Grotto was disgorging a number of drunken patrons. As Peter approached the saloon, he thought he heard footsteps coming up behind him and turned around for a look. Although he saw no one, he felt a sudden sensation of unease as if someone was lightly running the blade of a knife down his spine. He turned back around and kept walking. He was just passing the Grotto when the sensation returned, and this time for good reason. Three large men armed with cudgels had emerged from the saloon and were coming up fast toward Peter in a way that suggested very unfriendly intentions.

Peter was well built, made strong by years of hard labor, and more than capable of defending himself, but he didn't like the odds. Strong-armed robbers were known to hang around saloons late at night, looking for drunks who could be knocked unconscious and relieved of their valuables. Peter carried a small pocketknife and took it out, not sure what good it would to in a fight with three thugs, but it was the only weapon he had.

"You would be Peter Nichols, I imagine," the bruiser in charge of the trio said as they surrounded their quarry. "It's time to say your prayers, for you about to leave this world."

Peter realized at once who'd sent the men—it had to be Dowd, presumably on orders from Chase—and it was no robbery they were planning. He swung his knife toward the men, hoping to scare them off, but it did no good. "Why, lookee here," said the chief thug. "He has a knife. Let us see, boys, if we can make him eat it."

The men raised their cudgels, ready to strike Peter, just as a gunshot rang out behind them. Suddenly, there was another man on the scene, armed with long-barreled revolver. All went silent except for the distinctive sound of a trigger being cocked behind the ear of the man who'd threatened Peter.

"Don't try anything," said the man with the revolver. Peter recognized him at once. Hans Borgstrom was a bearded giant who worked as a loader at the Perfection Mill, where he routinely handled hundred-pound bags of flour as though they were filled with nothing more substantial than pixie dust. He also worked occasionally as a bouncer at the Grotto.

"You boys should be home with your mothers instead of up to mischief in the dead of night," Borgstrom said. "I am not a man to spill blood, but I will lay out your brains right here if I must."

The assailant with a gun to his head said, "We don't want no trouble, mister. We'll be leaving now if that is all right."

"Damned right you will," Borgstrom said. "But be warned: If you try to harm my friend here again, I will come for you and when I find you, you will not like what happens. Now, run if you value your lives."

Uninterested in further mayhem, the would-be attackers scattered into the night as Peter gulped in a deep breath to calm his pounding heart. It had been a very close call. "I would have been in for a time of it if you hadn't helped out," he told Borgstrom. "It was lucky you came along."

"It wasn't luck," Borgstrom said. "I've been watching you. Come along now. I'll walk you home. You never know who might be lurking in the dark."

Peter wanted to know how Borgstrom had come to be his guardian in the night and pressed him with questions. The big man, however, didn't reveal much. "Let's just say I was told to keep an eye on you. That's all I can tell you."

But by the time Peter finally settled into bed, safe in his own house, he was pretty sure who'd hired Borgstrom to watch over him.

*

Thomas Dowd had hired the three "strong-armers," as he called them, to take care of Peter once and for all. But they'd failed, thanks to Peter's guardian angel. This suggested to Dowd that Peter was smarter than he'd given him credit for. He must have smelled a rat when he was assigned to the night shift and so hired someone to watch his back. That was the only explanation that seemed to make sense. And if Peter was indeed on high alert, that made Dowd's job much more difficult.

Worse yet, Dowd wasn't sure exactly what his job was supposed to be or how it would end. He felt caught up in a scheme he didn't fully understand, and that made him uncharacteristically nervous. As Dowd mulled over his situation, a disturbing new idea crept into his head. Perhaps Peter Nichols wasn't in fact the great schemer behind the campaign against Chase. Perhaps it was instead that mother of his. Dowd had always thought of women as soft and pliant, the little tarts he frolicked with in brothels, but perhaps Sophia Westerly was made of different stuff. He would have to find out, and quickly. But first there was the matter of Jonathan Hobson and the bad things that could happen to an old man in a leaky boat in the roaring rapids below St. Anthony Falls.

*

Stoddard Chase, like Dowd, was feeling ill at ease. As he sat that evening in the tower room of his mansion, alone in the dimming light, he had a sense that his life, which he'd constructed as carefully as his mill, was somehow coming undone. For nearly a quarter century, going back to the May afternoon in 1852 when he first laid eyes on St. Anthony Falls, Chase had worked tirelessly with the aim of becoming the greatest, and wealthiest, flour miller on the continent. He was close now—the new mill he planned would dwarf any that had come before—but doubt was floating in the air, and to Chase doubt was as dangerous as the explosive flour dust that could turn even the mightiest mill into an instant ruin. All it took was a spark.

Could Bridget be that spark, he wondered, the destroyer of his dreams? Chase didn't know, but he desperately wanted to find out. The usually reliable Dowd had failed him, missing an opportunity to snatch Bridget from the home of the Sisterhood. Now that damned Westerly woman and her son were hiding her somewhere, and Dowd seemed to have no clue where she might be. Chase believed himself to be a master of calculation, always a step ahead of his rivals, but Bridget was a puzzle. Why had she left him so suddenly and what exactly did she want? Money? A divorce? Vengeance for something she thought he'd done?

Chase hated the uncertainty because it made him feel impotent, a man no longer able to command his world. Bridget had been a terrible mistake, the one time in his life he'd fallen victim to what he thought of us as low animal desire. Now she promised to cause him nothing but trouble, perhaps even putting all his great plans in jeopardy. By the time Chase finally fell into a fitful slumber he was more certain than ever what he would do once he found his missing wife.

11.
CONFRONTATION AND DENIAL

THE DAY AFTER BEING WAYLAID outside the Grotto Bar, Peter went to his mother's home for lunch. He was eager to talk about his adventures the night before and the man who had quite possibly saved his life.

"You sent Hans Borgstrom to protect me, didn't you?" he said.

Sophia couldn't deny it. "Yes. I was worried about you, and I thought Mr. Borgstrom would be just the man to help out. He's a force, isn't he? I'd hired him earlier to protect the actor who undertook that little performance for me at the Academy. So I hired him again to keep watch over you."

"But how did you know I might be attacked?"

"I didn't, but when you told me you'd suddenly been ordered to work night shifts, I became suspicious. I have no doubt Chase was behind it. He wanted to punish you, or perhaps even have you murdered, because he knows we've been looking into Mr. Everleigh's death."

Peter said, "Sometimes you amaze me, Mother."

"Of what use is a mother if she cannot protect her children?" Sophia said. "It is that simple. But let us speak of it no more. I have some news of far more consequence. I have received an invitation from Stoddard Chase."

"What do you mean?"

"See for yourself." She handed Peter a note that had arrived an hour earlier. "Mrs. Westerly, I wish to speak with you and your son," the note said. "If both of you would be so kind as to call at my home on Thursday evening at seven, I am hopeful we can come to terms on matters that affect us."

"Why, that's July fourth," Peter said.

Sophia said, "Yes, and perhaps we should be expecting fireworks."

"Well, I don't think we should go. It's like a wolf inviting us to his lair."

"I disagree. Let us see what Chase wants. But we mustn't tip our hand. I suspect he wishes to probe us to find out how much we know about the two murders he's committed."

"But what if it's a trap of some kind? He's already murdered twice, as you said, and I see no reason why he'd hesitate to murder again."

"No, I think not. It would be too hard for him to cover up our deaths. Even so, it would not hurt to take precautions. I still have your father's old revolver. We'll bring it along just in case."

*

Sophia and Peter arrived at Stoddard Chase's mansion at precisely seven o'clock. A few fireworks were already exploding overhead, but it would be two hours before night fell and the celebrating began in earnest. With its Cyclopean masonry, block piled upon mighty block, the mansion was testament to Chase's might, and Sophia had always found it cold and uninviting. Its massive front tower was especially daunting, jutting out as aggressively as a club in the hands of a street brawler.

"Chase must think of himself as the lord of all he surveys, our very own flour king," Sophia said. "But even a king can be toppled from his throne, and that is what I intend to do."

"Well, you know what I think," Peter said. "Just don't underestimate how much power he has in this city."

"You are my cautious counsel, Peter, and I love you for it. But caution will not win us the day."

A grave-looking butler in a long black coat and starched white shirt met Sophia and Peter at the front door, which was solid oak and thick enough to repel any invader. "Mr. Chase is in the tower's library," the butler said as he ushered them into a darkly paneled foyer. "I will show you to the manlift, as it is the easiest way to go there."

The lift was at one side of the foyer, set back several feet behind a decorative iron grill door that guarded the opening. The lift did not appear to be moving—there was presumably a switch somewhere that engaged it—and Peter, mindful of what had happened to Elizabeth Chase, said, "We'll take the stairs."

"Now, now, Peter, let's go for a ride," Sophia said to her son's surprise. "It will be an adventure."

"Then please follow me," the butler said, "and I will show you how to board."

The butler opened the grill door and pushed a lever on the wall, causing a small steam engine in the basement to chug to life and put the lift in motion. Small wooden platforms or steps just large enough to stand on were attached to a continuous belt every ten feet or so, with handholds above. It was, Sophia thought, quite a contraption, and she recalled reading somewhere that Chase had designed it himself to be a unique feature of his mansion.

"As you can see, it goes very slowly, less than a mile an hour, or so I am told," the butler said. "Just step out on one of the platforms and grab hold. It will take about a minute to reach the top. You'll see a bright light as you near the tower room. Step off there and Mr. Chase will see you in the library."

Sophia said, "It looks safe enough, but I must ask: Were you here when the first Mrs. Chase had her fatal accident? I have read the newspaper accounts, but they say only that she must have slipped and fallen. I do wonder how that happened."

"I cannot say," the butler replied, his face a stoic mask. "Mr. Chase will meet you at the top."

Sophia boarded first and Peter followed her on the next moving step. The lift rose through a brick-walled shaft lit by gas sconces that provided dim light at best. As she ascended, Sophia had the eerie sensation of being transported to some mysterious place beyond the usual earthly bounds. But when she looked down into the depths of the shaft she felt a chill, for she could imagine Elizabeth Chase, with a push from her husband, plummeting to her death, perhaps a scream marking the last terrifying moment of her life.

Midway up the shaft, Sophia passed a doorway that gave access to rooms on the second floor. Then, as she neared the top, she saw Chase staring down at her from another brightly lit opening. "Be careful now," he said and offered her his hand, but she ignored the gesture and stepped off on her own. Peter soon joined her. A grilled door like the one on the main floor guarded the entrance to the lift. Chase opened it, pushed down a nearby lever to stop the lift, and said, "I am pleased you are here. We have much to talk about."

So now I'm up close to the devil himself, Sophia thought as Chase led them into the library. She and Peter took chairs across from Chase, who seemed eager to speak with them but also wary. He wore a black suit with gray stripes, matching the colors of his heavy beard, and his eyes were black, too, and baleful. His broad, heavy body reminded Sophia of her second and third husbands, men of wealth whose money seemed to have settled into their stomachs, like meals that could not quite be digested.

Sophia had never been in the tower before, and the library was smaller than she had imagined it to be. One wall was taken up by the grilled door they'd just come through, an identical one next to it that guarded a short hallway, and past that a spiral staircase Sophia assumed led down to the mansion's second floor. To their left as they entered the room a pair of glass doors opened out onto a balcony. The other two walls consisted largely of shelves bearing the sort of expensive tomes rich men like Chase usually bought as a form of adornment. There were encyclopedias, multivolume histories, philosophical treatises, and row upon row of "great authors," from the Greeks and Romans on through Thackeray and Dickens. A heavy film of dust had collected on them all, suggesting that no one in the household was much of a reader.

Sophia was surprised to see a large oil portrait of Elizabeth Chase hanging between two of the bookshelves. The portrait showed her in a seated pose, wearing a long gown and a string of pearls around her neck. Her expression was hard to read, but Sophia interpreted as a mix of wistfulness and fear, the look of a woman who knew she'd married the wrong man.

"May I offer you a libation?" Chase asked, playing the part of a welcoming host. "I have some very nice French brandy, if that would suit you."

"We need nothing from you," Sophia said curtly, "except for a confession."

Chase stared at her as though she's just uttered a particularly disgusting vulgarity, and said, "And what would I be confessing to, may I ask?"

"Why, murder," Sophia said, meeting Chase's stare. "We know you murdered Elizabeth and Mr. Everleigh, and we will prove it."

Sophia could almost see steam rising from Chase's collar as he said, in an aggrieved and angry voice, "That is a lie! I loved Elizabeth, and her death will always haunt me. As for Mr. Everleigh, I will not pretend we enjoyed a good relationship, but I certainly never wished to see him die. And yet it is clear you are utterly intent on persecuting me. You sent that note to me. You put that notice in the *Tribune.* And you also staged that vile scene at the Academy of Music. I can only assume you have been listening to Bridget and have come to believe her lies."

"I believe in the truth," Sophia said, "with which you hardly seem acquainted. But your lies will no longer save you."

Chase said, "Very well then, what is your evidence that I am a murderer? Whatever you think it is, I will easily refute it."

"I doubt that. You will hear our evidence soon enough, and you will be convicted of your crimes."

"Is that so? Then let me tell you this: I will not be slandered by you or, for that matter, by my wife, with whom you are obviously plotting. I shall let my lawyers loose and they will exact a steep price for all the falsehoods told against me."

"We will see about that," Sophia said. "You are not the only person with lawyers. I have some very good ones and I expect they will discover much of interest when they interrogate your henchman, Mr. Dowd."

Peter hadn't heard his mother mention lawyers before, but he chimed in anyway. "That's right. Rats always sing in the end."

Chase rose to his feet and said, "Enough! I can see it was a mistake to invite the two of you here. It is obvious you have become utterly deranged and I will not waste any more of my time trying to disabuse you of your mad ideas. You will be hearing from my attorneys shortly. Now, it will be my great pleasure to show you out."

"And our even greater pleasure to leave," Sophia said. "I will only add that if there is madness in this room, it is not my son and I who are afflicted by it."

"Bah!" Chase said with a snort and pointed them toward the room's second grilled door, which was adjacent to the spiral staircase but separated from it by a solid wall. Chase restarted the lift with a push of its control lever, opened the door, and said, "Go along the hall and around the corner. You can take the lift down from there."

Sophia followed Peter along the hall until it made a ninety-degree turn to the right. There, a small waiting area provided access to the lift's downward side. The library and its resident ogre were now out of view, and Sophia felt relieved as she waited for Peter to step aboard the lift. Her confrontation with Chase had not been especially revealing, but at least she'd looked the murderer in the eye and, she hoped, instilled more fear in his dark heart.

Once Peter boarded, Sophia took the next step, and as she grabbed onto the handhold a strange thought arrived out of nowhere like a knock on the door at three o'clock in the morning. There was, she realized, something she should have seen but didn't, and it unsettled her. By the time she and Peter left the mansion, she was so lost in thought that she barely spoke to her son all the way home.

12.
A NEW IDEA

ON THE AFTERNOON OF THE FIFTH, the city quiet after a day of speechifying and celebration, Sophia went to see Bridget. Thinking Chase's agents, perhaps even Dowd himself, might be watching her, she took precautions so as not to be followed. After slipping out the back door of her mansion, she walked two blocks away to Washington Avenue and hailed a hack.

"I will be going over to St. Anthony," she told the driver. "Keep an eye out for anyone behind us. I do not wish my destination to be known, and I trust a five-dollar gold piece will secure your silence if any inquiries are made."

"For five dollars, ma'am, I wouldn't say nothing to nobody," came the reply.

The ride took Sophia across the Mississippi on the Hennepin Avenue suspension bridge, still the sole connection to the old village of St. Anthony, which had only a few months earlier merged with Minneapolis. The falls lay just to the south, and Sophia could hear the tumbling waters and the whine of saws as the hack's weary horse clattered along the bridge's narrow, crowded roadway. Sophia had been in Minneapolis for almost fifteen years, and every time she crossed the bridge and saw the untidy collection of sawmills that draped the falls, along with the much larger flour mills looming up nearby, she felt a twinge of sadness at what progress had wrought.

It was all for the best, she supposed, for without the doings of eager men there would be no city where Minneapolis stood, nor the mansion that allowed her a comfortable life. And yet she always remembered what Jonathan Hobson had told her one day when he came to her mansion in search of a handout. A maid had wanted to shoo him away, but Sophia, whose late husband had always given the old man a silver dollar when he appeared at their door, said it was all right. Sophia had stayed a moment to talk with Hobson after making the usual donation.

"You are a kind woman," he said, "and there is not much of that in this world. Look around you, Mrs. Westerly, and you will see the awful truth, that men are takers and destroyers. They steal the world from us, and account it a good thing. They took the falls, of course, and now look at it! But you are a giver, and the day will come when the takers find there is nothing left to take. Only then will Eden be restored to us, as Almighty God intends! I pray you will join Him one day there, for Eden is our true heaven."

"Then I look forward to that day," Sophia said, so struck by Hobson's words that she added a ten-dollar gold piece to her contribution.

Eden on earth seemed far lovelier to her than some vague heaven above where insubstantial bodies floated in the clouds. And if indeed there was a loving God, as Hobson so devoutly believed, then perhaps that old, splendid world might one day be restored to humanity. Or perhaps not, Sophia thought, for who could foresee what the long unwinding of time might bring?

She remained lost in her thoughts while the hack crossed a small bridge spanning the river's east channel, then proceeded south toward the campus of the state university, near which some of St. Anthony's pioneers had built fine houses. Sophia's friend, Mary Ames, was among those old settlers. She lived in a stately Greek Revival house, and it was there, after the usual courtesies, that Sophia and Bridget sat down for another talk.

*

"My son and I met with your husband yesterday," Sophia said over a cup of black tea. "He asked us to the mansion."

"Oh my, that is a surprise. Whatever did he want?"

Sophia described her conversation with Chase, adding, "It was interesting to see the library. I must say I was surprised to find a portrait of Elizabeth there."

"Yes, it seems strange, doesn't it," Bridget said. "But it is just the sort of thing Mr. Chase would do. He has the blackest of hearts. I imagine he smiles to himself every time he looks at it."

"Perhaps he does. Incidentally, my son and I rode that lift. How awful it must have been for Elizabeth to die as she did. Are you absolutely sure about what Sally Sharpe saw?"

"Of course. I have a perfect memory for such things. But why do you ask?"

"I ask because it is clear your husband will never admit to his crime, and I am beginning to worry that my strategy of trying to turn the public against him will not succeed. We may have no choice now but for you to make Sally's story known. If you were to give a sworn affidavit to my attorneys and take it to the police, we could force them to investigate Elizabeth's death. You may be sure the newspapers would soon learn of it as well."

"Do you really think so? Mr. Chase is one of the most powerful men in this city, and as I told you, he and the chief of police are as thick as thieves. I have begun to think my best course of action would be to contact Mr. Chase and ask to be released from our marriage on the promise that I would leave this city and never return. He might accept that, just to be done with me."

"And what of his crimes?"

"You know I would like nothing more than to see him pay for what I believe he has done. But I do not see how that will happen, and I cannot fight him forever."

*

When Sophia returned home, she found she had little appetite for dinner. She had spent the last month hounding Stoddard Chase, but she wasn't sure anymore that she was fighting the right battle. Doubt, the great seducer, was inviting her into its bed, and she knew that if she succumbed, she might never find her way to the truth. So she spent a restless night arranging all the pieces of the puzzle in her head and looking at them from every angle she could think of. And when she arose at dawn the next morning, Sophia felt utterly refreshed, for a remarkable idea had come to her out of the darkness.

*

As the duly elected coroner of Hennepin County, Charles Chilstrom held an office but didn't have one he actually occupied. Instead, he operated out of his home on Eighth Street, where he maintained his practice as a homeopath, offering ointments, creams, gels, tablets, and numerous other medicines of uncertain provenance aimed at curing the innumerable afflictions bedeviling mankind. But cutting into a dead body was another matter entirely, and in those rare instances when autopsies had to be done, Chilstrom brought in a trained physician to perform the task.

With her new idea shining before her like a beacon, Sophia went to see Chilstrom that afternoon. She had several questions on her mind and a newly struck double eagle in her purse, since she'd discovered long ago how money could lubricate reluctant vocal cords. She found Chilstrom ensconced in his small consulting room, as he called it, which was outfitted with an array of beakers, flasks, bottle, jars, and tubes designed to suggest his medicinal prowess. He was a gangly, long-limbed man with a face scarred by youthful acne and the bright, eager eyes of a salesman, and he greeted Sophia warmly when he ushered her to a seat across from his desk.

"Why, Mrs. Westerly, how nice to see you," he said. "How can I be of help? Ladies are my specialty, and if there is something causing you distress, I am sure I will be able to offer a successful course of treatment. Indeed, I have—"

"I am here in search of information," Sophia said, interrupting him. "What can you tell me about Elizabeth Chase's death? I presume you removed her body from the scene. Was an autopsy by chance performed?"

Chilstrom sat back in his chair, as though trying to distance himself from Sophia, and said, "I regret to say I cannot discuss such matters with you. Mrs. Chase's death was, of course, very tragic, but as the case is now closed, I see no reason to delve further into it. I am sure Mr. Chase would agree."

"I wouldn't know about that," Sophia said, removing the double eagle from her purse and setting it on Chilstrom's desk. Twenty dollars was a tidy sum in those days, and Chilstrom stared at the coin as a hungry man might eye a choice sirloin.

"May I ask why you're seeking this information?"

"I have my reasons," Sophia said, "but I prefer not to speak of them at the moment. All you need to know is that I do not intend to cause any trouble for you or Mr. Chase. Now then, speak freely and this lovely coin will be yours."

"All right," Chilstrom said. "I guess there would be no harm in it, so long as I can trust that your word is good."

"It is," Sophia said, "as good as gold. Now tell me all you know. Was there, for instance, an autopsy?"

"There was. Dr. Franklin over at the Cottage Hospital performed it."

"So you must have suspected foul play."

"No, not really. But Mr. Chase wanted it done, perhaps to remove any doubt it was indeed an accident."

"And what were the results?"

Chilstrom began to fidget in his chair as though he'd just sat on a tack. "Well, I'm not sure—"

Sophia cut in: "You agreed to tell me everything and you must do so. I would hate to leave with that double eagle in my purse."

"Very well. Dr. Franklin did find something unexpected, but I beg of you to keep what I am about to say in the strictest confidence."

"You have my promise of that."

Chilstrom let out a sigh, stared at the gold coin that amounted to a month's worth of his usual income, and then revealed something so unexpected that Sophia could scarcely believe it.

"You are sure of this?" Sophia asked.

"Absolutely. It was obvious once Dr. Franklin began the autopsy."

"You have been a great help," Sophia said and pushed the gold piece across the desk. "May I assume that you, like me, will never speak of our conversation to anyone. It would hardly look good for you if you were accused of taking a bribe."

"Well, I don't think of it in that way," Chilstrom said, "and I am offended you would say so. I was merely trying to be of help to you, and it is very kind that you have given me a small token of your gratitude."

Sophia smiled and said, "Yes, and silence is golden, isn't it?"

"Very golden," he agreed and gave a slight bow as Sophia left.

*

As Sophia spoke with the coroner, Stoddard Chase was at work in his home office but finding it hard to concentrate amid all his troubles. But when his butler arrived with a surprising message, Chase began to feel better. The message was from Bridget, who proposed a meeting. "I have much to explain," she wrote, rather cryptically. "I will come by the mansion this evening, and we will talk then."

*

"Guess who's here," said Thomas Dowd as he burst through the door of Henry Hobson's shack on Spirit Island. "It's time we had nice talk, don't you think?"

It was the evening of July 6, exactly one month after Dowd had murdered Everleigh and the same day Sophia had paid a call on the coroner. In Dowd's view, Hobson—no matter how crazy he seemed—was a threat. As the only witness to Everleigh's murder, he might start babbling out his tale one day, and Dowd simply couldn't allow that to happen.

Dowd had reached the island on a small rowboat commandeered from a storage shed at the Perfection Mill. He'd started out just before dark, long after the day shift at the mill was over, and there'd been no one around when he shoved off from shore and fought the current as he rowed across the narrow channel leading to the island. Clambering up the cliff that led to Hobson's shack, Dowd had been struck at once by how wet and noisy the island was. Heavy rains had caused the Mississippi to run exceptionally high and fast, and the falls gave out a pulsing, thunderous roar as it drenched the island in a steady spray. Only a lunatic, Dowd thought, could live in such an environment.

Hobson was asleep when Dowd, who'd brought along a lantern, woke him up. The shanty itself was disgusting, at least in Dowd's view. Its thin walls—cobbled together from driftwood and fugitive pieces of lumber—did little to muffle the sound of the falls, and Dowd wondered how Hobson could sleep amid the ceaseless din. Water dribbled down from a leaky tarpaper roof, but Hobson had cleverly avoided the possibility of inundation by cutting channels into the shack's limestone floor to draw the water away. A bed protected by a canvas canopy, two wooden chairs and a small chest constituted the shack's furnishings, along with crucifixes that adorned all four walls.

As soon he awoke to the sight of Dowd's harsh, pockmarked face in the glow of the lantern, Hobson said, "I see I am looking at the devil. I suppose you have come here to murder me, as you murdered Mr. Everleigh."

"That is the general idea," Dowd said with a smile as he drew a revolver from his coat pocket. "You have seen too much, Mr. Hobson, and there is a price to be paid. I must apologize, of course, for what is about to happen, but there is simply no way around it. Besides, death must be welcome to a man of your faith. Yes indeed, the Lord awaits you. Now, why don't you get out of that nightgown and put on some clothes?"

"And why don't you pull that trigger right now and send yourself to perdition? You are right that the Lord will receive me in His loving arms. As for you, you will soon enough be in Satan's iron grip, and he will have a fine time tormenting you for all eternity."

"Well, I guess we'll both have to see about that, won't we? Now, put on the stupid robe you always wear. We have business to conduct."

"And what would that be?"

"Why, you are going to take your skiff out for a little ride. But I fear it will sink, as will you. Accidents, you see, happen all the time."

Once Hobson had dressed and fetched the shepherd's crook he used as walking stick, Dowd began marching him at gunpoint to the eastern edge of the island, which overlooked the main channel of the river as it descended through a series of treacherous rapids between jagged slabs of limestone. Not long before, two men had fallen from a logging platform and died in the rapids, their bodies as battered as if they'd received severe beatings. Dowd intended a similar fate for Hobson. A quick blow to the back of the head would send him tumbling unconscious into the wild waters. Then Dowd would untie the old man's skiff and launch it downriver to be torn up on the rocks. Poor old Hobson, everyone would say. He fell from his leaky little boat and drowned. It was, Dowd told himself, a flawless plan.

Spirit Island was all rock, and as Dowd shoved Hobson along, he found it hard to keep his footing on the wet, slippery limestone. Hobson, in his bare feet, moved far more easily, for he knew every inch of the island by heart, even in the mist and darkness. One of the island's most prominent features was a slab of rock jutting out twenty feet above the rapids. Boys who occasionally explored the island had dubbed it the "lookout," and in the light of day it offered a dramatic view of the row of sawmills that formed an industrial village at the brink of the falls.

But the mills were invisible now, lost in the night. The mist grew heavier as Dowd and Hobson approached the lookout, and Dowd had to wipe off his face every few feet so that he could see where they were going. His lantern was also befogged, its light all but swallowed by the dense mist, and so thunderous was the sound of the falls that he could not hear himself speak. So it was that Dowd, who enjoyed dispatching his victims with a few choice observations on the regrettable brevity of life, offered no words of parting as he forced Hobson out onto the overlook and raised his pistol to deliver the blow that would send the old man to eternity.

To Dowd's amazement, the old man saved him the trouble by suddenly leaping off the rock and into the river. Or so Dowd assumed. What he didn't know was that a ledge lay a few feet beneath the overlook, and Hobson, who was remarkably spry for his age, landed squarely on his feet. What happened next would constitute the final surprise of Dowd's life. Hobson used his crook to hook Dowd's ankle and pull him off the overlook.

With no time to regain his balance, Dowd struck the ledge, firing off a futile shot before he went headfirst into the river, where the rapids took him as swiftly as if he was being dragged behind a runaway horse. Dowd was a man of many skills, but swimming was not among them. He managed to keep his head above the frothing waters for a few seconds before he felt himself being pulled down into the wet, roaring blackness all around him.

When his body turned up the next day, two miles downstream, with the badly damaged rowboat Hobson had sent after him afloat nearby, the newspapers duly noted his demise, the *Tribune* describing it as a "a rather mysterious accident." But Dowd's death was all but forgotten a few days later, when the press became consumed by astonishing events that had occurred at the mansion of Stoddard Chase.

13.
SECRETS AND LIES

Sophia Westerly was enjoying a late lunch in her mansion's bright sunroom when she came across the news of Thomas Dowd's death in the *Tribune.* It was a shocking development, but how had it happened? She doubted his death was an accident—what could Dowd possibly have been doing in a small boat in the rapids below the falls?—and she wondered whether Jonathan Hobson was somehow involved. Her thoughts were soon interrupted by the arrival of an unexpected visitor.

"I do hope I am not disturbing you," Bridget Chase said when Sophia came to greet her at the front door. "I had to see you because I have some important news."

"I see. Well, come along to the sunroom and we'll talk. Would you like some lunch?"

"Oh no, I'm so excited I don't think I could eat a thing," she said as they settled into chairs. "I came to tell you I have gone back to Mr. Chase."

Sophia said, "I had a suspicion you might. You talked of it the last time we met. What convinced you to do so?"

"As I told you then, I could see no other choice. So I decided to speak with him last night and offer the possibility of a divorce. But he showed me something very surprising, and I know now that I was terribly mistaken about him."

"Really? What did he show you?"

Bridget, who wore a stylish pink outfit and a fancy new hairdo that suggested she was happy to back in the good graces of her wealthy husband, removed a folded letter from her purse and handed it to Sophia. "Mr. Chase showed me this. It's Elizabeth's testament, if you could call it that."

"The one you looked for but couldn't find?"

"Yes. Mr. Chase had it all along, but he never told anyone about it. When we talked, I said I wished to leave him because of my suspicions about Elizabeth's death. That's when he finally grasped why I had fled from him, and he showed me what Elizabeth had written. Read it if you would. You will see that Elizabeth was not of sound mind. I am certain now that the poor woman committed suicide."

Sophia unfolded the letter and read its rambling words, written in a thin, wavering hand. Ghosts haunted the Chase mansion, or so Elizabeth wrote, and voices spoke to her from the walls. Her husband, her house servants, even her carriage driver were plotting against her. Often, she wished to die. "There is no hope for me," she wrote, "and I do not think I can stand this life much longer."

"And you know this is Elizabeth's handwriting?" Sophia asked.

"I do. I have seen other letters she wrote."

"But what of Sally Sharpe's story that she saw Chase murder Elizabeth?"

"She must have made it up because she was angry that Mr. Chase dismissed her for her thievery. And I know it to be true that she did steal things now and then."

Sophia said, "This is most interesting. Yet there's also the matter of Mr. Everleigh? Do you also believe now that your husband was in fact not behind his murder?"

"I very much do. When I told Mr. Chase about what that old man who lives on the island had seen, he was quite astonished. But as he thought about it, he told me it made sense. Apparently that awful man Dowd bore a deep grudge against Mr. Everleigh over some financial matter—I understand that a good deal of money was involved—and so murdered him."

"And now, of course, Dowd is dead. I assume you've heard the news. "

"Yes. The newspapers are saying it could have been an accident."

"The newspapers are often wrong," Sophia said. "In any event, I take it you now intend to fully reunite with your husband."

"Yes. As I said, I was mistaken about him. He is not the evil man I thought him to be. I do not wish to be forward, but I do think you owe him an apology, and I know Mr. Chase would readily accept it."

"I am not ready for that," Sophia said. "I still have unanswered questions."

Bridget offered her most winning smile and said, "I understand. Perhaps there is a way we could put your mind at ease. Why don't you come see Mr. Chase tonight? I am sure he could explain everything to your satisfaction. Would seven o'clock be all right?"

"Will you be there as well?"

"Certainly."

"Then seven would fine."

"Excellent! We will see you then. I am just so pleased to put this terrible business to rest, and I'm sure you must be, too."

"Yes," Sophia said. "That would be wonderful."

*

Sophia had agreed to the meeting thinking that Peter would be able to accompany her, unannounced. But when she sent a message to him at the mill, she learned he wasn't at work. Instead, he was off helping a millwright who'd been maimed in a gruesome accident. The man had nearly bled to death after losing an arm, and Peter had gone with him to the hospital. Sophia sent a message there, but to no avail, and by five o'clock she still hadn't been able to reach him. She then left an urgent message at his house, telling him to come to the Chase mansion at seven o'clock if he could. Otherwise, Sophia would be on her own when she met with the Chases, and she knew there could be trouble.

Sophia decided she had to chance it. She'd come a long way since the news of Ransom Everleigh's death bruised her heart, and she needed to know the truth once and for all. After a quick dinner, she went up to her bedroom to dress. She also removed a family heirloom of sorts from a closet shelf and put it in her purse. Back downstairs, she wrote out a note to Peter, sealed it in an envelope, then left for Chase's mansion.

When Sophia reached the mansion, just three blocks from her own, Bridget answered the bell and invited her in. An unsettling hush prevailed inside the house, and Sophia felt as though she'd entered a tomb, but not necessarily of the kind where the dead rest alone in their eternal slumbers.

"The servants have the night off," Bridget explained, "so I'm back to being a maid for a while. Come along. Mr. Chase is up in the library. He'll be very happy to see you. If you want, you can leave your purse here."

"No, I'll hang on to it. There's something I wish to show your husband."

"May I ask what it is? I do hope it's not something that will trouble Mr. Chase."

"It's just a document that might be of interest to him," Sophia said.

"Good, then there's no cause for worry," Bridget said. "Now, shall we take the lift?"

"I'd prefer the staircase," Sophia said. "I find the lift rather confining."

"Yes, I've heard that's true of some people. We'll take the steps then."

The mansion's main staircase was broad and ornate, its black walnut balusters carved to resemble sheaves of wheat, the ultimate source of Chase's fortune. The treads squeaked as Sophia followed Bridget up to the second floor, but there was no other sound in the house. At the top of the staircase, a wall mural depicted St. Anthony Falls running free and wild, as Chase would have seen it in the early 1850s.

"Mr. Chase loved this picture," Bridget said as she stopped in front of it. "But it's too big, don't you think? I'd prefer a portrait here."

"Whose portrait would that be?" Sophia asked.

"Why, my own, of course," Bridget said with a girlish giggle. "Don't you think it would be pretty?"

"I'm sure it would."

When they reached the spiral steps, which were tucked away at the end of a short hall, Sophia looked up and saw that she had a long climb ahead of her.

"Twenty-five steps," Bridget said. "The same as my age. Isn't that funny? I'll go first."

"All right, I'll follow as best I can."

Bridget ascended quickly, Sophia trailing behind. Near the top, where Chase presumably waited for them, Sophia stopped for a moment to catch her breath. When she finally reached the library, she realized she had made a possibly fatal miscalculation.

*

As she stepped off the stairs, Sophia gasped. The body of Stoddard Chase lay face up on the floor in the middle of the library, his white shirt soaked with blood from two small wounds to his chest. He wasn't moving and his dark eyes, once so fierce and commanding, were wide open in a kind of blank astonishment, as though he'd barely had time to realize that he was about to die. Bridget had momentarily disappeared, but then Sophia saw her standing in the hallway by the lift. She was pointing a revolver at Sophia, and it looked very familiar. "Have a seat," she said, motioning Sophia toward a chair next to one of the bookcases. "You must be very surprised."

"Perhaps not as much as you think," Sophia said as she sat down. "I have known for some time that you are a liar and a murderer."

This was true, but Sophia hadn't anticipated Chase's death. She'd come to the mansion believing Bridget had murdered Elizabeth, Everleigh, and perhaps Sally Sharpe as well. She was fairly certain Chase didn't know what Bridget had done, and she'd hoped to convince him of his wife's guilt. Although Sophia knew it might be risky confronting Chase with the truth, which is why she'd wanted Peter to join her, she didn't think Bridget would be foolish enough to resort to more violence. Now Sophia saw that she was the fool, outmaneuvered as so many others had been by the pretty young woman pointing a gun at her chest.

"No, you must be honest and admit you were taken in," Bridget said. "People have always underestimated me."

"Yes, I can see that they have," Sophia said, choosing her words carefully. She was trying to sound calm despite her racing heart and the sight of the body lying a few paces away on the floor. "You have planned everything out very nicely, and you used me like everyone else. When you saw how much I despised Mr. Chase, how I had gone so far as to accuse him of murder, you thought I'd make a perfect dupe, and that's why you've lured me into your scheme. Will the story be that I had an unhappy affair with your husband and shot him before turning the gun on myself? Or will it be that I killed him to avenge Mr. Everleigh's death and then took my own life to avoid prison or the hangman?"

"One or the other, I'd guess," Bridget said nonchalantly. "The newspapers love a tragic heroine. Why, you'll be in the newspapers for days."

"Perhaps I will, or perhaps you will be the one in the press tomorrow. You see, you've made some mistakes, Bridget, and they will be your downfall. I've noted them in a letter that will go the police. You weren't quite as clever as you think you are."

"Nor are you. I'm thinking the letter is in your purse because you wanted to show it to Mr. Chase. We'll have to see about that, won't we? But go ahead and tell me about all the mistakes I supposedly made."

"That story about Sally witnessing Elizabeth's murder was obviously false, for one. When my son and I spoke to your husband three days ago, I noticed that the entry to the lift isn't visible from anywhere in the library. You claimed Sally told you that she came up the spiral stairs and immediately saw Chase throw Elizabeth down the shaft. But she simply couldn't have seen that, not unless she went down a hall and around the corner to the lift's entry. And if she had done that, why wouldn't Chase have killed her too?"

"I must say, that was very observant of you, Sophia. You are a clever woman and I really do like you. It is too bad we won't be friends. What else gave me away?"

"The books," Sophia said.

Bridget looked genuinely puzzled. "What do you mean?"

"You're almost too good a liar," Sophia said. "You spin and spin your tales, always inserting a nice little detail or two, as when you told me you'd taken down all the books here to look for Elizabeth's supposed testament, which I imagine you forged as part of your scheming. But as you can see, all the books here have a thick layer of dust, which means you lied about searching through them."

"Oh my goodness, you really are sharp-eyed, aren't you? I do believe you would make a good detective like that fellow in the Poe stories. The 'Rue Morgue' is my favorite."

"Yes, when I think of morgues, you come to mind," Sophia said. "There is one other problem with your account of Elizabeth's death. You see, I had a talk with the coroner yesterday."

"Did you now? And what did he tell you?"

"He told me, as you well know, that Elizabeth was with child when she died. When I learned of that, it dawned on me who'd pushed her to her death. It must have been you. I imagine Elizabeth regarded you as a trusted confidante and so told you about her condition before informing Mr. Chase of the good news. Only from your point of view it must have been very bad news. You were determined to make yourself Mr. Chase's wife, but you knew that would never happen if Elizabeth delivered the boy he'd always wanted."

"Perhaps. Do tell me more."

"Mr. Chase ordered an autopsy—something you probably didn't expect—and it must have crushed him to learn he'd lost his chance to have a child. You, on the other hand, stood to gain a husband, so you were there to console him and soon enough lure him into your bed."

"True, but men are easy, poor fools that they are. They will do anything to have a woman. The trick, if you're the woman, is to keep them. Mr. Chase liked me very much in the bedroom but told me marriage would be out of the question. I managed to convince him otherwise."

"By threats of scandal and blackmail, I suppose."

"Let us just say he saw it would be in his best interest to marry me."

"But now you've killed him. You must have come to despise him."

"What woman wouldn't? He was a fat, disgusting pig, interested in only one thing from me. I knew I couldn't stand to live the rest of my life with him."

Sophia, who was coming to see how the beautiful monster in front of her had used men as a hunter might an eager spaniel, said, "And now we come to Ransom Everleigh. You slept with him, didn't you?"

"I did. He was quite the lover, that man."

"Yes, I know," Sophia said.

Bridget smiled and said, "Why, my dear Sophia! Who would suspect a fine woman such as yourself was one of his conquests?"

"Perhaps it was the other way around. Unlike you, he actually believed in the possibility of love. But why did you want to sleep with him?"

"It was a bit of a lark. I simply like a handsome man in my bed now and then. There is nothing else like it, as you know. But Ransom turned out to be troublesome."

"How so?"

"He became suspicious of me. It seems he ran across that tart Sally Sharpe one evening at a saloon and she told him something she shouldn't have."

"Let me guess," Sophia said, her mind now working with exceptional clarity. "She told him she'd seen you in the library—not Chase—on the night you murdered Elizabeth. Sally couldn't actually have seen you push Elizabeth, but she must have arrived in the library in time to hear her scream as she fell to her death. I'm sure you claimed to Sally that it had all been a terrible accident. But in time she must have begun to wonder if it was really true."

"Yes, Sally wasn't as stupid as she looked, and she always talked too much."

"So much that you had her killed?"

"No, she managed to die a miserable death on her own. Be that as it may, Mr. Everleigh told me what Sally had told him about Elizabeth's death. Of course, I tried to persuade him that Sally was hallucinating from the nerve tonic she drank, but he remained suspicious nonetheless. I worried he might tell Mr. Chase about our little dalliance and, worse, publicly accuse me of Elizabeth's murder. In that event, Mr. Chase would certainly have sought a divorce and probably tried to disinherit me as well. As you can see, I had no choice but to take action."

"To commit another murder, you mean. So you hired Dowd for the job, the idea being that he would kill Mr. Everleigh in a way that would inevitably cast suspicion on your husband. Did you pay Dowd for his work, or did he take it out in trade, as it were?"

"Are you questioning my virtue?" Bridget said with mock horror. "Shame on you. But does it really matter? I will simply say that Mr. Dowd was amply rewarded for his work. And now, alas, he is gone. You will be pleased to know I had nothing to do with his death, but it is a gift, is it not? He will not be around to blackmail me, as I'm sure he planned to do."

Sophia didn't want the conversation to lag, not yet, and poked a stick at the scorpion. "You of all people would know about blackmail and intrigue. It is all you really know, isn't it? That and how to lie. 'Bridget the Liar' should be carved on your tombstone, if you get one."

"No!" Bridget said, her voice rising in anger. "No! It is the world that lied to me from the very beginning. Why wasn't I born to a better life, the one I deserved? Of what good was my beauty in the filth and stench of the cesspool where I was raised? It was unjust, and I would not accept such a life. Fate is what we make for ourselves, and I have made mine. Soon I shall be as the queen of this city, adored for my beauty and elegance."

Sophia studied Bridget's gorgeous face, as perfect as a face could be, and saw the frightening emptiness in her eyes. She was from another world, one where murder and greed were virtues and conscience did not exist. *She will kill me now,* Sophia thought, *unless I kill her first.*

"There's one thing you seem to have forgotten," Sophia said. She felt a strange sense of calm, as though the world had stopped moving, the stars fixed for a moment in the heavens. This was to be her moment, either the last or the first of a new beginning.

"I have not forgotten," Bridget said, sure it was to be her moment, not Sophia's. "I have watched you clutch at your purse. You have the letter in there, don't you, the one you'd like to send to the police."

"I don't have the letter," Sophia said truthfully.

"Now you are the liar," Bridget said. "Give it to me, Sophia, or I will have to take it from your dead body."

"Can't we talk? There is no need—"

"The letter. I will not ask again."

"Very well," Sophia said. She reached into her purse, but not for a letter. The "family heirloom" she'd brought along was a fully loaded revolver. When Bridget saw the gun, she stepped back and fired wildly. Sophia would later tell Peter that she heard the bullet go past, a lethal bee buzzing by her left ear, just before she fired her own shot. Unlike Bridget, her aim was true. Looking startled, as people always do when death has the audacity to find them, Bridget said, "No, no," then dropped to the floor beside her late husband, a bullet in her chest.

Sophia sat still for an instant, staring at the two bodies as though they were fascinating works of art in the grand museum of human folly. It occurred to her that Chase in his own way had been an artist, sculpting his mighty mill out of stone and iron, with a river running through it. Yet stone and iron had proved no match for Bridget's much darker art, founded on ambition and greed, and with sex, that old dangerous magic, at the heart of it.

Practical thoughts quickly intruded on Sophia's reveries, for there was much she had to do if she hoped to avoid an unpleasant encounter with the law. She knelt by Bridget's body and felt for a pulse. There was none, nor was she breathing. Sophia picked up Bridget's revolver, which she'd recognized as soon it was pointed at her. The revolver was a seven-shot, .22 caliber Smith & Wesson, a very common weapon. By a fortunate coincidence, Sophia's revolver was the identical model, and she saw at once how she could stage the murder-suicide scene Bridget had planned for her and Chase.

Sophia tilted up the barrel of the revolver to inspect the cylinder. Bridget had fired three rounds, the two that killed Chase and the one that nearly killed Sophia. The third shot could now become the one Bridget had supposedly fired into her own chest. Like the Minneapolis police in 1872, Sophia knew nothing of ballistics analysis, and she believed, correctly, that the bullet from her gun would easily pass for one from Bridget's revolver.

But what of the bullet Bridget had fired at Sophia? It had to be retrieved or the scene would not make sense. Sophia went over to the bookcase behind the chair she'd been sitting in, and saw that the bullet had, by a nice twist of fate, lodged in *Bleak House,* an apt name for Chase's mansion. The leather-bound tome was so thick that the .22 slug hadn't made it all the way through. Sophia retrieved the book and put it in her purse along with her revolver. Then, after one last look around, she went down the spiral staircase and left the mansion, where death now ruled.

*

Much later, long after the police had concluded that Bridget shot her husband and herself, Sophia would watch as a new mill, built by the Washburns, replaced the Perfection to become the largest in the world. Across the river the Pillsburys would soon build an even bigger mill, and for decades to come Minneapolis flour would feed a hungry nation. But that was all in the future, and of little concern to Sophia.

As she left the Chase mansion and came out into the cool air, she heard the distant susurration of the falls, whispering to her out of the darkness. She took comfort in its sound, in the knowledge that the Mississippi, no matter what men did to it, would always be there, flowing through time. Her doings, she thought, would be of no consequence to the river as it made its journey to the sea, indifferent to her as it was to all the creatures of the earth.

Walking back to her mansion along quiet streets, a half-moon overhead, Sophia marveled as she always did at all the lives—past, present, and to come—moving with a moment's breath beneath the stars, propelled by hopes and dreams. Her own life had come to seem as mysterious as the divided moon, caught between light and darkness, with revelations yet to come. She did not know what lay ahead, for the future is always a mist, impenetrable to mortal eyes. But she was sure her heart remained steadfast, beating life into her body, and she intended to spend whatever time she had left tending to its vital needs. After all, she had a wonderful son and his soon-to-be wife to love, a few good friends to cherish, and sublime memories to occupy her nights, when Ransom Everleigh would rise from his grave and touch her like a spring breeze.

A WILDE NIGHT AT THE NICOLLET HOUSE

"Truth is never pure, and rarely simple."

—OSCAR WILDE

1.
THE CELEBRITY

There is only one thing in the world worse than being talked about, and that is not being talked about.
—OSCAR WILDE

ON THE NIGHT OF MARCH 15, 1882, at the Nicollet House Hotel, I was plunged into a murder investigation that proved to be among the great adventures of my life, all the while accompanied by the most fascinating man I have ever known, Oscar Wilde. Now that Oscar, as he insisted I call him, has left this world, I have decided to tell the full story of the case that came to be known in the newspapers as "The Bell Captain Slaying." The events I am about to narrate remain as fresh in my mind as though they happened yesterday, a circumstance I can only account for by the fact that Oscar burns in my memory like a powerful lamp that can never be extinguished.

I am well aware of the disgrace now attached to Oscar's name, but I prefer not to speak of the unfortunate business that brought him low, except to say that in my long experience as a hotel detective, I have encountered all too many men undone by the urgings of the flesh in their many varieties. "Innocence is a beautiful seed," Oscar told me on the night of our adventure, "but sin is its inevitable bloom." So it was in his case, although I will leave it to the Almighty to be Oscar's final judge and jury.

What I can say is that the young Oscar who so dazzled me was no languid fop. He was, in fact, a formidable man in his own distinctive way. Indeed, had he not chosen a literary life, he might have been a detective in the manner of Sherlock Holmes, for he possessed high intelligence along with wonderful powers of observation and memory, as I saw firsthand during our brief time together.

The case of the murdered bell captain, a young man named Jimmy Jones, is little remembered today. Had Oscar's role in solving it become widely known (I will explain in due time why that did not happen), I have no doubt the case would have garnered publicity across the globe. Oscar himself never made much of his detective work, later dismissing the murder as "hardly a work of art, which is what all good murders should be." Yet in a candid moment, as we said our goodbyes, he admitted he would always remember his night in Minneapolis as "quite extraordinary," and I hope readers will agree.

*

I will say right out that I didn't think much of Oscar the first time I laid eyes on him at the Nicollet House on the afternoon of his arrival. It was about four o'clock, as I recall, when he sashayed into the hotel lobby, having come up from Chicago by train. He was accompanied by a swarthy road manager, a Negro valet, and enough luggage for a trip around the world. A gaggle of young women bearing lilies and sunflowers were there to greet him as though he was as some god come down from the heavens, and everyone else in the lobby took time from their usual idling to have a look at the great aesthete.

Certainly, I had never seen a man like him before. He wore a heavy green coat trimmed with white fur and a black slouch hat set at a rakish angle atop his head, and he carried a knobbed cane that he twirled about like a dancer performing on stage. Thick brown hair, carefully divided by a part, fell to his shoulders, and on his long, clean-shaven face was the knowing smile of a man entirely satisfied with himself. Advertised as the "Apostle of Beauty," he seemed about as dandy as a man could be, and compared to the usual habitués of the Nicollet House, he looked as out of place as cream frosting on a biscuit.

Yet I sensed from the start that he was not quite the delicate flower the press had made him out to be. For one thing he was surprisingly tall, an inch or two over six feet, and well enough put together that he looked as though he could handle himself in a tight situation. There was also more than a hint of steel in his grayish-blue eyes, which as I was to discover could bear down hard on a man if that was what needed to be done.

I imagine few people recall now what a celebrity Oscar was at that time. Before reaching Minneapolis, he'd been traveling around the country on a lecture tour for two months, growing more famous by the day thanks to a constant blaze of publicity. The press delighted in following his every move, either to proclaim his brilliance or, more commonly, to cast him in the role of a holy idiot spouting nonsense. The Minneapolis newspapers happily participated in the Oscar show, although they didn't have much good to say about him as he made his rounds.

Here, for example, is what the *Evening Journal*—in my opinion a newspaper run and read by snobs—had to say: "Mr. Wilde's beauty is the beauty of hideousness. His philosophy is reactionary, and not progressive, and while he may draw after him a large following of shallow fools, it will not take him long to discover that the mass of the people of this country regard him and his teaching with immeasurable contempt." The *Tribune,* meanwhile, dubbed Oscar the "ass-thete," not the cleverest pun I've ever heard, even as its writers promoted his lecture that night at the Academy of Music.

I doubt that Oscar, who was very canny when it came to making his name known, took much heed of the unflattering comments in the press. As he said to me: "Publicity is what puts a man at the head of the table, no matter how execrable the food may be. I will dine contentedly on swill so long as I am the center of attention." And he definitely was that from the moment he strolled into the hotel, for he was one of those electric people who seem to brighten and intensify everything around them, and to whom others are drawn as the moth to the flame.

I didn't have much to do with Oscar at the time of his arrival. My job at that point was simply to go about my usual work. Here I must note that a hotel detective should never be confused with a policeman of the same title. The police detective investigates crime, whereas the hotel detective works diligently to prevent it so as to keep guests feeling safe and comfortable. Pickpockets, room thieves, confidence men, and prostitutes are the chief enemies of the hotel detective, and all four are like flies at a screen door, trying their best to get inside. I'm the man with the swatter.

So it was that when Oscar and his retinue made their appearance, I observed from a distance, especially looking to see if pickpockets were on hand, but I didn't see any finger-smiths I recognized. The lobby of the Nicollet House is always busy, but Oscar's grand arrival made for a packed house, as though everyone in the city had come to get a glimpse of the exotic peacock. Smitten young women constituted much of the crowd, although it would be a safe bet that few of them were interested in Oscar's flowery verse or his aesthetic doctrines. It was simply beautiful Oscar himself that they wanted to see. Yet even the weary-eyed drummers hanging out in the lobby appeared fascinated by Oscar, if for no other reason than his life must have seemed so much more exciting than their own.

Oscar addressed a few words to the adoring throng, accepted an outsized sunflower from one particularly fetching girl, then headed to the front desk to check in. Jimmy Jones, looking very snappy in his red and gold uniform, was waiting for him there along with David Hutchinson, the hotel's manager, who greeted Oscar in his usual florid way.

"The Nicollet House is honored by your presence," he said, making a small bow. "Be assured that we will do all in our power to make your stay a comfortable one."

"How kind of you, Mr. Hutchinson," Oscar said, presumably having spotted the brass name tag on Hutchinson's black jacket. "And who is this handsome bellman I see before me in such splendid livery?"

Hutchinson came around from behind the desk, put a hand on Jones's shoulder, and said, "This is Mr. Jones, our bell captain, and a fine young man. He will take you up to your suite on the second floor and provide any assistance you may need."

"Well, that will be lovely," Oscar said. "I do like a man in uniform, so long as he isn't shooting at me across the line of battle."

"Don't worry, I won't be shooting nobody," Jones said. "Now, just follow me, Mr. Wilde, and I'll show you to your suite."

Jones wasn't my favorite hotel employee. He'd risen rapidly through the ranks to become the bell captain at just twenty-three years old, perhaps in part because he cut a strikingly handsome figure in his uniform, so much so that I often saw guests, especially women, look him over as though they had something indecent in mind.

Jones was also a maneuverer, devious and secretive by nature, and he'd found many ways to supplement his meager wages. He was the man to see for "special services," such as providing information on where a guest might find a nearby gambling parlor or after-hours drinking joint. An even more lucrative sideline was procuring prostitutes for guests. By the time of Oscar's arrival, I'd caught Jones on several occasions sneaking a prostitute up to a room. He should have been fired, but for whatever reason he was a golden boy, seemingly able to get away with almost anything.

I tagged along as Jones, beaming at the prospect of a hefty tip, escorted Oscar to the hotel's sole elevator and told the operator, "Mr. Wilde will be going to suite 113. Make sure you level off nicely when you get to the second floor."

Once Oscar and his valet reached their suite, I waited outside in the hallway while he settled in, just to be sure no one would bother him. Jones soon emerged from the suite jingling a pair of silver dollars in his hand.

"Two bucks," he said to me as he headed back to the elevator. "Usually, I'm lucky to get a dime."

"I guess there's more money in being an apostle of beauty than I thought," I said. "By the way, Jimmy, I don't want to see you bringing any girls up here. That's trouble we don't need."

"Is that so? How about you keep out of my business, Dobsy. You're not my boss."

I was tempted to respond by punching Jones in the nose, but

I let it go, since I wouldn't have done myself any good by making a scene. "Just watch yourself, Jimmy. You're not as clever as you think you are."

"Cleverer than you," he said and then went whistling down the hallway.

I hung around for a while and had to shoo away a number of Oscar's female admirers, among them two very young girls who had sneaked up a back staircase in hopes of seeing their idol. Before long, a reporter I knew from the *Tribune* named Billy Clark came down the hall.

"Going to interview the apostle of good taste?" I asked.

"Yeah," Billy said. "I'm hoping he'll have something funny to say. Or better yet, something insulting. Readers will eat it up if he calls Minneapolis a frozen backwater."

"They'll be delightfully outraged," I agreed. "Well, go to it, Billy."

"I will. Say, I've always wondered. How come you left the *Trib*? Old man Shaw still thinks you're the best writer he ever had."

"That's lovely to hear. Trouble is, Shaw in his capacity as editor in chief declined to back up that sentiment with a raise, so I sought out greener pastures. I like it here just fine. Lots of interesting people and nothing to write on deadline with Shaw staring over my shoulder like a vulture."

"So have you met the pretty boy yet?"

"No, but I intend to. Well, good luck with your interview, Billy."

"Thanks. I must say I feel a bit underdressed compared to the great Oscar."

"Don't we all," said I.

*

Whatever else Oscar was, he was certainly good for the hotel's business. When I went back downstairs to check the register at the front desk, I saw that we had close to a full house, which was unusual for a Wednesday.

"Too bad we can't get the English fellow here every night," Hutchinson said as he came up for a chat. "He seems to bring out a crowd, and that is a wonderful thing."

Hutchinson was himself a well-known figure in the city, as hotelkeepers often were in those days. Described by one newspaper as "Mr. Bonhomie of Minneapolis" by virtue of his bluff and hearty manner, he was somewhere in his forties, broad and barrel-chested, with sandy hair long since in retreat and bright, welcoming eyes. Like any good hotel manager, his work consisted of coddling guests and terrorizing the staff, at both of which he excelled. However, he'd learned that, unlike bellboys and maids, I couldn't be bullied, so we got on well enough.

I now looked at the room assignments to see who would be in the suites adjoining Oscar's. On one side, in suite 111, was someone named Pluto Conklin. With a name like that, I figured he had to be rich. On the other side, in 115, was Chauncey Montague, who sounded like an English swell. Neither man was familiar to me.

"Well, it looks like our famous aesthete will be wedged between a banker and a fancy-pants," I said. "Hard to know which of the three is worse."

"What a cynic you are!" Hutchinson said. "Besides, you must think of Mr. Wilde as entertainment, Dobsy, and people like nothing better than to be entertained. The bar is already packed, and there will be more than a hundred people for the big banquet in his honor tonight. And not just any people. We are talking about Pillsburys and Washburns and Morrisons. The cream of the crop, as it were. The kind of people who are not afraid to spend money."

"Well, they certainly have it. I guess flour is gold in this city. What are you going to feed the hungry rich?"

"See for yourself," he said, handing me a menu specially printed for the grand dinner.

Mock turtle soup, broiled whitefish, turkey giblets with gravy, filet of beef, larded peas, sweetbread, peaches à la Richelieu and a chocolate mousse were among the highlights. "I am happy to see the guests won't be starving," I said. "I was worried about that."

"Hah! Now, listen up, Dobsy. The banquet starts at six, and I fear some disreputable characters will be in the vicinity looking for gravy of their own. You must evict them as soon as you spot them. And needless to say, we cannot have any ladies of the evening going about their business."

"Don't worry. I'll make sure there are no problems."

"Excellent," said Hutchinson. "This will be one of the biggest nights we've ever had, and we can't afford to let anything go wrong."

*

At six o'clock, Oscar made his next appearance, emerging from the hotel's recently installed elevator with his manager, a smallish man named Stanley Vale, who appeared to be in a state of constant agitation. I could only imagine what wrangling Oscar must have been like, and I gave Vale a sympathetic nod as he and his charge came out into the lobby. Vale responded with an eye roll and a slight shake of the head, as though he deserved the sympathy of the world for taking on an impossible task.

By this time, the banquet crowd had already assembled in the main dining room, which was decorated with pink and gold bouquets, garlands, swags, and even a plaster replica of a Greek statue someone had dug up from an art studio at the university. It was all very swanky, as was the crowd. The men—drawn from the city's business, professional, and political elite—wore evening clothes, while their wives vied to outdo one another in the glory of their gowns and the glimmer of their jewels. It was amusing to see so much wealth assembled to fete a man who preached, even if he didn't seem to practice, the virtues of simplicity.

I wasn't well acquainted with the city's upper crust, but I recognized some of the tuxedoed men from previous events at the hotel. Among the women, however, only one stood out, and that was Mrs. Sophia Westerly, whom I'd first encountered ten years earlier when I covered the notorious murder of Ransom Everleigh for the *Tribune.* She had pushed mightily to find Everleigh's killer, and I'd developed great respect for her. Long a widow, she was at the banquet with a man I didn't recognize, but as the night unfolded and another baffling murder shocked the city, Mrs. Westerly was to prove a valuable ally.

Oscar now made his way into the dining room, like a prince ready to be feted by his adoring—or possibly mystified—subjects, and he wasn't underdressed for the occasion. He wore a cutaway coat of black velvet, fluffy white shirt, light blue cravat, brown knee breeches, and patent leather shoes so shiny I almost had to squint to look at them. I'd read about his peculiar apparel, but seeing him in full garb was quite the experience. I stationed myself at the back of the dining room as Oscar waltzed in, all eyes focused on the sheer spectacle of his presence.

I will not trouble readers with a detailed account of the banquet, which like all such affairs entailed much speechifying and even more eating. The mayor formally welcomed Oscar, various nabobs expressed their pleasure that so an exalted a figure had come to Minneapolis, Oscar pronounced himself deeply pleased to be among so many lovers of the artistic and beautiful, and the chocolate mousse, I was told, was really quite excellent. Oscar did at least toss out a few witticisms to keep the crowd from choking on their giblets. Asked what he thought about Minneapolis, he said, "I am fairly optimistic there will be a city here someday," but he drew more far more enthusiastic laughter when he remarked that "the chief value of a reputation is to see how utterly delighted people are when you fail to live up to it."

I have been to three-hour-long banquets that would test any man's endurance, but this one lasted only half that long because Oscar was due to deliver his lecture on the English Renaissance, a topic that has always managed to elude my purview, at eight o'clock at the Academy of Music. Those who are of a certain age undoubtedly remember the old Academy, which was just across the street from the hotel at Hennepin and Washington Avenues. It was then the largest hall in the city, seating up to 1,300 people for performances of all kinds. Like so many of the entertainment venues of its time it met a fiery end when it burned down on Christmas Day in 1884, having stood for just twelve years.

As the banquet wrapped up, I kept a close watch on Oscar and those around him, and there soon occurred an incident that caused me to earn his favor. Oscar and Vale were heading through the lobby on the way to the elevator when I spotted a known pickpocket named "Fast Willie" Mueller lurking nearby. The crowd was so thick that I wasn't able to lay my hands on Mueller before he slipped into the elevator cab, the kind of tight space pickpockets love.

The elevator was very slow, so I raced up the main lobby stairs to get ahead of it. Oscar and Vale were just exiting the cab when I arrived. Mueller, trying to look as inconspicuous as he could, followed them out, but I grabbed him before he could make an escape.

"What's this?" Oscar asked as I shoved Mueller, who was quick of hand but otherwise not much of a physical specimen, up against a wall and began going through his coat pockets, where I found three wallets, two of brown leather and the other of black.

"Fast Willie here is a pickpocket," I said. "Do any of these wallets look familiar?"

"My God, that black one is mine," said Vale, just as Mueller made a sudden move and darted away. I grabbed the wallets but didn't bother to go after him, knowing that he'd flee the hotel. I'd let the police deal with him in due time.

Oscar, who appeared to be entertained by the proceedings, said to his manager, "Why, Mr. Vale, you have just encountered a genuine American criminal and something of an artist in his own way. What delicate fingers that fellow must have!" Then he turned to me and said, "I must account you our savior, sir. May I ask who you are?"

"Robert McGuire, but everybody calls me Dobsy. I'm the house dick here."

"Well now, there is a title any man could be proud of," Oscar said with a naughty grin. "I fear to think what might have happened had that fellow escaped with Mr. Vale's wallet. To whom do you suppose the other ones belong?"

"Banquet goers, I'm sure. Pickpockets aren't stupid. They go where the money is."

"As do I," Wilde said. "One needs a great deal of money, after all, to lead a modest life. Well, now that you have performed a heroic deed, why don't you come along with us to my suite. I should like to hear more about you before I go off to deliver words of profound wisdom to the benighted residents of Minneapolis."

Oscar's suite, number 113, was one of the largest in the hotel, consisting of a parlor, two bedrooms, a small dressing area and a private bath, which back in the 1880s was a real luxury. Although his lecture was scheduled to begin in just twenty minutes, Oscar didn't seem to be in any hurry as he sat down on a sofa in the parlor and lit a cigar. He said to Vale, "Why don't you arouse Mr. Davenport from his slumbers and tell him I'll need my maroon coat for the lecture and a white scarf. And make sure he carefully brushes the velvet."

After Vale went into the adjoining bedroom, Oscar said, "Have you seen Mr. Davenport? He is my Negro valet and quite the fellow, though I sometimes think he would be much happier if I were dead. Dressing me would be so much easier then."

"And he'd only have to do it once," I noted.

"Yes, but it would have to be done exceptionally well. Indeed, I've often wondered how one should dress for eternity. Everyone is sent off in their best clothes, for that good coffin look, yet it seems the occupants of heaven all wear white robes, if the painters are to be believed. I should think that must be quite tedious. Of course, I am confident I will end up in hell, if it comes to that, where all the interesting people will surely be. Now then, Dobsy, may I offer you a small token of my gratitude for your splendid work in fending off that cutpurse?"

"The pickpocket, you mean? No, I was just doing my job."

"So tell me, how does one end up in the glorious role of 'house dick'? I imagine a sturdy-looking man such as yourself was probably a policeman at some point."

"I was, back in Chicago, but not for long."

"Chicago is quite the place, isn't it. Big and crude in a distinctively American way. I rather liked it, but I was also glad to leave. I found the city exhausting. Everyone seemed to be rushing about as though they had a train to catch in five minutes. Do you by chance hail from Chicago?"

I was surprised by Oscar's interest in my hardly remarkable life, but he was insistent that I describe my background, which I will share here so that readers may know a little about me. My parents were Irish immigrants who settled in Chicago in the 1840s. My father worked on the big canal project there, like many another poor Irishman. Our family was large—I had nine siblings—and by the time I came of age I was ready for adventure, so I went off on the last days of the War of the Rebellion to serve with an Illinois regiment, seeing little combat but much disease and death.

After the war, I struck out on my own. As I was big and strong and not afraid to mix it up with anyone, I tried my hand at police work in Chicago, but found the job of a patrolman to be mostly tedium interrupted by occasional gunplay or fistfights. Possessed with a certain gift for words, I quit the police force and began writing for the *Rock Island Argus* in Illinois, soon becoming its city editor. By 1871 I was ready for a change of scenery and came up to Minneapolis, where I took a job with the *Tribune.* The work was to my liking, but the pay was poor, and so in late 1878 I hired on as the Nicollet House's night detective. I was to hold the job for twenty years and I greatly enjoyed it, for few other lines of work afford so many interesting encounters with humanity in all its variety.

As I was finishing my impromptu autobiography, Vale returned to the parlor, his normal look of agitation replaced by the wide-eyed panic of a man about to have a molar yanked out.

"For God's sake, Oscar, it's nearly five to eight. Hurry now, get dressed. Davenport has your outfit ready. I'm going over to the hall to tell them you'll be there shortly."

After Vale rushed out, Oscar lifted himself off the couch and said, "Duty calls, Dobsy. But before you go, let me show you something."

He went over to a side table and came back with handful of trade cards, all of which featured his image. "It seems America now needs me to sell things. Have a look at this one."

The card was for something called "Mrs. Brundage's Bosom Beautifier and Bust Enlarger," and it featured a small photograph of Oscar, his lips painted ruby red, beneath an image of a blonde-haired maiden watering sunflowers.

"The picture is one of several Mr. Sarony, the celebrated New York photographer, took before I started my tour, and now the damned things are everywhere. I am also peddling coats, shirts, shoes, liquor, and furniture, but I am at a loss to know why I am also promoting bosom enhancement, however much I favor the concept."

"I guess people think of you as a ladies' man," I said.

"Ha, if only they knew!"

Davenport appeared at the bedroom door and said, "Please get in here, sir, and dress. You're already late. Mr. Vale must be having a fit."

"Coming," Oscar said. "Well, Dobsy, it has been a pleasure making your acquaintance. I shall rely on you as my faithful Hibernian so long as I remain in this fair city. I must be off to the Academy. Public lectures, alas, are generally a matter of the uninteresting speaking to the uninterested, but I shall strive not to be the former. Wish me luck."

I did so, then said, "And you'll be off to St. Paul in the morning, I hear."

"That is the plan," he said, "but I have learned on my travels that one must be flexible. What is an itinerary, after all, except hope with a schedule attached? I relish the unexpected. Surprise is life's most delightful elixir, don't you think?"

"It depends on the surprise," I said, not knowing then what lay in store for us upon Oscar's return.

*

While Oscar performed his act across the street at the Academy, I kept to my usual routine of roaming around the hotel on the lookout for trouble. With the banquet ended, most of the swells had gone back to their mansions or off to Oscar's lecture. But some remained in the lobby or had moved on to the bar, and I had to make sure none of Mueller's coworkers, if they could be called that, were lurking in the shadows.

A word here about the layout of the Nicollet House may be in order, as some readers may be unfamiliar with the establishment. It was built in the 1850s, only a few years after Minneapolis was founded. The hotel was then, or so I have been told, among the largest buildings in the city, rising to five stories and offering nearly one hundred rooms. Around 1870 an addition more than doubled the size of the hotel. Then came various remodelings and reconstructions, and by the time of Oscar's arrival the hotel was, as it is today, an intricate maze of corridors, narrow back passages, winding staircases, abandoned rooms, and hidden alcoves where mischief can readily flourish.

The hotel has two dining rooms, one fancy and the other not, along with a bar. All three are served by a large kitchen located across a small open courtyard from the lobby. A hallway used only by employees runs along one side of the courtyard, connecting the lobby and kitchen before branching off into another passage that leads to an employee entrance on Nicollet Avenue. At about quarter past eight, with Oscar droning away at the Academy, I headed down the hall, which is narrow and ill-lit, to grab a sandwich in the kitchen. Usually, the hall reeks of food and grease, but as I walked along I caught a surprising whiff of perfume.

I knew at once where the scent must have come from, since ladies of the evening had been known to slip into the hotel via the back entrance with the help of a bellboy, porter, or some other employee. The entrance was supposed to be kept locked at all times, a bell being rung to secure admission, but I knew from experience that the door was often left open. I went down to check the entrance, which was indeed unlocked, and when I pushed open the door, I ran straight into Jones, smoking a cigar out on the sidewalk.

"Taking a little break, are you, Jimmy?" I said.

"Yeah, what does it look like I'm doing?" he replied in his usual smart way.

"You know, Jimmy boy, one of these days I'm going to have to teach you some manners."

"Is that so? What are you going to do, take a poke at me?"

"The thought has crossed my mind."

"I wouldn't try it if I were you."

"And why is that?"

"You'll see. I've got plenty of friends around here."

"Including that woman you just let in?"

For once, the little schemer was taken by surprise, a hint of alarm evident in his pale blue eyes. But he quickly assumed a pose of nonchalance. "I don't know what you're talking about."

"Is that so? Maybe I imagined that perfume I smelled in the hallway, although I don't think so. What do you charge to let her in?"

"I'm going back to work," Jones said, stepping past me. "Make sure you lock the door behind you."

I let him go—he wasn't the type to admit anything—and watched him head toward the lobby while I went into the kitchen for my sandwich. After I'd wolfed down some ham and cheese on pumpernickel, I went back along the hall. The scent of perfume was all but gone by the time I reached the lobby. There, only a few steps away, I found Mrs. Westerly, sitting alone at a low table and sipping a glass of white wine. Her position was such that she had a direct view down the hall if the door was opened, and it gave me an idea, so I went over to say hello.

She was wearing a long black dress accented by a necklace of lustrous pearls, and although I guessed her to be well into her sixties, she looked as slender and elegant as I remembered her from a decade earlier. Her eyes took me in with interest when I approached.

"Why, Mr. McGuire, it has been a long time," she said. "Are you still writing for the *Tribune,* or have you graduated to bigger and better things?"

"Well, I don't know that being a hotel detective is bigger or better, but that's what I'm doing now. May I join you for a minute?"

"Of course."

I took a seat and said, "I saw you earlier with a gentleman. Am I to assume you've remarried?"

"You are not," she said with a sly smile. "Three husbands are enough for any woman. No, he is simply a man I allow to escort me around now and then. But he wasn't feeling well—something in the soup, perhaps—so I sent him home. I don't mind being by myself, although it causes all too many eager men to think I must be a damsel in distress."

I could easily imagine that. She was reputed to be one of the richest widows in the city, and fending off suitors hoping to share in that wealth probably kept her busy. I said, "I'm trying to recall the last time we talked. It must have been after that awful business at Stoddard Chase's mansion. That was just about the craziest murder-suicide I ever covered. I sometimes wonder if there was more to the story than we'll ever know."

"The past is always a mystery, if you think about it. I prefer to stay in the present. And by the look in your eye, Mr. McGuire, I have a suspicion there is something you want of me at this very moment."

"Am I that obvious? Well, you're right. I'm just curious if you might have seen anyone a bit earlier coming from the hall over there."

"I am sorry to say I did," she said without hesitation. "It was a young woman I once tried to help. Her name is Louise Merriman and she's a prostitute, I'm afraid."

I knew Louise. She went by Merry, and she was young and pretty enough to have a select clientele. I'd run her out of the hotel a few times but hadn't made a big deal of it to the police. Just a week earlier, however, I'd told her that I would call the coppers if I caught her in the hotel again. Obviously, my warning hadn't done much good.

"Did you speak to her?"

"No. As soon as she saw me, she rushed away. I could only assume she was going to meet a customer somewhere here in the hotel. It is very sad, what happens to girls like her, and disgusting that so many men are eager to exploit them to satisfy their lust. But I have found that once a young woman is lured into prostitution, it is a very hard for her to escape that life. Your job, I imagine, is to keep women like Louise out of the hotel."

"It is, but it's a constant battle. Did you happen to see where she went?"

"Yes, and it was rather odd, I thought. She was in the lobby for only a moment. Once she came out of that hallway, she walked directly to that other door over there and went inside. That was all I saw of her."

The "other door" in this case led to another hallway primarily serving the hotel's laundry. But the corridor also provided access to a back staircase that winds all the way up to the hotel's attic. From the stairway, Merriman could easily reach any room in the hotel, meaning I'd have no easy way to find her.

"Thanks for your help, Mrs. Westerly," I said. "I'll see if I can track her down. The management would like to think this place isn't a brothel."

I went to the back stairs, thinking that like a bloodhound I might be able to follow Merriman by the smell of her perfume. But the scent had faded by the time I reached the second floor, where Oscar's suite was located. The corridor there was clear—Oscar's admirers were presumably at the lecture—and since I couldn't very well go to every room on the floor and inquire whether its occupant was romping with a prostitute, I gave up the hunt. When I got back to the lobby, I alerted Hutchinson to the situation and told him I'd evict Merriman if I could find her.

"Yes, please do," he said. "Women like her are a scourge as far as I'm concerned."

"I agree," I said. "Too bad not all of our guests feel the same way."

*

I was hanging around the lobby at half past ten when Oscar returned from his lecture with Vale in tow. "It's not your fault," the little man was saying. "There's just no culture in a place like this."

Oscar spotted me and came over for a chat as Vale fussed nearby. "Dobsy, I have bad news. I have lost some money tonight for Mr. D'Oyly Carte, who's sponsoring my tour, although I doubt it will bankrupt him. Have you heard of him?"

I said I hadn't.

"Well, he's the fellow who puts on the Gilbert and Sullivan extravaganzas. I fear I am small change in comparison, but he still expects me to turn a profit for him. Alas, the noble citizens of Minneapolis were not eager to hear my message. What were the proceeds again, Stanley?"

"Two thirty-seven at a dollar a head," Vale said. "The house takes half, so we didn't clear much."

"There you have it, Dobsy. Only two hundred and thirty-seven souls wished to hear me tonight. I would be devastated if it were not for the fact there were several handsome young people in the audience I was able to flirt with. I positively melted them with my ineffable charm. Or perhaps they were simply mocking me with their batted eyelashes. One never knows, does one, if being famous is all that different from being foolish. Well, perhaps St. Paul will be better tomorrow. I have heard there are many Irish there."

"That's true," I said, "and they like to drink."

"They are Hibernians after my own heart then. Speaking of alcohol, I will need some extra refreshment tonight. I can only hope the hotel's cellar is well stocked. Well, it is off to nurse my wounded pride."

I watched as Oscar and Vale went to the elevator, thinking that the night's big show was over. Minutes later, a desk clerk called me over. "Mr. Wilde would like to see you in his room at once," the clerk said. "He said it's urgent."

For once, as I soon discovered, Oscar wasn't exaggerating.

2.
OSCAR FINDS A BODY

Murder is always a mistake. One should never do anything that one can't talk about after dinner.
—OSCAR WILDE

AFTER BEING TOLD I WAS URGENTLY NEEDED in Oscar's suite, I went right up and knocked on the door. Oscar answered, poked his head out to survey the hallway, then said in a calm voice, "Dobsy, I am very glad you're here. You'd better come in and tell me what to do. You see, there is a dead bellman in my room. Or perhaps I should say he very much looks to be deceased. The poor chap is on the carpet by the sofa, and I have no idea how he got there. Neither does Mr. Davenport."

Oscar wasn't kidding. I stepped inside and saw Jones lying prone on the floor. His legs were spread slightly apart, his uniform was in some disarray, his eyes were fixed wide open, and his tongue hung out at a strange angle. Nasty bruises were visible on his neck, suggesting someone had choked him with great force. I went over to feel for a pulse but found none. A brass button torn from his double-breasted uniform jacket lay on the floor next to his body. The hat that formed part of his uniform was also on the floor.

"We'll have to call the police," I said. "It's obvious he was murdered. Is this how you found him?"

"Yes. I'd just chatted with you down in the lobby after my lecture, and I came straight up here, opened the door, and there he was. I do not mind saying it was quite a shock. Of course, I recognized him at once, which made it doubly shocking. He's Mr. Jones, the same bellman who brought us up here after we checked in. Seemed like a nice enough fellow."

"Maybe he seemed that way if you didn't know him," I said.

"Ah, I sense some drama in your reply," Oscar said. "Well, in any case here we are, contemplating a corpse. I must say I have encountered many hopelessly dead minds in my day, but a dead body is a new experience, and a rather thrilling one at that."

I'd seen all too many corpses over the years and "thrilling" wasn't how I'd describe the experience. "Believe me, Oscar, you won't be so thrilled when the cops show up," I said.

"I suppose not. I'm sure they'll be thoroughly unpleasant. How do you suppose Mr. Jones ended up like this?" Oscar was staring intently at the body as though he was trying to will Jones back to life.

"I don't know, but you can bet the police will have a lot of questions for you, so stick around. Where's that valet of yours, by the way?"

"He's in the rear bedroom saying his prayers. He's deathly afraid he'll be blamed. He was in his room, you see, while I was about my business at the Academy. But he tells me he was sound asleep and didn't hear a thing. Indeed, I had to wake him up after I found Mr. Jones."

"Well, the police will be suspicious, especially since he's a Negro. All right, just stay put and don't open your door for anybody until I get back. And don't touch the body either."

"Your wish is my command. I shall await your return. Where are you going?"

"I need to get the hotel manager here. I'll be right back."

Although Hutchinson had a private apartment a few doors down from Oscar's suite, I figured he'd still be at work in the hotel's office, so I hustled downstairs to find him. He was at his desk, snappily attired in a dark red jacket as he worked through the usual pile of paperwork. When I barged in he said, "Jesus, Dobsy, what's up? You look like you've seen a ghost."

"Oh, it's much worse than that," I said before delivering the kind of news no hotel manager ever wants to hear.

"Good God! Jimmy, you say? Murdered? How could such a thing happen?" A pause followed before whatever sympathy Hutchinson might have felt quickly turned to calculation. "This will look terrible, Dobsy. Absolutely terrible! A murder here at the hotel! It has never happened before. I suppose we'll have to notify the police."

"Yes, Hutch, they do like to be informed when someone has been murdered," I said. "We can't cover this up. Let me handle it. I know most of the coppers. I'll try to keep them from stomping around here like a herd of elephants, but don't count on it."

I rang up the operator to speak with the police. I explained the situation and asked for as much discretion as possible, although I doubted the coppers would heed my request. Any murder was big news in Minneapolis, but a victim found dead in the hotel room of a man as famous as Oscar was sure to bring out most of the police department, no doubt led by the chief himself, not to mention every newspaper reporter within a hundred miles.

"Brace yourself," I said to Hutchinson. "It's going to be a very long night. I'm going back to Oscar's room before the mob arrives."

"I'll come with," Hutchinson said. "This is most distressing, and I wish to assure Mr. Wilde that the hotel will do all it can to keep his name out of this unfortunate business."

"Somehow I think that's the last thing he'd ever wish for," I said, "but you do what you want."

Oscar admitted us to his suite and said to Hutchinson, "Ah, management is here. As I recall, you are Mister—"

"Hutchinson. David Hutchinson. I checked you in."

"Of course you did. Well, you have some managing to do tonight. I do not suppose a dead bellman is a regular occurrence at your establishment."

"Oh no, it most certainly is not," said Hutchinson, who erupted with a gush of apologies before he even bothered to look at Jones's body. He then went on to assure Oscar that no scandal would be attached to his name. "You are merely an innocent bystander in this sorry business, and I have no doubt the police can be persuaded to exercise the utmost discretion in handling the matter."

True to form, Oscar replied, "Discretion, Mr. Hutchinson, is like whiskey without the alcohol, and thus of little use. Besides, I rather like the idea of being linked to a murder most foul. My name has been connected to all manner of crimes against good taste, common sense, and whatnot, but never to murder. I find it quite exhilarating!"

I'd been around Oscar just long enough to know the pride he took in being perverse, so his words didn't surprise me. Hutchinson, on the other hand, was thoroughly nonplussed. "Ah, you are joking, Mr. Wilde," he said. "Surely you don't mean that."

"I always mean what I say, my dear man. Otherwise, how would people know that I'm lying?"

While Oscar was busy baffling Hutchinson, I went through Jones's pockets. I found the two silver dollars he'd received from Oscar, plus a five-dollar gold piece. Was it, too, a tip? If so, it probably would have qualified as the biggest of Jones's life, since five dollars was a lot of money in those days, and I wondered what he'd done to merit such largesse. His pockets also yielded one of the hotel's distinctive passkeys, an item he wasn't supposed to have.

"Looks like Jimmy was running around with a passkey," I said to Hutchinson. "I doubt he was using it for the benefit of guests."

"My God, do you think he was sneaking into rooms and stealing things?"

"That would be my guess."

After I'd finished exploring Jones's pockets, I made note of a small puncture wound on the ring finger of his left hand. The wound was near the tip of the finger, behind the nail, and it had produced just enough blood to form a thin smear on the surrounding skin. It appeared to be the kind of mark made by a pinprick, or perhaps even a needle.

Oscar came over for a look and said, "That's peculiar, isn't it. As I know of few men who sew, I doubt it came from a needle. I should guess he was stuck with a pin."

"Looks that way. It must have happened just before he was murdered. Jimmy always prided himself on being neat. If he'd accidentally pricked a finger, he would have taken care to wash off the blood. There's something else to think about. Do you see those two lines in the carpet that extend from Jimmy's feet to the communicating door over there?"

"Yes, I noticed them. I assume that door leads to an adjoining suite."

"It does. Number 111, to be exact. And those lines must be drag marks left by Jimmy's heels. Looks to me like somebody pulled his body in here from that suite. As I recall, a fellow named Conklin is in one eleven, isn't that right, Hutch?"

"Yes. Mr. Pluto Conklin."

"You know anything about him?"

"Not really. I believe he's a banker from St. Paul here on some sort of business. He was alone."

"Well, let's see if he's home," I said and went to the communicating door, which was unlocked.

"Did you open this?" I asked Oscar as I swung open the door, revealing a second door directly behind it. The two doors are meant to provide security, the idea being that the occupants of both suites have to open their doors from the inside if they want to create a connection.

"Never touched it, Dobsy. I have spent my life trying not to communicate with bankers, particularly ones named Pluto. With a name like that, I picture him as a rotund man with a walrus mustache, a monocle, and a soul unacquainted with beauty."

"Pity him," I said as I announced myself and knocked on the second door. There was no answer. I knocked again without effect, then gave the door a push. It was open, so in I went. The suite was much like Oscar's, with a parlor and beyond that a bedroom and a bath.

The banker was nowhere to be found, but there were signs of a recent disturbance in the parlor. An ice bucket with an uncorked bottle of champagne sat on a low table in front of a sofa, and the carpet beneath was wet. This suggested that the champagne or ice or both had been spilled at some point. The table itself was angled slightly away from the sofa, as though it had been moved and then not quite restored to its usual spot, as indicated by indentations in the carpet where the legs normally rested. But it was something else visible in the carpet—drag marks extending from near the sofa to the communicating doors—that left little doubt as to where Jones had been murdered.

"Why, I do believe we have discovered the scene of crime," said Oscar, who'd come up behind me with Hutchinson.

"It looks that way," I agreed. "There must have been a struggle, and Jimmy didn't come out on top."

Oscar began to explore the rest of the room, flitting around like a bee in search of nectar, and before long he found a black porkpie hat, decorated with two feathers, that hung on a hook next to the suite's entrance door. He picked up the hat, examined it carefully, and said, "Judging from the size of it, not to mention the duck feathers, this is a woman's hat. It is of indifferent quality and certainly not the sort of hat that would be worn by any ladies of my acquaintance."

"Maybe you don't know the right kind of ladies," I said. "Okay, just put it back where you found it. I don't want the coppers to think we've been tampering with evidence."

"I am all for tampering, but I suppose you're right. But you must agree, Dobsy, that this hat is most interesting. Methinks Pluto had a visitor tonight, and it was in all likelihood not a Roman goddess."

"That's one way of putting it," I said. "Let's check out the rest of the suite."

The tiny bathroom yielded no obvious clues. The bedroom, however, was interesting. The sheets and blankets on the four-poster bed were in disarray, as though Conklin had been thrashing about. I also noted small stains on the bottom sheet. I'd spent enough time working at the hotel to know what the stains indicated.

"It appears our banker made an unauthorized deposit, if you could call it that," Oscar said with a delighted grin. "I am beginning to think more highly of Pluto, who obviously has been a naughty fellow this evening."

"Yeah, it looks that way," I said, "but we won't know for sure until we find him and see what he has to say for himself."

When we returned to the parlor Oscar said, "I am no detective, but I wonder why Mr. Jones was placed in my suite. Could it be that someone, as you Americans say, is trying to 'frame' me?"

"Maybe," I said, "but it won't work because you have an unshakable alibi. I saw Jimmy downstairs not long after you left for your lecture. Also, I talked with you in the lobby when you returned. It couldn't have been more than a minute or two after that when you called to report finding the body. No, the police shouldn't have any reason to suspect you. But that valet of yours is a different story. Is he still there in the back bedroom?"

"Yes, but I can assure you Davenport is no murderer, even if he regularly commits crimes against the English language. He's a capital fellow in my estimation, and I may take him on permanently when I return to England."

"Mind if I talk to him?" I asked.

"Go right ahead. As I said, he's terribly afraid he may become a scapegoat in this unfortunate business."

*

I found Davenport in the suite's small back bedroom after passing through Oscar's much larger sleeping chamber. The valet, who was as dark-skinned a Negro as I had ever seen, looked to be in his early thirties, and what I most remember about him to this day was how wary he looked, as though he always expected being ill-used by strangers. He sat on his bed, one leg shaking violently as he wrung his hands and swayed from side to side. Small beads of sweat were visible on his brow, and when he saw me, he said, "Are you the police? Believe me, sir, I know nothing about what happened here tonight."

"I'm not the police," I said and introduced myself. "But the coppers will be here soon, and they'll want to talk to you."

"They'll blame me for sure," he said in a deep voice with more than a trace of New York in it. "They always do when they see a Black man such as myself."

"I don't think Oscar will let the police browbeat you," I said. "Just tell me anything you can."

"I was sleeping in here, that's God's truth, so help me. I enjoy working for Mr. Wilde, but he don't keep regular hours, no sir, he does not. So I try to doze off when I get the chance. I need my rest like everybody else. I was surprised something terrible when Mr. Wilde woke me up and showed me that boy's body. Made me sick to see it."

"So you were sleeping the whole time Oscar was giving his speech?"

"Oh yes, and a mighty good sleep it was. Only woke up once."

"What woke you up?"

"Well now, I thought I heard voices, only I figured it was a dream."

"What kind of voices?"

"Sounded like two men arguing about something. They were loud, but I couldn't make out any words. It went quiet pretty quick after that. The next thing I know, I'm back asleep, and that was that."

"What time was this?"

"I can't say, I really can't. I guess it could be any time after I nodded off."

"Did you close the door to this room before you went to sleep?"

"I surely did. I wanted things nice and quiet, on account of it's never that way when Mr. Wilde is around."

"I'm discovering that," I said.

Nothing about Davenport's demeanor or his story gave me pause. He had no obvious motive for murdering Jones, nor did it seem odd that he would have gone to sleep when he did, since I could readily imagine that tending to a man like Oscar was exhausting work. But if Davenport had indeed been roused briefly from his slumbers by the sound of voices, whose were they?

"All right, Mr. Davenport, just try to stay calm and tell the police what you told me. But try to make sure Oscar is around when they question you. Otherwise, they'll probably want to get rough."

"I know all about that," he said. "Yes, sir, I do indeed."

*

By my watch it was a bit after eleven when the police arrived in the form of two uniformed patrolmen and a detective named Walter Jackson, whom I knew well enough from my days as reporter. Jackson was a big man, like most coppers, rough and tenacious, with eyes that came at you like bullets. He was not, however, the possessor of an elegant intellect. Bulldozing was his style, and he was particularly fond of questioning suspects with his fists.

"Hello, Walt," I said. "Looks like you're going to have your hands full here. I assume the chief is on his way."

"Of course he is. The reporters will be with him, like birds hitching a ride on the back of a crocodile. So, the stiff is a bellboy?"

"Bell captain. His name is Jimmy Jones."

Jackson went over for a closer look at the body. "Yeah, that's Jimmy all right. I've run into him a few times. So where's this Wilde character everybody's been talking about?"

"Right here," said Oscar, coming in from his bedroom. He was still attired in the velvet coat and knee breeches he'd worn to his lecture. "It's a pleasure to meet you, Detective, despite the unfortunate circumstances. Naturally, I'll do all I can to be of assistance."

"Sure you will," Jackson said, with the quizzical look of a man who'd just spotted a flamingo and couldn't fathom how it had reached Minneapolis. "What's the story?"

I stepped in to tell Jackson what we'd found out so far and to let him know that Oscar couldn't have committed the crime. "It appears as though Mr. Jones was killed in the adjoining suite and then dragged in here."

"And why would anybody do that?" Jackson asked.

"No idea," I said.

Jackson had barely started in on his investigation when the police chief, A. S. Munger, arrived with two reporters in tow, including Billy Clark from the *Tribune* and a fellow from the *Pioneer Press.* I regarded Munger as being reasonably honest if not particularly capable, but he did his best to direct the operation as more coppers appeared, no doubt drawn to the scene by the fact that the case was certain to be sensational fodder for the newspapers. Oscar happily entertained the reporters with his usual run of witticisms—talk, I suppose you could say, was his greatest art—while I nosed around for any clues the police might be overlooking.

As Davenport had predicted, the coppers, Jackson in particular, immediately homed in on him as the likely suspect. "You can't trust them Negroes," Jackson announced, only "Negroes" wasn't the word he used. Oscar, to his credit, stood by his valet and insisted it was "utterly ridiculous" to think Davenport had anything to do with the crime. I could tell Jackson wanted to run Davenport in for a good working over, but Oscar wouldn't hear of it.

"I should have to make a big case of it," he said to Jackson, "and you would not come out looking well."

"Is that so? What are you going to do, throw flowers at me?"

"I was thinking more along the lines of a left hook," said Oscar.

That remark amused Jackson, who said, "Is that so? Try it, boy, and I'll drop you like a stone."

Not wishing Oscar to end up on the floor, I stepped in and said, "We don't need a big set-to, gentlemen, although I'm sure the fellows here from the press would greatly enjoy it. Walt, what say you start looking into Mr. Conklin? It seems to me he's the one who has a lot to answer for."

"Yeah, and he will," Jackson said as Oscar and I followed him into Conklin's suite, where the chief was already snooping around. "We've just got to find him first."

As if on cue, a uniformed copper appeared with Conklin in tow and said, "Found him down in the bar. Claims he's been drinking there for hours."

"Just what in blazes is going on?" Conklin said as he surveyed the scene.

"Murder," said Jackson, "and you're going to tell us all about it."

*

There are people who look like their names, and Pluto Conklin was one of them. He was short and fat, with more beard than face, and cold black eyes of the kind that only a glittering pile of gold could warm. However, the monocle Oscar had predicted was not in evidence. I put Conklin's age at about fifty-five, but his toupée was much younger. He wore the customary banker's uniform—dark pin-striped suit, vest, tie, gold watch chain—yet he seemed disheveled. His tie was loose, his shirt collar was slightly torn, and his bulbous nose didn't sit quite right on his face.

"Why, this is an outrage!" Conklin said by way of an opening statement. "All of you must leave my room at once."

Munger said, "That will not be possible, I'm afraid."

"And who the devil are you?" Conklin asked.

The chief made introductions, then said, "I regret to tell you that there has been a murder. Please have a seat and let me introduce you to Detective Jackson. I am sure he would like to ask you a few questions."

"Murder?" Conklin said with what sounded like a genuine gasp of surprise. "What on earth has that got to do with me?"

"That's what we're here to find out," said Jackson. "You see, there's a dead fellow next door and it looks like he was killed in your suite. Maybe you can explain how that happened. And while you're at it, maybe you can explain why you don't look so good. What happened to your nose?"

Conklin attributed his misaligned nose, not very convincingly, to an unfortunate mishap with a swinging door.

"Looks to me like somebody punched you," Jackson observed, his own crooked nose being testimony to just such an event.

"Well, that's not what happened," Conklin insisted, adding, "and what business is it of yours anyway?"

"I am also struck by your damaged proboscis," said Oscar. "Did some poor widow deliver a left jab when you foreclosed on her home? Or have you been brawling downstairs in the bar like a naughty fellow? In any event, I welcome you to the chaos, Mr. Conklin, or should I call you Pluto? I am sure the police will cherish your every word."

"Don't be ridiculous," Conklin said, glaring at Oscar as though he'd just found a cockroach in his soup. "You must be that English fellow who's being paid to talk nonsense here, there, and everywhere."

"Yes, and if I talked sense, I shouldn't get paid nearly as much."

"Bah," said Conklin by way of a clever riposte. "As I said, this is outrageous. I'll have you know I am president of the Second National Bank of St. Paul, and I do not need to answer to the likes of you."

Oscar smiled and said, "The Second National Bank, you say? Oh dear, what happened to the First? Did it fail? Financial irregularities, perhaps?"

"Why, I will not be slandered! My attorneys—"

"Oh, the both of you shut up," Jackson said, a sentiment I heartily endorsed. "Now, come with me, Mr. Conklin, I want to show you something."

Jackson led the way to Jones's body. "Recognize this fellow?" he asked.

Conklin appeared to be taken aback but quickly regained his composure. "He is a bellboy, I assume. What happened to him?"

"He was strangled," Jackson said, "and like I said it seems to have happened in your room. Now, why don't you start telling us the truth?"

So began a long back and forth between the detective and the banker. The gist of it was this: Conklin said he'd attended a bankers' meeting earlier in the day, then checked into the hotel at around four because he had another meeting scheduled in the morning and thought it would be inconvenient to go home to St. Paul only to return to Minneapolis early the next day. Jones, he believed, had been the bellboy who took him up to his suite but that was his only contact with him. Conklin said he'd dined at the hotel, then gone back to his room for a time before heading off to the bar. As for the murder, he knew nothing of it.

"What about the champagne in your suite?" Jackson asked. "Did you order it?"

"No. I have no idea how it got there."

Oscar, who'd been watching Conklin closely, said, "In my experience champagne is what men give to women when they do not wish them to be ladies. You're a married man, are you not?"

"Yes, but I do not see—" Conklin suddenly braked to a stop, like an engineer seeing trouble ahead on the tracks, and went silent for several seconds. Then he reached into his vest pocket and took out a gold wedding band. "It's gotten a bit tight so I sometimes have to take it off," he explained. "But I was wearing it earlier this evening."

"Oh, I very much doubt that," Oscar said. "No, you entertained a woman of the evening here. Thus the champagne, and that hat over there. You'd need a head shrinker to make it fit you. Also, feathers aren't your best look."

"This is all perfectly absurd," Conklin replied. "I do not cavort with scarlet women. What kind of man do you think I am?"

"A banker on holiday. Besides, if men were faithful to their wives, or wives to the husbands, of what possible interest would marriage be?"

There was something mesmerizing about Oscar—the musical baritone, the flowing wit, the boyish exuberance—and even Jackson had temporarily fallen under his spell. But he finally freed himself and said, "I'll do the questioning here, Mr. Wilde. You can do us all a favor by butting out."

"I prefer to stay right where I am. Surely you can see that our banker friend is keeping a secret in his vault. I fear Mr. Conklin has been a very bad boy this evening."

Oscar of course had no intention of "butting out," so I did my best to shush him, which was like trying to throw a blanket over an erupting volcano. Jackson, who preferred deeds to words, now undertook a direct solution. He grabbed Oscar by the lapels and escorted him none too gently out into the hall. "Stay there if you know what's good of you," he said, and slammed the door.

As it turned out, Oscar didn't miss much during his exile. Conklin stuck to his story, no matter how hard Jackson tried to shake it. The hat, he contended, was as much a mystery to him as the other clues found in his suite, and he repeatedly denied being with a prostitute. Jackson finally backed off, but not before cautioning Conklin to remain in the hotel until further notice.

Hutchinson, who'd been busy whining that the murder threatened to blemish the hotel's "spotless reputation"—a risible notion if there ever was one—also underwent questioning. But he couldn't provide any useful information as to where Jones had been during his evening shift. At that point I stepped in to describe my encounter with Jones by the employee entrance and my belief that he'd sneaked Louise Merriman into the hotel to service a guest.

This naturally piqued Jackson's curiosity, and he spent the better part of fifteen minutes questioning me in painstaking detail, as though I was a sentence in need of careful parsing. But I couldn't tell him what he most wanted to know, which was whose room Merriman had gone to and where she might be at the moment. Jackson had had enough of me by the time the coroner and two heavy lifters arrived to take charge of the body.

While the coroner was making his examination, I slipped out into the hallway to check on Oscar. He was smoking a small cigar, the ashes decorating the carpet around his feet, and when he saw me, he said, "Dobsy, I was listening at the door while that detective grilled you. My God, what a plodder he is! It is a transatlantic voyage for him to go from A to B. Too bad you had to book passage on the same ship. I must say that the police here do not remind me of Scotland Yard."

"They're more like junkyard dogs," I said. "But don't be fooled. Walt Jackson may not be a genius, but he's a pit bull, and if he gets you in his jaws you won't be happy."

"Then I shall endeavor not to be masticated. Still, I think you will agree we have before us a murder case with some interesting features. The problem is the police, who are always around when you don't need them. I therefore have a proposition for you, Dobsy. What say we look into this business while the police bumble about? I confess to an ulterior motive, which of course is the only kind worth having. You see, I should like to find out if solving a murder is as satisfying as committing one must be."

"Well, I'm encouraged that you're at least not admitting to murder," I said.

"Not yet, but one never knows. Indeed, I have often thought how bracing it would be to eliminate a few of those execrable literary critics who write for the English newspapers. Murderers, I suspect, are much like them, only kinder. But let us return to the subject at hand. What harm would there be in conducting our own investigation into Mr. Jones's demise?"

"The coppers won't like it," I said, "but then they don't much like me much as it is. I'm your man, Oscar. Let's see what we can find out."

*

Before we could get underway, Vale came rushing down the hall. "My God," he said, struggling to catch his breath, "somebody in the bar said there was a 'death' in your room. I am relieved—"

"To find me alive?" said Oscar. "Well, I am pleased you prefer a living Oscar to a dead one, as do I. Besides, my demise would fatally compromise our itinerary, and we can't have that happen, can we?"

"What's going on then? Did somebody really die?"

Oscar explained the situation to Vale, who did not take the news well, his swarthy face turning ashen. He looked, I thought, like a man who'd just swallowed a snake and was trying to digest it. "Oh, this is terrible, as terrible as can be. We cannot afford to have any scandal associated with your name."

"No scandal?" said Oscar, as though he'd been refused butter on his toast. "Don't be ridiculous. My dear Mr. Vale, scandal is a wonderful thing! It is the shortest route to fame, and I highly recommend it to any man who wishes to be in the public eye, as I most assuredly do. I can already see the headline: 'Mr. Oscar Wilde, Traveling Aesthete, Finds Dead Man in His Hotel Room. Police Investigating.' I guarantee you that once the story gets out, I will double my crowds, for most people are far more interested in a good murder than whatever advice I may offer on choosing the correct wallpaper."

Oscar soon managed to calm Vale and advised him to head back downstairs to the bar.

"I didn't know you were a wallpaper expert," I said to Oscar.

"I'm not but keep that between us. You see, I am selling 'good taste,' Dobsy, and that is what everyone wishes to claim for themselves, as opposed to no taste at all, which is what most people actually have."

"Is that so? Then I guess I won't let you into my apartment. Even I know the wallpaper is hideous."

*

We were discussing how to proceed with our rump investigation when a tall, thin man in a brown tweed coat came down the hallway in our direction. He was smoking a meerschaum pipe with a fancy carved bowl but tamped it out as he drew closer. He looked to be in his fifties, and he had one of those long, pinched faces that seemed almost too narrow to accommodate his features. His pointy nose had a slight uplift, as though he could breathe only rarefied air.

"Why, Mr. Wilde, fancy meeting you here," the man said, ignoring me. "Too bad you had such a small crowd at your lecture, or so I've heard. Ah, but where are my manners? I am Chauncey Montague, professor of rhetoric at the university here. Several of my students attended your lecture. Alas, I had other business and was unable to join them. I am sure I would have enjoyed it, despite your, shall we say, unorthodox ideas."

With his supercilious manner, Montague was instantly irritating, and I figured he'd be red meat for Oscar. I wasn't disappointed.

"The orthodox," Oscar replied smoothly, "is for teetotalers. I prefer stronger stuff. But I am pleased to hear your students were at my lecture. The opportunity to learn something is a rare treat for students condemned to university life, don't you agree?"

"I will have to inquire what they learned," Montague said, his voice tightening, "although I doubt it was of great value. Vague theories of the beautiful, after all, are hardly a substitute for genuine knowledge."

"Nor, Mr. Montague, is knowledge a substitute for the bright, sudden rush of beauty as it seizes a man's heart."

The talk was getting pretty thick for my blood, and I was relieved when Jackson came out of Oscar's suite and said to Montague in his usual charming way, "And who might you be?"

Once Jackson learned that Montague occupied an adjoining suite, he ushered him inside for an interview, which I guessed would be oddly entertaining for both of them.

"Mr. Montague is an old dry book, isn't he?" Oscar said. "That's what happens to a man who possesses learning but no inspiration. Still, I have a strong suspicion he isn't quite as orthodox as he pretends to be."

"What do you mean?"

"Did you notice the carving on his pipe bowl?"

"Can't say that I did."

"You must be more observant, Dobsy. The carving depicted the head of a very young man, perhaps even a boy. I've never seen a pipe like it before. Pirates, Indian chiefs, soldiers, sea captains, even good old Zeus are the usual figures one sees on meerschaums, and they're almost always fully bewhiskered. But instead of these standbys, Mr. Montague has a smooth-faced, Apollonian lad carved on his pipe."

"Well, I guess we'd better notify Jackson at once. Obviously, the man is a dangerous criminal."

"Oh, don't be silly. What I'm telling you is that both the pipe and Mr. Montague's demeanor are quite revealing."

"How so?"

"Dare I explain to you, Dobsy, that there are many different kinds of love and that society, in its infinite wisdom, frowns on certain of them?"

"So you're saying Mr. Montague likes men better than women, is that it?"

"Ah, so you are no mere innocent, I see."

"You can't work as a house detective and be an innocent. Pretty much everything you can think of, and maybe some things you can't, goes on in these rooms."

"Yes, I suppose it does. And what of you, Dobsy? What do you do for love?"

"I have a lady friend. I'll leave it at that."

"Were you ever married?"

"No, never had time for it. Besides, I don't like to be tied down."

"Yes, marriage can be a trap, can't it. The problem is that men really want only one thing from women, whereas women want many things from men. It does not generally make for happiness all around."

"Not much does," I said. "Well, if we're going to be investigators, we'd better get to it."

"I couldn't agree more," Oscar said. "Now, let me review what we know. Mr. Jones was murdered sometime between eight o'clock, when I left for my lecture, and ten thirty when I returned and found his body. It is also apparent that the murder was committed in the delightful Mr. Conklin's suite. Mr. Jones's body was then dragged into my suite through the communicating doors, for reasons unknown. Furthermore, we know from the champagne bottle and ice bucket in Mr. Conklin's suite that he, or perhaps someone else, had entertained a visitor. The feathered hat indicates that this visitor was a woman. In addition, we know from your testimony and that of your friend Mrs. Westerly that a lady of the evening named Louise Merriman had been admitted to the hotel, presumably by Jones, sometime after eight. These facts, I think you will agree, pose several interesting questions."

Oscar paused to light a new cigar, then said, "I am also quite fascinated by that pinprick on Mr. Jones's finger. It's very odd, don't you think? I have a sense that if we can discover how he got it, we shall find his murderer."

"You could be right, but it's also possible Jimmy pricked his finger by accident and it doesn't have anything to do with his murder. In any case, we need to concentrate now on identifying the woman Mr. Conklin entertained in his suite, since it's obvious he's lying when he claims he did no such thing. I'd put my money on Miss Merriman as the woman he was cavorting with. She's not a streetwalker or a brothel girl. She's expensive and she strictly works the hotels. A rich old bird like Conklin would be her typical customer."

"I agree, but how do we prove that?"

"Well, Conklin won't admit anything to us if he's not admitting anything to the police. We need to find Merriman. If she was with him in his suite tonight, she's the key to everything."

"Any idea where she might be now?"

"Maybe," I said, "but it might not be easy to get her to talk. Are you willing to go out on a little expedition this evening? There could be some danger."

"Why, Dobsy, a little danger is always stimulating. By the way, do you carry a pistol?"

"Not always, but where we're going tonight is the kind of place where it never hurts to be armed."

"Excellent. Do you know that I'm a very good marksman with pistol and shotgun? I've done quite a bit of hunting in my day. Indeed, I have a revolver in one of my bags."

"Best to leave it there," I said. "Gunplay and poetry don't mix."

3.
ENCOUNTER WITH A PRINCE

Good people exasperate one's reason; bad people stir one's imagination.
—OSCAR WILDE

As Oscar and I were laying our plans for the rest of the night, Hutchinson came out into the hall, worry etched into his big pasty face. "The police are being entirely unreasonable," he said. "They are positively in league with those awful newspapermen. I can only imagine how ruinous the publicity will be for the hotel."

"Au contraire," said Oscar. "The masses will flock to this establishment in the days to come to inhale the rich scent of murder most foul. If I were you, sir, I would begin offering tours, for a small consideration, of course, of the scene of the crime."

"What a disgusting idea," Hutchinson said.

"Precisely. Disgust is merely love turned on its head, and who among us does not find it curiously appealing?"

"I'm thinking I don't," I said. "So, Hutch, what are the coppers saying in there?"

"They seem to be debating whether Mr. Conklin or that Negro valet is the guilty party. They're giving the Negro the third degree right now."

"Damn!" said Oscar, abandoning his usual cool detachment for an instant of genuine emotion. "That is not right. I must go in there and give those policemen a good dressing down. Mr. Davenport would not harm a flea."

Oscar moved toward the door to his suite, but I stepped in front of him. "Coppers don't much like being 'dressed down.' Let me handle this. I agree that Mr. Davenport isn't the murderer. The big thing now is to make sure the coppers don't drag him into their lair. They could beat a confession out of the Pope if it came to that. I'll talk to Chief Munger and see what I can do."

I found Jackson and Munger in the suite's back bedroom, peppering the poor valet with questions and doing their best to put guilty words in his mouth. I pulled Munger aside and tried to talk some sense into him.

"Look," I said, "you and I both know Mr. Davenport had no possible motive for murdering Jimmy Jones. But if you and your boys decide to pound a confession out of him, here's what will happen: Oscar will open his brilliant mouth and condemn you and the entire police department to high heaven, and every newspaper from New York to San Francisco will carry the story in big bold headlines. Do you really want that? It would be smarter to leave Mr. Davenport alone for the time being, and no rough stuff. Besides, he's not going anywhere tonight. If you do find real evidence against him, you can always arrest him later."

Like every police chief in those days, Munger was no more than a politician with a badge, and I knew he hated bad press. After a while, I got him to agree to my approach because, as I told him, "What have you got to lose?" Then I went back out to tell Oscar that his valet was safe for the moment.

"Dobsy, you are a fine fellow," he said. "Now, are we ready to go about our business?"

"What business is that?" Hutchinson asked.

"We're just going to nose around a bit," I said. "Don't worry. We'll do everything we can to put the hotel in a good light."

"Yes, you do that. In the meantime, I'll keep an eye on the police and those damn newsmen. I simply couldn't bear to see the good name of the Nicollet House sullied in any way."

*

It was approaching midnight now and time to go in search of Louise Merriman. "I have an idea how to track her down," I told Oscar. "Go fetch your outer coat and we'll take a little walk."

Oscar went into his suite, where the coppers were still conducting their business, and soon returned wearing a heavy green coat lined with enough dark fur to have cost numerous minks their lives. "I am pleased to report that the police are no longer molesting Mr. Davenport," he said. "He is safe for the time being. All right, Dobsy, what's the plan?"

The best way to locate Merriman, I believed, was to pay a call on her procurer, Dickie Prince. He controlled, often by the cruelest means, a group of prostitutes whom he dispatched to hotels to entertain the likes of Pluto Conklin. Jones, I believed, had been Prince's agent at the Nicollet House, taking requests from guests and then contacting Prince to send over one of his "rentals," as he always called them. I knew Prince by sight—he'd occasionally show up at the hotel to deal with troublesome customers—and he could be plenty rough with any man who refused to pay up in full for services rendered. I immediately tossed him out whenever I found him in the hotel, but I couldn't be everywhere and he had ways of sneaking in to do his dirty business.

I told Oscar about my plans as we walked down to the hotel lobby. "Mr. Prince sounds like a nasty character," he said. "Will he talk to us?"

"We might have to persuade him."

"Am I right in thinking that the sort of persuasion you have in mind will not entail any rhetorical devices?"

"Good guess."

"Where does this ogre reside?"

"Not sure, but there's a joint not far from here where he usually hangs out at this time of night. You might say it's his office. From what I've heard, he receives a request, usually from a hotel guest, contacts one of his girls, and then dispatches her to the client. I understand he does quite a business."

"But surely the police know what he's up to."

"Yeah, they know. But Dickie's got friends in the right places, and he passes around enough money to keep the coppers at bay. He's a sly one."

"Well, I must say, if honesty is indeed the best policy, as the guardians of morality never tire of informing us, you'd think it would be more widely in evidence by now."

"They also claim crime never pays, which makes me wonder why there are so many criminals."

Oscar broke out in a great, snorting laugh and said, "Dobsy, you are a veritable philosopher of the streets. I should take you back with me to England, where you could make a tidy fortune on the lecture circuit as a homespun American original."

"No thanks. England has always sounded gray and depressing to me. But let's get back to the business at hand. Dickie Prince is a dangerous customer, and the people he hangs around with aren't any better. If we do find him, we could be in for a rough time. Are you sure you want to be a part of it?"

"Why, my dear Dobsy, I wouldn't miss it for the world. I have been on tour now for two months, delivering the gospel of good taste to America's great unwashed masses, with results that can best be described as checkered, and it has all become rather wearying. I should definitely like some excitement."

"Well, you may get it. Just stick close to me. I'd hate to lose my job because you got killed."

"What a kindly sentiment! I assure you, I would be even more upset by my demise. Now, where is this 'joint' you speak of?"

"Three blocks from here. It's called Ma Swenson's, and it doesn't attract a choice clientele."

We went through the lobby, which was quiet, and out to Washington Avenue, in those days downtown's busiest street. We crossed Nicollet and headed toward Third Avenue South, where Ma Swenson operated her saloon across from the Chicago, St. Paul & Milwaukee depot. The horsecars that traversed Washington had stopped running at eleven, so there weren't that many people out on the street, and the cool night air felt refreshing.

There were easily two dozen saloons within a few blocks of the Nicollet House, most of them tied to local breweries that either owned them outright or helped finance their operation. Ma Swenson's place was typical—a stand-up joint offering cheap beer, cheaper whiskey, and not much in the way of decor. Like other establishments of its ilk, Ma's place didn't advertise itself by name but rather by the brand of beer it served. A sign above the saloon, which occupied the ground floor of a narrow brick building, announced that "Gluek Beer" was the brew a drinking man would get for his nickel.

By the time we strolled in just after midnight, the place was thinly populated with a handful of sturdy drinkers pursuing oblivion at the oak bar. Their well-lubricated faces were reflected in a long mirror mounted behind a shelf displaying liquor bottles, which appeared to consist of whiskey and not much else. The place offered the standard saloon scent concocted from cigar smoke, tobacco juice, beer, and the rich bodily aromas of men not overly fastidious about bathing. At the far end of the bar was an open door that led to a back room where hoodlums like Prince gambled with cards or dice and busily plotted whatever illegal enterprises their scheming minds could conjure up.

Our arrival was greeted by dumbfounded stares from the patrons, who clearly had never seen a genuine aesthete before, least of all one well over six feet tall sporting shoulder-length hair and a pea-green ulster trimmed with fancy fur. I doubt Queen Victoria in the flesh would have occasioned a more startled reaction. Ma Swenson, a woman of ample dimensions and dyspeptic disposition known to evict unruly drinkers with the aid of a shotgun, had apparently retired for the evening, and a lone bartender I didn't recognize was in charge.

"Good evening, gentlemen," Oscar announced before I could stop him. "Mr. McGuire and I are here on a most important mission. We are looking for Mr. Dickie Prince. Is he somewhere on the premises?"

It was not, as they say, an auspicious beginning. The men at the bar, all rough laborers by the looks of them, responded to Oscar's request with a collective hoot. One of them, a wide-bodied brute who appeared as though he could easily outwrestle a bear, said, "Well, boys, would you listen to this. We got ourselves some sort of a limey. I hate limeys."

I was thinking it might be time to step right back outside and reconsider our situation, but Oscar had other ideas. "Why, my dear fellow, I am no limey," he said without hesitation. "I am as Irish as the green hills of County Mayo. Dublin-born and proud of it. And what of you, sir? Do you claim the Emerald Isle as your place of birth? I am guessing a stout fellow such as yourself must have the good blood of an Irishman, and there is no better blood than that."

Oscar's willingness to engage so readily and on so friendly a basis with the man gave evidence to one of his most endearing qualities. In his pose as the world's most languorous aesthete, singing the praises of high-toned beauty and passing out bright witticisms like chocolate bonbons, he seemed at first glance to be the perfect snob. Yet I found time and again that he possessed what is often called the "common touch." He was never obnoxious or overweening when it came to dealing with everyday people well below his station in life, and he'd treated me as an equal from the moment we met.

I'd quizzed him about this seeming contradiction, and he said, "The thing you must know about me, Dobsy, is that while I hobnob with all manner of the rich and titled, I will never be one of them at heart. The lords and ladies I entertain in England are really quite despicable, once you have the displeasure of getting to know them. Indeed, I think of them not as the upper crust but rather as moldy bread, buttered with wealth to disguise their rotten taste. I much prefer a good honest workman to the lot of them."

And now here was a "good honest workman" who looked as though he was about to commit mayhem on Oscar's person. But he didn't. Instead, the bruiser grinned and said, "I am Paddy O'Shea, and it is County Cork I hail from. And who might you be?"

Although Oscar was probably offended that someone in America had failed to recognize him, he didn't pout about it. "I am Oscar Wilde," he said with an exaggerated stage bow, "and this is Mr. McGuire, chief dick at the Nicollet House."

"House dick," I said. "We're not here to cause you or your friends any trouble."

"Of course we're not," Oscar said with a wave of his hand. "But as I said, we are here on an urgent matter. However, it is not so urgent that we cannot enjoy a libation first." He promptly ordered "two rounds of the nectar of the gods"—whiskey—and when he opined with a sly grin that "I think you fellows will agree that work is the curse of the drinking man," he'd won the place over.

The bartender, a small man with thinning red hair and a nose of similar color, wasn't as accommodating when we asked about Prince. "He ain't here," he claimed, adding, "You fellows can leave anytime."

"We're not leaving, not yet," I said. "There's been a murder at the hotel, and we need to talk to Dickie. We'll just go to the back and have a look for ourselves."

At that instant our quarry appeared at the door to the back room and said to the barman, "What's all this, Fred?" Then he caught sight of me and Oscar and said, "Why, Dobsy, what are you doing here? Looking for a nightly rental? And who's the big lug with you?"

Prince was a wiry man, about forty, with the lean look of a hunting hound, and he wore his usual costume—red velvet jacket, frilled shirt with diamond studs, dark trousers, and well-shined shoes. A gold tooth provided additional decoration. I knew him to be a man without conscience or care, and very treacherous, a derringer always hidden somewhere on his person.

"Well, I do not think I have ever been called a 'lug' before," Oscar responded before identifying himself. "You must be the pimp we're looking for."

"I don't much like that word," Prince said, his dark eyes fixed on Oscar, "and I ain't got time for no English poof, so the two of you can scram."

If you're in a tight situation, the first thing to know is who to keep your eyes on, and mine weren't on Prince. Instead, I was watching the bartender. I saw him reach under the bar, but he wasn't as quick as I was. "Don't do that," I said, slipping a revolver from my coat pocket and leveling it at him. "Just put your hands on the bar and leave them there. You fellows at the bar can do the same."

"Oh my," said Oscar. "Isn't this thrilling?"

The men at the bar took in the scene with interest but showed no sign that they might intervene, especially since Oscar was paying for their drinks. It simply wasn't their fight. As for Prince, I didn't figure he'd try anything, at least for the moment, and I was right.

I said in a voice loud enough for everyone to hear, "Mr. Wilde and I are going to have a little chat with Dickie in his lair. I don't expect trouble from any of you. Just go about your business and everything will be fine."

We escorted Prince into the back room, which offered a pair of well-scuffed round tables with chairs, small paintings of underdressed women adorning the walls, and a hand-printed sign that read, "Don't Spit on the Floor." To my surprise there was also a telephone on one of the tables. Phones were still a novelty at the time—the first one at the Nicollet House had been installed only two years earlier. I assumed Prince had found the device useful enough for his business to justify the cost. A deck of cards, a bottle of rye, and a vase of bright yellow daisies also sat atop the table where Prince had been sitting before we so rudely interrupted his evening.

"Have a seat," I said to Prince as I locked the door behind us. There was a second door, a rear entrance to the saloon, and I locked that too. "You can put that derringer you carry on the floor and kick it away."

Prince did so, smiled, and said, "Whatever you say, Dobsy. But why the roust? You ain't got no jurisdiction over me."

"Murder is our jurisdiction," said Oscar, not the first time I'd heard him say something that didn't make much sense.

Prince said to Oscar, "You don't look like no copper I ever met. What the hell are you doing here?"

"A deep philosophical question if there ever was one," Oscar replied. "I often wonder why any of us are here. But I must say, your flowers are lovely. Are you a fancier of daisies, Mr. Prince?"

"He isn't," I said. "He has his girls pin one on so customers can be sure who they are."

"What a terrible misuse of the beautiful," Oscar said.

"Does he always talk strange like this?" Prince asked me, studying Oscar as he might someone newly arrived from Timbuktu.

"Pretty much," I said. "You get used to it after a while."

"So what do the two of you want? I got no beef with you, Dobsy, but here you are pointing a gun at me. And what's this talk about murder?"

I told Prince what had happened at the hotel and asked if he had an alibi for that time. I'm pretty good at reading faces, but Prince didn't give away much.

"Well, that's too bad about Jimmy, but I don't know nothing about it," Prince said. "I've been here since, oh, six or so. Fred out at the bar will vouch for me."

I had no doubt Fred would, and I didn't see any point in trying to break Prince's alibi. The coppers would do that if the time came. I said, "I think you do know what happened, Dickie. Louise Merriman was seen at the hotel tonight. We know for sure"—this was a lie, since we weren't really certain—"that she was servicing a customer named Pluto Conklin. You worked with Jimmy to set it all up. But there was a problem, wasn't there? Jimmy wanted a bigger cut of the action, so you went to the hotel to straighten him out. There was a fight in Conklin's suite, and the next thing you know Jimmy is dead."

"Dobsy speaks God's truth," Oscar said, although he knew I was engaged in pure, unvarnished speculation. "It will not go well for you, Dickie boy, if you try to cover up your crime."

I couldn't help but laugh. *"Dickie boy?"* Oscar clearly was enjoying himself.

"Jesus," Prince blurted out. "Where did you find this mutt?"

"He found me," I said. "But he's right. Your best hope is to be truthful with us."

Prince, who was hardly a fool, called my bluff. "Sounds like you're just guessing, Dobsy. Nothing like what you say happened."

So I bluffed in return. "I'm not guessing. Mr. Conklin saw you and Jimmy together and so did Merry. We'll be talking to her next. You could save us some trouble by telling us where she is. Who knows, maybe she'll put you in the clear. Otherwise, I don't like your chances, Dickie. The coppers will be here soon enough. I'm betting they think you strangled Jimmy, and they won't be as polite as we are."

"The coppers don't scare me, and neither do you," Prince said, but I caught a glimmer of fear in his eyes. Obviously, he knew something about Merriman and her possible connection to Jones's murder. He also realized big trouble was heading his way, and that made him doubly dangerous, as we momentarily discovered.

"Go to hell," he said with an angry snarl, suddenly lifting the flimsy table and using it like a ram to push Oscar and me off our chairs. As we tumbled to the floor, my revolver fell from my hand and skidded away. Meanwhile, Prince made a beeline toward the back door. I scrambled back to my feet and grabbed him around the collar before he managed to unlock the door. A sort of dance followed, the two of us spinning around like a regular ballroom couple. Then came a nasty surprise. Prince managed to reach into his coat pocket, and I saw the lethal glint of a knife in his hand.

That's when Oscar very possibly saved my life. He picked up the heavy ceramic vase that had fallen from the table and wielded it as a weapon. My back was turned to him, but I saw his arms reach over me as he smashed the vase with full force on Prince's head, knocking him insensible.

"Are you all right, Dobsy?" Oscar asked as I started to regain my breath.

I picked up the knife—its well-honed blade sharp enough to have delivered me to the next world—and said, "I'm okay, but that was a close call. Oscar, I will forever be in your debt. He could have killed me."

"Well, I couldn't let that happen, could I? But I do regret to say that the daisies are probably dead. I trust that the same cannot be said of Dickie boy."

I bent down to look at Prince, who lay sprawled amid the daisies. Blood poured from his head, but I'd seen worse, and he was breathing well enough.

"He'll survive," I said, "but I guess we won't be getting any information from him tonight."

We heard pounding at the door leading into the barroom. "What's going on in there?" a voice asked. I assumed it was the bartender.

I retrieved my revolver, dusted off my coat, and said to Oscar, "Time for us to leave."

"So it would seem. But we've had a great adventure, haven't we?"

"I guess you could call it that, but I'd prefer a bit less adventure in my life from now on."

Revolver in hand, I unlocked the door and found the bartender and several patrons gathered in a small circle like bystanders at a street fight. "Call the police and an ambulance," I said. "Mr. Prince jumped us, and we had to subdue him."

"With a vase," Oscar added. "Indeed, you might say he was deflowered."

"You couldn't resist that, could you?" I said. "Now, if everybody will make room, we'll be on our way. The police will know where to find us if need be."

"I'll drink to that," said the big man from County Cork, and with that final toast to send us on our way, we went out into the night.

*

"Dobsy, I do believe you are rapidly becoming my favorite person in the world," Oscar said as we hoofed around the corner on Third and headed back up Washington to the hotel. "What a marvelous time that was! I always find wicked people like Mr. Prince to be quite fascinating. They make one realize how tiresome goodness can be. Incidentally, are you aware that today is the Ides of March? Fortunately, unlike Caesar, you didn't get Brute-d, as it were."

"Well, I almost did, and I'd just as soon not be compared to old Julius. A knife to the gut wouldn't be a pleasant way to die."

"True, but then again, what would be a pleasant way?"

"In your case, I'd say drowning in a vat of rose petals."

"No, I think not. Too much struggling for air. I should prefer to breathe my last in flagrante delicto, but of course we never get to die the way we want, do we? I imagine I shall probably expire in some dreary room, surrounded by enemies gleefully commending me to Satan."

I glanced up at the big lighted clock outside the Chicago, Milwaukee & St. Paul depot, where clumps of passengers were disgorging from a late train. "It's half-past midnight, Oscar. The Ides have passed."

"Then we must begin the next stage of our adventure. The night is yet young, Dobsy."

The night didn't feel all that young to me. Oscar, on the other hand, seemed to possess the energy of a two-year-old chasing bubbles. "So what's next? Finding Louise Merriman perhaps?"

"Yeah, that would be nice, but I really don't know where to look. Dickie was the one person who could have told us how to locate her."

"What about the police? Perhaps they know her whereabouts."

"Maybe, but if they do, they won't be sharing that information with us. Besides, for all we know, Jackson and his boys may already have her in custody. We'll see when we get back to the hotel."

The Nicollet House, like many hotels, once had a separate entrance for unaccompanied women, apparently because it was thought they'd be molested by the rough class of men who sometimes hung around the main doors. But women like Sophia Westerly took umbrage at this arrangement and routinely ignored it. By the time I took over as house detective the "ladies" entrance, located on the Hennepin Avenue side of the hotel, had been closed for want of use. Even so, my master key still worked on the door, and I decided to use the old entrance so as not to be seen by the police.

"Oh, I do so like skullduggery," Oscar said as I opened the door and we stepped into a narrow hallway. "I take it we are sneaking in because you fear the police would interfere with our investigation."

"Something like that. The coppers know their work, but they don't have much imagination. There's something off about Jimmy's murder, and I don't trust the coppers to figure it out."

"I entirely agree. Indeed, I have a certain suspicion when it comes to Mr. Jones."

"And what would that be?"

"I'm not ready to reveal it quite yet."

"You can't libel the dead," I noted.

"Untrue, my dear Dobsy. How could history be written otherwise? In any case, it's possible Miss Merriman could confirm my suspicions, if we can find her. What do you propose to do next?"

"I propose a quick visit to the front office, so long as any coppers aren't in sight. If Hutch is back there by now, he could fill us in on what they've been doing."

The hallway led in one direction to the lobby and in the other to the hotel laundry and a back staircase. It was the same hallway Mrs. Westerly had seen Merriman entering earlier in the evening. Once we reached the lobby, I gave it a good eyeballing and didn't see anyone who looked like a copper, so we went to the front desk.

"Is Hutch in his office?" I asked the night clerk, a freckle-faced young fellow whom I'd always found to be reliable.

"Yeah, I don't think he ever sleeps."

"What about the coppers?"

"They've left, as far as I know. Oh, and I have a message for you," the clerk added, handing me a folded sheet of paper. "A lady left it off around eleven."

I opened the message, which offered intriguing news: "Spoke briefly with L. Merriman after you left. Ran across her in the ladies' room about 9:30. She had a bruised eye & looked very frightened. It is clear something bad happened to her tonight. She may still be hiding in the hotel, as she hinted as much to me before she ran off. Try to find her if you can & let her know I can be of help to her if she will let me." It was signed "S. Westerly."

I showed the message to Oscar, who gave out a low whistle, and said, "It is manna from heaven, Dobsy."

"Maybe. Let's talk to Hutch first."

We found Hutchinson at his big rolltop desk, leaning back in his chair and appearing quite satisfied with himself, whereas he usually had the put-out look common to all hotelkeepers, whose job entails the daily orchestration of chaos.

"Ah, here the two of you are," he said. "There is good news. The police have left, and I am most happy to tell you that you may return to your suite, Mr. Wilde. On behalf of the Nicollet House, may I offer you my sincerest apologies for the most unfortunate events of this evening."

"Why, I require no apology, Mr. Hutchinson. Instead, you have my profoundest gratitude. Dobsy and I are having an absolutely splendid time. I find murder to be most stimulating."

Hutchinson reacted to this Oscarism with a disbelieving stare. "I see," he said, although it was obvious he didn't.

I said, "So how did the coppers leave the situation? Do they still think Oscar's valet must be the culprit? Or is Mr. Conklin their main suspect?"

"They seem undecided," Hutchinson said. "But they told both men not to leave the city until the matter is resolved. Mr. Conklin wasn't happy about that, of course, but I moved him down the hall to suite 103 and did my best to calm him."

"Well, I will simply not allow Mr. Davenport to be held hostage here beyond tomorrow," Oscar protested. "I have a schedule to keep, and I cannot possibly be without my valet."

"I hear there are fellows who somehow manage to survive without one," I noted.

"Yes, and they are men who lack an adequate wardrobe. I do not suffer from that deficiency."

"All right, let's not worry about apparel for the moment," I said, turning to Hutchinson. "My ace detective Oscar here would like to resolve this business tonight, and so would I. Let me show you something."

I handed him Mrs. Westerly's note and as he read it, I said, "If Louise Merriman is somewhere in the hotel, we need to find her. She may well have witnessed Jimmy's murder."

"Yes, yes, I can see that. But without a room key, I don't know—"

I cut in. "I may have an idea about where she is. My guess is that if she really is here, she's hiding out somewhere in the attic."

The "attic," as it was called, was the top floor of the old section of the hotel that had originally been used to house employees such as maids, cooks, and bellboys. Although it had been closed off in the 1870s, employees were known to sneak up to one of the rooms for amorous encounters or other forbidden activities. I'd caught Jones up there a couple of times doing God knows what, and I'd even had to give the heave-ho to the occasional squatter.

Hutchinson said, "But why would she be in the attic? There's no heat up there, and all the old rooms are locked."

"Half the skeleton keys in the city probably fit those locks," I said. "I'll have a look there just in case."

"A capital idea," Oscar said. "But first I'd like to check on Mr. Davenport. I do hope the police weren't too hard on him. He really is a fine fellow, you know."

"Okay, you do that while I go up to the attic."

"Why, Dobsy, you will do no such thing. Come along with me to my suite. It will take but a few minutes. Besides, I think we should have a look for ourselves at the scene of the crime now that Mr. Conklin has vacated it. Perhaps we'll find something the police missed."

"All right, but let's be quick about it. I don't want to miss out on a chance to find Merry. She's the key to this business."

*

Davenport was elated to see us when we returned to Oscar's suite, and he quickly explained how he had thwarted the police as they tried to make him "the villain," as he put it.

"I stood my ground, that's what I did," he said. " 'Why would I kill a bellboy?' I asked them over and over, and they had no answer. No sir, they had no answer. But I do believe, I surely do, that they would have whaled on me something fierce if you hadn't vouched for me like you did."

"Think nothing of it," Oscar said. "What else did the police do before they left?"

"Well, they spent a lot of time with that banker fellow in the adjoining suite. I heard some yelling, but I couldn't tell you what was said. From the way that big policeman acted when he came back in here, I think he's pretty convinced the banker did it."

"And he could be right," I said.

Davenport said, "Oh, I forgot to mention that the police talked to Mr. Vale, too, on account of he was hanging around."

"Is that so?" Oscar said. "What was he doing here? I thought he was down in the bar romancing a bottle of whiskey, as is his usual wont."

"Well, he came back. I guess he just wanted to find out what the police were up to, but he was acting all nervous and jumpy, like something was itching at him, if you know what I mean."

Vale was largely unknown to me, so I asked Oscar about him.

"Mr. Vale was assigned to me by D'Oyly Carte as my tour manager," Oscar said, "much like a keeper might be put in charge of a prized specimen at the Regent Park's Zoo. His job is to keep me on schedule and make travel arrangements. He also collects the proceeds, however meager, from my lectures, and rewards me with a pitiful allowance. Most important, he is supposed to prevent me from doing anything scandalous. Indeed, I fear he would make a gelding out of me if he could. I find him to be a rather unlikable. Then again, someone must be in charge of me, Dobsy, or this whole ridiculous tour would fly off the rails. Mr. Vale's job, I will admit, is not easy, and it is hardly surprising that he consoles himself nightly in the hotel bar. I would do the same in his situation, only with a better quality of liquor."

Hardly had Oscar finished his little disquisition when there was knock at the door. I opened it and there stood Vale himself, with bloodshot eyes and the desperate look of a man who'd just lost a prized puppy. But when he saw Oscar, he instantly brightened.

"My dear Oscar," he said, rushing past me as if I was a station where the express train never stopped. "I am so relieved to see you. What a horrible business this is! Absolutely horrible! But we will go on, as we must. I have already talked with the newspapermen who were here, and they assure me your good name will not be sullied."

"I am distressed to learn, Mr. Vale, that you are under the mistaken impression that I have a good name. There is nothing that will drag a man down faster than having an impeccable reputation, for of what value is goodness in a world that so rarely rewards it?"

"A question for the ages," I said, "but not exactly relevant at the moment. Come on, let's get moving. We have things to do."

"Ah, yes, the hunt for a lady of the evening. But let us have another look at the scene of the crime first. Those policemen did not impress me with their acumen. I should not be surprised if they overlooked some obvious clue in Mr. Conklin's suite."

"It's possible," I said, "but I wouldn't count on it. The coppers aren't as dumb as you think they are."

"How fortunate for them," Oscar said. "Well, let us see if you're right about the local constabulary. Now then, Mr. Davenport, you may retire to your room as I shall not require your services before morning. As for you, Mr. Vale, you are on your own, but I suggest you get some rest as well. We will be leaving for St. Paul tomorrow. Who knows, it could be an exhausting journey."

"It's a half-hour trip to St. Paul," I pointed out. "I doubt it will be taxing."

"Excellent," said Oscar, who seemed to be growing more bright-eyed and alert by the moment, even as I longed for a nice bout of shuteye. "Then we won't need any sleep tonight, will we? Lead the way, Dobsy. I am sure more adventure awaits us."

4.
MERRY TELLS HER TALE

Everything in the world is about sex, except sex. Sex is about power.
—OSCAR WILDE

THE SUITE OCCUPIED EARLIER by Pluto Conklin, and where Jones had presumably been murdered, gave ample evidence of a police search. The parlor was in especially bad shape. Like unruly children, the coppers had made a mess without bothering to clean up after themselves. They'd pulled out drawers, removed couch and chair cushions, lifted portions of the carpeting, and even taken down a window curtain for some reason. But as far as I could tell, the only item they'd removed was the woman's porkpie hat. The bedroom was in better condition, although the coppers had ransacked the wardrobe in search of who knew what.

"It looks as though the Huns have invaded," Oscar said. "Are the police always so untidy?"

"They are," I said. "I doubt we'll find any clues in this mess."

"We'll see about that. Most people are blind to the world, whereas as I am quite good at noticing even the smallest of things. My eyesight, if I must say so myself, is exceptionally keen."

"Then go to it," I said as Oscar started looking around.

Before long he got down on his hands and knees and began a close inspection of the carpet. It made for an amusing picture—the great celebrity crawling around like a child in search of a lost penny. But as it turned out, Oscar wasn't lying about his eyesight. He was in front of the sofa, doing his best to peek under it, when he reached for something on the carpet.

"Aha, look what we have here," he said as he got back to his feet.

I had to look closely to see that he was holding three black threads.

"Okay, you've found some threads. What about them should interest me?"

"I know my fabrics," Oscar said. "These threads—yarn actually—look to be wool worsted. They could be from a man's suit."

"All right, but so what? Lots of guys wear wool suits. The threads could have been here for days or weeks, for all we know."

"Perhaps, but threads like these don't just fall off suits. Worsted is a smooth, tight weave. You'd have trouble pulling out a thread if you tried. But in a struggle, one man grabbing at another, these threads could somehow have been scratched loose. Trouble is, I don't recall seeing anyone tonight who was wearing a black suit."

"Really? Didn't Conklin have on a dark suit?"

"Yes, but it wasn't the midnight black color of these threads."

To my amazement, Oscar now proceeded to describe in minute detail the apparel of every man we'd met at the hotel during the course of the evening. Once he'd finished his sartorial review, he said, "I have always had what is called a photographic memory, my dear Dobsy. It is a curse, actually, because much of what I see in this world I would greatly prefer to forget."

"Wouldn't we all," I said.

Oscar's expression suddenly changed, and he looked upward, as though he'd experienced a vision from the heavens. "Good Lord, I just had a little flash in my mind. Perhaps I did see a suitcoat from which these threads could have come."

"Really? Well, don't be shy. Spill the beans."

"Not yet. I have to be sure. Unfortunately, I wasn't paying as much attention as I should have been. Let me think upon it for a bit. In the meantime, we can move on, Dobsy. The infamous attic awaits us."

*

The attic was a peculiar place. It had been built to house unmarried employees in rooms that had all the charm of prison cells. To guard against any nefarious mingling, the rooms had originally been divided into separate sections for men and women, with a solid wall between them. Each side also came with its own staircase and bathroom. The rooms were tiny, ill-heated, and so low-ceilinged that a man over six feet, such as Oscar, was in constant danger of hitting his head.

When a new fire chief who wasn't inclined to take bribes finally had the audacity to inspect the attic in 1875, he found it to be what it had always been—a perfect firetrap and no fit place for anyone to live. Much to the dismay of the hotel's owners, the chief said the two sides of the attic had to be connected with a door so as to provide a second way out in the event of fire. The door was duly installed, but so much hanky-panky ensued that the good Methodists who owned the hotel soon decided to close off the attic for good rather than tolerate an arrangement that encouraged immoral behavior.

Since then, the doors to the attic were supposed to be kept locked at all times, but on my regular rounds I'd often found one or both open. I'd also found evidence that some of the old beds in the rooms were being used, presumably by employees, for purposes other than sleeping. To discourage such activity, I'd suggested more than once to Hutchinson that all the beds be removed, but he'd never gotten around to doing it.

It was close to 2 a.m. by the time we left Oscar's suite and headed downstairs so that I could fetch a pair of lanterns, since the attic had no working lights. The broad corridor outside the suite was empty for a change—coppers, the coroner, newspapermen, miscellaneous guests, and Oscar's female admirers all gone—and the silence felt strange. Somehow, with Oscar, I always expected a crowd.

The sleepy clerk at the front desk who provided us with lanterns said Hutchinson had gone to bed, and I envied him. Oscar was wearing me out, and I was pretty sure now that I'd go the rest of the night without any rest. The lobby was blessedly empty except for an old gent snoozing in an overstuffed chair, and our footsteps echoed on the tile floor as we walked across to the hallway where we'd reentered the hotel after our vase-crashing interview with Dickie Prince.

"There's a back staircase at the end of the hallway that will take us to what used to be the women's side of the attic," I said. "Be prepared for a long climb. The attic is five stories up." As we walked down the hall, I told Oscar a bit about the attic's infamous reputation. Naturally, he was delighted to hear of it.

"They say cream rises to the top," he said, "and it is encouraging to know that the same may be true of sin. I had no idea this hotel was such a hothouse of carnal activity."

"Well, you'll find out soon enough that the attic is no hothouse at this time of year. Also, when you get up there, watch your head. The ceilings are very low."

The wooden staircase was narrow, winding, steep, poorly lit, and little used, least of all in the wee hours of the morning. No sooner had we reached it than we heard the clattering of footsteps far above.

"It would appear we are not alone," Oscar said. "Perhaps a guest is taking a shortcut."

"I doubt it. Employees are normally the only one who use these stairs, but not at two in the morning."

The footsteps almost immediately went silent, followed by a faint squeaking sound, and then silence.

"I know that squeak," I said. "That was the attic door. Come on, let's move."

I raced up the steps, Oscar not far behind. After climbing seventy steps (I'd counted them many times), we reached a small landing, where a door led into the attic.

"We made it," Oscar said, bending over to catch his breath. "Now what?"

"We find out who's inside," I said as I lit the small lantern that had been attached to my belt. "Something definitely is not right."

As though eager to confirm the wisdom of my remark, a woman somewhere in the darkness beyond the door let out a scream.

*

"Who's inside there?" I shouted as I yanked at the door, only to find it locked. Oscar by now had lit his lantern, and he shined it toward the lock while I fumbled for my passkey. There was another scream, followed by the sound of racing footsteps. I was still trying to find my key when Oscar stepped back and put a shoulder to the door, all but knocking it off its hinges.

"That does it," he said triumphantly, gazing for a moment on his well-splintered handiwork before rushing through the opening. All I could do was follow. Past the door was a claustrophobic hallway perhaps forty feet long and barely wide enough for two people to pass. The hallway gave access to the old employee rooms—there were a dozen or so—along with a bathroom.

Oscar had barely made it into the hallway before he dented a ceiling beam with his forehead. He gave out a pained yelp accompanied by several colorful expletives. "Christ," he said, dropping to his knees. "Who used to live up here, Tom Thumb?"

I looked past Oscar, who was busy rubbing his battered forehead, and saw a thin slice of light coming from one of the rooms along the hall. Of even more interest was a shadowy figure—almost surely a man—who was hurrying toward the far end of the hall, where it made a sharp turn before connecting to the other side of the attic. The man held a lantern, which looked like a small lighthouse in the gloom, but both he and his light quickly vanished around the corner.

"Stop!" I shouted at the figure, a futile command if there ever was one.

"See if there's anybody in that room with the light on," I said to Oscar as I squeezed past him. "I'm going after that man I saw."

"Will do," Oscar said, "assuming my head doesn't explode in the next few seconds."

I ran down the hall and turned the corner. Just past it was the door that had been installed at the insistence of the fire chief. The door was closed but unlocked. I pulled it open and entered another cramped hallway lined with rooms in what had once been the all-male section of the attic, reached by its own staircase. The hall was empty, and for a moment I wondered if the man I was after had hidden himself in one of the rooms. But as I came farther down the hall I saw that the door to the staircase was swinging shut, signaling that the man had taken to the stairs.

When I reached the staircase, I heard the man's footsteps below, and I guessed he was heading for the ground floor, perhaps to escape the hotel via the employee entrance. But it was also possible he intended to hide somewhere in the hotel, since the stairs connected through fire doors on every floor to the main corridors serving guest rooms. I hightailed it down to the fourth floor and then to the third, where I stopped to listen for footsteps. Silence prevailed, leading me to believe the man might have exited the staircase on the second floor. What I found next confirmed my suspicion. The fire door on the second floor was slightly ajar, as though it had just been opened but hadn't fully closed. Wary now of an ambush, I carefully pushed open the door.

I fully expected to spot my man in the corridor, running away, but I saw no one, and all I could hear was the soft hiss of gas from the sconces along the walls. The corridor here, on the opposite side of the hotel from Oscar's suite, was very long, and its only other exit—to the hotel's main staircase and elevator—was a good sixty feet away. Had my quarry gone into one of the guest rooms that lined the corridor? It seemed the only explanation, but now what? I couldn't very well go knocking on dozens of doors at two in the morning without causing a great many guests to be exceedingly unhappy. And if I did so, how would I even know whether I'd found the right man, since I hadn't seen his face?

As I went down the corridor, I realized that I was coming up on 103, the suite to which Pluto Conklin had been moved after Jones's murder. Could he have been the man I was chasing? The only way to find out was to knock at his door, despite the lateness of the hour. I gave the door a few good raps but received no reply. Either Conklin was a very deep sleeper or he was ignoring me, assuming he was indeed in the suite. I debated whether to open the door with my passkey, but entering an occupied room in that way was strictly forbidden absent some evidence of a dire emergency, and I'd be in serious trouble if Conklin raised a stink about it. I finally decided it would be best to leave Conklin to himself for the time being.

After a quick tour down the length of the corridor to check the main stairs and elevator, neither of which gave any sign of activity, I abandoned the chase and returned to the attic. There, in the room where I'd seen the sliver of light, its door now wide open, I discovered that Oscar had made quite a find.

*

"Ah, Dobsy, I was hoping you'd be back soon," Oscar said, an arm wrapped around the shivering shoulders of Louise Merriman as they huddled together on the bare mattress of a broken-down bed.

A flickering kerosene lamp, its reservoir almost empty, sat on a small table next to Oscar's lantern. "This is Miss Louise Merriman, and she has a most remarkable story to tell."

"I'd love to hear it," I said. "But let's find a warmer place first."

"Amen to that," Oscar said. "By the way, you will be pleased to know that we may have saved Miss Merriman from a terrible fate by arriving on the scene when we did. Apparently that man you saw in the hallway was about to molest her, or worse. I take it you didn't find him."

"No. He disappeared on the second floor, maybe into one of the guest rooms." I then told Oscar about my suspicions regarding Conklin, but he wasn't impressed by my reasoning.

"I have trouble imagining that the portly banker could outrun a fit man such as yourself, unless the wings of Mercury were attached to his shoes."

"I didn't see enough of him to spot any wings," I said, "but I'll keep that in mind."

Oscar said, "Well, wings or no, couldn't the man you pursued be another guest at the hotel or perhaps even an employee with a passkey that allowed him to slip into one of the rooms?"

"It's possible," I acknowledged, "but we're just guessing now." I said to Merriman, "Did you get any kind of look at the fellow?"

She shook her head. "I was in here when I heard someone coming down the hall," she said, her voice barely a whisper. "I didn't know who it was, and I was very frightened. I tried to close the door, but it wouldn't shut all the way. Someone started pushing at the door, and then all of a sudden there was a big commotion out in the hall. The next thing I know, there's Mr. Wilde at the door. I couldn't believe it, a famous man like him come to rescue me."

"Oscar is full of surprises," I said.

"How did you know I'd be here?" she asked.

"You have Mrs. Westerly to thank for that," I said. "She left a message saying she'd talked with you and that you might be hiding in the hotel. Why didn't you let her help you? I'm sure she would have taken you home with her."

"No, no, I didn't want a fine lady like her to become involved in my awful business."

"Well, we're involved now," I said. "A man has been murdered, and you will need to tell us everything you know about it."

Most of the night women who plied their trade at the hotel were hard cases, deadened by years of physical abuse and heavy drug use, be it alcohol, laudanum, or opium. Merriman, I believed, hadn't arrived at that dreary end station yet, and I'd more than once tried to set her on a better path even as I was booting her from the hotel. Now, she seemed more like a lost child than anything else. She wasn't much more than twenty-five, with a lush head of blonde hair, delicate features, and blue eyes of the sort that inspire poetic rapture. But there was no poetry in the black circle around her left eye or the dark bruise on her neck.

"It looks like you've had a tough night of it," I said to her. The room was ice cold, and her thin gray coat would have done little to keep her warm. "All right, let's get going before we all freeze to death up here."

"My suite is available," Oscar said.

"Oh, I don't think I should go back there," Merriman said. "If the police—"

"Go back?" I said. "So you were in his suite earlier, I take it."

"She was," Oscar said, "while I was out preaching to the dubious. I have yet to hear her full story, but I have learned that she was not wearing a brooch of any kind tonight, nor did she have a hatpin in her possession. That means we shall have to look elsewhere for the source of the pinprick on Mr. Jones's finger. And as for the police, Miss Merriman, have no fear. They are gone, retired to their bone-filled lairs to dine on criminals, and they won't cause you any trouble if we can help it. Isn't that right, Dobsy?"

"There are no guarantees when it come to the coppers," I said. "But Oscar is right. We're here to help you if we can and to find out what happened tonight."

*

We wound our way back down to the second floor and slipped unseen into the warmth of Oscar's suite. Davenport was presumably fast asleep in the back bedroom, so we had the parlor to ourselves.

"I'll make some tea," Oscar said. "I have my own Earl Grey. It's quite decent."

Merriman still looked very cold, so I retrieved a blanket from Oscar's bedroom and wrapped her in it while he fussed with the tea.

"You are very kind," she said. "I do not see much of that."

"No, I imagine you don't. Let's get some hot tea in us and we'll all feel much better."

Once Oscar had the tea ready—I soon learned that he traveled with his own exquisite china, lesser varieties apparently being unsuitable for his refined palate—we sipped from our delicate cups as Merriman told a harrowing story.

As I suspected, she'd been sent to the hotel by Dickie Prince around eight thirty to entertain Pluto Conklin in his suite. Jimmy Jones had admitted her via the employee entrance, and I'd just missed her, catching a whiff of her perfume as I went to the kitchen for a sandwich. Jones, of course, had lied to me when I found him lolling about the entrance, but there hadn't been much then that I could do about it.

Once Merriman arrived at Conklin's suite, the usual activities occurred, and all went smoothly until the time came for Merriman to leave. That's when she sprang a surprise on her customer.

"Dickie has this little trick of his to get more money," she told us. "Me and the other girls, we have to demand an extra five dollars before we leave. We're to say that if the customer doesn't pay, we'll tell his wife what happened."

"A little blackmail, in other words," I said.

"I'm curious," said Oscar. "How much do you usually charge for your, let us say, encounters?"

"Ten dollars, but I only get two and Jimmy gets one. The rest goes to Dickie. But he pays my rent and buys me clothes."

It sounded like cruel exploitation, and it was, although few if any legitimate jobs available to a single woman would have paid Merriman anywhere near as much. It was the devil's bargain, as so many things are.

"I gather Mr. Conklin wasn't interested in shelling out another five bucks," I said.

"No, and he got real mad and said he wouldn't pay me one penny more."

Oscar said, "Sounds like a banker, doesn't it? After all, there is nothing like having money to make a man cheap."

"What happened next?" I asked.

Merriman pointed to her black eye and said, "That's what happened. He grabbed me by the throat, punched me right in the face, and called me all kinds of nasty names. My hat fell off, and when I tried to pick it up he kicked me and told me how stupid and disgusting I was."

She started to tear up, and Oscar did his best to comfort her. I was surprised by how tender he could be, given the coldhearted cynicism of so many of his observations. But I guess he was a showman first and foremost, and so mostly he had to play the role expected of him. "Now, now, it will be all right," he said, to Merriman, although I wasn't so sure things would ever be much good for her.

I said, "After he hit you, what happened?"

"He threw me out of the room, saying more awful things."

"The man sounds like a perfect cad," Oscar said. "I think I should very much like to punch him in the nose."

"That's probably not a good idea," I said, "but I share the sentiment." I said to Merriman, "So now you're out in the hallway, and I imagine you're worried because if you don't collect that extra five dollars, Dickie will be very unhappy with you."

"Yes, he would hurt me for sure. He always thinks me and the other girls are trying to shortchange him."

"What did you do next?"

"Well, that's when Jimmy came out of this very room, Mr. Wilde, and asked me what the trouble was. He must have heard all the commotion."

"My God!" said Oscar. "What was he doing in my suite?"

"Looking for loot, I imagine," I said. "Remember, we found a passkey he wasn't supposed to have in his pocket. That's how he got in. He knew you'd be off at your well-publicized lecture, so why not take a quick look around? We've had a problem with thefts from unoccupied rooms over the past few months. Jimmy must have been the culprit. I never did trust the little weasel. Maybe he was after your china, Oscar."

"I am a tolerant man, Dobsy, but purloining china is beyond the pale. However, I don't think the scoundrel got any of it."

"Well, that's a relief," I said. "So, Merry, what happened after Jimmy found you in the corridor?"

"He was angry when he saw my black eye and I told him what Mr. Conklin had done. Jimmy hated the swells who stayed at the hotel, flashing money and acting like big shots. He told me once he'd kill them all if he could."

"A not wholly unreasonable sentiment," said Oscar, ignoring his own spectacular swellness. "But pray, go on, Miss Merriman."

"Well, Jimmy said he'd take care of Mr. Conklin, so he brought me in here and told me to wait. 'That dirty old bastard will pay five dollars and plenty more,' that's how he put it. Then he opened the communicating doors and rushed right at Mr. Conklin like a mad bull. He knocked him straight to the floor. Jimmy got on top of him and kind of held him by the throat and told him to pay up or else. They were screaming at each other. I was really scared. I couldn't look, so I closed the door. Jimmy was acting so crazy I was afraid he'd kill Mr. Conklin."

"Well, clearly he didn't. Mr. Conklin is alive and more or less well," I said. "In any event, you're hiding behind closed doors while the titans do battle. Even so, you must have heard what was going on."

"Yes, and I was petrified. It sounded terrible, the way Jimmy was yelling. I could hardly stand it. After a while, I heard a door slam shut. Then Jimmy came back in here and said Mr. Conklin had paid up and was gone. Jimmy gave me the five dollars—he was always good to me that way—and said I should leave, too, so I did."

"What time was this?"

"I think it was close to ten, maybe a little earlier."

"And what about Jimmy?"

"He said he wanted to look around a little more."

"In other words, to look around for something to steal," Oscar said.

"I guess so, but I didn't want any part of that. I'm not a thief."

"I'm sure you're not," I said, although in my experience prostitutes weren't averse to pinching an item or two while on the job. "In any case, you left. Did you happen to see anyone out in the hallway?"

"I did catch a glimpse of someone coming down from where the elevator is, but I didn't hang around for a good look. I just got out of there as fast as I could in the opposite direction, toward the back stairs."

Both Oscar and I had the same thought. He said, "Aha, now we are at the nub of the matter. That could have been Mr. Jones's killer arriving on the scene. Describe this mysterious figure, if you would."

"I'm sorry, but I can't. It was just a glimpse, like I said, and he was pretty far away."

"So it was a man," I said. "Big, small, tall, short? Wearing a suit, a uniform, work clothes?"

Merriman shook her head. "Oh, I wish I could help you, but I can't. Do you know how it is when you just catch a flicker of something out of the corner of your eye? Well, that's how it was. I do think it was a man for some reason, but I couldn't possibly identify him."

"I fear that looking for a flicker is like hunting for a nobleman's conscience," Oscar said. "It may be there, but it is very elusive. Still, I am not ready to give up. I have some idea, you see, as to the identity of the Specter in the Hallway, if he can be called that. Now then, is there anything else you can tell us, Miss Merriman?"

There wasn't, other than that after fleeing Oscar's suite she went downstairs to the women's toilet room, intending to hide out for a time while she figured out what to do next. There, she'd encountered Mrs. Westerly before going up to the attic.

"Well, Miss Merriman, you have certainly tantalized us," Oscar said. "A shadowy murderer stalks the Nicollet House! It makes for quite a tale."

"It does," I agreed, "and I'd love to know the ending."

*

By now it was approaching three, when even a busy hotel like the Nicollet is normally locked into deep quiet, the guests snoozing in their beds and only a skeletal staff on hand to deal with the occasional night owl lurking in the darkness. The lateness of the hour—I was stifling a constant urge to yawn while Merriman was nodding off in her chair—had no effect on Oscar, who seemed to grow more energized by the minute.

"Well, Dobsy," he said, "I believe we are very close now, very close. I am convinced the murderer is still here in the hotel, and I shall be very disappointed if we fail to demonstrate his guilt by the time the sun comes up. I have been thinking—a pastime, alas, that is foreign to much of humanity—and there are at least two clues that point to the identity of the miscreant."

"And they are?"

"Need you ask? I am of course talking about the blacks threads I found in Mr. Conklin's suite and that pinprick on Mr. Jones's finger. If I'm right, they are related and point to a singular suspect."

"Well, if you're ready to name the murderer, I'm all ears. Who is it?"

Oscar smiled, took out a cigarillo, lit it, and said after he took his first puff, "While I believe I can identify the murderer, that is not the same as knowing beyond all doubt. Until I do, I would rather keep my ideas to myself, lest I be revealed as a fool."

"Well, we certainly couldn't let that happen," I said.

"You are teasing me, Dobsy, but I am quite serious. After all, the people who think they're never wrong are usually the ones who are seldom right, and I wish to be right about this matter."

"As do I. So, what would it take for you to know 'beyond all doubt,' as you put, that you've identified the guilty party?"

"There is one man who is the keeper of secrets in this business, and we must talk to him, the sooner the better."

"That would be our friend, Mr. Conklin, I suppose."

"Yes. Perhaps we should go pound on his door."

"Maybe, but who's to say he'll be in the mood to answer? As I told you, he didn't reply when I knocked at his door, and I'd probably be fired if we waltzed into his suite with my passkey and found him sleeping like a babe."

"Bankers don't sleep like babes," Oscar said. "I imagine them more as crocodiles lying in a dark swamp, happily digesting their profits. But if we say some magic words at Mr. Conklin's door, he'll let us in. I'm sure of it."

" 'Open sesame'— is that what you have in mind?"

"No, I was thinking of threatening him with poetry."

I'd heard many strange statements from Oscar since his arrival, but this was the topper. "So a little verse, you think, will turn Conklin to jelly and make him blurt out the truth? Well, I'll be eager to see that."

"And you shall. Poetry spoken aloud, even if mere doggerel, always gets a man's attention. It is like music in that regard. But it can't be just any poem. It must address what a man like Mr. Conklin fears more than anything else."

"And what would that be?"

"Exposure, Dobsy, exposure. Our reticent banker, I should imagine, is a community pillar respected by all if loved by none, a faithful churchgoer—Presbyterian, no doubt—and a family man with the sort of wife who knows everything and forgives nothing. For such a man, the appearance of rectitude, if not its actuality, is all. But if the world, not to mention his wife, discovers that Mr. Conklin has been consorting with prostitutes, he will suffer profound embarrassment, and from his point of view that would be as death, though without the bothersome expense of a funeral."

This ornate little speech was pure Oscar, a rolling wave of words, and after I'd been duly inundated, I came up for air. "All well and good," I said, "but where's the poem you say will cause Conklin to tremble with fear?"

"Ah, the poem. I am sure I can come up with a few suitable lines."

Oscar went over to the suite's writing desk, got out paper and pencil, then quickly scribbled out a few words. "Yes, this will do nicely," he said, folding the sheet of paper and putting it in his jacket pocket. "Time to pay a call on Mr. Conklin."

"Okay, I'm game for whatever crazy thing you have in mind, but first we have practical matters to attend to. We need to find a room where we can stash away Miss Merriman for a while. The coppers will be back here in the morning, and I'd like to keep her on ice until I know where we stand with our own investigation. I'll run downstairs and see what's available."

I was on good terms with the clerk manning the front desk, and I gave some story about needing to check on a troublesome guest as an excuse to scan the room occupancy sheet. I saw that several rooms on the third floor were open, and when I returned to Oscar's suite I woke up Merriman and advised her of my plan.

"Just stay in the room until morning, and then we'll figure out our next move. You'll have to talk to the coppers at some point and tell them what you told us. But until then, don't let anybody except me or Oscar into your room. Is that understood?"

"Yes, but you must know I am terrified of the police. What if they accuse me of murdering Jimmy?"

"They won't," I said. "There's no way you could have overpowered him. It would have taken a strong man to do that."

Once we'd settled Merriman in her room, we headed for suite 103 to give Pluto Conklin a lesson in the power of poetry, Oscar style.

5.
PLUTO SPEAKS

No man is rich enough to buy back his past.
—OSCAR WILDE

MY WATCH WAS JUST TICKING to half-past three when we arrived at the door to Conklin's suite. Entertaining as I thought a poetic performance from Oscar might be, I hoped it wouldn't come to that, so I announced myself, rapped at the door several times and called out Conklin's name, although not so loudly that I'd wake up other guests on the floor. I received no answer.

"Maybe he's not in there," Oscar said. "Maybe he's on the lam, as you Americans so quaintly say. What is the 'lam' anyway? It sounds so ovine."

" 'Ovine'?"

"Yes, you know, sheepish."

"Oscar, you never cease to amaze me. But if Conklin has up and left, I'd be surprised. Remember, the coppers told him to stick around until morning, and he'd look mighty suspicious if he ran off during the night."

"Then the time has come to sound the trumpet of poesy and force his hand."

"Fine, but try not to awaken the entire floor."

Oscar, however, ignored my cautionary words, immediately breaking out into "poesy" with his sonorous baritone: "Pluto, weep for your sins, admit that you lied / For the truth alone will conquer your shame / Speak to us now of the bellman who died / Or risk the death of your own good name."

He followed his poetic recital with some plainspoken prose: "This is Oscar Wilde, Mr. Conklin, and I will not be denied. You must talk to Mr. McGuire and me at this very moment or come morning I shall make you the subject of a most revealing lecture in the hotel lobby. The press, I am sure, will report every word of it, and your good name will be as horse manure in the mud. Now open up or face the consequences!"

Well, it was something to hear—the world's greatest traveling aesthete dispensing poetry and threats in a voice booming enough to rouse the dead from their tombs—and before long doorways began to open all along the corridor to reveal men in sleeping gowns and nightcaps wondering what the godawful fuss was about.

"Say, keep it down, you idiots," said one of them, while another, who clearly recognized Oscar, offered some friendly advice: "Shut up, you damn fool, and go back to England."

I was about ready to extend my humblest apologies when the door to Conklin's suite swung open, and there stood the banker, wearing the same suit we'd seen him in earlier. Disgust soured his face.

"What the hell is wrong with you?" he said. "Go away and leave me alone."

"I don't think so," I said, inserting a foot in the door. "For your own sake, you need to talk to us right now."

"Get out at once," Conklin growled, trying to push me out the door. I pushed back, Oscar right behind me, and we more or less manhandled Conklin toward a sofa, where we deposited him with a final shove.

The suite was drabber in color than Oscar's but otherwise quite similar in its furnishing. A half-empty bottle of gin sat on a table next to the sofa, and I could tell by Conklin's bloodshot eyes—not to mention that he was still in his dark pin-striped suit—that he'd spent a sleepless night with his distilled companion.

"I, I will not stand for this," Conklin sputtered as he glared up at us from the sofa.

"Of course you won't," Oscar said. "You're sitting down. Now, be so kind as to shut up while we explain why you are in trouble so deep that not even your underworld connections can be of help to you."

I had no idea what Oscar meant until he saw my baffled expression and said, "You know, Dobsy, Pluto. God of the underworld and all of that."

"Good to know," I said, "but let's try to stay out of Hades if we can."

Conklin started to protest again, but I cut him off and said, "Here's the situation. I'm going to talk and you're going to listen. Otherwise, I might have to put a new dent in that big red nose of yours."

That threat seemed to drain the defiance from Conklin, and so I went ahead and described, point by point, what Louise Merriman had told us. "So you see," I concluded, "you're smack dab in the middle of a murder case, Mr. Conklin, and you can't buy your way out of it. When the coppers talk to Miss Merriman, as they surely will today, you're going to be front page news, and not in a good way."

Oscar observed, unhelpfully, "Very true, although I have always contended that publicity is rather like alcohol in that even a bad drink is better than none at all."

I let that one pass and said to Conklin, "But if you come clean with us, maybe, just maybe, you can go back to St. Paul tomorrow with no one the wiser about your little escapade with Miss Merriman."

Conklin's eyes began to dart like fish in a bowl as he considered the possibilities, much as he might calculate the compound interest on a loan in hopes of securing the utmost profit. "Very well," he finally said, "but you must promise me that my name will be kept out of this."

"I can't make that promise, but I can put in a good word for you with the coppers if you cooperate now. And if you were to express your gratitude in the right way—to the police, that is—you might just skate out of this mess."

Oscar added, "You should also apologize to Miss Merriman for your beastly conduct. I believe that, say, one hundred dollars would show how genuine your regret is."

"One hundred dollars!" Conklin exclaimed, as though he'd just been asked to hand over his bulging wallet to a beggar. "Why, that is ridiculous!"

"Life is ridiculous," said Oscar. "Otherwise, how could we stand it?"

"How about we leave the philosophy to Aristotle," I said, hoping to avert one of Oscar's long excursions into the lush realm of his wit. "What will it be, Mr. Conklin? The truth now, or the coppers making your life extremely miserable?"

"All right, all right," Conklin said. "But you must know that I had nothing to do with the death of the bellboy, whatever his name was."

"Bell captain," I said. "His name was Jimmy Jones. Now, start from the beginning. You asked him to arrange for some companionship, and he agreed to send up a girl to your suite and that it would cost ten dollars, correct?"

"Yes, and why not? A man is entitled to a bit of fun now and then."

"I'm sure your wife would agree. So Jimmy sends up Miss Merriman, the two of you have your 'fun,' but when the time comes for her to leave she wants an extra five dollars."

"The little whore didn't ask for the money, she demanded it. Naturally, I refused. Contrary to what she told you, it was she who attacked me, and I had to defend myself."

"By trying to strangle her and punching her in the eye," said Oscar. "Why, not even Leonidas and the Spartans displayed more bravery in the face of overwhelming odds. I salute you, sir!"

"Ignore the boy genius here," I told Conklin, "and go on. There was an altercation, you toss her out of your suite, then Jimmy suddenly appears and he's fighting mad."

"He was absolutely insane. He came rushing out of the adjoining suite, the one occupied by this English twit"—here Conklin gave Oscar a contemptuous glance—"and before I knew it that damned bastard was assaulting me. He nearly broke my nose."

"Too bad I wasn't there," Oscar said, "I would have broken it with pleasure. I am quite capable, you know, when it comes to fisticuffs."

"Oscar, I'm sure you're John L. Sullivan in the flesh," I said, "but please, I'd like to hear the rest of Mr. Conklin's story without further interruptions."

"As you wish. However, I do hope it will be fact and not fiction. One author in the room is enough."

Or perhaps one too many, I thought. Be that as it may, what Conklin said next corresponded to what Merriman had told us. After being assaulted by Jones, he forked over the extra five dollars, collected himself, and left his suite, having had enough "entertainment" for the evening.

"About what time did you leave?"

"Quarter to ten. I looked at my watch."

"And Jones at that point was uninjured, as far as you know?"

"Of course. He was the one who injured me. I did no harm to him."

"When you left your suite, did you see anyone in the hallway?"

"No."

"Where did you go next?'

"Downstairs, to the bar. I needed a drink."

"Several, I imagine. Did you take the stairs or the elevator?"

"The elevator."

"Was anyone getting off as you got on?"

"Let me think."

"Don't strain yourself," Oscar said.

"Pay no attention to the world's greatest wit," I said as I scowled at Oscar. "He's not always as funny as he thinks he is. Just take your time, Mr. Conklin, and try to recall if you saw anybody in the elevator."

"Come to think of it, I did. He got out as I was getting in."

Conklin said he didn't recognize the man, but he was able to provide a good enough description that Oscar said at once, "Sounds like my neighbor in the far suite, Mr. Montague."

"Never heard of him," Conklin said.

"Did you say anything to Mr. Montague?"

"No, why would I?"

"Not one for idle conversation, are you?" Oscar said. "In which direction did he go when he left the elevator?"

"To the right, I think."

"Toward your suite and mine, in other words?"

"Yes."

Conklin went on to say that after boarding the elevator, he went down to the lobby and then straight to the bar, where he drank for several hours. The bartenders there, he said, would vouch for his presence.

"Weren't you tempted to complain to the management about what had happened?" Oscar asked. "I would have. After all, I'm sure this fine hostelry does not countenance its bellmen assaulting guests. It might well do grave harm to return business."

Conklin delivered another lethal glare at Oscar and said, "How could I say anything? There'd just be another scene, and I hardly needed that. I just wanted to get away from the whole business. Besides, I didn't see that fellow who runs the place at the front desk."

"Mr. Hutchinson, you mean," I said.

"That's him. As far as I'm concerned, he's running a damn zoo here, not a hotel."

"Yes, and the animals are restless tonight," Oscar said. "I'm surprised you don't carry a whip, Dobsy, to keep them under control."

"I'll stick with my revolver. All right, is there anything else you can tell us, Mr. Conklin?"

But the banker had little more of value to offer. After a few more perfunctory questions, we abandoned him to his gin and worries, promising that we wouldn't expose his activities to the press. As for the police, he'd have to make his own arrangements.

"You seem to believe him," Oscar said as we headed back to his suite.

"I do. His story holds together. Besides, I just don't picture him having the strength to strangle Jimmy. Too old, too fat, too much booze."

"And there, in a nutshell, you have the story of every man's life as he approaches the abyss."

"That's a happy thought," I said. "But if Conklin is telling the truth—and I think he is—we need to talk with Mr. Montague. He may have seen something. Or maybe even done something."

"Like murdering Mr. Jones?" Oscar said. "I suppose that is possible, given that Mr. Montague is one of at least two men we've run across tonight with a big secret that dare not be revealed."

"Is that so? What's his 'big secret,' if I may ask?"

"I must regard it as being my secret as well for the moment. But let's have a chat with him posthaste and see what he has to say for himself."

"It's almost four in the morning," I reminded Oscar. "I doubt Mr. Montague will be in the mood for conversation."

"Then we shall put him in the mood. After all, who wouldn't enjoy our delightful company, no matter how inconvenient the hour?"

"Most of humanity," I said, "but since we're trying to catch a murderer, I guess we can give it a try."

"Now you're talking, Dobsy. We're like the hounds of Zeus. No one can stop us."

"I'll take your word for it," I said, since Zeus and his pets were unfamiliar to me. "By the way, has anyone ever told you, Oscar, that you are a very strange man?"

"Oh yes. I've been told that many times. It would be quite awful if I were not so entirely lovable."

*

We made our way down empty, silent corridors to Oscar's suite and then to Montague's just beyond. I knocked firmly on his door three times, identifying myself as the house detective, and asked to speak to Montague on what I described as an "urgent matter." I received no answer. Another series of knocks also failed to get a response.

"I guess we shall have to resort to poetry again," Oscar said.

"Over my dead body. I don't want to wake up half the people on this floor a second time. Tell you what. I'll open the door and stand watch out here while you go inside and look around for anything that might indicate Mr. Montague was involved in the murder. If you do find him in there asleep, leave at once. If you awaken him, say you entered his suite by mistake, then leave. And if he happens to show up out here in the hall, I'll knock twice and then distract him while you make your getaway. In any case, don't spend more than a few minutes in there, all right?"

"Oh, this will be marvelous," Oscar said. "Besides, I know exactly what to look for, and it won't take me long."

I slid my passkey in the lock and opened the door for Oscar, who was smiling like a boy about to go on a holiday at the beach. "Wish me luck," he said as he disappeared into the suite, where no lights appeared to be on.

Five minutes went by, then ten, and I was about to go in to see what Oscar was up to when he reappeared at the door, looking very satisfied with himself.

"All done," he said. "There was no sign of Mr. Montague, but I did make two finds of interest. Let's go to my suite and I'll tell you all about it."

Once we were back in his suite, Oscar put on some coffee—I desperately needed a jolt—and launched into an account of his adventure in what he called "burgling for a good cause."

"Once I saw that Mr. Montague was gone—and of course I wondered where he could be at this hour—I searched the wardrobe in his bedroom. However, there was no black jacket or other item of apparel matching the color of the threads I found at the scene of Mr. Jones's murder. And as you may recall, Mr. Montague was wearing a navy jacket when we saw him earlier. Ergo, if he is our murderer, he must have hidden a black jacket somewhere other than in his suite."

"Or he's fled the hotel with it," I suggested.

"No, I think not. I found clothes, jewelry, and toiletry items in his suite. He is most likely elsewhere in the hotel, in the company of another person."

I assumed Oscar meant Montague must be with a woman. Perhaps another prostitute supplied by Prince and Jones? It seemed plausible. But when I put that notion to Oscar, he slowly shook his head and said, "Mr. Montague, I am of a mind, does not consort with the female of the species. You see, as I was poking around his suite, I found a scrawled message on the nightstand by his bed. It said, 'Thomas, room 412, ten p.m., five dollars.' It sounds as though Mr. Montague has engaged a rent boy for the evening."

"Rent boy" wasn't a term I'd heard, but at the same time I wasn't ignorant of what goes on in the world. "Okay, that makes Mr. Montague a pervert but not necessarily a murderer."

Oscar said, "I should be careful whom I call a 'pervert.' I personally find a number of things—foxhunting comes immediately to mind—far more perverse than whatever our esteemed professor of rhetoric may be doing at the moment. However, society does indeed frown upon it as a crime against nature, although I have always thought that nature is in many ways a crime against us."

"I'm not sure I follow that dazzling train of thought," I said, "but no matter. The question is what to do next. Maybe we'll have to go up to room four twelve and interrupt the proceedings."

"We could," Oscar said, "but it would accomplish nothing. In any event, do you really believe Mr. Montague could have committed the murder? I do not. Remember, he is professor of rhetoric. Words are his weapon, not his hands or a knife or a pistol. Besides, he strikes me as a cold fish, content to circulate in the chill waters of indifference. On the other hand, I believe that the man we are looking for must have loved Mr. Jones enough to kill him."

"Loved him? He had a funny way of showing it."

"Perhaps, but why bother to kill someone you care nothing about? I assure you, Dobsy, there is no better motive for murder than love. And that is why Mr. Conklin can't be the killer either. There is no love in him, other than for lucre. And as you have said, our banking friend probably lacks the physical wherewithal to have throttled Mr. Jones. All of which leaves us with just one person, in my estimation, who could have done the deed."

"All right, I'll bite. Who's the guilty party?"

Oscar now identified his prime suspect, and I will admit to being shocked when he uttered the name. But as Oscar explained his theory, marshaling his arguments like a prosecutor before a jury, I couldn't deny that he might be onto something.

"Okay, let's say you're right," I said. "Where's the hard evidence? You've put a lot of circumstantial stuff together but nothing that would have a ghost of a chance of standing up in court."

"True, which I why I'm going to need your help, and your pass-key, of course."

When Oscar explained his plan, I saw big trouble ahead if he was wrong. But somehow I couldn't refuse him, even if it cost me my job. That was the thing about Oscar—he could make even the most outrageous ideas seem charming, so that if he told you arsenic was the food of the gods, you just might believe him. Now I was ready to go ahead and sip what Oscar had to offer, hoping it wouldn't turn out to be poison.

6.
OSCAR GETS HIS MAN

The man had killed the thing he loved.
—OSCAR WILDE

AT SIX O'CLOCK, sunrise still an hour and a half away, Oscar and I went down to the lobby. He idled about near the elevator while I walked over to the front desk. Guests with early business to conduct or trains to catch were lining up to check out, so I went around the desk to ask a crucial question of the overnight clerk before he left. His answer proved enlightening. I thanked him and then asked if Hutchinson was in his office.

"Yeah, you know him. He's always the early bird. Say, can you tell me anything more about Jimmy? Who do you suppose did it?"

"I'm working on it," I said as I reached up to scratch a nonexistent itch on my head, signaling Oscar to continue with our plan. "In fact, I'm going to update Hutch on the situation right now. Also, I expect Oscar Wilde will show up here in a little bit. When he does, send him back to the office."

"Sure thing. I hear that Wilde fellow is really something. I missed seeing him when he came back last night. What does he look like?"

"Oh, you'll recognize him," I said. "He stands out in a crowd."

Hutchinson's office was always kept meticulously neat, like Hutchinson himself. The furnishings included a rolltop desk, the usual gathering of file cabinets, a pair of side chairs, and a plush sofa, where I found Hutchinson sprawled out with a glass of whiskey in one hand and a cigar in the other. He was normally the very definition of dapper, his suits meticulously tailored, his shirts perfectly starched, his ties precisely knotted. But now he'd discarded his coat and tie, and he had the bedraggled look of a man desperately in need of a good shave and a lot of sleep.

"Ah, Dobsy, it has been quite a night, hasn't it?" he said. "Care for a drink? Help yourself."

"Why not," I said and poured out a shot from the nearly empty bottle of Old Crow Hutchinson had been drinking. It was strange to see him imbibing at so early an hour. Then again, given the night's events, I couldn't blame him. I took a seat on one of the side chairs but didn't let myself get too comfortable.

"I'm glad you came by," Hutchinson said. "I've been thinking about what happened to poor Jimmy. It's a real mystery, isn't it? The police seem to think that banker did it, but I don't know. What do you think?'

"It wasn't Mr. Conklin."

"How do you know that?"

"Oscar and I had a nice chat with him not long ago," I said and then recounted what Conklin had told us about his nasty encounter with Jones.

"My goodness, that's just awful," Hutchinson said when I'd finished. "I'm appalled that Jimmy could act in such a way. But are you sure Mr. Conklin is telling the truth?"

"He's not an admirable character," I said, "but Oscar and I don't believe he's a murderer. He doesn't have it in him."

"I see. Is there someone else you suspect?"

"There is," I said. "You see, we also talked with Louise Merriman. She was hiding in the attic, just as I suspected, and it's fortunate we got to her when we did. There was a man up there, no doubt the murderer, and my guess is that he intended to do her harm."

Hutchinson shook his head and said, "It just keep getting worse, doesn't it? Did you get a good look at the man?"

"Afraid not."

"Too bad," Hutchinson said, swirling his glass before taking a big gulp. "So, who's this suspect of yours?"

"I'm not ready to say quite yet."

"Ah, so you're still gathering evidence, is that it?"

"That's right. Oscar is at it as we speak. As a matter of fact, I expect him here shortly."

"Is that so? Well, I can't picture that fop as a detective. Where's he looking for this evidence?"

"Here in the hotel. If he's right, we'll know for sure who murdered Jimmy soon enough. In the meantime, there's something I've always wondered about when it comes to Jimmy, and maybe you can help me out."

Hutchinson drank the last of his whiskey and set the glass down with a firm thud, as though he'd suddenly decided to embrace sobriety. Suspicion lurked in his eyes. "All right, I'll help you if I can."

"Good. Here's the thing I wonder about. You always treated Jimmy as the golden boy around here even though you knew as well as I that he was no good. I told you more than once how I suspected him of bringing prostitutes into the hotel and stealing valuables from guests' rooms. But you never called him to account. Instead, you made him the bell captain. That seems odd to me."

Hutchinson rose to his feet, and I thought he might be trying to leave, but instead he went to his desk, took a cigar out of its box, and lit it. "There's nothing like a good cigar, is there? You know, if I were headed for the gallows and they offered me a last meal,

I'd say, 'No, sir, all I need is a cigar. A good cigar.' How about you? What would you want?"

"I don't plan on going to the gallows," I said. "But what say we get back to Jimmy. Why didn't you fire him?"

Hutchinson sat down at the desk, took in a satisfying draw of smoke, and said, "Well, first off, I didn't believe Jimmy was 'no good,' as you say. To the contrary, I'd found him to be an excellent bellboy, very responsible and efficient. I advanced him to captain because I thought he deserved the job. I know you had your suspicions about him, but let's be honest, you didn't come to me with any proof. I did talk to Jimmy, and he denied any wrongdoing. What was I to do, Dobsy? I couldn't let him go just because you didn't like him."

I'd seen Hutchinson fire bellboys and maids on the faintest suspicion of thievery, and I didn't find his explanation at all that convincing.

"I disliked Jimmy because he was a crooked operator," I said. "I find it hard to believe you didn't know that."

"Well, I didn't. Let's just leave it at that."

"There was no personal motive behind his preferred treatment?"

"What do you mean?"

"Well, maybe you had certain feelings toward him," I said, aware that I was entering dangerous territory. "After all, Jimmy was a very handsome young man."

We're all dentists now and then, striking a nerve, and the startled look on Hutchinson's face left little doubt that I'd drilled into a very sensitive spot. A yelp of denial followed.

"Why, that is an outrageous thing to suggest!"

"I'm not making any accusations. I'm just trying to figure out why you thought so highly of a little criminal like Jimmy. You must have loved him, that's all I can figure."

I'd drilled down to the pulp now, and Hutchinson, whose fabled geniality disguised a fierce temper, reacted explosively.

"How dare you!" he screamed before hurling a few indelicate oaths at me. "What do you think I am? Get out and don't come back!"

Before I could reply, Oscar stepped into the office, a black jacket flung over one shoulder and a large manila envelope in his right hand. "There is no need to shout, Mr. Hutchinson," he said. "You're frightening the desk clerks out there. If you'll just stay calm, Dobsy and I will be pleased to hear your confession now. I'm quite sure you didn't intend to kill Mr. Jones, but I fear there can be no doubt whatsoever that you did."

*

The drama that unfolded over the next half hour or so will always stay with me, one of those moment-by-moment memories too clear and sharp to ever be erased. I conferred briefly with Oscar, telling him what I'd learned from the overnight clerk. Then Oscar took center stage, speaking as only he could—the words tumbling out in easy abundance like gold coins falling from the sky. Yet their glimmer couldn't disguise the hard reasoning behind Oscar's words, and I doubt any prosecutor before a jury ever delivered a more precise or well-reasoned argument.

Oscar had hardly begun before Hutchinson interrupted the proceedings to proclaim his innocence, adding, "I will not sit here and listen to my good name being sullied by absurd accusations. I want both of you out of my office immediately."

We stayed put. "If we leave, we're going straight to the police, and I don't think you want that," I said. "You're in a tough spot, even if you won't admit it. Just listen to what Oscar has to say, and then you can deny everything if you so choose."

"You'd better believe I will," Hutchinson said, folding his arms and staring at us defiantly. "I had absolutely nothing to do with Jimmy's death."

"I disagree," Oscar said in a measured voice as he removed the jacket slung over his shoulder and held it out in front of him like a tailor displaying his handiwork. "Indeed, there are several things that gave you away, Mr. Hutchinson, beginning with this black jacket of yours. I took the liberty of retrieving it from your apartment with the help of Dobsy's passkey."

"Why, you are nothing but a common thief," Hutchinson said. "What else have you taken?"

"Your good name, I'm afraid," Oscar said, "and that you will never get back. You see, I found three black threads on the carpet in Mr. Conklin's suite, and as it turns out they match the threads of your jacket perfectly as to color, size, and texture. Moreover, there is a small tear in the jacket, at the right breast, thereby accounting for the lost threads."

Oscar had predicted to me that he'd find a torn black jacket in Hutchinson's apartment. Even so, I was amazed to see it. I was amazed, too, by how Oscar had turned a seemingly insignificant observation into evidence of murder.

"But the threads really are a minor feature of the plot when it comes to the telltale story of this jacket," Oscar continued as his magnetic eyes bored in on Hutchinson. "Something else about it is of far greater import. As I'm sure you recall, you were wearing it when I arrived at the hotel yesterday afternoon. I notice such things, and really, what is life except noticing things? But when I next saw you, after Mr. Jones's body so inconveniently appeared in my suite, you were attired in the red jacket I see lying there by the sofa."

"What of it?" Hutchinson said. "I often change my jacket."

Oscar nodded and said, "Yes, it's an inconsequential thing, as you say, for a man can change his jacket whenever he pleases. But there was one other point that drew my attention. When you came into my suite to gaze in mock surprise upon the man you'd just murdered, I had to pause for a moment to put a name to your face, as I had seen you only once before. Later, it struck me why I wasn't immediately able to identify you. It was because you weren't wearing this," Oscar said with a dramatic flourish as he took a brass name tag from his jacket pocket.

He held up the tag as though it was a precious offering to the gods of vengeance, and said, "You will note that it identifies the wearer as 'G. Hutchinson, manager.' It is indisputably yours. Yet you will also note that the long safety pin by which the tag attaches to a jacket is so badly bent as to make it unusable. That alone is hardly dispositive, as barristers like to say when they are busily engaged in hoodwinking a jury, but the blood is a different matter."

Oscar had told me earlier that he believed the pinprick on Jones's finger might have come from Hutchinson's name tag as it was being torn from his jacket during a struggle. I'd thought the idea was far-fetched—an intuitive leap into the thinnest of air. Now it was obvious Oscar had been right, for a small smear of dried blood coated the end of the mangled pin.

His eyes still fixed on Hutchinson, Oscar said, "I imagine Mr. Jones tore the name tag from your black coat and pricked his finger in the process as you strangled the life out of him in Mr. Conklin's suite. You retrieved it after you killed him, but instead of tossing it down a sewer or otherwise disposing of it so that it would never be found, you brought it back to your apartment, where I found it resting unceremoniously in a rubbish bin. If one is to be a successful murderer, tidying up is essential, and I fear you failed in that regard."

"This is all nonsense, a fairy tale," Hutchinson said, yet I sensed that his defiance was a show, the last snarling stand of a man caught in a very bad corner.

"Yes, and in this tale of mine, you're the ogre," said Oscar, who then related what Louise Merriman had told us about her encounter with Conklin, including how Jones had come to her defense after Conklin roughed her up and how she'd spotted a man coming down the hallway as she fled.

Oscar went on, talking as easily as if was reciting one of his poems to a rapt audience. "Now let me set the next scene for you. Mr. Conklin, duly chastened, has been vanquished to the bar. Mr. Jones then sets about looking for valuables in his suite in the same way that he had been rummaging through mine. And that is where, quite by chance, you enter the picture, Mr. Hutchinson. At approximately quarter to ten, you told the overnight clerk—he has just verified this to us—that you were going to take a brief rest in your apartment. But as you were on your way there, you were startled to see Miss Merriman emerging from my suite and walking toward the back staircase. She also saw you, of course."

This was a fib. As we both knew, she hadn't been able to identify the man in the hall. I thought it was a smart move on Oscar's part to make Hutchinson believe he'd been spotted so as to ratchet up the pressure in him.

Oscar continued: "You knew, Mr. Hutchinson, that I was still at the Academy of Music, so your suspicions were immediately aroused when you saw Miss Merriman leaving my suite. And so we come to the fateful moment. You enter my suite to see if anyone else is skulking about, and lo and behold, you spot Mr. Jones in the adjoining suite through the open communicating doors. There is an immediate confrontation as you demand to know what he is doing. Mr. Jones, judging from what I have heard about him, probably responds to you with the utmost impudence. Anger boils up within you and you throttle him until he stops breathing and dies. How does that sound to you?"

Hutchinson wasn't ready to crumble, at least not yet. "It's quite a story," he said in a flat voice. "But where's the proof?"

I had to admit Hutchinson had a point. I thought Oscar was absolutely right about what had happened, but I'd seen plenty of smart defense attorneys operate in my day, and the reality was that we didn't have anywhere near enough evidence to convict Hutchison of murder or, for that matter, even cause charges to be brought against him.

"Oh, there is more proof to come, as you shall see," Oscar said. "But first let us go back to what happened after you strangled Mr. Jones. Of course, you are horrified by what you've done, yet you are a man capable of calculation, and so you start thinking about how to cover your tracks. You soon hit upon a brilliant idea, which was to drag Mr. Jones into my suite, along with his hat and the button torn from his jacket. You did this knowing there would be a mighty uproar when I discovered the corpse upon returning from my lecture. After tidying up Mr. Conklin's suite, which was in some disarray after his fight with Mr. Jones, you depart the scene. Your hope is that the police and the press and everyone else will become so entangled in Oscarmania—dare I use that term?—that the murder investigation will inevitably founder, leaving you in the clear. But then a new problem presented itself, didn't it?"

"And just what would that be?" Hutchinson asked.

"Why, the problem of what to do about Miss Merriman. You feared she'd seen you coming down the hallway as she left my suite. It was something to worry about and became more so when you learned from us, as we'd learned from Mrs. Westerly, that Miss Merriman might be hiding out in the hotel, very probably in the attic. And so, while we were otherwise engaged, you went up to look for her, perhaps to buy her off or even to silence her permanently. But Dobsy and I arrived on the scene to thwart your plans, and I must say you were lucky to get away."

I had told Oscar that Hutchinson, who was shrewd and not given to panic, probably wouldn't admit to anything absent overwhelming evidence against him, and I was right. "Well, this has all been very fascinating," he said, rising from his chair and walking toward the door. "But you have proved nothing, Mr. Wilde. Exactly nothing! As for you, Dobsy, collect your things and get out. I have no use for you here anymore."

Oscar wasn't finished, however. He stepped over to the door, blocking Hutchinson's path, and said, as casually as if he'd just noticed a loose shoelace, "Did I mention I found some extremely interesting photographs in your apartment?"

Hutchinson stopped, as though an abyss had suddenly opened up before him and he dare not take another step. A stricken look engulfed his features, and he said softly, "What photographs?"

"Photographs of Mr. Jones," Oscar said, "and they're very revealing. If you think about it, photographs are a wonder, don't you agree? The famed Mr. Sarony in New York took quite a few of me for publicity purposes before I embarked on my adventures here in America, and I think he caught my rather ruthless charm quite nicely. But I must say the photographs from your apartment are far more explicit in nature."

I wasn't sure what Oscar was talking about. As far as I knew, he'd gone to Hutchinson's apartment in search of murder clues, specifically the black jacket and name tag. Now, he was making a big thing of some photographs, and I wondered why.

Oscar still had the manila envelope in his hand. He unclasped it, took out an eight-by-ten-inch print, and showed it to Hutchinson and me. I am not easily shocked, but I was at that moment. The photograph showed Jones stark naked, in a pose that I will describe as suggestive and leave at that.

"I believe there are half a dozen or more like this in the little studio and darkroom you maintain in your apartment," Oscar said, "and I must compliment you on the excellence of your work. The albumen prints are very nicely done as to lighting, composition, and tone. And of course they make it obvious that you and Mr. Jones had a most intimate relationship."

A moment comes in every man's life when he realizes he is sunk, that the fates have found him and whatever disaster looms before him like some nightmarish beast can no longer be avoided. So it was with Hutchinson. The defiance drained out of him like water from a burst dam, and he began to sob. "It never should have happened," he said, "I, I was just so mad."

"I understand," Oscar said, displaying genuine sympathy. "You cared deeply about Mr. Jones. Dare I say you loved him. And yet angry love is the most powerful love of all, isn't it? You saw in that fatal moment that Jimmy was not as you believed him to be, that he was in fact a scheming little criminal, and it hurt you to the core. And so you put your hands around his neck and loved him to death."

"I didn't mean to hurt him," Hutchinson said through choking sobs. "I really didn't. It just happened so fast. He was a beautiful young man."

"Yes, and the beautiful die young, or so the poets tell us," Oscar said.

We all sat silent for a time until Hutchinson regained his composure, his tears giving way to the sober realization of what lay ahead.

"I am ruined," Hutchinson finally said in a quiet voice, "ruined forever, and I will surely go to hell for my sins."

"Hell is what we want it to be," Oscar replied, "and I see no special place for you there. Love is usually a mistake, Mr. Hutchinson, but it is rarely a sin. Still, I fear you are indeed ruined. Murder is your offense, and for that you must pay. As for your form of affection, I do not see that it has to become a matter of public knowledge. Don't you concur, Dobsy?"

I saw no reason to humiliate Hutchinson beyond what he would endure for being tried for murder. But I also knew that the photographs were a form of leverage that we needed to use. "If you'll write out a full and accurate confession right now," I said to Hutchinson, "then I don't care what happens to the photographs."

It was clear that the prospect of being exposed for his unnatural love weighed for more heavily on Hutchinson than the threat of a murder charge, and after a bit of prompting he wrote out his confession, which confirmed our theory as to how and why the crime had been committed. The confession made no mention of his lover's relationship with Jones. Instead, he stated only that he'd strangled Jones in a "moment of ungovernable rage" after finding him up to no good in Conklin's suite.

Afterward we accompanied Hutchinson to his apartment and watched as he collected all the revealing photographs of Jones from his files and burned them, with the doleful reluctance of a man destroying his greatest treasure.

*

And so the case of Jimmy Jones's murder played itself out. Oscar and I handed Hutchinson and his confession over to Chief Munger when he arrived at the hotel later that morning. The press was suitably agog, and although Oscar very much wanted to proclaim his own genius in solving the case, I talked him out of it.

"The coppers will not only hate you, and me, if we take credit for fingering Hutch as the murderer, they'll flat out deny we had any big role in it. The press will take their side, and pretty soon everybody will be making fun of you as the silly ass who thought he solved a murder when he didn't. Trust me on this one, Oscar. I know how things work around here."

"Dobsy, you are a veritable font of cynicism," Oscar replied with a grin, "which is why I must trust your judgment in this matter. I shall simply say to the reporters that I provided what little assistance I could to the police and that I am grateful for their most excellent work. Besides, I have always found the telling of lies in public to be quite bracing. It gives one renewed respect for the truth, whatever that may be."

"Well, I'm sure you'll lie very convincingly. Now, there's one thing I'm curious about. You told me last night, well before we got the goods on Hutch, that you believed Jimmy had been his lover. What made you suspect that?"

"Let us just say, Dobsy, that the two of them gave out signals, and that I saw the lights flashing from the moment I entered the hotel. I could not help but notice, for example, that when Mr. Jones was assigned to take me to my suite, Mr. Hutchinson hurried around from behind the desk, laid a hand on the young man's shoulder and rubbed it ever so softly. Did you observe that?"

"I guess I did, but I didn't think anything of it."

"Nor, I imagine, did anyone else except me. As it was, I found Mr. Hutchinson's gesture to be quite telling. The simple truth is that love is a rare thing, like some elusive bird in the jungle. But it's a colorful bird, and I am always startled when I make a rare sighting. So it was with our two love birds. I just knew, by the way Mr. Hutchinson touched the young bellman, that there was some profound connection between them."

I believed Oscar, strange as it may sound. In our time together, I'd come to realize that he had an unusually keen awareness of the world around him, seeing past what most of us do and into the hearts and minds of others. And yet, as I look back on his achievement and follies, I'm inclined to think he never made as much of his gift as he might have, if only because he could never quite escape the wit he wore like armor.

By early afternoon, with the reporters off to write their stories and Hutchinson deposited in the county jail, Oscar was ready to take his leave of Minneapolis and of me. He gave me a hug, we shook hands, and just before he went off in a hack with his valet and his tour manager and his piles of luggage, he said, "Dobsy, you must always remember me, for I will always remember you." I never saw or spoke to him again.

I read all the news accounts that followed over the next few days but found no mention of Pluto Conklin. Oscar's well-known observation that "no man is rich enough to buy back his past" didn't seem to hold true in Conklin's case. The banker, I figured, had managed to spread around enough money to keep his name out of the whole sordid business. I later sent him a note suggesting, in the strongest possible terms, that he never stay at the Nicollet House again, and as far as I know he took that advice. I did see Chauncey Montague a few more times at the hotel, but never spotted him with any "rent boys."

*

Oscar's next stop, in St. Paul, proved to be one of the highlights of his American tour. He delivered a standard lecture on the sixteenth of March but stayed over for St. Paddy's Day, always a big event in a city well stocked with Irishmen. The newspapers reported that he delivered a rousing impromptu speech on the genius of Irish culture and the imperative for Irish independence. His efforts, it was said, earned him "thunderous applause."

My last communication with Oscar came a week or so later, when I received a letter postmarked from Omaha. "My dearest Dobsy," he wrote, "I am ensconced in a city, if it can be called that, which smells like cattle, preparing to address a crowd that promises to be equally bovine in character. I write you only to say that I have been thinking about our adventures in Minneapolis and am of a mind to write a play about the murder and mayhem we so delightfully encountered. Then again I may not, for like most men I am very good at finding ways not to do things, thereby saving myself much trouble.

"I should also tell you that even in this wretched outpost I am continually besieged by news reporters, who seem quite fascinated by me, although not to the extent that I am. Fame of course is an intoxicant and I am drinking freely of it now, hoping that the glass will never be emptied. But one never knows, does one? Tomorrow I will be heading off to the Wild West, where cowboys and Indians and stampeding buffalo promise much excitement. Wish me well! Yours forever, Oscar."

Oscar did all right out West—the highlight being his legendary underground encounter with silver miners in Leadville, Colorado, during which he helped consume a "dinner" consisting entirely of whiskey. By the time he finally returned to England in late December 1882 he was basking in the kind of fame most men can only dream of.

Well before Oscar departed these shores, Hutchinson was sentenced to prison, but only for ten years, his attorneys having convinced a jury he was guilty of manslaughter but not of cold-blooded murder. It seemed a fair enough verdict to me. He was released after seven and a half years and left for points unknown, never to be heard from again. As for Louise Merriman, she went to live in a home for "rescued" women, with Mrs. Westerly making the arrangements. But I guess the cure didn't take and I heard she eventually went back to her old line of work, although I never saw her again at the Nicollet House. There was better news regarding Dickie Prince. He took a knife in the chest from one of his criminal companions at Ma Swenson's saloon. "A good friend will always stab you in the front," Oscar once said, and so it was with Prince.

I still think a lot about Oscar and all that brought him low. Maybe he deserved his fate, although I'm not one for harsh judgments anymore. For all his cutting wit and avowed cynicism, there was something impossibly romantic at his core, and it was perhaps fitting that at the bitter end he died for love. And for those who believe he was an unrepentant sodomite, forever lost to heaven, I suggest they read his words from "The Ballad of Reading Gaol," the finest poem he ever wrote:

How else may man make straight his plan
And cleanse his soul from Sin?
How else but through a broken heart
May Lord Christ enter in?

Rest in peace, dear Oscar.

THE DEATH COMMITTEE

"I've searched all the parks in all the cities and found no statues of committees."

—G. K. CHESTERTON

1.
THE LOTTERY

$10,000 REWARD FOR DISCOVERING MY MURDERER!

So read an astonishing headline that appeared on the morning of September 1, 1896, atop the front page of the *Minneapolis Tribune.* The newspaper's faithful readers could scarcely believe the headline, for who had ever heard of a dead man pursuing justice from the grave and promising a fortune to anyone who could deliver it? The notice that followed provided details of the extraordinary offer.

"I, George Wallace Pemberton, need your help in solving a terrible crime. A few days ago, I was murdered, even though my death was undoubtedly made to look accidental. I had been well aware before the fatal event that someone wished me dead and would go to any and all lengths to achieve that goal. Incidents occurring in July and August of this year demonstrated the malignant intent of my enemy, and it was only by good fortune that I survived those attempts on my life. But now that my enemy has accomplished the dark deed and sent me off to whatever eternity may hold, I fervently wish that justice be done.

"I have no faith in the police of this city, nor in the corrupt politicians who control them, and I am certain that they will never undertake a thorough investigation into my murder. Indeed, you may be certain they are pleased to be rid of me. With that in mind, I am calling upon the people of Minneapolis to investigate my demise, convinced as I am of the wisdom and intelligence of the common people without whom this city would be nothing. To this end, I have made provisions for a lottery to be held, whereby three people will be selected, at random, to form a special Committee of Justice charged with the task of identifying my murderer.

"If you live in Minneapolis, are at least twenty-one years of age, and belong to the ranks of the working class, and if you believe you are well equipped to serve as an investigator on my behalf, you are invited to enter the lottery. To do so, submit your name, address, occupation, and age by 5 P.M. TOMORROW at Temple Court, corner of Washington and Hennepin Aves.

"On Friday, the fourth of September, at two o'clock in the afternoon, a drawing will be held in the offices of Michael Gozzard, attorney-at-law, 301 Temple Court, to select the three individuals who will become my Committee of Justice. Members will receive a generous stipend while they investigate and will have one month to do their work. If their efforts result in the conviction of the guilty party, they shall each receive $10,000 along with my eternal gratitude and that of all the good people of Minneapolis."

As might be imagined, Pemberton's offer caused a great sensation, and in cramped working-class households from Cedar-Riverside to the Near North to the Bohemian Flats people could talk of little else. Ten thousand dollars in those hard times amounted to a fortune, enough to lift a man or woman out of whatever hole they'd been born in and up into the light of a much better existence. And so, over simple dinners where potatoes and coarse bread appeared far more frequently than choice cuts of meat, thousands of Minneapolitans reached the same conclusion: "I will put in my name, for what have I to lose?"

*

Pemberton's death three days earlier had prompted a substantial story in the *Tribune,* not only because he was a prominent figure but also because of the sudden and unexpected way in which he'd met his end. But the *Tribune*'s account, which was part news story and part obituary, did not suggest that his death had been anything other than a tragic mishap.

"George Pemberton, a well-known lawyer who championed the working people of Minneapolis, was found dead early Saturday morning, having fallen down the basement steps in his home at Central Park Terrace. He was found, insensible, at the bottom of the staircase by his daughter, Miranda, when she returned home late that evening. She immediately summoned aid and Mr. Pemberton was rushed to the city hospital, where he never regained consciousness and succumbed to his injuries shortly thereafter.

"The police were called to the scene to delve into the circumstances of the death, but Chief Smith stated there was no evidence of foul play. 'The stairway is steep and poorly lit, and it appears Mr. Pemberton stumbled and fell as he started down the steps. It has all the hallmarks of a tragic accident.'

"Mr. Pemberton, who was in his late fifties, had long represented the interests of the city's unions and served as general counsel for the Minnesota State Federation of Labor. He also served as defense counsel in several prominent criminal cases. He was known for his pugnacity in the courtroom and for his fiery orations on behalf of union causes. During the railway strike in 1894, he represented several men charged with rioting and secured their acquittals while exposing irregularities in the police department that led to the resignation of Chief Albert Garvin.

"Long active in politics, Mr. Pemberton was a staunch Democrat and ran twice for Congress, losing both times. In July, he delivered a well-received speech on behalf of William Jennings Bryan at the Democratic National Convention in Chicago.

"A native of Massachusetts, Mr. Pemberton arrived in Minneapolis in the 1870s and immediately opened a law practice. He later began investing in real estate and was so successful that he was reputed to be one of the city's wealthiest property owners. He was a member of several law firms over the years, most recently being in partnership with Thomas Blair, who stated this morning that he was shocked by his partner's untimely death. 'Mr. Pemberton was a dear friend, a superb lawyer, and a man of deep and genuine convictions,' Blair said. 'I can only cherish his memory now.'

"His daughter is Mr. Pemberton's sole survivor, his wife having died last year. Funeral arrangements are pending."

*

The press saw in Pemberton's notice the making of a once-in-a-lifetime story, and Gozzard was instantly besieged by reporters, much to his delight. Known around the courthouse as "Gozzard the Buzzard," he was a rough-hewn and flamboyant defense attorney whose stable of clients included saloonkeepers, madams, gamblers, and anyone else who, as he liked to say, "isn't threatened by respectability."

Still, the press openly wondered why Gozzard—rather than Pemberton's longtime law partner, Blair—had been given the task of carrying out his final wishes. Although Blair refused to speak to reporters about the situation, it was known in legal circles, if not yet to the newspapers, that the partners had had a falling out some months earlier and were supposedly preparing to dissolve their relationship. But as to what had caused the sudden breakup, no one seemed to know.

When asked by a reporter why Pemberton had hired him, Gozzard said, "Can't say that I know for sure, but I guess he believed he could trust me. He represented the common man, and so do I. We were very similar in that regard."

"So the two of you were friends?"

"No. I hardly knew him. But it's something isn't it, what he's done? It's going to be an adventure, and I'm glad to be part of it."

"Do you believe Mr. Pemberton was murdered?" the reporter asked.

"I have no idea," Gozzard said. "We'll just have to see, won't we."

Hardly had the first copies of the *Tribune* hit the streets before hopefuls began appearing at Temple Court. There, in the building's expansive atrium, they were directed to long tables equipped with pencils, paper, and envelopes of identical size and make. Under the watchful eyes of guards, candidates for the committee were told to write out the necessary information on the paper provided, seal it in an envelope, and then deposit the envelope in an outsized wicker basket.

A line quickly formed, for there were then many unemployed men in the city with time on their hands, and extra guards were called in to manage the crowd. By late afternoon—as mills and factories disgorged their workers, teamsters parked their drays, laborers dropped their shovels, and seamstresses abandoned their sewing machines—a new wave of hopefuls arrived at Temple Court, the line growing so long that it snaked around the atrium and out the building's main doors onto Washington Avenue.

Newspaper reporters trolled the line, fishing for tales of sadness and woe. There were men who'd been out of work since the great crash of ninety-three, widows struggling to feed their children, wage slaves staring at a life with no hope of surcease from their labors, and the usual lost souls and dreamers who collected like dust in the dark corners of the city. Ten thousand dollars! Why, it would be as the touch of God's own hand, a miraculous balm for all the harsh ailments of existence, and every man and woman in line believed they deserved the prize as much as anyone else, and perhaps more so.

The newsies also pursued Pemberton's daughter, Miranda, but she steadfastly refused to make any statement. As his only surviving child, Miranda had been as surprised as anyone by the lottery plan. She'd also been deeply hurt. Even though she was her father's sole surviving flesh and blood, he'd decided to bring in three strangers to investigate his death, leaving her out in the cold, and she wondered why.

"Sorry, but I can't explain why your father did what he did," Gozzard said when Miranda reached him by telephone. "It's as much as mystery to me as it must be to you. But he made a point of telling me that you and Mr. Dixon are to be present when the committee is convened. So perhaps he has something in mind for you. He also asked his bookkeeper, Mr. Ledger, to attend the meeting."

In addition to being Pemberton's private secretary, Paul Dixon was Miranda's fiancé, and she was pleased to hear that they would not be entirely shut out of the proceedings. "Well, that is something, I suppose," Miranda said. "Still, this lottery business is so bizarre that I must wonder whether Father was of sound mind when he conceived of it."

"I can only tell you that he seemed plenty sharp the last time I spoke with him," Gozzard said.

"Let us hope that was the case. Now, I have one other question for you. Did Father say anything to you about his will?"

"We had some discussions about it, which were in confidence. I am not at liberty to say more."

"I find that very strange. You must have seen the will. I assume the entire estate will go to me."

"That might be a safe assumption."

Miranda was hardly satisfied by that answer. "You are sounding rather evasive, Mr. Gozzard. I need to see the will. I haven't been able to find it among my father's possessions or in his safe-deposit box at the bank. Do you have it at your office?"

"No, but I'm confident it will turn up."

"What happens if it doesn't?"

"Then it will become a matter for the probate court. But as his sole heir, the estate would be yours alone under the law, absent some disqualifying circumstance."

"What do you mean by a 'disqualifying circumstance'?"

"Well, if it were discovered, say, that you had murdered your father—a perfectly ridiculous idea, of course—then you could not inherit. But as I said, I wouldn't fret too much over the will. I'm sure everything will work out for you."

"I hope you're right. But I do not mind saying that I find all of this very distressing. First, my father decides to secrete his will in a place where no one can find it and then he orders up an utterly absurd investigation into his death. Tell me, when is this death committee, as the newspapers are calling it, to be convened?"

"As soon as possible after the lottery. I will keep you informed."

"You do that," Miranda said, and only later did it occur to Gozzard that at no point during their conversation had she expressed grief over her father's death.

*

After Miranda's phone call, Gozzard thought back to his first and only meeting with George Pemberton a fortnight before his death. Gozzard had been surprised when Pemberton called to request the meeting, since they were barely acquainted. Pemberton had appeared gaunt and ashen when he arrived at Gozzard's office, attributing his stricken appearance to a gastrointestinal disturbance that had left him violently ill for days.

"I am recovering now," he said, "but I fear I was poisoned—arsenic probably—and I may not be long for this world, which is why I have come to see you, Mr. Gozzard. There are things you need to do for me, and I must insist that you carry out my wishes exactly. If you do so, you will receive a handsome fee for your work."

"How handsome?"

"I should think two thousand dollars would suffice."

"Yes, that would do nicely. But I'm curious why you want me to represent you in whatever this matter is. Our paths have not really crossed before."

"Let's just say I believe you're the perfect man for the job, given your reputation as a lawyer who isn't afraid of a little trickery, if that's what it takes to win a case. And trickery is very much what I have in mind."

"I see. Just what is it you want me to do?"

Pemberton then explained his plan, beginning with the notice to be placed in the *Tribune*. The plan seemed more than a little cockeyed to Gozzard, but he had to admit he was impressed. Pemberton had thought through everything down to the last detail.

"Well, that's quite a scheme," Gozzard said. "But is it legal? I could see a case being made for fraud."

"It cannot be fraud if everything is made good in the end, as it will be."

"Very well, but I'm still rather confused. If you truly believe you are about to be murdered, or indeed that you've been poisoned, you should go to the police and tell them what you know. I presume you suspect someone."

"I suspect a number of people," Pemberton said, "but I lack proof. As for the police, they are worthless, as I wrote in the notice. Now, can I count on you, Mr. Gozzard? Will you carry out my plan?"

Many lawyers would have wanted no part of what Pemberton intended to do, but Gozzard was intrigued, if cautious.

"I could get in big trouble over this," he said.

"Yes, but it could also make you the most famous lawyer in this city, and that would hardly be bad for business, would it."

True enough, Gozzard thought. "All right, I'll do it, Mr. Pemberton. But what if you aren't murdered, as you fear, and live for many more years?"

"Then we shall have to revisit this matter, I suppose," Pemberton said. "But I sincerely doubt that will happen."

*

Once Pemberton died, just as he had predicted, Gozzard set to work. He sent the notice, word for word as Pemberton had written it, to the *Tribune* and then began preparing for the lottery, which turned into a huge public spectacle. By the time the entry deadline was reached, so many envelopes had piled up in the wicker basket at Temple Court that it required two men to bring it up to Gozzard's office, where per Pemberton's instructions it was kept under lock and key, with a guard stationed outside around the clock.

As the time for the two o'clock drawing approached, news reporters gathered outside Gozzard's office along with a curious crowd eager to learn who would gain the chance to win $10,000. Miranda and Dixon arrived at one thirty and had to elbow their way into the office as the reporters swarmed around them. Gozzard welcomed them inside and told them they could watch the drawing from a small anteroom to avoid the press. At ten to two, Gozzard finally admitted reporters and a few members of the crowd to his office, where the basket filled with entries rested atop a low table.

At precisely two o'clock Gozzard raised his arms to quiet the buzzing crowd and said, "We are here today, in accord with the wishes of Mr. George Pemberton, to select the names of three people who will investigate his death. I do not know why Mr. Pemberton decided upon this course of action, nor can I speculate on the circumstances that led up to his death last month. I am simply here to do as he asked me."

Without further comment, Gozzard reached into the basket, which contained several thousand entries, fished his hand around, and pulled out an envelope. Reporters crowded up close to the table as Gozzard slit open the envelope, removed the slip of paper inside, and, with the studied solemnity of a minister at a funeral, said, "The first person selected to serve on the committee is Mrs. Annie Nichols, 525 Sixth Avenue South, union organizer by occupation."

"Why, that is Peter Nichols's widow," said a voice from the crowd.

"Silence please," Gozzard commanded as he picked out another envelope and read the name inside. "Mr. Walter Snook, 111 Ninth Street South, teamster by occupation." The final selection was Frances Reed, identified as a seamstress who lived on Fifth Street South.

Once Reed's name been announced, a ripple of disbelief ran through the virtually all-male crowd. "What a mistake," muttered one man. "How does anyone expect two women to be of use?"

Gozzard again hushed the crowd and said, "Now then, here is what will happen next. First, I will take steps to verify the identity of the three people who have been selected. Assuming they are legitimate, I will meet privately with them to lay out the process by which they are to investigate Mr. Pemberton's death in accord with his instructions. After that, they will conduct the investigation as they see fit over the course of one month. The committee members will be required to submit a final report on their findings, regardless of whether they discover evidence of foul play in Mr. Pemberton's death. That is all I have to say for the moment. Good afternoon."

The drawing had come just in time to allow the *Minneapolis Journal* to incorporate a brief story in its late afternoon edition. ONE MAN AND TWO WOMEN ON PEMBERTON DEATH COMMITTEE, said the headline. The story below listed the names and addresses of the committee members but otherwise provided little information.

*

That evening, Annie Nichols returned home from her day's work as an organizer for the American Federation of Labor. Her daughter, Sophia, greeted her excitedly at the door, a copy of the *Journal* in her hand.

"Look at this, Mother," she said. "It says here you're on Mr. Pemberton's death committee. Won't that be exciting!"

"Whatever are you talking about?"

"Just read the article. You'll see."

"All right, sweetheart," Nichols said as she took off her coat. "Give me a minute and I'll look at it." She went to her favorite chair, removed the shoes that were pinching her sore feet, and asked Sophia to make some tea. "Now then, show me the article."

When Nichols read it, she was stunned, for the simple reason that she had not entered her name in the lottery.

2.
A SECRET REVEALED

THE DAY AFTER her obviously fraudulent selection as a member of the committee, Nichols paid a call on Gozzard. Like her late husband, Peter, and her deceased mother-in-law, Sophia Westerly, Nichols was a forceful personality who wasn't afraid to speak her mind. But a lingering sadness had clouded her days and nights since Peter's death two years earlier, at age fifty-two, from a kidney ailment. Her grief had been compounded when Mrs. Westerly passed away, at eighty-three, only a month later.

Afterward, Nichols threw herself into her union work and caring for her daughter. Although she'd inherited the bulk of her mother-in-law's multimillion-dollar estate, including a towering old mansion, Nichols remained in the modest home she and Peter had shared for years. She sold the mansion, established charitable funds with her newly acquired fortune, and at age fifty found herself fending off a procession of much younger suitors hoping to strike it rich. The newspapers were taken with her story, the *Minneapolis Journal* dubbing her "the wealthiest working woman in Minneapolis" while commenting on how strange it was for her to be living "a simple life" when she could "easily afford luxuries of every kind."

But no matter how busy Nichols kept herself, it wasn't enough to chase away the grief that haunted her. During her long nights alone,

Peter's warm presence beside her forever gone, she often felt lost in a dark fog that refused to lift, and she had come to believe that her heart would never heal. Curiously, the surprising news that she'd "won" a lottery she hadn't entered served to buoy her spirits. It was a mystery, something to occupy her thoughts instead of dreadful memories. She called Gozzard and demanded to see him at once.

"Clearly, a fraud has been committed, and I am wondering why I should be a party to it," she told Gozzard after the lawyer, who smelled of alcohol and cigars, ushered her into his office. Gozzard was in his early forties, clean shaven, with coal-black hair that he obviously dyed, and lively brown eyes. He somehow reminded Nichols of a carnival barker, the kind who could convince you to pay your hard-earned dollar to see the bearded lady.

For his part, Gozzard was immediately impressed with Nichols. She was quite attractive, with a fine Irish face, auburn hair going to gray, and a pleasing figure beneath a teal dress accented at the sleeves and bodice with patterned white lace. "Elegant" was the word that came to his mind. But there was no Irish twinkle in her eyes, which were steel gray and so probing that when she looked at Gozzard he felt as though he was in the witness box and about to be stripped naked by an intense cross-examination.

"I fear I don't know what you mean by fraud," Gozzard said.

Nichols tried to read his expression, hunting for a lie, but his eyes gave nothing away. "Oh, come now. You are surely aware that I did not enter the lottery."

"Is that so? Well, that *is* a mystery, isn't it. Perhaps someone else entered your name. There would be no way of knowing, of course, if that was the case."

"Why would someone do that?"

Gozzard shrugged. "Who can say? Perhaps you have a secret friend."

"I doubt that. And what of the other two people on the committee? Were they really selected at random?"

"I can't comment on the workings of the lottery, other than to say that I followed Mr. Pemberton's instructions in every respect."

"You didn't answer my question."

"I answered it insofar as I am able."

Nichols said, "Why don't you tell me what's really going on here? You do know, of course, that Mr. Pemberton and I were acquainted."

"That is news to me. How did you come to know him?"

Nichols sighed and said, "All right, I'll play your little game. He represented my late husband, Peter, in that terrible business at the Huntington Mill."

*

The "terrible business" was an explosion in 1886 that leveled the flour mill, killing a night watchman. Coming just weeks after the deadly Haymarket affair in Chicago, the explosion had at first been blamed on "labor saboteurs." Amid much speculation and finger-pointing in the newspapers, suspicion immediately fell on Peter Nichols, who worked at the mill and who had been attempting to organize its workers into a union. Despite a lack of evidence, Peter Nichols might well have been brought up on charges had not Pemberton stepped in to represent him. With his client's help, Pemberton soon exposed the mill's lax safety protocols, and the explosion was ultimately ruled an accident.

Annie Nichols had gotten to know Pemberton well during those difficult days and learned they had much in common. Both had been born to impoverished families in the old industrial town of Haverhill, Massachusetts, although they'd never met there. At sixteen, Pemberton had gone to work in a tannery beside the poisoned waters of the Merrimack River, while Nichols labored in one of the city's many shoe factories.

Smart and ambitious, Pemberton had by age nineteen talked his way into a job clerking for a lawyer who'd befriended his parents, and he proved so good at the work that he realized he'd found his calling. Like thousands of other New Englanders, he eventually made his way west, finally settling in Minneapolis, where he married after establishing a lucrative legal practice and then began to invest with great shrewdness in real estate.

Nichols, née Doherty, had managed to escape Haverhill in her twenties, when she migrated to Minneapolis and found work in the offices of one of the big milling companies. She'd met and married

Peter Nichols a few years later, and over time they'd become a kind of union power couple, despised by employers but much admired by the working people they represented.

Although Nichols would always appreciate what Pemberton had done for her husband, she'd never been entirely comfortable in the lawyer's presence. He was a man with a roving eye, and she'd always had the feeling he hoped to seduce her one day. After Peter's death, Pemberton had made advances, but Nichols had spurned them, and for good reason. Pemberton, she knew, was a serial womanizer who'd cheated for years on his long-suffering wife.

Nichols had learned of his disreputable behavior some years earlier after he came to her out of the blue with a request for help. He told her he'd gotten into a big jam that had all the makings of a ruinous scandal. A prostitute at one of the city's more opulent sporting palaces claimed he'd fathered a child by her. She wanted Pemberton to pay for an abortion, and she also wanted thousands of dollars in hush money.

"I have found you to be quite an exceptional woman," Pemberton told Nichols, "and I believe you could help me, just as I helped your husband at a dire moment." Nichols didn't like the idea of wading into Pemberton's sleazy business, but she felt she owed it to him because of his work on behalf of her husband. So it was that she agreed to help.

By dint of shrewd questioning and some digging into the prostitute's very checkered background, Nichols was able to demonstrate that she was lying about her pregnancy and was simply trying to blackmail Pemberton. Nichols threatened the woman with criminal prosecution, and she quickly withdrew her paternity claim. Pemberton was so grateful he sent Nichols a huge bouquet of flowers, addressed to "my favorite detective." But Nichols went out of her way afterward to avoid Pemberton, feeling she'd dirtied her hands by coming to his aid in such an unsavory matter.

Now, Pemberton wanted Nichols to investigate his death but had asked for her help in a bizarre, roundabout way. It was all very curious, and Nichols wasn't sure what to think.

*

"Yes, I vaguely recall what happened at the mill," Gozzard said as Nichols forced her thoughts back into the present, "but the fact that you knew Mr. Pemberton is irrelevant to the matter at hand. As I have said, you were selected quite by chance to serve on the committee."

"And what if I say 'no' to this sham?"

"Well, no one can force you to serve. If you wish to decline, another name will be drawn. However, given that Mr. Pemberton did such good work on your late husband's behalf, I should think you would have an interest in investigating his death."

"Do you believe he was murdered?"

"I have no opinion on that question. It will be up to the committee to arrive at an answer."

Nichols was of two minds about her mysterious appointment—for that is how she viewed it—to the committee. On one hand, she still felt she owed Pemberton for his signal service on her husband's behalf. Yet she greatly disliked the underhanded means by which she had been placed on the committee. And, for that matter, could she really trust anything Gozzard had told her?

"If Mr. Pemberton, as it seems, wanted me to look into his death, why didn't he simply ask that I do so? Why this great charade instead?"

"It is not a charade," Gozzard insisted. "But as to Mr. Pemberton's motives in establishing the committee, I confess ignorance. All I know is that he wanted it done and that he asked me to carry out his wishes. And now that you're here, I can fulfill another one of my instructions from Mr. Pemberton by giving you this. I was told you were to receive it, in private, prior to the committee's first meeting."

Gozzard took a sealed envelope bearing Nichols's name from his desk drawer and handed it to her. Inside, she found a handwritten note, which offered yet one more surprise. She read it slowly while Gozzard did his best to appear nonchalant.

"My dear Mrs. Nichols, now that you have been selected for my death committee, I imagine that you are wondering why I did so. The explanation is simple. As I told you during that unfortunate blackmail matter, I believe you to be a woman of exceptional intelligence, and I need you more than anyone else to be on my committee. You will find the committee to be a most interesting group, for there are secrets to be uncovered, and you are the one person I can trust to pursue the truth, wherever it may lead. My murderer is close at hand, of that I am certain, and if you and certain other committee members can bring him (or her) to justice, you will have my undying gratitude. With the utmost respect, I am faithfully yours, George Pemberton."

Nichols read the note a second time, then folded it back into its envelope, while Gozzard offered a vague smile. He said, "Of course, I do not know the contents of the letter, but I am hopeful it will help convince you to serve on the committee."

"We'll see," Nichols said. "I still find this business very strange."

"I agree, but here we are. In any event, I can tell you that the committee will receive further instructions from Mr. Pemberton at its first meeting. Perhaps then the situation will be clarified."

"And if it isn't, then what? Am I to tell the other committee members, for example, that I don't believe my name was drawn at random?"

Gozzard lifted his hands, palms upward, in a gesture of resignation. "I really don't know, Mrs. Nichols. But I must ask you again whether you will agree to serve. If not, I will make arrangements to select a replacement."

Curiosity can be as hard to ignore as a bee sting, and Nichols felt its sharp incursion under her skin. Pemberton's carefully composed private letter had intensified her curiosity. It featured one odd phrase, about how she and "certain other committee members" could bring the murderer to justice. Why hadn't Pemberton simply referred to "the committee"? Instead, he seemed to be hinting that not everyone on the committee would be of use in the investigation. But as to what that might mean, Nichols wasn't sure.

Still, Nichols had to admit that the chance to solve a mystery, just as her beloved mother-in-law had done long ago in the murder of Ransom Everleigh, was an exciting opportunity. And maybe playing detective would help her find her way out of the gloom that had hovered around her like a powerful scent since Peter's death.

"All right," she said, "I will serve, but I will not be a party to any further deceits."

"Fair enough," Gozzard said. "The first committee meeting will be held at two o'clock on Monday at Mr. Pemberton's residence. His apartment is at 116 Willow Street, in Central Park Terrace. Do you need directions?"

"No, I know where it is," Nichols said. "I will see you tomorrow."

3.
THE COMMITTEE

CENTRAL PARK TERRACE was one of a handful of luxurious row houses that had sprung up in Minneapolis in the 1880s. Built of brick and sandstone, it sported a not always harmonious array of bays, towers, dormers, and gables in the grand Victorian manner, and so picturesque was its appearance that locals soon dubbed it "The Castle." Its ten-room apartments, spread over three stories, featured fine woodwork, parquet floors, tiled fireplaces, and stained-glass windows. Pemberton's spacious corner apartment overlooked Loring Park, which had been known as Central Park at the time the row house was completed.

Nichols appeared at Pemberton's apartment at the appointed hour. She was surprised to see a uniformed police officer guarding the stone steps leading up to the front door. The copper asked who she was and when she gave her name he nodded and told her to go ahead. She went up to the front door and rang the bell.

Gozzard answered. "Ah, Mrs. Nichols, welcome. I hope the policeman outside didn't disturb you, but I thought it wise to take precautions."

"Against what?"

"Newspapermen. They've been nosing around. One of them even tried to sneak into the apartment, hoping to find God knows what. In any case, come along. We'll get started shortly."

Reporters had also been pestering Nichols, who'd shooed them away without comment. However, another committee member—Snook—had given multiple interviews to the newspapers in which he promised that the committee, no doubt under his brilliant leadership, would find Pemberton's killer.

Gozzard led her into the front parlor, which was outfitted with a fireplace, bookcases, oriental rugs, floor lamps, and furniture of the massive sort favored by Victorian gentlemen. Under normal circumstances, the room's tall windows would have admitted a decent amount of daylight, but heavy drapes were drawn shut, presumably to prevent curious newshounds from trying to peek inside. Nichols found to her surprise that she was one of six people who had been summoned to meet with Gozzard, and she wasn't sure why. The committee, as far as she knew, was to consist of only three members.

Gozzard soon made introductions, giving Nichols a chance to make quick study of the group, beginning with Walter Snook. About forty, he was short and slender, with wide-set brown eyes, a full head of hair, and a pencil mustache. Nichols knew quite a few teamsters, who were usually rough, profane, and headstrong, the sort of men always ready for a good brawl. But Snook, who wore a well-fitted blue suit, looked more like a clerk or salesman than the burly teamster Nichols had expected him to be. As the only man on the committee, he'd assume that he would be in charge, but Nichols had other ideas.

Frances Reed was quite striking, taller than most women, with long black hair cascading down to her shoulders, and full-figured in a way that conveyed a voluptuary air. She wore a simple but elegant gray dress, presumably of her own making. Nichols found Reed's beautiful oval face hard to read, but her intense hazel eyes suggested both shrewdness and passion. She might prove to be a useful ally, Nichols thought, especially if Snook became troublesome.

When Reed was introduced, however, Miranda Pemberton shook her head with a look of disgust, then whispered something in her fiancé's ear. Nichols didn't hear what she said, but it seemed obvious that Miranda knew Reed well enough to deeply dislike her. Miranda then asked a surprising question as she turned back to stare at Reed. "Are you really sure, Mr. Gozzard, that all of these committee members were selected at random?"

"I can assure you, Miss Pemberton, that the lottery was conducted entirely in accord with your father's wishes," Gozzard replied. *An evasive answer if there ever was one,* Nichols thought, but Miranda didn't pursue the point.

Stanley Ledger, Pemberton's aptly named bookkeeper, was the next to be introduced. He was tall and lanky, perhaps thirty-five, with a long equine face and a thatch of thin red hair. His blue-gray eyes radiated a sense of self-satisfaction and surety, as though his judgments, financial or otherwise, were beyond reproach. "I really don't see why any of this is necessary," he told the group. "Mr. Pemberton is just playing with us for malicious fun, if you ask me. We all know how much he loved a good drama."

"That's a queer thing to say," Paul Dixon noted. "What do you mean by it?"

"Why, just that this is going to be a big show, and we're the actors. But what's the point of it?"

"I do not think of this as a show," Miranda protested. "It is a very serious business."

"Agreed," Gozzard said. "Now, let us move on."

Miranda Pemberton and her beau, Paul Dixon, were the last to be welcomed to the group. Clearly lovebirds, they sat next to each other on a settee, touching in a way that suggested to Nichols that they'd already been intimate. Miranda, still in a black mourning dress, was no great beauty but certainly attractive, with lustrous blonde hair, delicate features, and bright blue eyes. There was hint of poutiness about her, perhaps understandable given the circumstances. Nichols guessed that Miranda was no more than twenty-five, old enough to be on her own yet perhaps a bit too young to understand all that goes on in the world.

Paul Dixon was also in black, although a bright red tie offset the somber color of his suit. He was undeniably handsome and conveyed a sense of smooth, effortless urbanity. Perhaps ten years older than Miranda, he was dark-haired and dark-eyed and wore a neatly clipped Van Dyke beard. Showy rings—two flashing diamonds, another holding a big ruby—decorated his fingers, and Nichols suspected he'd come from a wealthy background. Given his elegant appearance and manners, it was not surprising that he'd won over Miranda.

Nichols was tempted to blow up the meeting by telling the truth about the sham lottery. Since she hadn't been selected by chance, it was no stretch to think that the same held true for Reed and Snook. But until she learned more, Nichols thought it best to keep playing out the fiction that the three of them had been put on the committee by the luck of the draw, if only because well-clothed lies could sometimes be more revealing than the naked truth.

Once the introductions were over, no one seemed interested in making small talk as Gozzard got up and went to an ornate library table that had been pulled into the center of the room. He removed a large manila envelope, sealed with wax, from the table's center drawer, and made a small show of opening it. Inside were four typewritten sheets titled "Instructions to the Investigators, to Be Followed Without Fail."

"Thank you all for being here," Gozzard said. "Now then, let us get down to business. I have before me Mr. Pemberton's instructions to the committee, which I am seeing for the first time. I will now read them to you. I ask that you reserve any questions until after I have finished. Thank you."

The instructions began with a greeting to the committee, followed by a general statement of purpose. "Your task, put simply, is to find out who murdered me. No matter how my death was made to appear, you may be certain that it was not accidental. Now, I am relying upon you to identify the calculating criminal who took my life."

Surprisingly, Pemberton offered no real explanation for his decision to stage the lottery. "You may be wondering why the three of you were selected in such a peculiar manner. Please believe me when I say I had very good reasons for doing so. You need not know those reasons at present, but in time they will become apparent."

Pemberton went on to state that Miranda, Dixon, and Ledger were to serve as "ex-officio members of the committee, privy to its work, but without voting power. You may regard it as strange that I have assigned a secondary role in this investigation to my dear Miranda. However, just as a physician is ill-advised to minister to a loved one, lest his emotions get the better of his judgment, so it is in this matter. I pray that Miranda will understand and respect my decision."

Miranda, however, wasn't assuaged. "Frankly, this in insulting," she said. "Surely my father knew he could trust me in all matters, and yet here he is clearly saying otherwise. I do not mind telling you I regard this so-called committee as a farce."

"Now, now, my dear, don't take umbrage," Dixon said, putting a hand on Miranda's shoulder. "I, too, feel left out of this business, but I'm sure your father sincerely believed it was the best thing to do."

"I must ask again that all of you refrain from any comments until I have finished," Gozzard said with a trace of irritation. "Now, let us continue."

The next part of Pemberton's instructions dealt with what he described as two "obvious attempts" on his life in the weeks before his death. On July 30, he wrote, he had "nearly been run down by a wagon whose driver clearly aimed to trample me under his team. I eluded the racing horses only at the last instant. I caught a mere glimpse of my assailant as he thundered past, but I am certain he was wearing an eye patch." Pemberton reported that the second attempt to kill him occurred in mid-August, when he became so ill that he "hovered at the brink of death. I believe someone tried to poison me, presumably with arsenic, and it was only due to my strong constitution that I survived."

Then came a bombshell as Pemberton identified the "prime suspect" in his alleged murder—Thomas Blair. "Mr. Blair, I discovered only recently, is a shameful, dishonest man who stole money from me and from our clients to support his vices, which are numerous. The committee should thoroughly investigate him, especially as to his whereabouts at the time of my death. But be warned: Mr. Blair is a slippery character, and he will be as a spooked fish, difficult to hook."

Miranda now interrupted again. "Well, this is news to me. Mr. Blair a thief? That seems very unlikely. Wouldn't you agree, Mr. Ledger?"

"Well, I, I could not say," Ledger stammered. "But if you are suggesting—"

Gozzard said, “Please, no more of this. Let me continue with the instructions.”

“The committee should not, however, limit its inquiries to Mr. Blair,” Pemberton wrote, “since he may have had help in undertaking his defalcations. As a result, it is possible that some other individual, highly secretive and with malignant intent, effected my demise. The committee must always be on the lookout for such a person as it goes about its work.” To Nichols, it seemed as though Pemberton must have known who this “malignant” actor was, yet he hadn’t named the person. She wondered why.

The next big reveal concerned a safe. “There is in the main bedroom of my residence a wall safe, behind a painting of a sailing scene on Lake Calhoun. The committee is to open this safe, in the presence of all its members, using the combination I will provide below. There is evidence in this safe that will be of use to you, and the sooner you examine it the more speedily your investigation will proceed.”

The remainder of the instructions covered a range of topics. The committee, Pemberton wrote, was free to set its own rules as to how it would proceed. The three voting members were to receive a stipend of $1,000 each for their work, which was to terminate at the end of thirty days, regardless of their findings. No police were to be involved in the investigation. Only upon a grand jury indictment of a murder suspect would the $10,000 prize be awarded to each committee member or “otherwise divided as the members see fit,” a clause that to Nichols seemed pregnant with mischief. Finally, Gozzard was to serve as a “legal adviser and facilitator” who would “assist the committee by all possible means” as it went about its work.

Pemberton’s instructions concluded with an exhortation. “My dear committee members, you are pursuers of the truth and agents of justice. Be fearless in your task and show the world what common men and women can do. I pray for your success.”

“Now then, are there any questions?” Gozzard asked.

Nichols could think of many, chief among them whether Snook and Reed were “plants” like her. Judging by her question to Gozzard, Miranda appeared to believe that Reed’s selection was hardly on the up-and-up. Nichols strongly suspected that Snook hadn't landed on the committee by accident either. She wondered once again if she should tell them both how she'd been handpicked by Pemberton. Perhaps they'd then be honest with her. But she couldn't make herself do it, at least not yet. Pemberton had gone to a lot of trouble to set up what might be an elaborate charade, but why?

Snook asked several questions focusing on how the committee members would be paid. Reed was also interested in the money, inquiring whether the $10,000 reward would be given out even if someone indicted for Pemberton's murder was ultimately acquitted. It would be, Gozzard assured her. She also asked what Nichols regarded as an excellent question: Did the committee have to act as a group, or could members investigate on their own?

"I cannot answer that for you," Gozzard said. "You are free to make your own rules. However, I think it would be wise for the committee to meet regularly and share information. Otherwise, well, there could be bad blood, as I'm sure you understand."

"I agree," Nichols said. "We should meet at least once a week. Mr. Snook and Miss Reed, do you agree?"

"I do," said Snook, "so long as you ladies don't try to interfere with me too much. I have my own way of doing things."

"As do I," Reed said, "and I certainly will feel no need to 'interfere' with you, Mr. Snook. But, yes, I agree, we should hold regular meetings. And we seem to have a starting point—that wagon driver with an eye patch. There can't be too many such men in the city."

"They're more common than you might think," Snook said. "I've run across several fellows like that over the years."

"Be that as it may, it shouldn't be too hard to track them down," Reed said.

"Maybe. I'll start nosing around."

"You do that," said Nichols. "Now, instead of more talk, I think it's time for action. Why don't we a take look at what's in that safe?"

4.
UNEXPECTED DISCOVERIES

When Miranda led the committee up to her father's second-floor bedroom, they encountered a disturbing sight. A man, perhaps in his fifties, dressed only in a union suit, was sprawled out on the bed, apparently asleep, an open jewel box and a bottle of whiskey beside him. With his dirty, unkempt hair, stubbled face, and bulbous red nose, the man looked like a habitué of the city's ever expanding skid row. But how had he found his way into George Pemberton's bedroom?

It was obvious that the man had been rummaging through the room before deciding to take a rest from his criminal labors. He'd pulled open all the drawers in a highboy, leaving clothes strewn about, and he'd also gone through a wardrobe, none too carefully. Of even more concern, he'd discovered the wall safe whose contents the committee had come to examine, although it didn't appear he'd been able to open it.

"This is an outrage," Gozzard said as he tried to herd the committee members back downstairs. "I will notify the police at once and have this man removed. He is a vagrant and a thief by the look of him."

"There is no need for that," Miranda said. She went over to the bed and shook the sleeping man, who reeked of alcohol. "All right, Freddie, wake up now. Come on, wake up."

The man's eyes slowly opened, then he sat up and said to Miranda, "I was just resting, my dear. Who the devil are these other people?"

"The more pertinent question," Gozzard said, "is who the devil are *you*?"

Miranda answered for him. "This is Freddie Pemberton, my uncle. Apparently, he has decided to take up a new career as a burglar. How did you get in here?"

"Why, I have a key," he said, slurring his words. "Georgie gave it to me. And I am certainly not a burglar. I was merely looking for something."

Freddie was George Pemberton's younger brother, a toper and a scamp who'd never made anything of himself. Instead, he'd relied for years on his older brother's largesse, living in a spare bedroom on the apartment's third floor. But as Freddie's binges grew ever more destructive, Pemberton had finally evicted him, telling Miranda, "I might as well just buy a saloon and let Freddie drink himself to death, as I see no hope that he will ever change."

After Freddie retrieved his trousers and shirt from the floor and made himself decent, he wobbled up to his feet and said, "You have disturbed my slumber. Now, go away, the lot of you!"

Miranda said, "You're the one who must go. You have no business being here."

"Why, I have every right. I am investigating, and you can't stop me. You see, Georgie was murdered. I am sure of it."

Miranda rolled her eyes and said, "Of course you are. I imagine you found all the clues you needed in that bottle of yours."

Dixon said, "I think it would be best if we escorted Freddie out. He's just looking for something to steal."

"Why, that is a damn lie and a slur upon my character!" Freddie protested. "I am no fool. I know things."

"I see. And you tried to open the wall safe, I suppose, to learn even more, is that it?" Miranda said, her words cutting like acid.

"No, I was just curious, that's all. Georgie had secrets, you know, plenty of them."

"We're wasting our time," Dixon said. "Come along, Freddie, time to leave."

"I won't! This is my house now."

"Don't be absurd," Miranda said. "This was never your house and never will be. Now, just what have you been stealing, you old drunk? Let's see what you have in your pockets."

As Miranda advanced toward him, Freddie backed away and swatted at her as if she was a noxious insect. A wrestling match between niece and uncle might have ensued had not Snook gotten behind Freddie and pinned his arms to his side. "Stop struggling," he said, "or I will have to lay you out."

While Snook kept Freddie under control, Miranda went through his pants pockets—a rather indelicate business for a woman, or so Nichols thought—and after some digging emerged with a gold pocket watch.

The watch was a family heirloom, given to George Pemberton by his father, and when Miranda found it she couldn't contain her anger. "Why, you rotten thief," she said, and slapped Freddie so hard that he nearly sobered up. "I should have you thrown in jail."

"Well, it was promised to me, that's all I have to say," Freddie replied as he tried, unsuccessfully, to slip away from Snook.

Gozzard said, "All right, I think that is quite enough. Miranda, is it your wish that your uncle be turned over to the police?"

"No, not this time. But if I ever find you here again, Freddie, I will see to it that you are sent straight to jail for trespass and burglary. Now, Mr. Snook, would you do me the favor of escorting Freddie from my house?"

"I can do that," Snook said, grabbing Freddie under one arm. "Come along now, and don't give me any trouble or you will regret it."

"I have every right to be here," Freddie insisted, but he didn't offer any resistance as Snook hustled him out of the room as though he was ejecting an unruly drinker from a saloon.

"I apologize to all of you," Miranda said when the hubbub was over. "Families are impossible sometimes."

*

With Freddie gone, Miranda began opening the wall safe. "Father used this small safe for his most private items," she said. "I didn't even know about it until a few months ago when he gave me the combination."

"Did he share the combination with anyone else?" Reed asked.

"I do not see how that is any of your business," Miranda said.

"Well, it is our business," Reed said, staring at Miranda. "Someone with access to this safe could have forged or altered the documents your father supposedly left for us."

"That is an outlandish accusation," Miranda said, "especially coming from you. I will not stand for—"

Gozzard broke in, "Come now, ladies, let us keep to the matter at hand. We are all eager to see the evidence Mr. Pemberton gathered."

Nichols, meanwhile, was baffled. Why was there so much bad blood between Miranda and Reed?

With a final spin of the dial, Miranda opened the safe. Inside was a large manila envelope with the words "Murder File" written on it in Pemberton's distinctive hand.

"Perhaps it would be best if I open this," Gozzard said, "and then we can all have a look at what's inside."

"Fine," Snook said. "But we'll be watching like hawks."

Ignoring the teamster's comments, Gozzard went over to a writing desk in one corner of the bedroom and opened the envelope as the committee members gathered around him like gawkers at an accident. He removed a thick document bristling with legal boilerplate and paged through it before passing it around to the committee members. After they'd read—or at least tried to read—the document, Gozzard said, "I fear the legal language may be hard to follow. However, I would be happy to explain in simple terms what these documents have to say."

The documents, Gozzard said, appeared to show that Blair had set up a sizable trust fund in a huge civil case involving the dissolution of a business partnership. "It is a standard sort of agreement where there is a large amount of money in dispute. The fund, of course, must be kept in a completely separate account. It cannot by law be commingled in any way with the law firm's own accounts."

"Okay, so what's the problem?" Snook asked.

"The problem may be that the fund was not maintained in proper fashion," Gozzard said as he dug back into the envelope and removed a series of bank statements along with two pages of handwritten notes.

"I'd like to see those statements, if you don't mind," Ledger said. His face took on a quizzical look as he pored over them. "This is quite incredible," he finally said. "I was aware of certain issues with the firm's books, but I have never seen any of these statements before."

"What do they show?" Nichols asked

"Well, they appear to show that Mr. Blair transferred money—some twenty thousand dollars in all—from the law firm's trust accounts into his personal account. That, of course, could be highly improper, depending on the circumstances."

"There's more," Gozzard said. "Mr. Pemberton attached notes to the statements, and they leave no doubt he believed his partner was guilty of theft."

"The fraud here is obvious," read one of Pemberton's comments, while another said, "The crook is getting bolder. He has no shame." A note dated July 15 was especially revealing: "My dear partner now suspects that I know what he is up to. He will pay a high price when I expose him, which will be very soon."

"Sounds like a motive for murder to me," said Snook.

"Yes, but I would remind you that a motive for murder is not proof of murder," Gozzard noted. "Besides, I am not even sure these documents prove malfeasance on Mr. Blair's part. There could have been legitimate reasons for the transfers he made."

"Like what?" Snook said. "Looks to me like this Blair fellow is a thief, pure and simple."

"I agree with Mr. Gozzard," Nichols said. "We should at least talk to Mr. Blair before jumping to conclusions."

"And I'm sure the committee will do so," Gozzard said. "In the meantime, there is something else to consider. Mr. Pemberton also left a note about his brother, dated July 28. Let me read it to you: 'I believe Freddie has been sneaking into the apartment, trying to steal things or perhaps even searching for a copy of my will. I would put nothing past him—even forgery, if it came to that.'"

"No wonder we found him here," Miranda said. "He was looking for the will."

"Well, there was no will in the safe, and I do not see how a man like your uncle Freddie could have managed to open the safe and remove it," Gozzard said.

"Unless he had the combination," Reed said.

"He did not," Miranda insisted, "and it is ridiculous to suggest that he did."

"Well, perhaps we should talk to him again just to be sure," Nichols said. "Mr. Snook, is it is possible Freddie is still hanging around outside?"

"No, I let him go as soon as we got out the door. It looked like he was heading over toward the park."

"Why don't you go see if you can find him?"

"I'll stay here, if you don't mind," Snook said. "The committee should stick together right now, the way I see it. So what's next?"

Nichols said, "I have a suggestion. Our next step should be to examine the basement stairs where Mr. Pemberton met his end."

"Haven't the police already looked there?" Reed asked.

"Yes, but we should have a look for ourselves," Nichols said. "The police could have missed something."

5.
THE STAIRS

MIRANDA LED EVERYONE back downstairs and into a short hallway at the rear of the house off the kitchen. A door on one side of the hall gave access to the stairs. "As you can see, there's a landing one step down, and then you turn to go straight down to the basement," Miranda said.

A single overhead light bulb, which Miranda switched on, illuminated the landing, where a curtained recess opposite the stairs provided storage space for mops, brooms, buckets, and other cleaning equipment. The stairs themselves were narrow and very steep, and it was easy to see how Pemberton could have taken a fall.

The committee members clustered around the landing as Miranda described what had happened to her father. "I found him at the bottom of the stairs, as the newspapers said. It looked very much like he had somehow slipped and fallen. I've nearly done so myself more than once. The steps are quite treacherous."

"What's down there?" Snook asked.

"Very little," Miranda said. "The basement is musty. It's not really suitable for storing much of anything, except wine. Father kept quite a few bottles there."

"Can we have a look?" Nichols asked.

"Be my guest. But be careful and hang on to the railing."

A large wooden wine rack, filled mostly with ports and Bordeaux, stood near the bottom of the steps. An upright bottle of port, its cork protruding, caught Nichols's eye. She went over for a look and saw that the bottle was less than half full.

"Did your father usually leave opened bottles of wine down here?" she asked Miranda.

"Not that I know of," she said, picking up the bottle. "That's rather strange. Well, shall we go back up?"

"Not yet," Nichols said. "I would like to have a look at the rest of the basement."

"What for?" Snook asked.

"We are supposed to be investigating," Nichols said, "and that means we must be thorough. I am curious, for example, whether Mr. Pemberton kept any rat poison or the like here."

"Ah, I get it," Ledger said. "There's arsenic in rat poison and that could have been used for the second attempt on Mr. Pemberton's life."

"If he was indeed deliberately poisoned," Dixon noted. "Both Miranda and I got a bit ill around that same time. It could simply have been a case of food poisoning."

"Well, in either case it's worth looking around," Nichols said. "Mr. Dixon, could you fetch a lantern for us?"

An old tin labeled "Rough on Rats" was soon located on a nearby shelf. The tin proved to be nearly empty. "Well, that's rather suspicious," Dixon said.

"Do you recall your father ever using this?" Nichols asked Miranda.

"I wouldn't know. But I will say I've never seen a rat here."

"Problem is, most everybody has rat poison around the house," Gozzard noted. "So just finding it here doesn't necessarily point to Mr. Pemberton's being poisoned."

"But we can't rule it out," Nichols said as the group headed back upstairs to consider how Pemberton had taken his fatal tumble.

Once everyone had reassembled in the hallway, Nichols said to

Miranda, "Did the police or the coroner establish a time when they think your father fell?"

"They believe it must have been around midnight. He'd gone out for the evening and then returned here at a late hour. His back door key was found on the kitchen table. He must have left it there after he came in."

"Why would he have gone down to the basement after returning home?" Nichols asked.

"I imagine it was to fetch a bottle of wine," Miranda said. "That was his preferred evening drink. The police believe he simply slipped and went headfirst down the steps."

Reed asked, "Do the police know where he was that night?"

Dixon answered. "Apparently not. They told Miranda and me that they weren't able to trace his movements."

"I'm not sure how hard they tried," Miranda added. "They were convinced it was an accident, so they didn't spend a lot of time investigating."

Nichols said, "May I ask, Miss Pemberton, where you were that evening before coming home to find your father?"

"Paul and I were out late, if you must know."

"I see. Were you by yourselves or out with company?"

Miranda shot Nichols a venomous glance and said, "We were together, as might be expected with any couple in our circumstances. I see no need to say more. It was about one in the morning when Paul dropped me off here. I went to the kitchen to get a glass of milk and saw that the light over the basement steps was on, which seemed odd. That's when I found my father. As you can imagine, it was a terrible shock."

Nichols said, "I am sure it was. In any event, since we are supposed to be investigating a possible murder, let us assume for the moment that someone pushed your father down these stairs. If so, it must have been someone he knew, someone perhaps with ready access to the apartment."

"Hold it right there," Snook said. "Why did it have to be somebody he knew? Could be he surprised a burglar. You know, some fellow just jimmied his way in, which isn't all that hard, or maybe a door was left unlocked. The old man comes home, there's a fight, and the next thing you know he gets tossed down the steps."

"Father was not an old man," Miranda said, glaring at Snook, "and for your information he always locked the doors and windows before he went out. He was very wary of burglars. Besides, the police checked for signs of a break-in and found nothing. Nor was anything taken from the apartment, as far as I can tell."

"Let's not forget that Mr. Pemberton thought someone was trying to murder him," Nichols said. "He wasn't worried about a random burglar. He believed he was being targeted. Since the police found no evidence of a break-in, the murderer—if indeed there was one—must have had a key to the apartment. Miss Pemberton, do you know who else had a key besides your father?"

"Well, of course, I have one," Miranda said, "and so does Paul. Our maid, Mrs. Engstrom, also has a key."

"And don't forget that crazy uncle of yours," Snook said.

"I should very much like to forget him," Miranda said. "But yes, he might have had a key as well."

"What about Mr. Blair?" Nichols asked.

"Oh, I see no reason why he would have a key. He and father were never close friends."

Nichols was puzzled by one aspect of Pemberton's behavior on the night of his death. She said to Miranda, "You mentioned that your father's back door key was found on the kitchen table, indicating that he had come in that way. He didn't have his own carriage, did he?"

"That's a funny question. No, he never wanted the bother or expense of owning a carriage. He took cabs everywhere."

"Then wouldn't a cab have left him off that night at the front door?"

"Yes, I suppose that would have been the usual case," Miranda admitted. "It is peculiar, now that you mention it. I really don't know why he would have gone all the way around to the back."

*

That evening, as Nichols was preparing for dinner, she had an unexpected visitor. Miranda Pemberton, carrying a parasol and wearing a rather formal peplum dress with long sleeves, appeared without notice at Nichols's front door.

"I don't wish to bother you," she said as Nichols invited her into the front parlor, "but there is something you should know. It concerns Mr. Ledger." Sophia was up in her room, no doubt reading one of her detective stories, so Nichols and Miranda had the parlor to themselves. Miranda was slightly flushed, and her eyes darted around as though she feared someone might overhear their conversation.

"Are you all right?" Nichols asked. "You seem anxious."

"Do I? No, it is just that, well, I have something to say that may be of great importance."

"Then I am all ears."

"Good. You see, after we were talking about rat poison this afternoon, something occurred to me. Do you know that Mr. Ledger worked in his father's pharmacy back in Chicago, where he's from? So he would know all about poisons."

"Yes, I suppose he would, but I don't see—"

"Why he would have wanted to kill my father? I may know why. It has to do with the books."

"Go on."

"It's simple, really. Father may have learned that Mr. Ledger was embezzling money."

"I thought his suspicions were directed at Mr. Blair."

"Yes, but I think Father was wrong. I have no great affection for Mr. Blair, but you should be aware that he brought more money into the law firm than Father ever did. I don't think he would have any reason to steal."

"What if he had gambling debts or the like, as you father seemed to suggest?"

"I wouldn't know about that. However, I do know that Mr. Ledger handled all the accounts for the law firm. He could have doctored those bank statements in some way to point the finger of guilt at Mr. Blair."

"What proof do you have of this?"

Miranda hesitated before she said, "Well, I don't have any real proof—yet—but I know for a fact that Father was looking for a new bookkeeper just before he died."

"Did he say why?"

"Yes. He told me he had doubts about Mr. Ledger."

"What sort of doubts?"

"Father didn't exactly say. But I did overhear him once having an argument with Mr. Ledger. They were in Father's office at the apartment. The door was closed, but from what I could hear it was quite a violent disagreement. Afterward, Mr. Ledger stormed out."

"When did this happen?"

"It was back in July, I think."

"Do you know what they argued about?"

"No, but it must have been about money. What else would they fight over? There is something else you should be aware of. Mr. Ledger has a bad temper, and he's the sort of man who holds a grudge."

"How do you know that?"

Miranda flushed slightly and said, "Well, if you must know, he wanted to marry me, but of course I said no. There is something about him that I find quite repulsive. After I turned him down, he could hardly be civil in my presence and made many nasty remarks. I'm sure all that really interested him was the money I'd inherit from Father."

Nichols said, "Speaking of which, did your father ever show you his will—the one that has gone missing?"

"No, but there can be no doubt that I will be his sole heir," Miranda said in a firm voice. "No doubt whatsoever."

"Let us hope, then, that the will turns up soon," Nichols said. "As for Mr. Ledger, I appreciate what you've told me, but it doesn't amount to proof of wrongdoing on his part. Now, is there anything else you'd like to share with me?"

"No, but I hope you will take my concerns seriously."

"I will, and I'll pass on what you've told me to Miss Reed and Mr. Snook."

"Oh no, don't do that," Miranda said. "You are the only person on the committee I have any confidence in. That hussy Reed in particular is not to be trusted. She's a snake hiding in the grass."

"Why do you say that?"

"You don't know?" Miranda said. "I'm surprised."

"Know what?"

Miranda's face held few secrets, and anger and contempt now spread across her features like cloud shadows. "She seduced my father, that is what I know. She's an evil, depraved woman. I hate her!"

"So you are telling me she had an affair with your father?"

"More than that. She was his kept woman. It is disgusting to even think about it. What I can't understand is how she finagled her way onto the committee. Do not trust her for a second, Mrs. Nichols. She will do anything to get her hands on that ten thousand dollars."

Nichols tried to learn more from Miranda, but it was as though the mere mention of Reed's name had been too much for her to bear. "I must leave," she said. "I have said enough."

*

Although she was known in Minneapolis as a fearless advocate capable of stirring a crowd into action, Annie Nichols had grown up so shy that her parents wondered if she would ever escape from her shell. The sixth of eight children, surrounded by feral siblings in Haverhill's Irish slums, she'd been the odd child out, taking refuge in books and dreams. In school, under the harsh rule of nuns who commanded their wild Irish charges with beatings and threats of eternal damnation, she'd invariably sat in the back of the class, the silent little girl who never got into trouble and who always paid attention to her lessons.

Much later, Peter had helped her blossom into a confident and outspoken woman, yet she never regretted her quiet, insular youth. Her shyness, she knew, had been its own gift, a shield but also a window through which she closely watched all those about her, like a scientist observing some strange new species in the jungle. All that watching had taught her much about people, and reading people was, as Sherlock Holmes so often demonstrated, a powerful kind of magic.

Nichols loved the Holmes stories and had read them eagerly as they came out. When she finally settled into bed for the night, she found sleep an impossibility. Instead, she tried her hand at playing Holmes. Nichols had closely observed her fellow committee members, and just as Holmes might have done, she'd come away with some initial impressions.

She thought Frances Reed was particularly interesting, with a sultriness about her that clearly fascinated the men at the meeting. It was no secret that Pemberton had taken a number of mistresses over the years, and so Miranda's angry claim that Reed was one of them rang true. But Nichols still had trouble understanding why Pemberton would have put Reed on the committee. Did she possess incriminating information about Miranda or someone else in the Pemberton household? Or, for that matter, about Blair?

Miranda, meanwhile, had struck Nichols as being upset not only about her father's extramarital activities but also because of the uncertainty surrounding his will, and there was something unseemly about how eagerly she appeared to covet her father's multimillion-dollar estate. The missing will had clearly set her on edge, and her worry over it suggested that she had some reason to believe it might not prove to be the windfall she hoped for. Nichols was also intrigued by Miranda's unsubstantiated claims against Ledger. She seemed downright eager to paint the bookkeeper in the worst possible light, but why? Nichols wasn't sure.

As for Paul Dixon, Nichols was of a mind that he was all veneer, like a propped-up stage set, and so she had no easy way to gauge his true character. The way he behaved around Miranda left little doubt that they were extremely close. But could the two of them, eager for their freedom and a fortune, have actually plotted Pemberton's death? Nichols thought it possible—greed was as powerful a motive as any for murder. Still, Nichols found it hard to believe that Miranda, no matter how troubled, could have gone so far as to kill her father, with or without her fiancé's help.

Stanley Ledger was turning out to be a mystery as well. Was he really, as Miranda had suggested on the basis of little evidence, an embezzler who'd been confronted by her father? Nichols intended to look into that allegation, but she had a hard time picturing Ledger as a cold-blooded killer. Yet clever criminals, she knew, came in all forms. Nichols also thought Ledger's statement about the committee being a "big show" was peculiar. It suggested that he wanted to downplay the committee's work as little more than a harmless entertainment devised by Pemberton, and that was cause for suspicion.

Then there was Walter Snook, who not only seemed out of place on the committee but who didn't really look or speak like the teamster he purported to be. Nichols had expected him to be roughhewn and profane, but he wasn't. He'd worn a surprisingly nice suit to the committee meeting, and there was an aura of sophistication about him at odds with his supposed line of work. But if he, too, had been deliberately placed on the committee, Nichols had no idea why, since she knew of no connection between him and Pemberton.

And finally, there was the wild card of the day, Freddie Pemberton. Nichols hadn't seen enough of him to know whether he was simply a hapless drunk or a man on a mission, aiming to secure his share of a family fortune. But Freddie's surprising appearance in his brother's bedroom, with the wall safe there exposed if unopened, was extremely suspicious. Nichols wanted to talk to Freddie, if she could find him, in hopes of learning much more about what he might know.

Before she finally fell asleep, Nichols had one last, unhappy thought, which was that she'd stumbled into a hall of mirrors, suspects reflecting on one another at every turn, with no clear way out.

6

INTERVIEWS

THE NEXT DAY, Nichols and Reed went to speak with Alma Engstrom, Pemberton's longtime maid, at his apartment. Snook had been invited along but said he had business elsewhere and would let his fellow committee members fill him in later on what Engstrom had to say.

"Just don't try to hide anything from me," he cautioned Nichols. "Remember, we're all supposed to be in this together, like we're friends."

"I don't believe friendship is one of the committee's responsibilities," Nichols replied, coolly, "but have no fear, Mr. Snook. We will keep you informed."

Reed lived in a handsome brick row house not far from Nichols's residence, and as the day was warm and sunny, the two women decided to walk together to Pemberton's apartment. Nichols found Reed to be a likable companion. She was thoughtful, obviously intelligent, and possessed the sort of dry, sardonic wit more commonly found in men than women.

Nichols very much wanted to quiz Reed about her past relationship with Pemberton. She was equally curious as to why Pemberton had placed Reed on the death committee, as must have been the case. Still, Nichols was leery of confronting Reed and demanding answers. She might simply lie about everything. *Better,* Nichols thought, *to see whether Reed would reveal the truth on her own.*

"It is quite a strange business we find ourselves in, isn't it?" Nichols said as they made their way toward Central Park Terrace. "I have begun to wonder whether it was pure luck that put us on the committee. What do you think?"

"I think luck is a wonderful thing to have. Are you implying the lottery was somehow rigged?"

"No, I really have no idea," Nichols lied. "I was just curious, that's all. It seems odd how we were all drawn into this. As you are aware, I was acquainted with Mr. Pemberton. Did you also happen to know him?"

"It is never wise to ask a lady about her past," Reed said, "but I see no point in trying to skirt the matter. Yes, I knew him. He was quite the silver-tongued lawyer. But, of course, he turned out to be a big liar, like every man I ever met."

"I take it you've had some bad experiences."

"What woman hasn't? It's just too bad men are necessary, when you think about it. Dogs are better companions than most men will ever be, and much easier to train."

Nichols was amused. "I've found that trying to train men is usually a waste of time. Better to manipulate them if you can."

"And did you manipulate your husband?"

"No, we were the best of friends. No manipulation required."

"Then you were lucky," Reed said. "But as to the Great Crusader, as I like to call Mr. Pemberton, I'm sure Miranda told you all about my involvement with him."

They were approaching Pemberton's apartment now, Loring Park and its pretty little pond visible at the end of street. Geese frequented the pond and one had taken flight overhead, honking madly as it gained altitude. Reed watched until it disappeared behind them, then said, "Don't you love birds? They are what I have always aspired to be, a free creature."

"And yet you were a kept woman, if Miranda is to be believed."

"Here is some free advice, Mrs. Nichols: don't trust Miranda. She is a schemer if there ever was one. But it's true that I was what polite society, if there is such a thing, likes to call a kept woman. I'm sure Mr. Pemberton saw me that way—his little bird in a cage. But I had other ideas. My wings are not for clipping."

"It sounds as though the two of you had a rather tumultuous relationship."

"Is that what Miranda told you?"

"No. She just said that you had been one his lovers."

"Then we will leave it at that for the time being, although I will say that love was hardly part of the equation."

"Still, Mr. Pemberton must have had strong feelings for you. Otherwise, it is hard to understand why he would have put you the committee."

Reed deflected the question. "It's a big sham, isn't it, this so-called death committee of ours," she said. "You, of course, were no more picked by chance than I was. Nor, I imagine, was the lovely Mr. Snook a random choice, although I have no clue as to why that's the case. I guess we'll just have to let the mystery be for a while."

*

Frances Reed had first met George Pemberton a year earlier while working at a jewelry store on Nicollet Avenue. When Pemberton appeared, oozing with salacious intentions while supposedly looking for a necklace for his wife, she knew at once that he might be worth her time.

"I do not believe I have seen you here before," he said, his eyes running over her with a kind of lurid, anticipatory gleam. "My, what a beautiful woman you are."

"How nice of you to say so, sir," she said with a demure smile. "Now, how can I be of help to such a fine gentleman as yourself?"

A relationship quickly developed, the usual dance of sex and money. Pemberton set her up in a nice apartment, paid regular visits, professed his love, and even hinted that they might marry one day after his sickly wife died. She murmured how lovely that would be, doubting it would ever happen.

Born into poverty in one of Chicago's grimmest slums, Reed had discovered early on that men were remarkably easy to manipulate when it came to sex, and that there was money to be had in the bargain. But after an angry wife threatened to drag Reed into unpleasant and very public divorce proceedings, she moved to Minneapolis, where she soon encountered Pemberton. Their boudoir adventuring went on for many months until Pemberton's wife finally died.

Hoping to secure the wealth and status she'd always dreamt of, Reed pressed for marriage, but Pemberton coldly informed her that "it wouldn't look right." A huge row ensued. Reed demanded a parting payment amounting to thousands of dollars, to which Pemberton responded by calling her vile names and slapping her hard across the face. She in turn threatened to sue him for false promises and emotional suffering, but he just laughed at her. "Try it," he said, "and the whole world will know that you are nothing but a moneygrubbing whore." A month later, Pemberton was dead.

Then came his postmortem lottery, which Reed entered on a lark, only to be utterly surprised when her name was drawn. Certain her selection couldn't have been pure chance, Reed wondered why Pemberton would have wanted her—his avowed enemy—on the committee. Her best guess was that it was snare of some kind and she was the target. Pemberton, she feared, might just be trying pin his murder on her.

Reed agreed to serve on the committee nonetheless, on the theory that it was better to know what the group was doing than to be in the dark. But she knew she needed to be careful, especially around Miranda, who in Reed's view was capable of causing all manner of trouble. Nichols was perhaps an even bigger problem. She was smart and relentless, with a nose for the truth, and Reed feared what she might dig up in all the dirt George Pemberton had left behind.

*

When Nichols and Reed arrived at Pemberton's apartment and rang the bell, Engstrom opened the door. "Is there something I can do for you?" she said with a pronounced Swedish accent.

After Nichols explained their mission, Engstrom invited them into the front parlor, where they all took seats. Engstrom, who looked to be in her mid-fifties, was stout and well-bosomed, with a plump, dimpled face and pale blue eyes.

"Ja, I have heard of this committee," she said. "Miss Miranda, she told me about it. She's not here now, but if—"

"It is you we wish to see," Nichols said. "We just have a few questions."

Mostly, Nichols wanted to find out what life in the Pemberton household had been like before his death. Engstrom wasn't especially forthcoming, but after some prodding, she admitted there had been tension over Miranda and Dixon's relationship. "Mr. Pemberton, I guess he didn't want her to marry. You know how it is with fathers. They want to keep their daughters to themselves, and no other man is good enough. So, ja, there was some arguing I heard."

"So it sounds like Miranda wasn't at all happy with her father. What about Mr. Dixon? Did he and Mr. Pemberton argue over Miranda?"

"Oh, I wouldn't know. But Mr. Dixon, he is always very calm, so I don't think there would be big fights. I—"

"Did I hear my name being taken in vain?" Dixon said with a smile as he slid open the door connecting the parlor to Pemberton's home office. "Mrs. Engstrom knows everything," Dixon continued. "She is the true queen of this household."

"We were just asking about you and Miranda," Nichols said as Engstrom excused herself and went to the kitchen. "It would seem Mr. Pemberton did not approve of your match with her."

"True," Dixon said, "but he was coming around."

"Why did he oppose the marriage?"

"I will be honest," Dixon said. "He thought for a long time that Miranda should marry Mr. Blair. Miranda, of course, had other ideas. But things changed after Mr. Ledger began looking into Mr. Blair's financial activities. Once Mr. Pemberton saw what his partner was up to, he had a change of heart and I became a more appealing marriage prospect."

"So you knew about the allegations against Mr. Blair."

"Just from what Mr. Ledger told me. I think he was still trying to sort everything out when Mr. Pemberton died. Of course, now that we've found those bank records, I wouldn't be surprised if Mr. Blair is charged with embezzlement. By the way, where's Mr. Snook? I thought the committee was supposed to work as a group."

"We're not sure where Mr. Snook is at the moment," Nichols said. "He seems to like being on his own."

"A bit of a lone wolf, eh? Or maybe he just doesn't want to work with two women. Some men are like that."

"Most men, I would say," Reed noted. "All right, we should be on our way."

"Then I wish you success," Dixon said, "and I look forward to our next committee meeting."

"That was interesting," Reed said as she and Nichols left the apartment. "Clearly, Miranda and her father were not always on the best of terms."

"No, but if Mr. Dixon is to be believed, Mr. Pemberton was ready just before he died to give his blessings to their marriage," Nichols said. "I'm curious what Mr. Blair has to say about all of this. What say we head over to his office right now for a little talk."

"Shouldn't we call him first?"

"Let's surprise him. After all, fortune favors the bold."

*

The offices of Blair and Pemberton occupied a suite on the sixth floor of the Guaranty Loan Building, the largest and most splendid office structure in the city. Nichols and Reed took an elevator up through the building's huge light court and then walked along a vertiginous glass-floored gallery to reach the offices. There, the lawyer's all-purpose assistant, Beatrice Emerson, told them Blair was busy and that they should schedule a meeting with him for another time.

"Why don't you tell Mr. Blair that Mrs. Annie Nichols and Miss Frances Reed have urgent business with him concerning the death of his former law partner. I believe he will want to see us at once."

Moments later, Blair emerged from his private office and said, "I was afraid you'd be coming by. Out to earn your ten thousand dollars, are you? Well, I wish you good luck, but I want no part of it. Where's that fellow, Snook, by the way? Isn't he the third member of your little group? Or is it just you two ladies who've decided to play dime-novel detectives?"

"I assure you we are not playing," Nichols said, suppressing an unladylike urge to punch Blair in the nose. "As for Mr. Snook, he is off on his own, but you can talk to us."

"I'm very busy. What is it you want?"

"A chair would be nice," Reed said.

"All right, sit down if you must," said Blair, who clearly wasn't interested in having a conversation. "As I said, I don't have a lot of time. I have a trial to prepare for."

Blair, who looked to be about fifty, was well built, with broad shoulders, a thick head of silvery hair, rather fierce eyes, and the kind of chiseled features that Nichols thought must have made him very attractive to women. His dark blue suit was of the best material and so meticulously tailored that it appeared to have been molded to his body. His voice, as smooth and weighty as a gold ingot, was made for the two great human pastimes of lying and persuasion, or so it seemed to Nichols.

"I really can't tell you anything," he said, without being prompted, "other than that George was a fool to create this committee of yours. I have no idea what he was thinking."

"He was thinking he might be murdered," Nichols said, "and perhaps he was right."

"I really doubt that. George had too much of an imagination. He always thought people were out to do him ill. He wasn't a very trusting sort of man."

"Did he trust you?" Reed asked, a question that appeared to catch Blair off guard.

Blair stared at Reed and said, "Of course he did. He had every reason to." Then he added, his voice dripping with sarcasm, "But what of you, Miss Reed? Do you suppose he trusted you?"

Nichols felt a wave of tension in the air, as though a chill breeze had suddenly blown in under the office door. Blair, she assumed, knew all about Pemberton's relationship with Reed.

"We are here to talk about you, sir, not me," Reed said. "And since trust seems to be an issue, you should know we have evidence that Mr. Pemberton did not trust you in the least."

"You are speaking nonsense. As I said—"

Reed cut him off. "The fact is, Mr. Pemberton believed you were embezzling money from your clients and the law firm."

Nichols didn't like where the interview was going, and she realized that she should have discussed strategy with Reed before talking to Blair. It would have been wiser, she thought, to have sounded out Blair about the alleged embezzlement rather than confronting him at once about it. Now, they had little chance of catching Blair in a lie. What they got instead was a vociferous denial.

"That is complete rot," Blair said, his voice rising in anger. "Utter, complete rot. Who have you been talking to? Has Miranda been feeding you lies? Or is it that lickspittle Ledger? If anybody was stealing money, it would be him."

"It was Mr. Pemberton himself who raised the issue, based on what he'd found in certain financial documents," Nichols said calmly.

"Is that so? Well, show me these documents. If they do indeed exist, they must be forgeries that George managed to concoct, probably with Ledger's help. I would not put it past him to defame me from the grave."

"Why would he go to all that trouble?" Reed said, appearing ready for a fight. "It makes no sense to me. Why don't you just tell us the truth?"

"Perhaps we will show you the documents later," Nichols said, trying to keep Blair from shutting down the interview. "Still, I'm curious why you think Mr. Pemberton would want to put you in a bad light. Did the two of you have a falling-out, perhaps over Miranda? I understand that Mr. Pemberton had at some point hoped you might marry her."

"I have nothing to say about Miranda, other than that she is no innocent maiden. But I warn you, if you try to pursue these unfounded allegations against me, I will take legal action, and you will not like the results."

Nichols said, "We are not accusing you of anything, Mr. Blair. We are simply making inquiries. But if there were any financial improprieties and there was a threat of exposure, then a reasonable person might regard that as a motive for murder."

Furious, Blair rose from his chair and said, "How dare you! How dare you! Get out, the both of you."

"All right, we'll leave," Nichols said, "but before we go perhaps you could be so good as to tell us where you were on the night Mr. Pemberton died."

"Out!" Blair repeated, "And don't come back."

*

"A little more subtlety would have been helpful," Nichols said to Reed as they rode the elevator down to the ground floor.

"What do you mean?"

"Well, directly accusing Blair of wrongdoing wasn't the best approach. It just got his back up, and now I don't see that he'll ever talk to us again."

"Maybe, but who cares? He'll just lie and lie anyway. Besides, I thought you'd relish a confrontation with him. You're a labor organizer, and there can't be much subtlety in that."

"More than you might imagine," Nichols said.

"Well, I have little use for subtlety anymore. It is the way of women, and we are in a man's world now."

"Yes, but we are not men. We must be clever if we hope to get anywhere with this business."

"I will not argue with you about that," Reed said. "By all means, let us be the clever ladies. Well, I will be on my way. It's been an interesting day. We must get together again soon. After all, two heads are better than one."

"Three heads," Nichols said. "You seem to have forgotten about Mr. Snook."

"Oh, I haven't forgotten about him, but I am of a mind that, like most men, he will prove in the end to be useless."

7.
SNOOK AND LEDGER

As Nichols and Reed went their separate ways, Walter Snook was at his apartment on South Ninth Street, trying to figure out his next move. The two women on the committee were a concern. They were too nosy for their own good, and Snook worried what they might dig up. He wondered, too, if they were "plants," just as he was.

It was clear to Snook that he hadn't ended up on the committee by a stroke of good fortune. The odds against that happening were simply too long. But why had Pemberton chosen him? Did the lawyer genuinely believe, given their past relationship, that Snook could help solve his murder? Or was something more sinister at work—a trap perhaps, with Snook the prime prey? It was hard to know.

Snook thought back to how he'd been hired by Pemberton for a peculiar job in early August, a few weeks before the lawyer's death. Snook had just delivered several cases of wine to the apartment at Central Park Terrace when Pemberton came out for a chat. The subject was Dan O'Malley, a teamster known to both men.

O'Malley was a notorious figure in Minneapolis. Known as One-eyed Dan, he wore a black patch over his missing left eye, which he'd lost the year before under gruesome circumstances in one of the low dives along Washington Avenue. He'd gotten into a struggle with a famously corrupt police detective, who used the barrel of his revolver to gouge out O'Malley's eye. Despite this unpleasant development, O'Malley managed to disarm the detective, after which he beat him to a pulp. "Better one eye than dead because the dead don't see nothing," was O'Malley's succinct assessment of the encounter.

Despite his claims of self-defense, O'Malley was soon brought up on assault charges and might have done a long stint in prison had not Pemberton stepped up to represent him on a pro bono basis. It was the kind of highly publicized case Pemberton occasionally took on to burnish his reputation as a defender of the common man. Pemberton eventually negotiated a deal that allowed O'Malley to serve six months in the county workhouse in exchange for his guilty plea. O'Malley did his time, but afterward he complained to anyone who would listen that Pemberton was a "dirty shyster" who'd betrayed him.

"What do you think of Mr. O'Malley?" Pemberton asked while Snook unloaded the last of the wine. "I know what you testified to, but tell me the real truth, if you would." Snook had given brief testimony as a character witness at O'Malley's trial, depicting him as just an ordinary, hardworking fellow who must have been provoked into the fight at the saloon.

"Dan is a rough customer," Snook replied, "but you already know that."

"How rough?"

"What do you mean?"

"I mean, is he the sort of man who, for enough money, would be willing to kill someone?"

Although Snook had no doubt that O'Malley would indeed murder for money, he said, "Like I said, Mr. Pemberton, Dan's a rough one, but I don't know how far he might go. Why do you ask?"

Pemberton's reply was startling. "I'm asking because I think it quite likely that O'Malley tried to kill me a few days ago."

"Is that so? What happened, if you don't mind me asking?"

Pemberton described how he'd nearly been run down and said, "I'm pretty sure I caught a glimpse of an eye patch as the driver raced past me. It must have been O'Malley."

"Well, ain't that something? Did you tell the police what happened?"

Pemberton responded with a low chuckle. "The police have no use for me, not after I had the audacity to represent O'Malley against one of their own. They would have preferred to see him hang, and they'd shed no tears if I joined him on the gallows. Be that as it may, I find myself in need of a private detective, as it were, to discover exactly why O'Malley tried to murder me."

"Maybe he was just sore over going to jail," Snook said.

"Yes, that's possible, I suppose, but I doubt it. I think it far more likely that someone hired him to do the deed. I should very much like to know who that person is, and that is where you might enter the picture, Mr. Snook. You strike me as a man of great native intelligence, and of course you are acquainted with O'Malley. Would you be interested in making further inquiries on my behalf? Naturally, I would pay you for your time. Would one hundred dollars suffice?"

The offer put Snook in a tricky position. The opportunity to make one hundred dollars—a handsome sum for a man of Snook's station—was deeply appealing, and in most circumstances he would have jumped at it. But fingering O'Malley for the attempt on Pemberton's life would be very unwise for any number of reasons. So, what to do? Snook was a practiced schemer, and after some quick thinking he saw a way out of his dilemma.

"All right," he said, "I can ask around. Maybe somebody knows something. But I will need fifty dollars up front to begin. O'Malley is a hard case, and it will take time to get him to crack."

"Well, do what you can," Pemberton said. "See my bookkeeper, Mr. Ledger, and he will pay you. I need to know who sent O'Malley after me. If you identify that person, I may even be able to give you a nice bonus."

"I'll do my best," Snook said, "but I can't make any promises."

A big stall ensued. Snook delivered regular reports to Pemberton, always claiming that he was making progress in identifying the man who'd hired O'Malley. It went on for nearly a month, until Pemberton took his deadly fall.

Now, Snook was back in the thick of the Pemberton business, with all manner of angles to calculate, this time with $10,000 on the line. It was a once-in-a-lifetime windfall, but it came with real peril. A wrong step, Snook knew, could plunge him into disaster, and instead of riches he'd be living on bread and water behind stone walls—or worse.

Late that afternoon, as Snook was preparing to head out for a night at the saloons, a boy arrived at his door with a message. "If you are Mr. Walter Snook," the boy said, "I have a message from Mr. Daniel O'Malley."

"I'm Snook. What's the message?"

"Meet me Thursday night at Beecher's," the boy recited. "Be there or you will regret it."

Beecher's was a saloon well known to Snook, who gave the boy a dime and sent him away. Snook had feared O'Malley might make a play. Now, it was happening, and Snook felt his stomach tighten. O'Malley was the very definition of trouble, and one way or another, Snook would have to deal with him.

*

Stanley Ledger worked out of a cramped old building on Washington Avenue that had been put up, quickly and none too well, in the early days of the city. His office was small and poorly heated in winter, but it had one great advantage, which was that the rent was cheap. Ledger was parsimonious by nature, and although he could have afforded nicer quarters, he preferred the warm feeling that came from knowing he was saving money on his overhead.

Ledger had built a decent practice since relocating to Minneapolis from his native Illinois, and his prospects greatly improved after he landed the firm of Pemberton and Blair as a client. But everything turned sour once Pemberton began to suspect his partner, and perhaps Ledger as well, of financial wrongdoing. The situation became so tense that Ledger wanted to quit as the firm's bookkeeper. Dixon, however, had urged him to stay on, lest his departure be taken as evidence of criminal behavior.

Then came Pemberton's sudden death, and Ledger felt a sense of relief. The accusations of financial impropriety, he believed, would melt away once Pemberton was in the ground. Instead, the wily lawyer had created his curious death committee, which instantly became a source of much anxiety for Ledger.

Two days after the committee's inaugural meeting, Ledger's discomfort grew when Nichols showed up at his office, unannounced, to interrogate him. Nichols had invited Reed along—Snook was still in the wind—but Reed had politely declined, saying she had other matters to attend to.

"I have been hearing things about you," Nichols said as Ledger offered her a chair across from his desk.

"Have you now? Who's been talking about me?"

"I would rather not say for the moment. But I have been told that you and Mr. Pemberton had a huge argument back in July. May I ask what it was about?"

"It was a personal matter," Ledger said, trying to stay calm even as his heart pounded wildly. How, he wondered, had Nichols learned about the argument? And what might she make of it?

"What sort of personal matter?"

"I do not wish to be impolite, Mrs. Nichols, but it really is none of your business."

"Oh, but it is my business. Mr. Pemberton accused you of embezzlement, didn't he, perhaps in cahoots with Mr. Blair, and then threatened to fire you."

Ledger erupted, spewing out the hot lava of denial. "That is a dirty lie, and I will not stand for it! I never stole so much as a cent from Mr. Pemberton or anyone else."

"I never said you did," Nichols replied evenly. "Mr. Pemberton could have been mistaken."

"Of course he was mistaken, and I told him so," Ledger said, thereby confirming that there had indeed been an argument. "Someone was putting ideas in his head. And where did you hear that he wanted to fire me? That is also a falsehood."

Ledger's heavily lidded eyes, which always made him look sleepy, suddenly opened wide, as though he'd seen a startling vision. "Oh, I know now. You've been talking to Miranda, haven't you? Well, don't believe her. She's had it in for me for a long time."

"Why is that?"

Ledger began to stammer, a trait Nichols had noticed at the committee's first meeting. "I, I, I, well, I just would rather not talk about it."

"Was it because of how you acted after she turned down your marriage proposal?"

"Another lie! I will admit to making advances, but I never proposed to her, no matter what she says. The truth is, she's a practiced dissembler, and I want nothing to do with her. I am not a thief, nor did I have anything to do with Mr. Pemberton's demise, if that is what you're thinking."

Nichols said, "May I ask where you were on the night he was murdered?"

"I was home, at my apartment."

"Did anyone see you there?"

"No, I live alone. I prefer it that way. Now, if there is nothing else, Mrs. Nichols, I need to get back to work."

"Certainly. But we will talk again. I think you will agree that there is still much to be learned."

"Not from me," Ledger insisted, rising to escort Nichols out. "I am an innocent party in all of this."

*

When Nichols returned home that evening, she had dinner with Sophia, who wanted to hear all there was to know about the committee and its work.

"Tell me everything," she said. "Have you found the murderer yet?"

"No, dear," Nichols said. "We're just beginning."

"But you suspect somebody, don't you? It must be thrilling, Mother, to be a detective, just like Sherlock Holmes. Wouldn't it be wonderful if he could be here? Why, he'd figure everything out in no time."

Sophia, who'd just turned sixteen, had read the first two volumes of Holmes stories with great enthusiasm. She would have been even more excited had she known that Holmes and Dr. Watson, under assumed identities, had in fact been in Minnesota almost exactly two years earlier to pursue the ruthless arsonist behind the lethal Hinckley forest fire in what would later become known as the case of the "Red Demon."

Nichols said, "Now, Sophia, just calm yourself. Life doesn't work like a detective story."

"Well, it should. Can't you at least tell me about the clues you've found so far? I bet there are quite a few."

Nichols smiled at her eager daughter and said, "Don't worry. If I find any big clues, I'll let you know."

Later, as bedtime approached, Nichols enjoyed a cup of hot chocolate with Sophia, then as the two of them always did, they checked to see that all the doors and windows were secure. But when Sophia went into the vestibule by the front door, she was surprised to find an envelope on the floor beneath the mail slot. The envelope bore no name or address, and Sophia thought it was all very mysterious.

"Look at his," she said when her mother came up behind her. "Somebody put it through the mail slot."

"Just now?"

"I don't know. It was here when I went to check the door."

"Well, that's certainly curious, isn't it."

When Nichols opened the envelope, she found four clippings carefully cut from the *Tribune,* with an attached handwritten note saying, "You should look into this." The clippings recounted the story of O'Malley's saloon brawl and subsequent trial. Nichols hadn't paid much attention to the trial at the time, but now, as she read the articles, she was surprised to discover that Snook had testified on O'Malley's behalf. Yet Snook had never mentioned this connection to anyone on the committee.

"Is it a clue?" Sophia asked.

"Oh yes," Nichols said. "It's definitely a clue."

8.
SWIRLING CURRENTS

Although George Pemberton cast himself as a crusader for justice and a great friend to the common man, his personal behavior rarely mirrored his public image. He lorded over his meek wife, slept with other women when it pleased him, stocked his cellar with expensive bottles of wine worth more than the average laborer made in a month, and attended fancy soirées where he lectured the rich on their duties to the poor while eating the choicest delicacies. An imperial autocrat under his own roof, he also clashed frequently with his headstrong daughter, expecting her to obey his every wish and whim while offering her little in the way of affection.

Even as Miranda came of age, he insisted on controlling every aspect of her life. "You must marry well," he told her on her twenty-first birthday, noting that "an older man" would make the ideal husband for her. He'd then tried to fix her up with Blair, a man whom Miranda had no interest in. After that debacle, the relationship between father and daughter had dropped off a cliff, to the point that they barely spoke to each other.

Paul Dixon proved to be Miranda's savior, or so she believed. He'd been hired the previous winter to help manage Pemberton's large portfolio of properties, having come highly recommended from a previous position with a wealthy businessman in Chicago. As smooth as a slab of polished marble, Dixon was well spoken, unfailingly discreet, and very good at overseeing Pemberton's many interests. More importantly from Miranda's point of view, he was handsome and charming. He'd bedded Miranda—or perhaps it was the other way around—within a few months of his hiring, and afterward they'd become secretly engaged, since it wasn't initially clear that Pemberton would approve of their match.

Busy trying to improve the world, Pemberton hadn't at first noticed what was happening under his own roof. Once he finally learned of the engagement, he was angry, not because he had any particular objections to Dixon but because Miranda had gone behind his back. A huge row followed, but Miranda refused to apologize to her father, saying he held no sway over her life anymore. "I am a free woman now," she told him bluntly, "and I shall do as I please."

Then came the attempts on Pemberton's life. Although he believed his thieving law partner was the prime suspect, Pemberton couldn't dismiss the possibility that his own daughter and her lover were somehow involved, and so he'd made certain last-minute arrangements with his will affecting Miranda's potential inheritance. He hated that he couldn't trust his own daughter, but he saw no other choice.

*

On the same day that Nichols interviewed Ledger, Miranda undertook the task of turning her father's apartment inside out, with Dixon's help. Mrs. Engstrom had been dismissed for the afternoon, giving the couple an opportunity to make one last search for Pemberton's will. If it wasn't in the apartment, Miranda feared, they might never find it.

She'd already exhausted several other possibilities. The will wasn't in her father's office in the Guaranty Loan Building, or so Blair had assured her after conducting what he described as a "thorough search." Nor was the will in Pemberton's safe deposit box at the First National Bank. The substantial Diebold safe in Pemberton's home office, to which Dixon had been entrusted with the combination, had also failed to yield the precious document. So, too, had the wall safe in Pemberton's bedroom, assuming Uncle Freddie hadn't managed to open it and steal the will. Yet Miranda remained doubtful that Freddie, whose only talent seemed to be holding his liquor, could have managed such a feat. All of which led Miranda to conclude that her father had deliberately hidden the will away before his death. The question was why.

By the time night settled in, Miranda and Dixon had come up empty in their search, and Miranda was in a foul mood. "We have run out of places to look," she told her fiancé as they sat in the parlor and drank some of her father's expensive wine. "Father, it seems, went out of his way to make matters difficult for us."

"Well, would it necessarily be a bad thing if no will is found?" Dixon said. "You would still inherit his estate."

"Yes, but think this through, Paul. He had a reason for hiding the will, and the only one that comes to mind is that it is not in my favor. You know how much of a falling out we had. And I'm still not sure he ever really approved of our marriage plans. So you see, he might have revised his will to leave me out of it, then hid it, perhaps believing I'd try to alter or even destroy it. He would have done it out of pure spite. Father was a hateful man, you know, a humanitarian with a cold heart, if there is such a thing."

Dixon paused to sip his wine, a very nice Bordeaux, then gave Miranda a kiss and said, "So if I am following your logic, you believe the will is going to turn up before long just as mysteriously as it disappeared."

"Yes, and the estate will go to some ridiculous charity or even my awful uncle or, for all I know, to one of his mistresses, perhaps even to that schemer, Reed. Why else would he have put her on his stupid committee? It is all very unfair to me."

"It is," Dixon agreed. "You deserve much better."

"I do. And if that awful Reed woman thinks she can steal my rightful inheritance, she is dead wrong."

"Do you really think she could do that?"

"Yes. After all, a clever woman who sleeps with a man can have great influence over him. Men are fools in that way."

"I hate to say it, but you're right," Dixon said with a grin. "I just hope you don't take me for a fool."

"Never," Miranda said, giving him a kiss.

"Thank you, my darling. Still, the question remains, what are we to do about the will? We must find it, for your sake."

"For both of our sakes," Miranda corrected. "Our life together will depend on it."

*

The next afternoon, Nichols ran into Dixon quite by chance at Donaldson's Glass Block, the city's largest department store. She was searching for a new necklace when she caught sight of Dixon at a nearby counter, looking at watches.

"Are you in need of a new timepiece?" she asked when she came up to him.

"Why, Mrs. Nichols, fancy meeting you here," he said. "Yes, I do like watches. Timeliness is next to godliness, my mother used to say. Mr. Pemberton felt the same way. He did not like me or anyone else being late for anything. But tell me, how is your investigation coming along?"

"Well, I'm not working alone, as you know. But we are making progress."

"Ah, there's a noncommittal answer if I ever heard one. Still, it seems to me you're the real force on the committee, Mrs. Nichols. Miss Reed and Mr. Snook hardly count, don't you think?"

"Why do you say that?"

Dixon delivered a charming smile and said, "Oh, you know what I'm talking about. That Snook fellow doesn't really seem interested in doing any work, from what I can see. And Miss Reed is—well, how shall I put it?—compromised, as you know. It's queer, isn't it, that Mr. Pemberton put her on the committee. I'd certainly not want an ex-lover investigating my death. Too much bad blood, if you know what I mean."

"And was there a lot of 'bad blood' between the two of them after the affair broke up?"

"I should say more like boiling blood, from what Miranda tells me. Miss Reed wanted a big settlement but didn't get it, of course. A woman in her position doesn't have much legal standing, as Mr. Pemberton was well aware, so there wasn't much she could do."

"Did you know Miss Reed at all?"

"No. The first committee meeting was our introduction. But I knew of her relationship with Mr. Pemberton. Miranda figured out what was going on. Women are so clever when it comes to sniffing out affairs, aren't they."

"Perhaps it's because they have so much practice at it."

"Ha! I will not deny that men can be perfect beasts sometimes. But they can also be faithful if they find the right woman. That's how I feel about Miranda. She's really quite wonderful."

"And perhaps soon to be quite rich."

"Yes, although who really knows what's in Mr. Pemberton's will? He did like his secrets."

"How did you come to work for him?"

"It was a bit of serendipity, I suppose you could say. I'd just come up here from Chicago in search of a new opportunity when I happened to encounter Miranda in the tearoom of this very store. I do not mind telling you it was love at first sight, at least in my case. I later learned from her that Mr. Pemberton was looking for a secretary to help manage his real estate holdings, and I landed the job."

"You also 'landed' Miranda, as it were."

"Yes. I have been very fortunate," Dixon said, flashing another smile. "But it is distressing to know that someone murdered Mr. Pemberton before he could walk Miranda down the aisle."

"Have the two of you set a wedding date?"

"Not yet. We're waiting for this terrible business to be resolved. May I ask if you have a prime suspect?"

"You may ask," Nichols said, "but I'd rather not answer."

"You're playing close to the vest, in other words. That's wise of you. But for my money, Mr. Blair is the one to watch. Mr. Pemberton was absolutely convinced Mr. Blair was stealing from the firm."

"And were you convinced as well?"

"Bookkeeping isn't my strong suit, but as I told you before, Mr. Ledger thought something was amiss," Dixon said as he consulted his pocket watch. "Ah, I must be on my way. Miranda and I are going out this evening, and I should get ready. It was nice talking with you, Mrs. Nichols, and I wish you success. It would be wonderful to put this awful business behind us."

"It would," Nichols agreed.

As she watched Dixon leave, she wondered about his relationship with Miranda. Was he truly a man in love or just a fortune hunter so smooth that it was hard to get a grip on his real character? In either case, he remained on her suspect list. Unfortunately, so did everyone else on the committee, and Nichols felt mired deep in uncertainty, still looking for the one key clue that might be a strong hand, pulling her out of the muck.

*

That evening, Snook went to Beecher's saloon to meet with O'Malley. The saloon was not among the ornaments of the city. It occupied the ground floor of a brick-veneer building on Washington Avenue North across from rail yards, warehouses, and, along the Mississippi, steam-powered sawmills turning into usable lumber what remained of Minnesota's ravaged pineries. Like most saloons of its day, Beecher's—named after its dyspeptic proprietor—was a stand-up joint that offered a long bar, nickel beer, cheap whiskey, and a back room where disreputable characters regularly assembled to play cards, drink, fight, and dream up criminal endeavors.

Snook arrived just before eight and found O'Malley in the back room, playing stud poker with three worthies who all looked as though they'd be at home in a rattlesnake den. Cigar smoke hung like a foul fog in the air, seasoned with the aroma of beer. Snook didn't know the other card players, but judging by the number of scuffed wooden chips O'Malley had managed to assemble, he was having a profitable evening.

When he saw Snook, O'Malley grinned and said, "These gentlemen of leisure have been doing their best to cheat me all night, thinking they can take advantage on account of me having only one eye. Problem is, they don't have nothing in the way of brains, so I'm ahead of them. Ain't that right, fellows?"

"Aw, you're full of it," said one of the card players as he looked up at Snook. "Will this gent be joining us?"

"No, he will not," O'Malley said, "though I'd be happy to take his money. Fact is, I have business with him. Private business. Come along, Snooky, we'll talk out back. I don't want these boys eavesdropping on us."

There was a tiny yard behind the saloon, protected by a wooden fence with boards that leaned this way and that like a bad set of teeth. The yard, strewn with trash, was guarded by an elderly beagle chained to a stake. The dog bayed loudly when Snook and O'Malley came out into the yard but went quiet as soon as O'Malley approached and gave it something from his coat pocket.

"This here is Mortimer," O'Malley said. "He's a good old fellow but he yaps too much, and that's why he don't get to stay inside. Some people are just like Mortimer. They yap a lot. But you know me. I can be quiet as a mouse. I'm sure you can too. Ain't that right, Snooky?"

Snook sensed that some sort of shakedown was coming. "All right," he said. "Cut the crap. What do you want?"

O'Malley grinned, revealing a few yellowed teeth among many gaps. "Well, let's see now. From what I read in the papers, you could be in for ten thousand dollars. Half of that would be a nice figure."

"Don't be a fool," Snook said, watching O'Malley's hands in case he was carrying a concealed pistol or knife. "How do you think I'm going to get that money?"

"Oh, I'm sure you can figure something out, Snooky. You always were the clever one. Maybe you can steer those nice ladies on the committee in the wrong direction. That shouldn't be hard. Or maybe there's another way to cash in, from whoever hired you for our little job."

The possibility of blackmail had already occurred to Snook, and he was weighing the possibilities. Blackmail was always dangerous and unpredictable, especially when murder was involved. Yet Snook also knew he might be able to double or even triple the $10,000 reward if he played his cards right.

"Listen, the best thing we can do right now is lay low," he told O'Malley. "This is a tricky business, and we could both end up in prison if you get greedy. Besides, this committee Pemberton put me on isn't a joke. That Nichols woman is a sharp one. She just might figure things out."

O'Malley sent a spray of tobacco juice into the dirt and said, "Don't tell me, Snooky, that you're afraid of some skirt."

"Look, I'm just telling you now isn't the time to stir things up."

"So you say. Well, you know what I think? I think you're just trying to put me off. I know you're playing an angle, Snooky, and I want in on it. Don't forget I'm a man with a box of dynamite, and I'll blow it up in your face if I have to."

"And you'll blow up with me. You understand that, don't you?"

"Better to die quick than slow is what I say. So what's it going to be, Snooky? Are you with me or not? There's money to be made, a lot of it, and you're the man who can make it for us. Think of us as partners in crime. Ain't that a pretty picture?"

It wasn't, but Snook needed to buy some time, so he said, "Just be patient. You'll get some money once I figure everything out."

"You do that, but it better not take too long."

"I'll see what I can do, and I'll get back to you. Can I find you here most nights?"

"Why, this is my cozy home away from home," O'Malley said. "See you again soon."

"Sure," Snook said as he turned to leave, prompting a howl from Mortimer. "It'll be my pleasure."

*

Annie Nichols, who lay resting at home that evening, was also eager to talk with Walter Snook, although she doubted he would be very forthcoming with her. The newspaper clippings slipped under her door led her to believe that, like her and Reed, Snook had been placed on the committee. As to why he'd been selected, Nichols thought it probably had something to do with his connection to Dan O'Malley. Beyond that, however, she could only guess. Nor was she sure who'd sent her the clippings, although she suspected they'd come from someone on the committee.

Nichols wanted to keep an open mind, but the more she thought about everything, the more likely it seemed to her that the committee had been carefully curated by Pemberton to investigate its own members. And she was to be the chief investigator, judging by the private note he'd left for her with Gozzard. Pemberton, she realized, had in effect secretly deputized her, but in such a way that she was in all likelihood working, quite literally, with his murderer.

What Nichols couldn't understand was why he'd chosen such a weirdly indirect approach and entangled her in it like a spider among spiders. It would have been far easier, and more sensible, if Pemberton had simply named a private investigator to look into his death and given that person a straightforward list of suspects to work with. Instead, he'd gone to great lengths to create a drama over which he loomed like a playfully malicious ghost.

Sophia arrived with hot milk and a plate of cookies and said, "I just knew you were up here thinking, Mother. I wish to hear your thoughts, and then I shall give you mine."

Nichols laughed and said, "So it is to be a trade, is it? Very well. My thoughts are for the moment quite confused. I find myself in the middle of something I don't understand, and I very much fear I will be going in circles before long if I'm not careful."

"Well, I may be of help. You see, I have been thinking how Mr. Sherlock Holmes would go about solving the case."

"Ah, and what would he do, in your considered opinion?"

"Why, if he was stumped like you are, he'd burglarize the houses of all the suspects and when he found incriminating documents, he'd mail them anonymously to the police. That always works when nothing else does."

"So you wish to make a criminal of me, is that it? Sorry, but I don't think I'll be committing any burglaries. Remember, Sherlock Holmes isn't real. Now, let's have a cookie or two, and then we'll get you off to bed."

9. TWO DEATHS

ON THE MORNING OF SEPTEMBER 13, nearly two weeks after George Pemberton's notice had appeared in the *Tribune,* Annie Nichols dug into the Sunday newspapers, as she always did. There had been numerous stories about the "death committee" since its formation, and many of them were either wildly speculative or badly ill-informed. Nichols was pleased when she opened the *Tribune* to find that the committee's work merited only a brief story, which offered the less than riveting news that there were "no new developments of any consequence to report." But another, much longer story on the next page left her in something close to state of shock. DAN O'MALLEY DEAD, said the headline. FOUND SHOT IN ALLEY. LOST EYE IN FAMOUS BARROOM BRAWL.

Nichols read the story carefully, not wanting to overlook any details. O'Malley's body, with what was described simply as a "fatal bullet wound," had been discovered the night before behind a saloon on Second Avenue North. Police were investigating, "but as

O'Malley was a known criminal with many unsavory connections, the list of suspects is likely to be long," the *Tribune* reported.

Nichols didn't believe O'Malley's murder could be a coincidence, for she strongly suspected that the one-eyed teamster was the wagon driver who'd tried to run down Pemberton back in July. If so, O'Malley probably knew something about Pemberton's subsequent murder, and it seemed likely that he'd been killed to ensure his silence. And that in turn meant that members of the committee—none more so than Snook—might also be in danger.

Nichols had been thinking a great deal about Snook and his relationship with O'Malley. Had the two been merely acquaintances, or had they in fact been coconspirators, plotting Pemberton's demise? It struck Nichols as possible, yet her theory came with a big question: why would Snook have wanted Pemberton dead? Nichols didn't have a good answer.

Meanwhile, Snook's disappearance—he hadn't been heard from for nearly a week—was troubling. Nichols wondered whether he'd gone into hiding to avoid uncomfortable questions about his possible role in Pemberton's murder. It was also possible he'd vanished out of fear for his own life because of what he knew. In either case, Nichols wanted to track him down, assuming he hadn't already left Minneapolis. Snook, she had come to believe, was the key to unlocking the mystery of Pemberton's murder.

But the next day, as Nichols set out to find Snook, the afternoon *Journal* reported on another death, and this time the tragic news came directly from Central Park Terrace.

*

The cobblestone courtyard at the rear of the Central Park Terrace included a two-story powerhouse equipped with coal-fired boilers that heated the apartments. The powerhouse, which was entirely separate from the apartments to minimize the risk of fire, included a lean-to shed that sheltered trash cans. A janitor whose duties included maintaining the boiler house went into the shed on the morning of September 14 to gather loose trash before garbagemen arrived to haul everything away. What he discovered inside would quickly put the death committee and its mission back on the front pages.

NEW MYSTERY IN PEMBERTON CASE, read the headline in the *Journal.* BROTHER OF GEORGE PEMBERTON FOUND DEAD. The story began as follows: "The sensational case of George Pemberton, the lawyer who convened a committee to investigate his own death, took a stunning turn yesterday with the discovery of his brother's body behind Central Park Terrace. Frederick Pemberton was found lifeless in a shed in a courtyard at the rear of the apartments, where George Pemberton had lived for many years.

"Chief Vernon Smith described the death as of 'unknown causes,' as Mr. Pemberton's body showed no evidence of foul play. 'We found a nearly empty whiskey bottle beside Mr. Pemberton, who was apparently a heavy drinker, and it is possible he was poisoned by an excess of alcohol. It will be up to the coroner to say how he died.'

"The Journal has thus far been unable to learn a great deal about Mr. Pemberton, who unlike his brother was not a well-known figure in Minneapolis. Miranda Pemberton, George's daughter, spoke to our reporter, stating she was 'shocked and saddened' by her uncle's untimely death. 'Uncle Freddie was a wonderful man, but unfortunately he had succumbed in recent years to the awful lure of alcohol. I saw him briefly last week and he seemed his usual self. I do not know what he was doing at Central Park Terrace, since he did not live there. I fear he may simply have had far too much to drink, and so succumbed.'

"Miss Pemberton went on to say that her uncle, who was in his early sixties, had always been on good terms with his brother, although the two were not close. Asked whether she thought his death might in some way be related to that of his brother, Miss Pemberton said, 'I do not think so. It is just another tragic accident for our family, as far as I can tell.'"

The story went on to suggest that the brothers' deaths must be related. "When two fatal events come so closely together, more than coincidence must be involved." But the *Journal* advanced no evidence in support of its theory, and when the coroner later ruled that Freddie had died of "acute alcohol intoxication," his death quickly faded from the news columns.

*

Nichols was deeply disturbed by Freddie's death, which she very much doubted was accidental. After all, what drunk would choose to do his drinking amid reeking piles of trash when so many saloons, among them numerous after-hours joints, were readily available?

Nichols placed a call to Gozzard early that afternoon and said, "I assume you saw the *Journal* today."

"I did," the lawyer replied. "Very strange, I must say. Mr. Snook feels the same way."

"He called you?"

"Yes. He sounded quite agitated. Wanted to know if I'd heard anything about it and whether the police believe foul play was involved. What could I tell him? After all, I'm hardly a friend of the police."

"Did Mr. Snook say anything else?"

"Just that he's sure something funny is going on. That's how he put it."

"More like something dangerous, I'd say."

The committee's second meeting was scheduled for later in the afternoon, and Nichols asked whether Snook would be on hand.

"He didn't say," Gozzard told her.

"Let us hope that for his sake, he shows up," Nichols said. "I am very worried about him and everyone else on the committee."

*

George Pemberton's apartment was once again the site of the meeting, which was convened at four o'clock. Snook, however, was absent, despite his earlier call to Gozzard. "Mr. Snook seems to be an elusive fellow," the lawyer said. "I asked him when we talked where I could reach him, but he said he was out and about and would call me if he felt the need to communicate further."

"He's just a lone wolf," Miranda said. "Let's proceed without him. Mr. Gozzard can fill him in later."

Freddie Pemberton's death was on everyone's mind, and Miranda offered a few tepid words of grief before stating that his death had almost surely been an unfortunate mishap. "It was bound to happen one day," she said. "Poor Uncle Freddie was a slave to the bottle."

Dixon backed her argument. "We all saw how drunk he was when we found him in Mr. Pemberton's bedroom. He could barely walk, and Mr. Snook had to help him out. It would not serve us well to make too much of this."

Nichols was unconvinced. "Do you really believe, Mr. Dixon, that Freddie was enjoying a night of drinking amid the stench of offal to the point that he passed out and died?"

"I do not see why that is a ridiculous idea."

"Nor do I," said Ledger. "Drunks do many disgusting things in my experience."

"Oh come, Stanley, what do you know about drinking?" Dixon said. "I wager you've never touched a drop in your life."

"Well, I for one do not think Freddie drank himself to death, as the police and coroner believe," Nichols said. "He could have found any number of more appealing places to nurse his whiskey. Hasn't it occurred to you that Freddie might have known something and was killed because of it?"

"I find that hard to believe," Miranda said. "All Uncle Freddie ever knew was what he found in liquor bottles."

"That's not entirely true," Ledger said. "I happened to run across him a few days before Mr. Pemberton's death, and he told me he was looking into the attempts on his brother's life. He believed there was 'a big conspiracy,' as he put it."

"And you're just telling us about this now?" Reed said. "That seems peculiar."

"Well, I didn't think it was important at the time, Freddie being Freddie. But now—"

"Did he explain this so-called conspiracy to you?" Nichols asked.

"No. All he said was that he'd found some interesting stuff in the newspapers, and then he shuffled off."

Nichols now thought she knew who'd sent her the news clippings about O'Malley's trial. It had to have been Freddie.

"Where did you talk with Freddie?" she asked Ledger.

"Up on Hennepin, near the library. He used to go there a lot."

"Really, must we continue with this nonsense?" Miranda said, her blue eyes boring in on Nichols. "The truth is, Freddie was a sot, and he died a sot's death. It's sad, but those are the facts."

"Again, I must beg to differ," Nichols said. "If Freddie was investigating his brother's death, as Mr. Ledger has just informed us, it adds to the suspicion that he was murdered in order to silence him. Assuming he was already two sheets to the wind last night, someone could easily have slipped a dose of poison into his bottle."

"Speculation," Miranda said with a dismissive wave. "Nothing but speculation."

Reed said, "Yes, we are speculating. Let's see what the coroner has to say about Freddie's death. Still, it does make me wonder. Maybe there's more to this whole business than we know."

"Oh, I'm sure of that," Nichols said. "The question is, now what? I do not mind telling you that I am very uneasy about what has happened. If Freddie was killed because of something he knew, then any of us could be next in line."

"I share Mrs. Nichols's concern," Reed said. "We all must be vigilant from now on."

"There's a mad killer on the loose, is that it?" Dixon said. "I do believe you ladies are being overly dramatic."

"Maybe," Nichols said, "but my dear husband, Peter, used to say that he could smell danger in the air, like the faint whiff of a distant fire, and I am smelling it now."

"Then you have a better nose than I do," Dixon said with a smile. "However, I concur with Miss Reed. Let's wait for the coroner to issue his findings before we become too alarmed."

"Fair enough," Nichols said. "I do have a few questions for Miranda, however. May I ask if you had any contact with Freddie after we found him in your father's bedroom last week?"

"So you don't believe what I told the newspapers, is that it?"

"Not at all. But I do know that the newspapers are not above making things up, so I just want to be certain."

"Very well, then I will confirm that I did not see him again. That was in no way unusual. Uncle Freddie was not much for keeping in touch."

"I see. Do you know where he lived?"

Miranda gave Nichols a probing look before she said, "No, I don't have an address. I think he had a small apartment, but I was never there. Maybe the police would know."

"Yes, maybe they would."

Nichols now waited to see whether anyone would bring up O'Malley's murder. Miranda must have known her father had represented O'Malley, but she made no mention of his murder, nor did anyone else on the committee. Had Snook been present, Nichols would have brought his connection to O'Malley out into the open. But she decided to keep her own counsel until she could chase down the missing teamster.

The meeting ended after the committee decided to meet again in a week, but without any agreement as to how, or even whether, they should work together. The subject hadn't even come up, which indicated to Nichols that no one on the committee was deeply interested in a group effort, perhaps because everyone had something to hide.

*

After the meeting, Nichols accompanied Reed on a walk back to her apartment amid a light drizzle that forced them to open their umbrellas. Nichols hoped their stroll would offer another opportunity to sound out Reed, who seemed to be in a talkative mood. Their conversation took an interesting turn as they approached Hudson's Jewelry Store near Sixth and Nicollet.

"I worked there for a while," Reed said. "Mr. Hudson liked the idea of an attractive woman peddling his wares. He said it would be good for business."

"Was it?"

"Let's just say business did not suffer, although the wealthy ladies weren't always happy to see me, especially if they were with their husbands. I must say I have little use for most rich people. What their money really buys is the privilege to lord over people like me. Otherwise, I wouldn't be of any interest to them."

"And that was the case with Mr. Pemberton, I assume."

"As I told you before, I was simply a bauble he acquired."

Nichols said, "I gathered that. But it is surprising to me that a beautiful woman such as yourself never married. Or did you at one time?"

"No, marriage is a prison sentence in my estimation."

"Not if you're married to the right man."

"Well, I never found that man. But let us talk of you, Mrs. Nichols. Why were you put on the committee? Is it possible you, too, were one of Mr. Pemberton's lovers?"

The blunt question caught Nichols off guard. "No, I wasn't one of his conquests. But as everyone is aware, he represented my husband in that Huntington Mill case and I did get to know him then, although we were never close friends. In fact, I found him rather off-putting."

"Why do you say that?"

"It was the way he sometimes looked at me. I could tell he wanted to lure me into bed, probably just for the thrill of it. Is that what happened to you, or was it the other way around?"

"Why, that is a most impolite question, don't you think? But since we are being honest with each other, I will say that Mr. Pemberton believed himself to be a god among women, apparently unaware that there are goddesses as well."

"Yes, there are," Nichols said with a smile. "But tell me, why do you think he wanted you on his committee?"

"Perhaps for the same reason he selected you. He liked to tell me how clever I was, although my intellect was hardly his chief preoccupation. I am sure he found you to be very clever as well. And so here we are, two clever ladies in search of a murderer. It is quite something, isn't it."

"It is. Would you care to tell me more about your relationship with Mr. Pemberton?"

"What would be the point? Besides, what you really want to know, I'm sure, is did we part on good terms? Oh, and also, did I kill him?"

"Why would I suspect that?"

"Because you and I both know there is something very peculiar about our committee. Mr. Pemberton was a lover of the theater—he performed in amateur productions all the time—and I sometimes think we're just players in a drama of his devising, with the murderer to be revealed in the last act. Mr. Ledger more or less said the same thing."

"Yes, it's all very strange," Nichols acknowledged. "There are things we haven't been told. Mr. Snook, for example, remains a mystery."

"He does. He must have been known Mr. Pemberton. Otherwise, why would he be on the committee?"

"Do you have any ideas about that?" Nichols asked, not revealing what she already knew.

"No," Reed said, perhaps too quickly. "I don't recall Mr. Pemberton ever mentioning his name."

Nichols wasn't certain that was true, but she also knew Reed was too canny to give anything away unless it suited her. "Well, we are in the middle of quite a puzzle, aren't we," she said, "and it seems to grow more puzzling by the moment."

"Yes, it is all very queer, isn't it?" Reed agreed. "We are supposed to be investigating a murder, and yet it seems we are all suspects at the same time. If it will do any good to say so, I assure you that I did not kill Mr. Pemberton. That leaves five suspects, if you count the charming Mr. Blair." Reed paused before adding, "Unless, of course, I really am the murderer, or you are."

"No, I'm not the murderer either," Nichols said with a smile. "Still, we are not in a situation conducive to trust, and we must all be looking over our shoulders, especially in light of Freddie's death. I am convinced he was murdered, no matter what the police say."

"Perhaps. But accidents can occur even when murder is in the wind," Reed said as they reached her row house, which was among the most elegant in the city.

"You have a lovely place," Nichols said.

"Yes," Reed said, smiling for the first time during their stroll. "Being a bad woman always pays if you are smart about it."

*

That evening, as she prepared for sleep, Nichols glanced at the most precious object in her bedroom—a large studio portrait of her and Peter taken a year or so before his death. How strong he was, she thought, and yet how kind, a man like few others. Grief had never left her but had burrowed deep into her core like a painful infection. She didn't suppose she'd ever free herself of it, nor did she really want to. Memory, no matter how much it hurt, was a form of proof, like the smudge of a fingerprint, evidence of a life gone and of all that Peter had meant to her.

Often, she'd ask herself what Peter might think about some important matter and what he might advise her to do. But his best advice had always been the same—take on the world with all your gifts of body and mind, never surrender to fear, and always trust yourself. It was time, she knew, to follow that advice. She had come to believe that none of her fellow committee members, a murderer quite possibly among them, could be relied upon. If the mystery was to be solved, she alone would have to be the one to do it.

10.
INVESTIGATING

NICHOLS BEGAN HER SOLO INVESTIGATION at the offices of Blair and Pemberton in the Guaranty Loan Building. She'd read in the *Tribune*'s daily legal roundup that Blair would be in court all week trying a civil case, and that gave Nichols a chance to quiz his longtime secretary, the redoubtable Beatrice Emerson. Although she was by title a secretary, Emerson functioned much like a paralegal, and Pemberton had once joked that if he knew half as much about the law as she did, he would be ready for a seat on the Supreme Court. Nichols had become acquainted with Emerson during the Huntington Mill case and had found her to be both highly intelligent and hilariously honest when it came to her assessment of the legal profession.

"Beatrice, how nice to see you," Nichols said when she walked into the office and found Emerson at her usual desk, which supported a great pile of documents rising tier by tier in the manner of a Hindu temple. Emerson was in her fifties, with a broad face, eyeglasses attached by a chain to her neck, and short curly hair dyed to a bright blond sheen. A cigarette burned close at hand in a metal ashtray already well stocked with butts. Pretending that her visit was for the purpose of seeing Blair, Nichols asked if he was in.

"No, the lawyer in chief is off in court trying a property dispute between two rich fellows who have nothing better to argue about," Emerson said. "He's going to lose and he knows it, but he'll still get paid, and so will I, and there you have what matters. And how are you, dearie?"

"I am well," Nichols said, "but as you can imagine, this business with the so-called death committee is quite a challenge."

"It's crazy, isn't it? But I wasn't surprised when I read about it. Sir George—that's what I liked to call him—loved being the center of attention, and I guess he just wanted things to stay that way after he died."

"I must ask: do you think he was murdered?"

"I really don't know, but he definitely thought somebody was after him. Maybe they were. After all, who likes a lawyer?"

"Do you have any suspects?"

"Not that I could testify to in court. Sir George kept his personal business to himself, which was fine by me. I've got enough to do without listening to people's problems all day long."

"Speaking of problems, can I be frank with you for a moment?"

"Not if you're going to tell me you've got a bad case of bunions."

Nichols smiled and said, "My feet are fine. No, I was just wondering how Mr. Pemberton and Mr. Blair got along. From what the committee has been told, they apparently had a big dispute of some kind over money."

Emerson removed her glasses and looked up at Nichols. "I do believe I am being interrogated," she said. "I will have to take the Fifth at this point. I'm sure you understand."

"Of course. But let's consider a hypothetical. A lawyer discovers that his partner, in order to pay off huge gambling debts, has begun to misappropriate funds from the firm's accounts and those of clients. The lawyer says he intends to expose his partner's wrongdoing and press charges against him. Fearful his career will be ruined, the thieving lawyer then murders his partner, making the death look like an accident."

"So that's the theory, is it? Well, how about this instead: Suppose this allegedly thieving partner is actually the sort of man who wouldn't be caught dead in a gambling den, since he'd rather play the ladies than the horses, if you know what I mean. And suppose he's also a notorious tightwad who'd never let himself fall deeply in debt. And while we're at it, dearie, suppose that this mythical law firm has a bookkeeper who handles all of its finances but maybe can't be trusted. But it's all hypothetical, as you say, unless you have some real evidence to bring to the table. Do you?"

Nichols couldn't help but laugh. "Beatrice, you really should have been a lawyer."

"Too much trouble. I like it where I am. But mark what I've told you. You really are barking up the wrong tree with this theory of yours."

"Very well, you've made your point. But wouldn't it be better if the two of us dropped all the pretense and spoke candidly about what went on between Mr. Pemberton and Mr. Blair?"

Emerson lit a new cigarette, took in a draw of smoke, and said, "Perhaps that would work for you, but not for me. I don't talk out of school. That can get a person fired, after all. Now, would you like to schedule an appointment with Mr. Blair? I'm sure he'd be willing to share some thoughts with you."

"We've already talked, as you know. That is why I came to you."

"And you've learned something, I trust, about not getting entangled in a theory that will lead you nowhere."

"Then perhaps you can offer a better theory when it comes to Mr. Pemberton's murder."

"Perhaps I could," Emerson said, "but perhaps my theory would be no better than yours, so why bother? My advice to you is to keep digging. I have always said that a courtroom is where the truth goes to hide but that a really smart lawyer can find it, sometimes in an unexpected place. You must do the same. Good luck, dearie."

*

Nichols was that rare woman of her day in Minneapolis who had sources in the police department and at city hall. Her work with the American Federation of Labor had brought her into contact with any number of rough characters, including some who carried badges. Following her talk with Emerson, Nichols walked over to police headquarters to consult a detective she knew named Earl Brantley.

She found him at his desk, working on the last of a cigar and looking, as he usually did, disgusted with the world. Brantley was a grumpy bear of a man, wide around the middle but a match for anyone in a brawl, and smarter than he let on. He brightened when he saw Nichols.

"Well now, if it ain't a member of the famous death committee. Here looking for advice?"

"Maybe," Nichols said. "How are you, Earl?"

"Just trying to keep the peace," he said. "It ain't easy, people being what they are."

"I don't imagine it is. I have a question for you, if you don't mind. Do you know where Freddie Pemberton was living at the time of his death?"

"He had a room over at the Brunswick, but I hear he spent most of his daylight hours at the library, like a lot of bums do. Maybe he was studying the history of alcohol. Say, why are you so interested in Freddie?"

"Just curious. Did you go through his room after his body was found? You know, just to see if anything seemed amiss."

"Yeah, we took a look, but didn't find nothing. Freddie was just an old drunk who died of drink. Happens all the time."

Freddie wasn't Nichols's only concern. Snook and O'Malley were also on her mind. She'd begun to form an idea that, if correct, would be like a powerful arrow, penetrating through layers of doubt toward the hidden truth. But was she aiming at the right target? Brantley, she thought, just might help her answer that question.

"I'm curious about something," she said. "As I'm sure you're aware, Walter Snook is one of my fellow committee members. Have the police ever had dealings with him?"

Brantley managed a chuckle as he crushed out his cigar. "Sure, we know Snooky. Kind of funny that he ended up on the committee. The papers said he's a teamster, which he is, but he also runs with a saloon crowd that pulls off small-time swindles. Some hayseed comes in from North Dakota, they rope him into a poker game, and lo and behold he loses his shirt. Happens all the time. But Snooky's a tricky fellow, and nobody's ever been able to pin anything on him."

"I understand he and Dan O'Malley were friends."

"Sure, the two of them ran in the same crowd. But how come you're interested in a dirty crumb like O'Malley?"

"I'm just trying to put some things together, Earl. Let me ask you this: Was O'Malley the sort of man who'd commit murder, or try to, if someone paid him to do the job?"

"Are you kidding? He'd have killed his sainted mother and chopped her body into mincemeat if there was money in it."

"Any suspects yet in his murder?"

"Sure. We've narrowed it down to half the lowlifes in the city."

"In other words, you have no idea."

"And why should we? Whoever put a bullet in him did the world a mighty favor."

"I disagree. Murder is never a good thing," Nichols said. "Do you happen to know where he lived?"

"He had a room in the old Dole house on Fourth Street. We tossed the dump, but it was a waste of time."

"I see. By the way, you may be interested to know that Mr. Snook seems to have gone missing."

"Is that so? I'll send out a posse right away. In the meantime, I'm thinking we could both use a little entertainment," Brantley said. "I've got tickets to *The New Boy* tonight at the Metropolitan. Care to join me? We could have some fun."

"Perhaps another time," Nichols said, knowing there would never be one with the detective, whose badge was about all that distinguished him from the hoodlums he arrested.

*

Nichols's next stop was at the Hotel Brunswick, a well-known establishment that dated back to the 1870s, at Fourth and Hennepin. There, she learned from a desk clerk that Miranda, presumably hunting for her father's will, had already cleared out Freddie's room. It was a disappointment but not a surprise.

After leaving the Brunswick, Nichols walked six blocks up Hennepin to the public library, a handsome brownstone pile that had opened only a few years earlier on Tenth Street. She soon engaged a predictably prim librarian, who told her that Freddie had indeed been a habitué of the reading room, where he'd spent hours going through newspapers. But after he'd been caught one afternoon, scissors in hand, cutting out clippings, he'd been banished.

"It was really quite disgusting," the librarian said. "He clearly gave no thought to other readers who rely on our newspaper collection."

Nichols thanked the librarian and went on her way, certain now who had left the clippings at her home. Freddie had been on to something, and she wondered if it had been enough to get him killed.

Coincidence is a bird that alights in unexpected places, and as Nichols left the library, it landed right before her eyes. She was walking down Ninth Street, toward her home, when she glanced up at a wooden tenement that housed eight small apartments. One of them displayed the number 111 over its door, and it caused Nichols to stop in her tracks. She had a fine memory for facts and figures, and she realized that this was Snook's address on Ninth, as published in the newspapers.

Serendipity was not to be denied, so Nichols decided to see if Snook was home. Nichols went up to the door, which was sheltered by a tiny porch, but received no answer when she rang the bell and knocked repeatedly. Nichols went over to a window near the door and peered inside. A gauzy curtain obscured her view, but from what she could tell, no one was at home. As she stood on the porch, Nichols felt the tug of curiosity pulling at her like a strong dog on a leash, and she had a crazy idea. She recalled what her daughter had said about Sherlock Holmes and his occasional resort to burglary.

Even though she'd denied to her daughter that she'd ever consider a criminal act à la Holmes, she was tempted to do just that.

Nichols walked around to the rear of the tenement, where malodorous privies sat in a trash-strewn yard behind a high wooden fence that deterred prying eyes. She went up to the back door of Snook's apartment and knocked several times, without effect. The door, which did not close tightly, appeared to have a simple lock, and Nichols wondered if she could open it. She took a long, bendy nail file from her purse, slid it between the door and its jamb and, to her surprise, easily retracted the latch bolt. Nichols took a deep breath, feeling very much like the criminal she'd become, and stepped inside.

The apartment was just as she'd suspected it would be—a haven of male indifference to housekeeping. There were beer bottles in the kitchen sink, clothes strewn in small piles, and stacks of yellowed newspapers providing what passed for colorful décor. Nichols moved quickly through the apartment's thinly furnished rooms, looking for desks, cabinets, shelves, or anyplace else where documents might be kept, although she had no clear idea of what she was looking for. Her basic plan was to go through drawers wherever she found them. She was disgusted at herself, knowing how outraged she'd be if someone went pawing through her things, yet she also found it thrilling to play the criminal, if only for a few minutes.

She made her first discovery—an envelope filled with newspaper clippings—in the bottom drawer of a dresser in the apartment's only bedroom. The clippings were from a newspaper in Kankakee, Illinois, called the *Democrat.* Most of the articles, dating to February and March 1893, concerned "a confidence ring" said to be operating in Kankakee. Members of the ring had defrauded several "prominent businessmen" by means of what was described as a "green goods scheme" involving counterfeit money. The ringleader, who went by the name of David DeKalb, had already left town, and the police in Kankakee reported that he "may have moved on to Chicago to continue his fraudulent activities."

There were also two clippings from the *Chicago Tribune* that referred to the death, in June 1894, of a wealthy associate of the hotel and retail magnate Potter Palmer. The first article said the man had been "found dead under suspicious circumstances" after losing thousands of dollars in a stock fraud scheme. A follow-up article said a swindler going by the name of Lincoln Decatur was believed to be behind the scheme and was also a suspect in the victim's death, which the Cook County coroner ruled had been due to arsenic poisoning.

Given Snook's history as a confidence man, Nichols wondered whether he was the swindler, and possibly murderer, cited in the news stories. If so, he was now the logical suspect in George Pemberton's murder and the others that followed. But there were problems with her theory. How could Snook have managed to defraud Pemberton, and what would he have gained by killing him? And why would Pemberton have put him on the death committee?

While Nichols puzzled over these questions, she continued searching the bedroom. She rummaged through a wardrobe and a battered old escritoire to no avail. Nor was there anything of interest under the mattress or bed. But a small wastebasket under the desk yielded a curious discovery in the form of a crumpled playbill from the Theater Comique, an establishment notorious for the scanty costumes of its "actresses," none of whom could be regarded as a master of the thespian arts.

The playbill advertised performances on August 17–29 of the "Minneapolis Follies," which was said to offer "a bevy of beautiful girls in a lively revue." The date was interesting—George Pemberton had been found dead on the thirtieth—but it was a note scrawled at the bottom of the playbill that really got Nichols's attention. It said, "Sammy says they were there on the 29th & left together."

Who were "they?" Nichols wondered, and why had Snook made a note of their theatergoing? Nichols knew Pemberton had been out late on the night he was murdered, and it occurred to her that he might have attended the show at the Theater Comique. But if that was true, who had been with him?

Nichols put the playbill in her coat pocket, then left the apartment the same way she'd entered. Back out on Ninth Street, she felt that sense of exhilaration that comes from doing something bold and dangerous. She also felt an urgent need to locate Snook, although she realized she would have to be very careful about confronting such a dangerous man. First, however, she intended to pay a visit to the Theater Comique.

*

Minneapolis was hardly large or sophisticated enough in those days to have a full-fledged demimonde, but what there was of it found a home at the Theater Comique. Operating under a protective umbrella of police bribery, the establishment, which was more of a club than a theater, offered the sort of entertainment that otherwise respectable men craved as antidote to the pious decencies of the day. Carved out of the upper two floors of a narrow building on Washington Avenue, the theater consisted of a warren of small rooms and private boxes surrounding a jerry-built stage where the display of legs and cleavage provided the principal attraction. The clientele included prostitutes cruising for customers, men of both high and low station devoted to the fine art of ogling, and even an occasional couple seeking a thrilling taste of sin.

Nichols went to the theater that evening, arriving just as it opened at eight o'clock. Since she wasn't dressed like a prostitute and was alone, the big bearded man tending the box office thought she must be making a mistake.

"I think you're in the wrong theater," he said. "This ain't no place for a lady."

"I couldn't agree more," Nichols said, "but I am here on business. I would like to speak with Sammy. Where can I find him?"

"What business would you have with him?" the man asked suspiciously.

"This sort of business," she said, putting a gold coin on the counter. "I'm sure you could use five dollars. Just direct me to him."

"Upstairs, second door to the left," the man said. "Sammy runs the joint. I'm sure he'll be happy to see you."

Nichols went up a narrow stairway reeking of alcohol and cheap perfume and knocked on the door she'd been directed to.

"What do you want?" a voice said.

"Information," Nichols replied. "Twenty dollars' worth of it."

The door opened to reveal a fat, balding man in his forties with a cigar attached to his bloated, pockmarked face. Presumably this was Sammy, whose last name Nichols later learned was Stutz and who managed the theater. He eyed Nichols as though he was inspecting a horse he intended to buy. "And who would you be?" he asked.

"I'm the person with twenty dollars," Nichols said, displaying a double eagle she'd taken from her purse. "Answer a few questions and it will be yours."

"All right, come in."

The office was a windowless cubicle with just enough room for a desk and a side chair. Photographs of women wearing bustiers and not much else adorned the walls. Nichols instantly felt unclean, as though she'd tumbled into a privy vault, but she held her nose and said, "I'm looking for information about the night of August twenty-ninth"—adding in what was simply a guess—"when George Pemberton was here with a friend."

Stutz, who didn't bother to introduce himself or inquire as to Nichols's name, said, "I don't remember that night so well. But if you can hand over that coin, my memory might improve."

"Or that coin might disappear into your pocket and you'll show me the door," Nichols said. She reached into her purse, took out a five-dollar gold piece, and put it on the desk. "Consider this a down payment. If you want another twenty, tell me what you know."

"Okay, let me think. August twenty-ninth, you say?"

"That's right. It was the same night Mr. Pemberton died."

"Oh yeah, I read about that. Put in my name for that committee of his but didn't hit the jackpot. Say, who are you anyway?"

"Annie Nichols. I'm on the committee."

"Is that so? Well, I'll be damned."

"You probably will," Nichols said, "but let's get back to my question. If it will help jog your memory, 'Minneapolis Follies' was playing that night. Did Mr. Pemberton take in the performance with someone?"

"Sure, sure. Now I remember. He did come for that show. Told me afterward it was one of the best he'd ever seen. He was a regular, you know. He liked the girls."

"So I've been told. Was he with a woman that night?"

"Yeah, he was with a dame. Quite the looker, she was."

"Do you know her name?"

"No."

"Could you describe her?"

"I could, but twenty dollars only goes so far."

"It won't go as far as your pocket unless you can give me a description."

With Nichols prodding him, Stutz manage to provide a fairly detailed description of the woman.

"Do you know what time they left?"

"Might have been around midnight, but I'm not sure."

"Did they hail a cab?"

"How would I know that? You'd have to ask one of the doormen."

Nichols forked over the double eagle and went back downstairs. She soon found a doorman who recalled hailing a cab for Pemberton and his striking companion. Better yet, he knew the hack who'd driven them that night and, for five dollars, provided his name.

Satisfied that her money had been well spent, Nichols had the doorman hail a cab for her and went home, where Sophia was waiting for her.

"Have you been out sleuthing?" she asked. "Do tell me all about it."

"I will, but not just yet, my dear. I have some things I have to think about first."

"But you know who did it, don't you?"

"Let's just say I'm beginning to form a picture of what happened," Nichols said. It was a picture that now included a prominent place for Frances Reed, whose description perfectly fit that of the woman with George Pemberton on the night he died.

11.
SNOOK ON THE RUN

WALTER SNOOK WAS USED TO MOVING AROUND, for he'd learned that the trick to being a successful confidence man was never to stay in one place for too long. He'd been on his own since he was fifteen, operating first out of his hometown of Kankakee, Illinois, and then in Chicago, Detroit, Milwaukee, and finally Minneapolis. He'd run all the usual cons over the years, as well as one of his own invention, which became known in the trade as the "Snodgrass Shuffle," after one of his many aliases.

Yet Snook's cleverest con, one that separated him from most of the low characters who cheated for a living, was that he always worked, albeit sparingly, as a teamster even as he went about his criminal endeavors. Teamsters were omnipresent and yet invisible, their carts and wagons crisscrossing the city without attracting much attention. Snook had found that spending a day or two a week hauling freight or ferrying passengers to and from railroad stations put him in contact with all manner of potential marks. It also allowed him to mingle freely with men like O'Malley, who had now become a troublesome coconspirator.

Snook was used to complicated situations—all good con games, after all, were a magician's cabinet full of clever tricks—but the Pemberton business was becoming a mighty challenge. So many angles were at play that Snook felt as though he was in a game of pool in which only carom shots counted, and trying to figure out all the angles was as difficult a task as he'd ever faced. Even so, Snook knew he had to stay in the game because the payoff promised to be extraordinary. He also knew that the ten-thousand-dollar prize was dangerous fruit, pulpy and beautiful but with a poisonous pit inside. Claiming it, he feared, could be the death of him.

And then there was that damned Nichols woman, her steely gray eyes as much of a warning as any. She was shrewd and dogged—the kind of person who could cause him great trouble. The question was what he should do about her.

*

Snook was once again absent when the death committee held its third meeting on September 17, two days after Nichols had made her many discoveries, culminating at the Theater Comique. As it had before, the committee assembled at Pemberton's apartment.

"I am very concerned about Mr. Snook," Gozzard said as everyone settled in. "No one seems to know where he is or why he's disappeared."

"Maybe he simply doesn't like our company," Dixon offered.

"Well, that may be, but the fact is, he's apparently decided to ignore the rest of the committee," Miranda said. "It's very rude, if you ask me."

Nichols said, "I think we're missing the point. Mr. Snook may be rude, but from what I know, he is very much interested in earning the ten-thousand-dollar reward. There must be some good reason why he is staying away. My belief is that he is afraid of someone."

Dixon was amused. "Why, I hardly think we are a fearsome lot. What could Mr. Snook possibly have to be afraid of?"

"Of being murdered," Nichols said. "Just like Freddie and another man who recently met his end."

"I fear you are talking in riddles," Dixon said. "Who is this other man you speak of?"

"I would ask the same question," Reed said. "Are you hiding something from us, Mrs. Nichols?"

Nichols looked at Reed, who'd engaged in her own feats of concealment, and considered how to answer. It wouldn't be wise, Nichols thought, to reveal everything she knew. Even so, she was of a mind that applying the right amount of pressure could finally force the case open, like prying the lid off a can of paint.

"Very well," Nichols said. "There is something I wish to bring before the committee. It concerns a certain Mr. Dan O'Malley, a teamster well known in this city. Does the name register with anyone?"

"Isn't he that thug who was murdered recently?" Dixon said. "I read about in the papers."

"Yes, he was shot in an alley by an unknown assailant."

Ledger said, "Well, that's certainly unfortunate, but what does this O'Malley fellow have to do with us?"

"Mr. Snook apparently knew him quite well," Nichols said.

"What of it?" Dixon asked. "They're both teamsters, are they not? It stands to reason they'd know each other."

"Yes, but there's something else the committee should know. You see, the police believe Mr. Snook is also a swindler who regularly orchestrates schemes with a ring of criminals, O'Malley very probably among them. Now, O'Malley is dead, shot down. A few days later Freddie Pemberton also dies, under mysterious circumstances. And then Mr. Snook suddenly disappears. I think it likely these events are related."

Dixon said, "Well, I suppose that's possible, but what's your point, Mrs. Nichols? What does any of this have to do with George Pemberton's death?"

"I must agree with Mr. Dixon," Reed said. "Mrs. Nichols, I fear, has gone off on a tangent. We should be concentrating on Mr. Pemberton's death and who if anyone is responsible rather than mucking about with the likes of Snook and O'Malley."

Nichols said, "But the fact remains Mr. Snook ended up on this committee. I do not think it was by chance."

"Whatever do you mean by that?" Miranda asked.

Nichols said, "Mr. Gozzard can perhaps answer your question. Tell Miranda, if you would, about the fake lottery."

Once Gozzard was forced to admit that the lottery had indeed been a sham, Miranda said, "I suspected as much. I can see why you were selected, Mrs. Nichols, since I know my father admired you. And, of course, he also knew Miss Reed, but in a very different sort of way. He must have wanted her close to him even in death. How revolting!"

"Oh, come now, Miranda, you're sounding like a child," Reed said. "You know as well as I that your father had many women in his life. I was simply one of them."

"Oh my, isn't this getting juicy?" Ledger said. "I had no idea."

"Then you must have been blind," Dixon said. "Mr. Pemberton's affairs were hardly a secret. Still, that leaves Mr. Snook. He's the odd person out, or so it would seem. Insofar as I know, his only connection to Mr. Pemberton was that he delivered wine here on occasion."

"I believe he did more than that for Mr. Pemberton," Nichols said.

"Then tell us what you know," Miranda said. "I should very much like an explanation for all of this."

"I'm afraid I don't have one yet, but I'm working on it."

"I must say, you are being rather enigmatic," Dixon said.

"I cannot help but be," Nichols said. "All I can tell you is that once we know why Mr. Snook was named to this committee, we may at last be able to identify Mr. Pemberton's murderer."

*

After the meeting ended, Nichols stopped at a Western Union office on her way back home and wrote out three telegrams. The first was to the Kankakee Police Department in Illinois. The telegram—which she signed "A. Nichols, private investigator"—requested a description of David DeKalb, the swindler who'd defrauded a merchant in Kankakee two years earlier. It also asked for descriptions of any of his known associates. To improve her chances of getting an answer, Nichols prepaid for a reply.

Her second telegram went to the police in Chicago. It, too, asked for a description, this time of Lincoln Decatur, the man suspected of bilking and then murdering one of Palmer Potter's associates. Nichols had come to suspect that DeKalb and Decatur might be one and the same—a master confidence man who went by many aliases.

Her final telegram requested a favor from an old union friend in Chicago. She wanted him to go back through the last fifteen years or so of city directories there in search of a man's name and occupation. She didn't know what the directories would reveal, but it would be a valuable clue even if the name couldn't be found.

*

After a fitful night of sleep, a mad dance of theories swirling in her head, Nichols decided on a new approach in hopes of finding Walter Snook. She'd already alerted Brantley and the police to be on the lookout for Snook, but she wanted to cast an even wider net, so she spread the word through her union sources that she would pay fifty dollars to anyone who could locate him. While waiting to see if her efforts would bear fruit, Nichols turned her attention to Dan O'Malley. Snook's apartment had yielded valuable information. Perhaps O'Malley's room in the Dole mansion on North Fourth Street might do the same.

Built in the 1870s by a lumber baron, the house was a hefty exercise in the French Second Empire style and one of the last old mansions left in the city's rapidly expanding warehouse district. More than thirty tenants were crammed into the mansion, occupying rooms barely large enough to hold a bed. Nichols rang the front doorbell just after two and told the elderly woman who answered that she wished to see O'Malley's room.

"Are you a relative?" the woman asked, appearing dubious that anyone as well dressed as Nichols could be kin to the likes of O'Malley.

"I was an acquaintance," Nichols said, pressing a ten-dollar gold piece into the woman's hand. "I'm sure this will make up for any inconvenience I might cause you."

"It would," the woman replied quickly. "I'll take you up there. He was on the third floor. Truth is, I never saw much of Mr. O'Malley. He kept strange hours. It was terrible what happened to him."

Nichols followed the woman up to O'Malley's room, which was in the attic beneath a steep mansard roof. "I haven't had a chance to clean out the room yet," the woman said as she unlocked the door. "It's quite a mess, I'm afraid. Do you need any help?"

"No, I can manage on my own," Nichols said, stepping inside. "I won't be long."

"May I ask what you're looking for?" the woman asked.

"Oh, just old personal letters," Nichols lied. "Mr. O'Malley and my late brother were friends and corresponded for a time. I'm looking for any letters from my brother he might have kept."

"Well, take all the time you want," the woman said. "I'll be downstairs if you need me."

The room was tiny, furnished with a bed, chest of drawers, a small side table and a slat-back chair. Like Snook, O'Malley hadn't made a virtue of tidiness, and the room was a kind of dumping ground, with clothes, newspapers, liquor bottles, and ashtrays littering the floor. The stench of tobacco hung in the air, making the room so thoroughly unpleasant that Nichols felt an urge to flee immediately. But she had work to do, and so she methodically went through the detritus of O'Malley's impoverished life, hoping to find something that might tie him to the Pemberton case.

She uncovered nothing that struck her as being of value in the chest of drawers, in the side table's only drawer, or in any of the clothes strewn on the floor. The room was uncarpeted, and Nichols looked for anything hidden under a loose floorboard, to no avail. She hated the idea of even touching the bed and its filthy mattress but told herself it had to be done. When she lifted the mattress, she discovered a booklet titled *Girls at Play*. She flipped through the book, which offered photographs of bare-breasted women in provocative poses, and found a folded sheet of paper that proved to be far more revealing than the half-naked models.

A crudely drawn floor plan took up the top half of the sheet. It showed a room labeled "kitchen" with a "back door" marked by an arrow on one side and a hallway leading to a staircase on the other. Across from the stairs was what looked to be a closet, with an "X" inside it.

The bottom half of the sheet was a list of instructions: "Arrive no later than 10 p.m. Key above back door. Bolt front door from inside. Turn on light above basement steps. Hide in closet marked X. He will come through kitchen. He will go to turn off light. When he does, you know what to do. Be sure to unbolt front door before you leave. I will be in touch afterward. **DO NOT FAIL THIS TIME.**"

Nichols was astounded. The floor plan clearly showed Pemberton's apartment, and the instructions left no doubt that O'Malley had been hired to push him to his death. What Nichols didn't yet know was who had sent O'Malley on his deadly mission.

*

Three days after sending out the three telegrams, Nichols received her first reply, from her fellow unionist in Chicago. The name she'd asked him to look for couldn't be found in Chicago directories going as far back as 1880. This was proof of sorts that Nichols had been lied to.

The next day, Nichols received responses to her other two telegrams. Per her request, Sgt. James Morton of the Kankakee Police Department provided a physical description of the confidence man suspected of defrauding a merchant in that city two years earlier. He also described an associate who worked with DeKalb. Barely an hour later, another telegram arrived, from a police detective named Edward Peck in Chicago. It gave a full description of Lincoln Decatur, who was suspected of fraud and murder in that city. The detective also stated that Decatur had worked with a "beautiful woman" as part of his scheme.

When Nichols read the description, which included one very distinctive element, a chill ran down her spine, for she knew at last who had masterminded the murder of George Pemberton, then killed two other men to cover their tracks.

*

After receiving the last telegram, Nichols immediately placed a call to Gozzard. "We have no time to waste," she told him. "I know the truth. You must call a final committee meeting for this evening. Telephone Mr. Blair and tell him it is imperative that he attend as well. Also, I need to speak with Miranda once you get hold of her."

Gozzard wasn't used to being ordered around by a woman, but he did as he was told, for he'd come to understand why Pemberton had believed so strongly in Nichols's abilities. Now it appeared his faith was about to be rewarded.

"All right, I'll work on getting the group together," Gozzard said. "Is there anyone else you think should be in attendance?"

"Yes, and I'm going to call him right now. I suggest we meet at seven, at Mr. Pemberton's apartment. Before that happens, we need to talk. I'll be at your office shortly."

*

"Let's be honest with each other," Nichols said when she sat down with Gozzard. "Tell me about Mr. Pemberton's will. I know you have it."

Like all good trial lawyers, Gozzard was a skilled at evasion, but the blunt statement caught him off guard. "Why do you assume—"

"I assume you have the will because it is the only arrangement that makes sense," Nichols said. "Mr. Pemberton feared his daughter could not be trusted to make the right decisions, so he gave you his will for safekeeping and told you to keep it under wraps until the committee had done its work. He worried, I imagine, that a forged version might surface if certain people got their hands on the real will."

"Well, I'm afraid—"

Nichols cut him off again. "There is no time for games, Mr. Gozzard. The hour is at hand and there is a killer among us. What does the will say?"

Gozzard's instinct was to offer a flat-out denial, but it seemed pointless to offer a lie he knew Nichols would never believe. "Very well, I do have the will. Mr. Pemberton entrusted it to me for the very reason you've stated. I can tell you that it leaves the bulk of his estate, as you might imagine, to Miranda, but only if certain conditions are met."

After Gozzard described the conditions, Nichols said, "It is just as I suspected. Mr. Pemberton, for all his faults, truly did love his daughter and he sought, as any good father would, to protect her from harm."

"So you think, then, that—"

"Yes, there can be no doubt about it. Let me show you telegrams I received from the police in Illinois regarding a swindler and very probably a murderer who operated there two years ago but was never apprehended. You will recognize him from the description."

Gozzard scanned the telegram and said, "Good Lord, there can be no doubt, as you say. We must be very careful this afternoon. "

"Yes, that is why I've asked a police detective of my acquaintance to be on hand for the committee meeting. If there is any trouble, he will handle it."

12.
THE UNRAVELING

Two guests—Detective Earl Brantley and Thomas Blair—were on hand for the committee's final meeting, but two other people were missing. Nichols had not expected to see Snook in attendance, but she was surprised when Frances Reed also failed to show up.

"I am very sorry to report I have had no luck whatsoever in reaching Miss Reed," Gozzard said. "Indeed, a messenger I sent to her apartment was told by the building manager that she moved out several days ago."

"How very curious," Miranda said. "Where do you suppose she went?"

"The manager had no idea," Gozzard said. "She apparently gave no forwarding address."

Blair said, "I really don't care where she went. Now, let us get on with this ridiculous business. You are all wasting my time."

"Well, this is all very interesting, if you ask me," Ledger said.

"I agree," said Dixon, who was seated on a side chair rather than next to Miranda on the couch, where Blair had taken a spot. "But what's this big police detective doing here? Are we in some danger?"

"We are," Nichols said as she rose from her chair and stood in front of the parlor's big fireplace. "Mr. Brantley is here to see that no trouble occurs."

It had been three weeks and a day since the committee's initial meeting, well within the one-month timeline Pemberton had allotted to solve his murder, and Nichols was now ready to do just that. "If I may have your full attention," she began, "I would like to begin by telling you the story of this very peculiar committee of ours. It was curated—if that is the right word—by Mr. Pemberton not only for the purpose of identifying his murderer but also because he believed the murderer must in fact be someone on the committee."

"You can't be serious," Miranda said, her voice rising in anger. "How could Father think I'd ever want to murder him?"

"Bear with me, if you would," Nichols said, "and I believe you'll understand. As we know, Mr. Pemberton was convinced that, in the event of his murder, the police would be of no use in identifying the culprit. He understood that the police hated him for his work on behalf of Mr. O'Malley and other criminals and so would conduct a perfunctory investigation at best. He therefore decided to establish this committee as a means of gathering all the suspects, as it were, and he asked me to be the chief investigator."

"Is that so?" Blair said. "I don't seem to recall him saying anything about that in his letter to the committee."

"He also left a private letter for Mrs. Nichols," Gozzard explained, "in which he asked her to take charge of the investigation."

"And what makes you so special?" Miranda asked, not in a friendly way.

"I was of help to him some years ago in a sensitive matter, and it led him to believe I was someone who could sort through all that happened and discover the truth. Time will tell if he was right. Now, back to the committee. Its four nonvoting members are, of course, either related to Mr. Pemberton or are people he worked with. But he also wanted Mr. Snook, Miss Reed, and me on the committee, and so he dreamed up the idea of a fake lottery."

"Why?" Ledger asked. "Why not just appoint them to the committee?"

"Two reasons, I think," Nichols said. "The first is that he suspected neither Mr. Snook nor Miss Reed would agree to serve on the committee, fearing where the investigation might lead. So he decided to dangle a ten-thousand-dollar carrot in front of them in hopes they'd agree to join the group. But he had another reason for staging the lottery, as Mr. Gozzard will tell you."

"I'm all ears," said Dixon. "This is getting more fascinating by the moment."

Gozzard said, "The second reason Mrs. Nichols mentioned is this: the lottery was never intended to be a complete sham. Mr. Pemberton really did want to share some of his fortune with the common people of this city. Once this business is over, I will make known the real purpose behind the original drawing. I will then announce that a second, legitimate drawing will be held, using the names already submitted. The three winners, who will indeed be selected at random, will each receive ten thousand dollars."

"This all sounds crazy," Miranda said.

"It is very strange," Nichols admitted. "But just remember how much your father loved drama. You might say that the 'Death Committee,' as the newspapers call it, is his posthumous contribution to the dramatic arts, even if it will never be performed on stage."

"Well then, let us get on with the drama," Blair said. "This is all growing very tiresome."

Nichols said, "Yes, let us proceed. I would now like to tell you a story of murder and deceit that began on the night of August thirtieth, when Mr. Pemberton attended a show at the Theater Comique. With him that evening was his mistress of the moment, Miss Reed."

"More like a whore, I should say," Miranda spat out.

"Please, try not to interrupt," Gozzard said. "You will all have an opportunity to speak once she's finished."

"Thank you. As I was saying, Mr. Pemberton and Miss Reed attended the show. I know this to be a fact from the theater's manager. They arrived at around eight and left in a cab at about eleven. It's possible Miss Reed came here with Mr. Pemberton, but I think it far more likely that he dropped her off first at her apartment. In any case, when the cab left Mr. Pemberton off here, he was surprised to discover that the front door was bolted shut. He knew that Miranda was out for the evening with Mr. Dixon and would not be back until very late. So he hiked around to the apartment's back door, in the kitchen, and was able to open it with his key.

"When he got inside, he noticed that the light over the basement steps had been left on. This was unusual, and he probably went to the landing at the top of stairs to see if someone was in the basement. And that was when Dan O'Malley, a hired killer, burst from his hiding place in the mop closet by the landing. How long O'Malley lay in waiting I don't know, but he had time to enjoy some wine, judging by that opened bottle we found in the basement. In any event, it would not have been difficult for O'Malley to burst from the closet and shove Mr. Pemberton down the stairs, causing his death."

Ignoring Gozzard's plea not to interrupt, Blair said, "How in blazes do you know that? Did O'Malley confess?"

"In a way," Nichols said. "You see, I took the liberty of going through Mr. O'Malley's room at the old Dole mansion after his death. I have made a copy of what I found under his mattress. Mr. Brantley has the original. You may all have a look, if you wish."

Once everyone had examined the set of instructions and the drawing that accompanied them, Nichols said, "I think you'll all agree that the plan depicts the rear portion of this apartment. As I said, Mr. O'Malley was merely a hired hand, but whoever gave him the instructions obviously was familiar with the apartment's layout."

"And that person would be?" Ledger asked.

"I will get to that. First, there is the matter of the two murders that followed Mr. Pemberton's. Mr. O'Malley's is the easiest to account for. He knew the murderer's identity, and I suspect he tried to parlay that knowledge into a blackmail payoff. Instead, when he met with the murderer, probably to collect his first payment, he was shot dead.

"Next came poor Freddie. Even though he'd been evicted from this apartment because of his drinking, he really did care deeply for his brother, who had long supported him. After his brother's death, Freddie became suspicious once the committee was established. He'd seen Mr. Snook delivering wine here, and he probably also knew of his brother's relationship with Miss Reed. The committee, he must have concluded, could not have been selected at random.

"I believe Freddie had also come to suspect, probably from idle talk at one of the saloons he frequented, that Mr. O'Malley was the wagon driver who'd nearly run down his brother. As Freddie began putting two and two together, he also remembered that Mr. O'Malley and Mr. Snook were more than passing acquaintances. So, Freddie took it upon himself to start investigating. Something, he knew, wasn't right."

"Wait a minute," said Ledger. "How did you find out all of this? Did you talk to Freddie?"

"No, but I believe he sent me, anonymously, a set of newspaper clippings showing that Mr. Snook testified at Mr. O'Malley's criminal trial last year on assault charges. As some of you may recall, Mr. Pemberton represented Mr. O'Malley at that trial. I also learned that Freddie spent a lot of time at the public library. When I went there, a librarian told me he'd been banished for cutting out articles from the *Tribune* and other newspapers. I think Freddie believed both men were somehow involved in his brother's death."

Dixon said, "And this suspicion was enough to get him killed—is that what you're saying?"

"Yes. Freddie didn't know the whole story, but he was getting close enough to the truth that he had to be eliminated. My guess is that he was lured here under some pretext, probably plied with wood alcohol or some other fatal substance mixed in with his whiskey, and then left to die in the rear courtyard, such that it was assumed he'd simply drunk himself to death."

"Then who killed him?" Miranda asked. "Was it Snook or O'Malley?"

"Neither," Nichols said. "But let us speak more of Mr. Snook. He was in many ways at the center of everything that happened. As you know, I learned from Detective Brantley that Mr. Snook was a confidence man who hailed from Kankakee, Illinois. I sent a telegram to the police there and learned that a man very much resembling Mr. Snook, along with a fellow criminal, were wanted for swindling a businessman in that city two years ago.

"Mr. Snook left town after that swindle and later came up to Minneapolis to continue his career, if you can call it that. He also worked occasionally as a teamster, a job that included delivering cases of wine to Mr. Pemberton. That's when Mr. Snook may have encountered by chance the brilliant confidence man he'd worked with back in Kankakee. It's also possible Mr. Snook may have reconnected with his old partner before then.

"Mr. Snook quickly joined up with his former partner to carry out his scheme. Indeed, I think it was Snook, acting as a middleman on instructions from his partner, who hired O'Malley to run down Mr. Pemberton. But after that attempt failed, something very strange happened. Mr. Pemberton, unaware what Snook had done, quite possibly hired him to gather evidence against O'Malley."

"Why on earth would he do that?" Miranda asked.

"My theory is that your father was convinced O'Malley had tried to run him down. One-eyed teamsters, after all, are hardly a common sight in Minneapolis. Your father may have thought that Mr. Snook, being a teamster himself, could get the goods on O'Malley. I also know from Mr. Ledger that your father authorized a special payment to Mr. Snook. That indicates to me that he'd hired him for a job of some kind."

"What proof do you have of any of this?" Dixon asked. "It all sounds far-fetched."

"Proof enough, I believe," Nichols said. "But what's also important to know is that Mr. Snook may have been hoping for a double payday. On one hand, he intended to collect the ten-thousand-dollar reward by working with his partner to ensure that the wrong man—Mr. Blair—was fingered for Mr. Pemberton's murder. To that end, certain accounting and bank documents were forged."

Blair stood up, pointed at Ledger, and said, "You did it, didn't you, you little weasel. You made false entries in the books to frame me."

"I did no such thing!" Ledger said, rising to his feet and approaching Blair. "Take that back or I swear I will—"

"You ain't going to do nothing," Brantley said as he quickly stepped between the men. "Now, sit down, the both of you, and shut up. Let the lady finish."

Nichols said, "Thank you, Detective. Since the accusations against you have come up, Mr. Ledger, I should tell you that the murderer, in an effort to frame you, went so far as to suggest you were the one who poisoned Mr. Pemberton with arsenic."

"Poisoned him?" Ledger repeated in disbelief. "Why, that is—"

"A lie," Nichols said. "I know. But it was insinuated to me that your father was a pharmacist in Chicago and that you therefore would have been familiar with poisons."

"My father ran a clothing store in Wheaton, Illinois," Ledger said. "Whoever told you he was a pharmacist?"

"That would be Miranda."

Ledger was dumbfounded. He turned to Miranda and said, "Why would you make up a story like that?"

Before Miranda could answer, Nichols said, "I think Miranda

believed it was true, and I'll explain why shortly. Suffice it to say for now that when I sent a telegram to a friend in Chicago and asked him to check city directories there, he found no evidence of a pharmacist named Ledger ever working there."

Miranda and Ledger began to talk over each other, and a mighty commotion might have ensued had not Gozzard—who possessed the deepest and loudest voice among the group—commanded, "Silence! Silence! Pray continue, Mrs. Nichols."

Nichols said, "Let me return to Mr. Snook. As I was saying, he hoped to receive a big payout for his work on the committee. But I suspect he also saw an opportunity to blackmail his partner when the time came. Mr. Snook believed his partner, who was about to become a very rich man, would pay handsomely to keep his crimes from becoming known. But after Freddie and O'Malley were killed, Mr. Snook realized that he, too, was in grave danger, which is why he went into hiding. It's even possible he's left the city."

"All right, out with it," Blair said. "Who's this criminal mastermind you're speaking of?"

"I was just getting to that," Nichols said calmly. "I also sent a telegram to the Chicago police requesting a description of the confidence man who'd worked with Mr. Snook in Kankakee. This same man—the mastermind, as you called him, Mr. Blair—was wanted for a grave crime in Chicago. The police there responded with an excellent description of the suspect. Let me read it to you."

Nichols removed the telegram from her purse, along with her reading glasses. "All right, here it is: 'Age about thirty-five. Six feet tall, slender build, dark hair cropped short, close-set blue eyes. No identifying scars or marks but known to wear gold ring with large inset ruby. Goes by aliases including DeKalb, Decatur, Darien. Known to work with a beautiful dark-haired woman who may be his mistress. Wanted here for murder and theft by swindle."

Miranda's face went white, and she turned toward her fiancé, staring at the jeweled ring on his left middle finger. "Paul, please tell me—"

Dixon responded by bolting from his seat and running toward the front door, with Brantley in hot pursuit. But when Dixon flung open the door, a burly uniformed police sergeant was waiting for him. There was a brief struggle before Brantley managed to pin Dixon's arms. The sergeant then removed a small revolver from Dixon's coat pocket.

"You ain't going nowhere but to the gallows," Brantley said as he handcuffed Dixon.

Miranda watched the scene with a look of stunned disbelief. "Oh my God," she said. "This can't be true."

"Oh, it's true," Nichols said. "You have been saved from marrying the man who murdered your father."

13.
FINAL ACTS

THE TUMULTUOUS WATERS of the Mississippi River below St. Anthony Falls were notoriously reluctant to give up their dead. A body could scrape along the river bottom for days, pushed miles downstream by the powerful current. But whether in the river due to misadventure or murder, a bloated corpse always surfaced eventually, like some damaged creature from the deep.

Two days after the death committee's final meeting, a ten-year-old boy wandered down into the river gorge near the mouth of Minnehaha Creek to enjoy a satisfactory afternoon of playing hooky. The boy liked to bushwhack through the underbrush along the river, where big catfish could sometimes be seen lurking in shallow pools. His explorations soon took him to a tiny slack water cove ringed by overhanging bushes, and there he made an awful discovery.

Late that same afternoon, as Nichols was preparing to go out for dinner with her daughter, Brantley called. "We fished a body out of the river late this afternoon down by Minnehaha Park. Been in the water for a few days. The newspapers will have all the details in the morning, but I thought you'd want to know right away. It was Walter Snook."

Nichols wasn't surprised. "I feared Mr. Snook might meet a bad end, and so he did. I can only assume Dixon killed him."

"Seems likely. Snooky took two bullets to the chest, so it wasn't no accident, that's for sure. A guy like him, it was bound to happen sooner or later."

"Yes, I suppose it was," Nichols said. "He was a man full of tricks, but he didn't see the last one coming his way."

*

The "real" lottery, as Gozzard called it, was held a week after Dixon's arrest. The lawyer penned a mea culpa to the newspapers, describing how he'd staged the fake lottery at Pemberton's behest in order to find his killer. The notice included a brief message from Pemberton, who wrote: "I apologize to one and all for my little deception, but if you are reading this, then you know that my murderer has indeed been found. My agent, Mr. Gozzard, will now select, at random, three names from those already entered in the lottery, and each winner will receive $10,000, with no strings attached. I wish all of you the best of luck."

With observers on hand to ensure that there would be no new chicanery, Gozzard went ahead and drew three new names. A laborer, a charwoman, and, much to the press's amusement, a resident of one of the city's most popular brothels were the lucky winners. All would later say their lives were transformed by Pemberton's generosity. Nichols also received $10,000 for her work once Dixon was indicted, but she donated all of it to a union fund providing financial assistance to workers injured on the job.

Dixon was also very much in the news in the weeks that followed his arrest. His real name remained a mystery until a bright police detective noticed that all his aliases were the names of towns in Illinois beginning with the letter "D." Before long it was discovered that Paul Dixon was actually Philippe Duchette and that he hailed from Danville, Illinois, where he'd run small-time scams before moving on to bigger game in Kankakee, Chicago, and finally Minneapolis.

Although authorities in Illinois wanted to extradite Duchette, prosecutors finally agreed that he should stand trial in Minneapolis due to the magnitude of his crimes there. He was indicted on two counts of first-degree murder in the deaths of George Pemberton and Dan O'Malley, but there wasn't enough evidence to charge him with the killings of Freddie and Snook. Duchette denied all the charges and hired Rutherford Cuddleton, a prominent criminal defense attorney from St. Paul, to represent him. The trial, which began in January 1897, was one of the most sensational in the history of Minneapolis.

Prosecutors alleged that upon arriving in Minneapolis from Chicago, Duchette began looking for a new mark after making contact with his old pal, Snook. One theory, never proved, was that Snook steered Duchette to Pemberton, and his daughter, as ripe targets for fraud. Testimony from Miranda and others revealed that Duchette seduced her, promised marriage, and then with her support charmed his way into a job as her father's private secretary, using false references to obtain the position. His next step was to arrange what would look like Pemberton's accidental death. After that, his plan grew even more sinister. He intended to marry Miranda, live with her for a suitable period, and then see to it that she, too, met with an unfortunate demise. After that, the Pemberton fortune would be his.

Cuddleton did his best to challenge the state's case, but a key piece of evidence proved hard to overcome. A nationally known graphologist from Chicago testified he was "one hundred percent certain" that the floor plan and instructions found in O'Malley's room were in Duchette's handwriting. Ledger also bolstered the prosecution's case, stating that Duchette had access to the firm of Pemberton and Blair's accounts and could have doctored the books to make it appear Blair, or Ledger himself, was a thief. Yet another witness unearthed by the prosecution revealed that he had seen Duchette and O'Malley together not long before the teamster was shot to death with what a ballistics expert later testified was a revolver of the same caliber as the one found in Duchette's coat pocket.

Although Cuddleton advised against it, Duchette took the stand to testify. He offered an array of ingenious explanations and cleverly concocted lies to account for the wealth of evidence pointing to his guilt. Cuddleton would later say that Duchette knew his case was hopeless—"they will hang me for sure," he admitted in a moment of candor—and he was right. After being duly convicted on both counts by a jury, he went to the gallows in March 1897. His final words, as reported by the *Tribune,* were: "I look forward to meeting the devil. I am sure he will be a most interesting fellow. All right, hangman, do the deed, and be quick about it."

*

Nichols's role in bringing Duchette to justice became the source of much commentary in the newspapers. Yet the local scribblers found it hard to accept that a woman had managed to untangle what one described as "the most intricate scheme of murder and deceit the people of Minneapolis are ever likely to see."

"The newspapers do not give you proper credit, Mother, and it's unfair," Sophia complained one evening as they sat together working a jigsaw puzzle—a new pastime they'd just discovered.

"You're right. The newspapers seem to believe women are incapable of rational thinking. So I must have used women's intuition, whatever that is, to solve the case. It is all very tiresome. The truth, of course, is that women really do make the best detectives, as a many a wayward husband has learned. "

"Well, I think you were splendid, just like Sherlock Holmes."

Nichols smiled and said, "I don't think I'd go that far. But it was a wonderful adventure, wasn't it?"

Sophia said, "Now that it's all over, what do you think Miranda Pemberton will do? She must have been crushed to learn the truth about her fiancé."

"Yes, I'm sure she was. But she is strong and spirited. She is also very rich, for she will receive her father's entire estate. She is bound to have many suitors now. I only hope that she will not make the wrong choice again."

*

Two mysteries remained to tantalize Annie Nichols. What had happened to Frances Reed, and what role if any had she played in Pemberton's murder? Nichols thought of the "beautiful dark-haired woman" the Chicago police had mentioned in their telegram. Could Reed have been that woman? It seemed possible, but Nichols had no proof.

Two months after Duchette's execution, Nichols received a postcard from, of all places, Havana, Cuba. "Dear Annie," it said, "hope all is well with you. Have met a gentleman here who owns a cigar factory and we have become good friends. Just learned of Mr. Duchette's fate. Too bad, but not a surprise. We all must pay for our sins sooner or later. Best, Frances."

Nichols wondered whether she should give the postcard to the police but realized there would be no point in doing so. Most of the witnesses who might have implicated Reed in Pemberton's murder were dead, and Nichols did not see how charges could ever be brought against her. She was, Nichols thought, the cleverest of the whole lot of carnivores who had made Pemberton their prey. As for the Cuban "gentleman" who had succumbed to her charms, Nichols could only hope he was smart and wary, lest he meet an untimely end.

LARRY MILLETT has written twenty-one books, including ten mystery novels featuring Sherlock Holmes and St. Paul detective Shadwell Rafferty. A longtime reporter and architecture critic for the *St. Paul Pioneer Press,* he has also written many books on Twin Cities architecture.